SMOKE & MIRRORS

OUTBREAK TASK FORCE
book two

Stephanie,

SMOKE & MIRRORS

OUTBREAK TASK FORCE
book two

JULIE ROWE

Great to meet you
in Reno!

Julie Rowe

Entangled Publishing, LLC
2614 South Timberline Road
Suite 105, PMB 159
Fort Collins, CO 80525
Visit our website at www.entangledpublishing.com.

Amara is an imprint of Entangled Publishing, LLC.

Edited by Robin Haseltine
Cover design by Mayhem Cover Creations
Cover art from iStock

Manufactured in the United States of America

First Edition February 2018

To Loen, my sister and my friend.

Chapter One

At one o'clock in the morning, the I-15 through the Utah desert gave the impression it had been abandoned for years. Lyle Smoke drove his jeep through the desolate moonlight, not another car in sight. Not even the slow, slumberous roll of tumbleweeds. Not even wildlife approaching the pavement looking for roadkill.

Nobody to listen.

Nobody to issue orders.

Nobody to guard his back.

Eight years in the army—breathing, eating, shitting that life. Gone.

He wasn't Sgt. Smoke, the soldier who could track ghosts, capture boogey-men, and keep his battle-brothers safe. He was Smoke, just smoke. Nothing and nobody and not here.

The quiet highway should have been soothing.

It wasn't.

A good soldier didn't trust the quiet. Smoke *hated* it.

He used to love it.

He'd spent summers on the reservation with the desert

as his backyard. He'd rode horses and dirt bikes through it, camped for days at a time, and hunted to feed himself. He'd learned to navigate by the stars and knew the location of every water source.

But those simple, quiet, satisfying days were long gone.

Now his days were nightmares of memories. Memories of pain and blood.

All that shit should have stayed in the fucking Afghan sandbox. Too bad his brain hadn't figured that out yet.

He passed the silver shrouded shadow of Jack Rabbit Rock on the right. The last time he'd been in this part of the desert, he'd taken Liam there. His son had sat in front of him in the saddle, his small body warm and trusting as he looked everywhere at once and pointed at everything.

"Papa," he'd said, his voice high with excitement. He pointed at something new and announced, "Papa."

Stopstopstopyoustupidfuckerstop.

Smoke clenched the steering wheel, gritted his teeth, and tried to shove the reminder that his son would *never* have a life out of his head.

He sucked in deep breaths and focused on the facts. The truth. Maybe if he recited reality often enough, he'd accept it.

The last time he'd been home had been for Liam and Lacey's funerals.

Liam and Lacey were dead. His son and the mother of his son were dead.

There. He'd thought it. Didn't make it any truer to him than five minutes ago.

He'd sworn to stay away until he'd accepted what had happened. Yet, here he was, not twenty miles from the epicenter of his pain. Here he was, ready to kill someone, but no enemies to gut in his mother's kitchen.

Reaching to rewrite the past was stupid, dangerous, and insane. Didn't stop him from reaching for it in his head, anyway. The past was a ghost not even he could track. Still… the desert held other memories for him. Memories of happier times.

He'd say hello tomorrow morning, kiss his mom, nod at his father, then pack his shit and go hunting for a week. Or three. Maybe that would cure him of his increasing need to choke the life out of something with his bare hands.

He drove through his hometown of Small Blind, Utah, to his parents' ranch-style house. He left his vehicle on the street and went around toward the back door. A car was parked at the back of the driveway. Rental plates? Someone visiting?

Then he saw the dent in the driver's side door. A monster-truck sized dent. The kind of dent you can only get if you've been T-boned by something big and mean and pissed off. Some of the scratches in the paint looked like letters.

Fuck off & die FBI.

What a fuckup. Not an FBI vehicle. Not an accident. Not dealing with smart assholes.

He took a look inside. The airbag on the driver's side was smeared with something dark. Blood. The driver would have a couple of black eyes. And a hospital bill.

What was a bloodied and bent car doing in his parents' driveway?

Stop stalling, pussy.

He opened the back door, stepped inside, and memories raked pain across his battered, bruised, and broken heart.

After the first stab of sharp steel, images of Liam became a dull, dishwater ache, settling into his chest as if they were moving in for the duration of his deployment.

No, he was home, not in a combat zone.

Fuck, was he ever going to catch up to reality?

He took a step, and when no improvised explosive devices—physical, emotional, or otherwise—went off, he took another step. His room was only twelve more steps away. Twelve teeny, tiny triggers that could blow him up from the inside out.

The darkness helped by shrouding everything in shadows. His room, his stuff, his bed were right where he left them. Okay, good. He could breathe a little easier now.

Smoke set his duffle on the floor and stripped. He kept his boxers on in case his mom walked in, but it was hot enough in the room that he didn't want any part of the pile of blankets on the other side of the bed.

He should have called first. His mother was going to give him hell for not giving her time to make the damn bed. He slid onto the mattress.

As he considered the ceiling, Smoke put his hands under his head. His pencil drawings of the constellations were still up there, faded and farther away than ever. He'd wanted to feel like Michelangelo, transform his ceiling the way he planned to transform his life. Transform the world.

Now, he was adrift between the stars unable to see a way to live past his week-old discharge.

. . .

Fuck, it was hot.

Smoke rose out of sleep at the pace of a snail.

Who the fuck was touching him?

His body knew when something hinky was happening, and it roused him the second some asshole thought he could put shaving cream on his face or snuggle up and take incriminating photos. He sure as hell should have woken up the second anyone put their hand on Smoke's chest.

A second away from dumping the soon-to-be-interrogated dude on the floor, his brain registered two things. One, the size of that hand. Small, dainty even. Two, the lavender with a bite of citrus scent.

It made him horny.

He glanced down. There was a woman in bed with him.

Christmas? Months away. Birthday? Months away. Hallucination? Months too soon.

He scrutinized the woman. The blanket had slipped off her as far as the top of her butt, leaving her back bare.

No top.

Naked.

Christ, she was lying partway over his chest with nothing covering her but skin and him.

Fuck.

His body tightened, hardened, and wasn't that a kick in the nads, because this was a no-go situation front to back.

He couldn't just shove her off of him. Despite the fact that he'd gone to sleep alone, this little gal was no threat to him. He'd have to slide out from under her carefully, so he didn't wake her, and sneak out of the room.

Waking her would be…awkward. She'd scream, and he'd be hard pressed to explain what the fuck he was doing in the same bed with her. The screaming he could have put up with; it was the explaining he wanted to avoid at all costs.

Decision made, he eased out from under her a couple of inches.

She sighed and shifted her body, ending up with more of her covering him than before.

Well, shit.

Now he knew she had big breasts. Both of them were pressed against his lower rib cage, a soft, sweet weight parts of him really wanted to get to know better.

His cock was all kinds of interested, but given the lack of room in his boxer-style briefs, she'd probably freak out if she opened her eyes. Her face was turned in the direction of his primary weapon.

He tried to ease out from under her again, but this time,

she woke up.

Her head rose a couple of inches above his chest then stopped. She froze, her body tensing.

Here it comes, the screaming, the yelling, the accusations. A special kind of hell for a man who didn't like explaining anything to anyone.

Not breathing, he waited for the uproar to begin.

She turned her head slowly, like she had all the time in the world and complete power over the mostly naked man under her.

Her gaze met his and she tilted her head to one side, a tiny furrow etched between her brows. Not angry or afraid, no, she wore the same stoic mask some of his team wore before going into an active combat zone. Prepared to engage with the enemy.

He could see danger in her dark brown eyes and full, curved mouth. It was her hair, a tumbled rush of dark curling waves over her shoulder that made him want to thread his hand into its mass and tug her to him.

She was fucking gorgeous.

Someone needed to shoot him. Now.

Fuck.

She lifted her head another fraction, and the shadows fled from her face enough for him to see the bruises. All around each of her eyes, turning her pupils into dark targets.

She'd been in that car, the one with the dent. The one that had a death threat scratched into the paint.

Sleep hadn't quite let go of her yet, and he really didn't want to scare her, so he should say something to put her at ease. Reassure her somehow.

"Who did it?"

She blinked, surprise replacing the determination on her face.

What the fuck had just come out of his mouth? And why

had he said it so it sounded like a threat?

"Who did…what?" she asked.

Her voice was breathy, soft, and sexy. His cock went from interested to lifetime commitment in a heartbeat.

"Who hit your car and hurt you?"

"I don't know." Her gaze went unfocused. "It all happened so fast. I don't remember seeing another car. I don't remember the crash. I do remember one of the sheriff's deputies asking me about what happened, but…"

He stared at those bruises, bruises that looked *wrong* on her skin. "Car, van, ice-cream truck, give me something."

"Why?"

Why? Why wasn't she angry? Why wasn't she scared? "Because whoever did this to you"—he lifted one hand and traced the bruise circles with one cautious finger—"I'm going to find the fucker and kill him."

Calm curiosity was chased off her face by a cold, rigid rage that rivaled his own.

"Not for me, you're not." She began wiggling away from him.

Everything that made him a soldier rebelled at the idea of this injured, vulnerable woman leaving his home, his room, his bed. He locked his hands in place. This was a battle he had to fight with words. Not his weapons of choice.

"And if they hit you with something bigger next time?" he asked.

She slid away a bit more. "It was just random kids. Graffiti."

"Followed up by attempted murder."

She rolled her eyes then winced. Yeah, those bruises looked like they went all the way down to the bone. "Do what you want. Your house, your bed, but don't use me to rationalize your violence." She paused. "You are Lyle Smoke, right?"

"Smoke," he said, watching in fascination as she managed to slither out of bed without flashing him once.

"Isn't that your last name?"

He shrugged. "Yeah."

She got to her feet, the blanket now around her like she was a Roman goddess.

He realized she'd asked him something. "What?"

One eyebrow rose and she smiled.

Busted.

She shook her head. "I said it's okay. I can take care of myself."

The words fell from her mouth like lead weights, dark, heavy, and cold.

She headed for the door.

"Alone is a dangerous place to be."

She paused, looking over her shoulder at him. Her eyes were wide for a second.

She didn't answer, just stared at him with those somber, bruised eyes. Then she turned away, picked something off the floor, and left the room.

She took all the fucking air with her.

He couldn't breathe, couldn't remember how to breathe.

The bathroom door closed. He stood next to his bed, sucking in air like it was laced with cocaine and he needed a hit.

Holy shit.

Holy, *holy* shit.

Who was she?

Why was she here?

He needed intel on this woman and he needed it now.

Chapter Two

Kini stared at her reflection in the bathroom mirror then poked her cheek with one finger. What just happened couldn't have been real. Could it?

Had she really fallen asleep alone, only to wake up draped over the body of the hottest man she'd ever seen? A six foot-something tall, muscled, *hung*, man with Caribbean blue eyes.

She'd been ready to knee him in the nuts until he offered to kill whoever crashed into her car yesterday. All it had taken was a glimpse of her bruises.

So much violence in his eyes, on his face. It almost took her back to the scariest moments of her childhood. When her father had been in a rage he could do anything, hurt anyone. Could and did. Safety was a mirage most people believed in without thought. She'd learned the truth much too young.

Her father never had control over his anger. Smoke looked as if he had too much. He should have inspired terror, but he'd looked so damn serious and sincere, all she'd felt was regret because he was too late.

Two decades too late.

He'd demanded to know who hurt her.

The first words out of his mouth weren't a slick hello or hey, baby, come here often? No, he offered to kill for her instead—in a deep baritone that sent shivers of pleasure slipping up her spine.

Who did that? Offer to start a war for a woman he'd just met.

It was stupid to believe heroes existed. Depending on another person to save you was setting yourself up for disappointment, and she knew better than that.

She'd known then he was Susan and Jim's son, the soldier who hadn't been home in a long time. They'd told her he'd been in the army for eight years. Her dad had only been in for four and had come out of it a broken, angry, violent man. Eight years... *God*, she couldn't imagine the shit he'd seen and done and couldn't forget.

Her reflection stared back at her, sadness framed in her downturned mouth and dull gaze.

That wouldn't do at all. The whole world thought she was endlessly cheerful and had few worries. Time to put her game face back on. The one with a mega-watt smile that made anyone who looked at her believe she was young, a little foolish, and completely harmless.

Kini dropped the blanket and stepped into the shower, struggling to push Smoke out of her mind. His skin had been warm under her hands, his muscles firm, and his scent, cedar and sand, had made her want to lick at his skin to taste the spice of him. He was a temptation she didn't need.

Smoke was hot, but she'd gotten as close to him as she was ever going to get. Besides, she was only going to be in the area another week, then it was back to Atlanta to write up her report. After that, it was off to her next assignment in another state.

She dressed in the clothes she'd nabbed on her way out of the bathroom, a pair of dark blue jeans and a Public Health T-shirt that identified her without making her look like she'd just walked out of a hospital.

Her current assignment was to collect patient histories and blood samples from at least two hundred local people from the rural areas of Utah. Most especially, from those of Native American descent.

She'd been here a couple of weeks already, and things were going slower than she liked.

Kini braided her wet hair then left the bathroom, hoping to grab a coffee and go.

Jim and Susan were in the dining room off the kitchen with Smoke. No one looked happy.

"Morning," she said with a bright smile before anyone else could say anything. "I'm late, so I'm just going to grab some coffee before I go." She matched actions to words, heading toward the coffee pot and filling her travel mug with liquid energy.

"I'm not sure when I'll be back tonight," she continued in the same upbeat tone. "Don't hold dinner for me." The issue of sleeping arrangements occurred to her.

"Um, should I sleep on the couch tonight?" She glanced up and found Jim and Susan glaring at their son.

Smoke was staring at her, but he finally met his parents' gazes before meeting hers again and saying slowly, "No."

That was all he said. No explanation, no additional information. Must be a regional trait. She had yet to meet a talkative resident in the whole state.

"Okay." She saluted him with her cup and was about to turn and head for the front door, but there was a flash of movement behind her and male hands slid over her hips, pulling her backward into a body larger than hers.

Adrenaline shot through her system, dumping all the

confusion, frustration, and irritation she was trying to suppress straight into her bloodstream. She didn't freeze, didn't think, didn't hesitate, pushing back into the man behind her, surprising him and forcing him back a step, then she turned to face him and brought her knee up as hard as she could into his groin.

He went down on a groan, first to his knees then fell onto his side.

The next second, Smoke was there, between her assailant and her, blocking the man's access to her.

"Nathan," Susan demanded of the man on the floor. "What did you do?"

Smoke glanced at the groaning Nathan then turned to her. "Okay?"

She focused on his face, surprised by the lack of violence there. Irritation, yes. Violence, no. "Um…yes."

Smoke looked at her hands, and his gaze stayed there. She glanced down to see what he was looking at. Her hands were shaking. Hard.

Damn it. Kini took in a deep breath then let it out slowly. She repeated that for a couple of seconds, enough time for her to pull out of the violent, vicious emotional soup her brain was floating in.

She looked at Nathan and cleared her throat. "Who's he?"

"My nephew," Susan said, putting her hands on her hips. "Nate, what on Earth possessed you to grab Kini like that?"

"I thought Smoke brought a girlfriend home," he answered through clenched teeth. He squinted at her. "Did you have to knee me so hard? I may never father children."

She shook her head. *What had he been thinking?* "You shouldn't sneak up and grab women like that."

"Idiot," Smoke said to his cousin. "Touch her again, and I'll rip your arms off."

Everyone stopped what they were doing to stare at Smoke like he had three heads.

Smoke turned to Kini, gave her a visual once-over, but didn't seem too satisfied, given the frown on his face. "Your coffee?"

She glanced at her empty hands then the floor. Her travel mug was halfway across the room, the contents of her cup sprayed all over the place.

"Oh crap, I'm so sorry." She darted toward the sink and grabbed the dish cloth then hurried over to begin mopping up the spill.

Smoke put out a hand to stop her. "Idiot is going to clean this, not you."

"Excuse me?" She was grateful for his support, but not letting her clean up a mess she'd made wasn't his decision to make.

"Nate scared you." Smoke's voice, a deep rumble, did something to her insides. Something she didn't want to dwell on. "Nate can clean it up."

A glance at the idiot told her something different. "Nate doesn't look like he's going to be up to too much hard labor for a while, and this floor needs to be cleaned now."

The big man frowned at her. "Then let me hel—"

"It's fine," she said, cutting him off and going around him. Susan tossed her a roll of paper towels while Jim guided Nathan into another room; he complained about the pain the whole way. Despite her giving Smoke a narrow-eye'd glance, he grabbed a wet cloth and wiped away more than half of the mess.

As soon as the floor was finished, she grabbed her work bag and left the house.

She'd find coffee, sanity, and security later.

Watching her drive away unsettled Smoke's stomach. He didn't like it. Not one bit.

"Son," his father said behind him.

Smoke turned. His dad had his arms across his chest and the *time for business* expression on his face—the one he wore when he had to give anyone bad news.

"Where *did* you sleep last night?"

"My bed."

"Kini was in your bed." His dad said every word like they weighed a thousand pounds each.

"Yeah." Smoke shrugged. "But until this morning, I thought I was alone."

"So…" His father's voice trailed off, but Smoke could read the rest of the sentence on his father's face. *So…did you sexually assault our guest?*

Why was this even a question? It was an insult to Smoke *and* Kini.

He crossed his arms over his own chest and asked, in a tone that was a weapon he used sparingly, "So, *what*?"

Whoa, why the hell was he going there with his father? It was a question his father *should* ask. He opened his mouth to apologize, but got interrupted.

"You slept with her?" Nate asked from behind him, his tone incredulous, as if Smoke had slept with a tank full of piranha.

"Didn't know she was there until I woke up," Smoke said. Again.

Nate grinned. "You've got balls, man."

"Better than yours, idiot." His cousin looked like he'd recovered enough for another ass-kicking.

"Hey, I just wanted in on that action. She's got a great ass."

Smoke headed for him, faster than his cousin expected because he glanced up, paled, then backpedaled right into a wall.

"Whoa, whoa, *whoa*," the idiot said, putting his palms up.

Smoke shoved his cousin's hands away and stuck a finger in his face. "What did I say?"

Nate swallowed. "That if I touched her, you'd rip my arms off."

Smoke smiled, showing his teeth.

"Come on, dude, that's just creepy."

"Leave her alone." The words came out of Smoke's mouth like he'd chewed them up and spit them out.

"I will," Nate promised in a whiny voice that made Smoke's teeth ache. "I will."

Smoke examined his cousin and decided that while Nate was an idiot, he wasn't suicidal.

"*Smoke?*" his dad asked. Not one question, but several all in one word.

"Nothing," he answered. "I...she..." He shrugged, lifting his hands in surrender. "Nothing."

His father grunted and went into the kitchen. The sound of the back door closing came from around the corner.

Nate hightailed it out of there, so Smoke went back into the kitchen to find his mother sitting at the table, drinking a cup of coffee, reading something off the tablet in her hand.

"What happened to the newspaper?" he asked, nodding at the tablet.

"It went digital," she said, waving the device. She put it down and patted Smoke's cheek. "Times are changing, son. Try to keep up."

"Funny."

He got up, poured a coffee for himself, and sat back down. To stare at his mother.

She glanced at him then put the tablet down. "What?"

"Kini?"

The corners of his mother's mouth tilted up. "We offered

her a place to stay while she's in the area. She's doing a CDC health study of the local population."

Smoke grunted. He'd gotten a call from his army buddy River not more than a day and a half after he'd been officially discharged, offering him a job with the CDC. Some kind of investigation team.

Did the CDC do a lot of public health research or education?

"Unfortunately, some folks have refused to even talk to her. They think she's part of some government cover-up or something equally ridiculous."

That kind of talk could be dangerous—most folks in this part of the country didn't like the government sticking its nose into their business.

"What's Kini's full name?" Smoke asked.

"Kini Kerek."

At his arched eyebrow, his mother smiled. "Her mother was Hawaiian."

"Was?"

His mother cocked her head. "Yes, that's how Kini put it."

Smoke nodded then kissed his mom on the cheek. "I'm going to make a call."

She reached out and took his face in her hands, holding him in place. "It's good to have you home." Though no tears were visible, her voice dripped them.

"It is good," he said quietly, covering her hands with his. "But…"

"But what?"

It was a lot harder to say out loud than he anticipated. "I'm not…"

He didn't finish the sentence, he couldn't. It would be admitting defeat, and he wasn't going there. Not ever.

"Of course you're not," she said so matter-of-factly it

startled him. "Eight years in the army, the deaths of your son and his mother, and your injuries last year would damage anyone's...*okay meter*." She pulled her hands away then hugged him. "I'd be worried if you tried to lie and say you were fine."

He squeezed her tight and whispered into her hair, "Can't fool you." She smelled of everything good in the world, coffee, bacon, and home.

She held him for another second or two then released him and dusted her hands as if she'd finished a particularly difficult task. "Do you have any plans for the next few weeks?"

"Camping and hunting in the desert."

"Your grandfather was out there a couple of weeks ago," she told him. "He said there were more people around, strangers, than usual."

"I can cope. Stay out of sight."

She snorted. "You learned how to do that when you were five years old." She crossed her arms and scowled at him. "The army just put a polish on it."

"Yes, ma'am." God, he'd missed her.

He strode down the hall and into his bedroom, closing the door so his call wouldn't be interrupted. Not that he thought his parents would, but Nate was dumb enough to try to keep talking to him. Hopefully the idiot had left the house for a while.

The man answered on the second ring. "River."

"I'll take the job."

"Smoke?" River didn't wait for confirmation. "Awesome, man. I think you'll like work."

"Tell me about Kini Kerek."

"Yeah, Kini is in your neck of the woods." River didn't sound surprised at all. "Hang on while I bring up her file."

Smoke could hear the soft click of keyboard strokes, then River said, "She's a nurse and a member of the Outbreak Task

Force doing a study that's twofold. First, she's collecting DNA samples and patient histories in order to track the incidence of diabetes and heart disease in the Native American population in Utah. The second part of it is attempting to track the incidence of infection and the development of antibodies in the same population for the hantavirus."

That was a lot of information to collect. "Why?"

"The CDC is considering developing a vaccine for the virus. They need to know a lot more about it first though. Most important: are people acquiring an immunity to it without developing the rapid onset pneumonia it can cause? Thirty-eight percent of cases die, so it's a damned dangerous infection."

And now for the important question. "Does the public know what she's doing?"

"They know about the first, but not the second."

"Are you sure?"

The pause on the other end of the phone was a long one. "What have you heard?"

"She's running into a sudden and solid lack of cooperation from the locals. Someone key'd her car with death threats, and she was T-boned yesterday. Right now, she looks like a very pissed off raccoon."

"That's not good."

River had always been a master at understatement.

"Put me on the payroll."

"You mean right *now*? Are you sure?" There was no missing the concern in River's voice. "You just got home. Have you even *seen* your parents yet?"

"I saw them. They're good."

"Smoke, man, I appreciate the dedication, but you and I both know you need some down time."

"Something isn't right with her."

River didn't respond right away. Smoke had always liked

that about the other man—he thought before he said shit. "What do you mean?"

"She's in trouble. I don't know what it is yet, but she looks…hunted." He knew the expression on a human being's face when they knew a bigger, nastier predator was after them. He'd been the predator more than once.

"Her background checks were okay. Nothing popped up."

"Trouble," Smoke repeated, then asked, "payroll?" Okay, it was more of a demand.

"Give me an hour or so to get it done. If you think you might have to run interference for her, I'd better get you your credentials pronto."

"Send them to my folks' address."

"Will do," River said, then paused before continuing. "You're not in the army anymore, and we're not cops or FBI agents, so don't kill anyone. Okay?"

What the fuck?

"It's Tuesday," Smoke told him with complete seriousness. "I don't like killing people indiscriminately on Tuesdays."

"No?" The smart-ass sounded surprised.

"No. I save random killing for Fridays and Saturdays."

"What about Sundays?" River asked, curiosity making his voice rise.

"Sundays, I just slap people around for the fun of it."

"That seems a bit harsh. What do you do on Mondays?"

"I punch smart-asses in the mouth."

"See you Monday then," River said cheerfully before he hung up.

Chapter Three

Kini wiped sweat off her brow and walked from her second rental car to the Smoke residence. It seemed to take half an hour rather than the few seconds it actually took. Having doors slammed in your face all day took a lot of energy out of a person.

"Hello?" she called out as she closed the screen door behind herself.

Susan popped out of the kitchen. "How'd it go today?"

Kini let her shoulders droop and said with a sigh, "Two. That's all I got. Two."

Susan frowned. "I'm sorry to hear that." She wiped her hands on a towel slung over her shoulder. "Why don't you grab a shower and relax. Tomorrow is a new day."

"That's an excellent idea," Kini said, heading toward the bathroom.

She stood under the water for a long time, letting the heat steam eight hours of frustration, exasperation, and dissatisfaction out through her pores. Damn paranoid people. She'd run into this sort of thing before in Texas and

Arkansas, but never this bad. If things didn't improve in the next couple of days, she was going to have to ask for help from someone local, someone she could take with her.

Or she could move to a different community in a different part of the state.

That was giving up, though, and giving up wasn't part of her world. She hadn't backed down when her father had—

She shoved the old anger, fear, and pain away. No, she hadn't given up when he'd destroyed their family, and she wasn't going to start now. Two more days, then she'd strategically retreat and redirect her study to a new population.

Kini finally left the shower, toweled off, and dressed in a T-shirt and shorts. In the kitchen, Susan was preparing a salad to go with steaks grilling on the barbeque in the backyard. Kini grabbed a glass of lemonade then went out the front door to sit on the front porch, shaded by a forest of plants.

The lack of city noise was nice. Peaceful. Relaxing. With a sigh, she reclined on the deck chair and let the quiet roll over her.

Movement from up the street caught her attention. A man walked this way. Smoke. His stride was long and liquid, with barely leashed energy. He looked around, taking in everything.

She had to admit, he sure was something sexy and scrumptious to watch.

A police car drove past him and down the street. A moment later it returned, pulling over in front of Smoke one house away. The lights weren't flashing, so it couldn't be a traffic stop. The man was walking, after all.

The officer got out of his car, slammed the door, and stepped onto the sidewalk in front of him.

"Well, well, look at what the cat dragged in." She had no trouble hearing what the cop said or the sneer in his voice.

"What the fuck are you doing back here?"

Smoke came to a stop a good ten feet away from the officer. "Visiting family."

At the word "family," the cop put his hand on his weapon. "I expect you to stay away from mine, you son of a bitch. You got that?"

Smoke remained still, silent, and stoic.

The cop shifted his weight on his feet, back and forth a couple of times. "If you so much as breathe the wrong way, I'll haul you in for questioning."

Smoke just watched him.

After a minute the cop muttered, "Fucking freak," got into his car, and drove off.

Smoke didn't move until the vehicle was out of sight.

He walked up to the house, his stride now full of power and menace. That threat hijacked her heartbeat and breathing, sending both on a hard sprint.

No. Not going to let the past drag her down into the dark depths of her nightmares. She wasn't a skinny ten-year-old kid anymore facing a trained killer. She was an adult with training of a different sort, and she didn't fucking bend for anyone.

She propped one foot on her other knee.

The movement pulled his attention as he reached the door, and he stopped to stare at her.

She stared back. "In trouble with the law?"

He didn't answer; then again, he didn't have to. His face told her no.

"I don't know," she said as if he'd spoken out loud. "That guy sounded like he has a hate on for you."

"Yeah." It was softly spoken, barely audible. Unlike the cop, Smoke didn't fidget or shift his weight; he just waited, his whole body seeming attuned to hers.

It was disconcerting, having someone's complete

attention like that. Uncomfortable. Then he let out a big breath. "It's a long story."

After a moment's consideration she asked, "A...*personal* story?"

He nodded.

"Fair enough." She sipped her lemonade. She had to give it to him. "We've all got one those."

He continued to stare at her. "Any trouble today?"

"Got the evil eye from the guy at the rental car place when I told them what happened to the first one and asked for a second one, but other than that, no."

He nodded and went into the house.

Kini laughed to herself. Smoke wasn't much of a talker, but he still managed to get his thoughts across with a combination of grunts, body language, and miniscule facial expressions.

That cop sure had plenty to say, and he didn't look like the forgiving sort. If he could have arrested Smoke, he would have. So, what was that story?

No use speculating. Neither party was likely to explain it to an outsider.

Kini got up and went inside. Here, she thought this was going to be an easy assignment.

Not.

• • •

Susan had chattered to Kini all through dinner, while Smoke and his dad ate silently. It could have been awkward, but when she asked Susan about who were the movers and shakers in town, she received a colorfully sarcastic rundown of who was who.

After dinner, she spent some time on her laptop catching up on reports. Smoke and his father left to return his rental car to the local office.

She wasn't keeping tabs on him, no she wasn't. After finishing up her reports, she read a book then went to bed early. In the living room. On the couch.

Sometime later, a voice dragged her out of sleep.

"What?" she asked as she rolled over.

Smoke stood a few feet away, his features shrouded by shadows. "You're on my bed."

She forced her eyes to focus on him. "I was on your bed last night. *This* isn't your bed."

"You're not sleeping here." He said the words like they were accepted fact.

No one had asked her. "Yes, I am."

"No, you're not."

Oh, for the love of Pete. "Why not?"

"Because it's not polite."

Did he just say what she thought he said? "Because I'm a *girl*?"

"Because you're a guest."

"That's a bullshit answer." She rolled back over. "You're not the boss of me."

"Move or be moved," he told her, a deep, dark demand.

A shiver rushed through her. He was serious; he would move her.

"Fine," she said with a huff, rolling off the couch. She wrapped the blanket she was using around her like a cape and walked into his bedroom. "You're several inches too tall for this couch. Don't blame me for your sore back tomorrow."

"I think I'll survive." It should have sounded like an offhand comment, but it didn't. It had weight, and it told her exactly where his head was at. *Survival.*

Kini stopped and turned to look at him. "Not good enough. This is your home; this is where you should *thrive*."

He stared at her, confusion stamped on his features for

an entire second before he wiped his face clean and lay down on the couch.

She went into his bedroom and lay down on his ginormous king-size bed. Sleep, when it came, was full of dark rooms and darker voices.

• • •

So far, this day sucked.

Yesterday, Kini had awoken on Smoke's naked chest, hot, bothered, and unsure if she was still sleeping. The man had looked like he came straight out of her naughtiest fantasies.

Today, she'd awoken cold, alone, and afraid to remember the nightmares she'd dreamed. From the time she'd gotten her coffee to the time she'd gotten to the tenth house on her list it had only gone downhill from there.

Kini pasted a smile on her face and slowly backed away from the front door she'd knocked on thirty seconds ago.

The owner of the house stood on the other side of the screen door, his hands on the collars of two large, loud, lethal dogs. Neither dog looked like any breed in particular, not that she was paying much attention to anything but their teeth as they snarled and barked at her.

"I don't care who you say you are," the homeowner shouted at her. "You're not coming in here and taking any of my blood."

Kini began to explain, "It's completely voluntary—"

"You government people seem to think you can go anywhere you want and take anything you want," the man said, interrupting her. "All you're doing is spreading diseases around and getting more people sick."

"Sick?" The hairs on the back of Kini's neck prickled. "What do you mean sick?"

"My sister-in-law died two weeks ago," he snarled. "Some

kind of viral thing. And two little kids on the next block last week." He all but spit the words at her. "If you work for the hospital, you have to know this."

Three deaths? What. The. Fuck.

"I'm sorry, but I *don't* know. I'm not affiliated with the hospital."

The man looked momentarily surprised then contemptuous. "Who the fuck do you work for then?"

Huh-oh. Something told her he wasn't going to like her answer. But now that he'd asked, she was obligated to tell him. "The CDC."

His jaw dropped.

His face morphed into an enraged mask.

Kini's hind brain told her to run while simultaneously hitting her internal gas and turbo charge buttons. The rest of her didn't argue. She pivoted on her right foot and shot across the dusty yard and dirty grass toward her car.

Behind her, the dogs barked even louder than before. She glanced over her shoulder in time to see both animals launch themselves through the screen door.

She got around the car, into the driver's seat, and slammed the door shut just before either dog could reach her.

They rammed themselves against the door, scratched at it, then rammed it some more.

A shout from the house jerked her head toward it.

The homeowner walked toward her, a rifle in his hands.

She screamed and jammed the keys in the ignition. As soon as the engine woke up she stomped on the gas. The vehicle careened down the road, barely missing several parked vehicles, heading for Main Street.

Panic receded after a few blocks, and she was able to pry her hands from the steering wheel.

Coffee, she needed coffee. Buckets and barrels and boats of coffee.

There was a little shop and bakery on the same street as the post office and police station. She ordered herself the largest coffee they had and some kind of cinnamon bun that was larger than her hand with her fingers spread out.

It took a few minutes for her thundering pulse to calm enough to realize everyone in the shop had gone completely quiet and were staring at her. Unhappy, unwelcome, unnerving. There was enough hostility in the air to choke a person, and all of it was directed at her.

Her stomach cramped up, and the thought of eating any more of the sticky confection made her nauseous. She took her coffee and left.

She managed to arrive at her next possible study participant's address without being chased down the street by people armed with pitchforks, getting a ticket for distracted driving, or getting shot at. The white-haired woman who answered the door invited her in and answered all her questions without hesitation.

She had to explain what she'd do with the woman's blood before she allowed Kini to take a sample, then the elderly woman explained that she'd been a nurse for thirty years. That started a conversation about vaccinations that lasted a half an hour.

Kini completed her paperwork then left the house and walked to her car, but something about it was off. As she rounded the hood, the problem became obvious—both tires on the driver's side were flat.

Not just flat, slashed.

She was pretty sure the car rental company only kept one spare in the trunk.

A sigh escaped her as she pulled out her cell phone, took a couple of pictures of the damage, then phoned Jim and Susan's house.

Susan answered. "Hello."

"Hi Susan, it's Kini." *How to explain this?* "Can you recommend a towing company in town?"

Susan's voice became alarmed. "Something happened to your car? Again?"

She ignored the second question. "Two flats. Looks like someone slashed my tires."

"What?" Susan asked, outrage turning the word into a curse. "This is crazy."

Kini was out of energy to get upset. "Yeah." She rubbed one throbbing temple.

"Jim's brother runs a mechanic shop," Susan said in a let's-take-care-of-business tone. "Give me your location, and I'll have him drive over to grab you and your car."

"Thanks. I really appreciate it."

She gave Susan the address then hung up and stared at the tires. How had she become enemy number one in this community? Her first rental car had been graffitied and T-boned, a guy sic'd his dogs on her, then everyone in the coffee shop watched her like she was carrying the plague, and now this.

No one's luck was this bad.

"Hey!"

Kini looked up at the shout. A young man, no more than twenty, strode toward her. Angry brows crowded his eyes, and he pointed a finger at her. "We don't want you here, Fed." He said the last word like it was dirty.

"I'm not with the federal government or the FBI," she said to him in a firm tone. "And I'd love to leave, but someone slashed my tires."

Rather than glance at the tires, the young man glanced up and down the road. Kini followed his gaze but didn't see anyone. Was this the guy who'd hacked up her tires?

He grinned at her, but it wasn't a nice expression, and said, "Too bad for you." He strode toward her, his gaze hot with anger.

She'd seen that expression on a man's face before, and it only meant one thing. Pain, for her.

Fear locked down her muscles momentarily, but she breathed through the response like her self-defense teacher taught her. Yesterday, she'd kneed Smoke's cousin in the nuts without giving it a second thought, but he'd surprised her. She could see this guy coming, and her imagination began cramming every possible catastrophe into her cranium.

The sample. She had to protect the sample she'd just taken.

She tucked the case under the car and stepped away. Getting caught between him and the vehicle would be a mistake.

He kept coming, his speed increasing as he got closer, with enough rage on his face to ensure he'd probably knock her out with one punch.

Panic tried to take over her breathing, narrow her vision, and send her running, but she fought the bitch off.

Her assailant was too close, if she ran he'd grab or tackle her, then she'd be in real trouble.

He pulled his right arm back as he got within reaching distance, but she stepped into him, spoiling his strike. Her knee came up between his legs, then she stomped on his running shoe with every ounce of force she could put into her cowboy boot. She felt the distinct snap of a bone breaking in his foot.

He howled in pain and stumbled back.

It worked. Those self-defense lessons actually *worked*.

The high of the success only lasted a few seconds, followed by nausea strong enough to knock her to her knees. With the threat disabled, her stomach seemed way too interested in throwing up all over the situation. Was this normal?

The young man screeched and cupped his groin while

hopping around and trying to hold his foot at the same time. "Fucking bitch," he wailed.

"You threw the first punch," she retorted, breathing deeply through her mouth to stave off vomiting.

"I'm going to fuck you up so bad, bitch," he snarled. Then tripped and landed on his side.

"Oh, stop being such a baby," she said, dizzy with relief, and sick and tired of the weird attitude the people of this town seemed to have. "It's just one little bone in your foot. No one will even put a cast on it."

He tried to stand, attack her, but as soon as he got to his feet, he howled in pain and fell on his butt.

The rumble of an engine caught her attention. A tow truck pulled up next to her car, sending a cloud of dust into the air. A man got out, walked around the large vehicle, and out of the haze.

Smoke.

He took in the car with its slashed tires, the sniveling whiner, and her kneeling on the ground. His face tightened as he looked her over, his gaze tactile and proprietary.

She shivered and stood. No man had ever looked at her like that before. Then she noticed his clenched fists and realized his expression also contained an enormous amount of rage.

She got to her feet and fought to stand her ground, to wait for him to regain control, and gave serious consideration to hissing a warning at the guy who attacked her. *His* life might be in danger.

"What happened?" Smoke asked at last.

Sucking in a breath, Kini was about to answer. Her attacker beat her to it.

"She broke my foot," the big baby said, pointing at her. "And flattened my balls."

Smoke looked at her accuser. "She's what, five feet tall

and you're six feet," he said. "In order for her to knee you in the nuts and stomp on your foot, you'd have to be standing *in* her personal space."

"He threw a punch at me," Kini said before Whiner could complain again.

Smoke grunted. "Your fault. She was defending herself."

Whiner didn't take that well. "I'm calling the cops."

"Okay." Smoke smiled—it oozed threat and dripped menace. It was the scariest expression she'd ever seen on a man's face.

She darted a look at Whiner.

He'd paled, but he pulled himself together and said, "I don't know you, dude, but this is my town. I have a lot of friends here, so there isn't anywhere you can go where I can't find you."

"Freddy." Smoke spoke the name slowly, as if savoring it. "Alvarez." He let the name hang in the air for a moment before continuing. "The last time I saw you, you were sitting in county jail for a break and enter on your aunt's house. I know exactly how many friends you have, and where they all live, too."

Freddy's eyes widened and he leaned away. "Smoke?"

Smoke's white teeth flashed in the too-bright sun.

Freddy didn't say anything, just stared at Smoke like he was the monster under the bed.

"Go, Freddy," Smoke said, his smile gone as if it had never been there. "Stay away from her."

Freddie swallowed hard. "Yeah, yeah, or the buzzards will be picking my bones clean out in the desert," he said as he got to his feet, wobbled, winced, then limped away.

Smoke didn't move until Freddy was out of sight, then he stalked toward her, so totally focused on her she took a step back before catching herself and planting her feet.

He stopped a couple of feet away, his gaze examining

her again. "Okay?" His tone was surprisingly tentative and gentle.

Good Lord, the force of his personality was enough to knock a body over. "I'm fine." Her voice sounded much too shaky. She managed to take in a breath and repeated, "I'm fine." In a tone that could be believed.

He reached out and cupped her face with one large, warm hand.

Breathing was optional, right?

He studied her carefully, as if looking for evidence that Freddy had hit her, nodded once, then dropped his hand. "Okay," he said as if finally satisfied she wasn't injured. He went to the truck.

Smoke turned the truck around and backed it up to her car. He got out and began hooking it up to the tow truck as if he'd done it a million times before. Hadn't he just gotten out of the army?

"You got a job with the mechanic?" she asked him as she grabbed her sample case off the ground.

"Nope, just borrowed his truck. He's busy."

"Oh." She let out a deep breath. Her shoulders hurt, and she rotated them to loosen the tension.

"Freddy hit you?" Smoke asked, and she realized he'd stopped moving to watch her.

"I don't think so. He tried, but I got in too close."

Smoke's intense gaze never left her face. "You know how to fight." It was a statement, not a question.

"Dirty," she qualified. "I know how to fight dirty."

He didn't move, didn't even blink.

She sighed. "I have a good self-defense instructor. It's something of a hobby."

"Ah," Smoke intoned as if she'd explained the one concept that was the meaning to everything.

He finished hooking up the car then nodded at her to get

into the truck's cab. At least, that's what she thought his nod meant.

She got in and so did he, but he didn't put the truck into gear, didn't even take it out of park. He looked out the windshield for several seconds then turned his head to make eye contact with her.

"Good."

Good? What was goo— Oh. Her fighting dirty. The expression on his face was so…satisfied.

He *loved* that she fought dirty.

Was that good or bad? She smiled weakly at him. He nodded, then he started the truck and drove down the street.

"What pissed Freddy off?" Smoke asked after a minute.

"I don't know. I'd just left my last study participant. I discovered the slashed tires and called your parents to find out about a towing company. Freddy came walking down the street and yelled at me to leave. He never said why or what made him angry in the first place."

Smoke grunted, but said nothing more.

"The house before that one was worse, though. The guy sent his dogs after me for no reason I could figure out."

"Dogs?"

"Yeah. Scared me half to death. They scratched up the door of my rental, too."

"Bad luck," Smoke said, driving into the parking lot of a long, low building surrounded by an unorganized assortment of vehicles. "Caution is good, too."

"Thanks," she muttered. "I've gotten better advice from a fortune cookie."

A strange sound came out of him.

She narrowed her eyes and studied his profile. Was he laughing?

He kept his face angled away from her, but his shoulders were relaxed in a way that only happened after a good laugh.

Jerk.

He backed the car into the garage then got out to unhook it, with a sneaky little smile on his face.

Some hero he was, snickering at her.

Kini got out, too, and stood to one side, uncertain of where she should wait.

"Hey, government lady," someone said behind her.

She ignored them. Why did everyone think she worked for the government? She wasn't even wearing a suit.

"Hey!"

Whoever it was sounded a lot closer, and a lot angrier.

She spun around then took several steps back from a middle-aged man charging toward her with a large wrench in his hand.

He lifted the tool and pointed it at her. "I've got a question for you."

Chapter Four

Smoke slid between the truck and the car and got in front of Kini before his uncle Terry could finish yelling at her.

The other man brought himself up short, glaring at his nephew. "What?"

That's all he got after being away for two years—what? "Put the tool down."

Terry rolled his eyes. "I wasn't going to hit her with it."

Smoke didn't say anything, just stared and crossed his arms over his chest.

A second later, his uncle dropped it at his feet.

Smoke glanced at Kini over his shoulder, noted her slack jaw, and stepped out of the way.

She looked at him, her head tilted slightly to one side.

He nodded at her unspoken question, answering it the same way.

She hesitated, surprise fliting across her face, then looked at his uncle. "Your question?"

"I just got a call from Dave." He glanced at Smoke. "Marlowe."

Smoke nodded once.

His uncle frowned at Kini. "He said you wrecked his screen door."

Both her eyebrows went up and her jaw dropped before she said, "If by wrecking you mean running for my life after his two dogs went through that door to attack me, then yes."

Terry's frown turned confused. "He said you wanted his blood."

"I asked if I could interview him, obtain his medical history, and take a small sample of blood. I made it clear that his name wouldn't appear on any of the material. This is a blind study. I collect the information, but the techs and research staff only see each person as a number in the study."

Terry took a half step back. "It's all over town that you're making people sick."

Kini's expression turned insulted. "That's ridiculous. To do that, I'd have to be sick myself and I'm not."

Uncle Terry opened his mouth then closed it before saying anything.

"Where did Mr. Marlowe get his information?" Kini asked.

"He didn't say," Terry mumbled.

"You said it was all over town?"

"Yeah, the gals at the post office are talking about it."

"That's how you define everyone?"

"Everyone goes to the post office," Smoke told her.

"Fabulous." Kini threw her hands up in the air. "Attacked by dogs, slashed tires, and now confronted by a man with a wrench demanding answers, and it's not even noon. What's next? A knife-throwing circus performer who thinks I'm his target?"

Her sarcasm made him want to chuckle. No one had ever made him want to lose enough control over himself to actually laugh out loud, but she was managing it. Repeatedly.

"So you're not the reason three people have shown up at the emergency room with some kind of freaky pneumonia?"

Smoke studied Terry's face. Nope, the man wasn't making that shit up. He glanced at Kini in time to see her face harden into the kind of determination he'd only ever seen on the faces of his fellow soldiers.

Target in sight. Go for takedown.

She headed for Terry, going around Smoke so fast he couldn't catch her before she was by him.

Fuck.

Terry backpedaled fast with the air of a man a hair's breadth away from running.

Kini stopped advancing. The look on her face could have started another ice age. "What did you just say?"

Terry looked at him with a *now, what do I do?* expression.

Smoke gestured toward her with an open hand. No sense in keeping the information from her. Out of practically everyone within a one hundred-mile radius, she should probably be informed.

"Three people showed up at the hospital with pneumonia today. The doctor won't say what he thinks it is, but people are saying hantavirus," Terry said in a much nicer tone than he'd used so far.

Kini's small hands clenched into tight fists.

She looked ready to commit murder.

Smoke sidled up to her and laid one hand on the small of her back. Not doing anything, just offering comfort. "Terry isn't the one you want to strangle."

She spun to glare at him. "Just who is it you think I should strangle?"

"Whoever started the rumors."

"Something tells me that wringing all the necks of the post office employees won't go over with the local law enforcement."

"They didn't start it. They're just the delivery system."

She reared back a little and searched his face. "That's... perceptive."

He shrugged.

"I never asked before. What did you do in the army?"

"Whatever I was ordered to do."

She crossed her arms over her chest and let out a huff. "That's not an answer."

"Most of the time, that's all I was ever able to say." River had ordered him to look after her. To do that, he needed her to trust him, to count on him, to communicate with him. "Special Forces," he added quietly. "A buddy of mine works for the CDC. He says he knows you. River."

"You served with River?"

At his nod, she let out a huge breath. "He set up my homestay with your parents. You two were in some of the same deployments?"

"Same unit," Smoke confirmed.

"So you've worked with dangerous microorganisms before?"

"Not directly, but protecting the people who were."

"Don't sell yourself short," she told him, then glanced at Terry and raised her voice. "Most people actually believe everything the media says about bacteria and viruses."

"What's that supposed to mean?" Terry asked.

She snorted. "They blow some things completely out of proportion, like Ebola." She shook her head. "Everyone was in a frenzy about it, but did they mention you have to be swimming in that stuff to get it? No, they made it seem like you could catch it easily."

"But all those cases in Africa—"

"They *were* swimming in it. Those shanty towns have no sanitation, so they're drinking, bathing, and washing in their own waste."

"She's right," Smoke said. "If your water is clean, the chance of a disease spreading is a hell of a lot smaller."

"How do you know that?" Kini asked.

"One of the first things you learn before you're deployed: ensure you have enough clean water and food with you to last the mission." He hesitated then added, "Though, when in doubt, always take additional ammunition and less food."

Terry looked uncomfortable. "So, those people in the ER...?"

"I'd bet hantavirus, too. It's endemic to most states west of the Mississippi and in this part of the country in particular." She frowned. "It *can* cause a catastrophic pneumonia-like response in the body that can kill in less than two days. Basically, you drown in your own fluids. Mice and rats carry the virus, and it's found in their droppings. If their droppings dry out and become part of the airborne dust, it's all too easy for you to breathe it in. It's not unusual for hotspots of infection to pop up from time to time." She hesitated. "But three at once, that's concerning." She frowned. "The guy with the dogs said there was a death two weeks ago and two deaths one week ago."

"That makes six," Smoke said. That wasn't good.

"That's a significant number." She turned to him. "I'll check in with my boss and see if the CDC has been informed."

He nodded, and she walked a short distance away before pulling out her cell phone.

Terry wandered over to stand next to him. "I fucked that up."

"Yup."

"I should have known better than to believe those harpies, but they had me and a bunch of other people convinced she was the source of some nasty shit."

Smoke slanted an *are you kidding me?* glance at his uncle. "She's not the serial killer type."

"I don't know, she looked like she was ready to fight tooth and nail with someone." Terry looked over at the rental car. "Did she say someone slashed her tires?"

"Yeah. Two. Can you put some new ones on for me?"

"Sure. My cost plus a piece of your mom's pie tonight."

"Done."

Terry headed into the shop to check the tires.

Kini closed her phone and came over. "There's been no official reports of any hantavirus cases here. None. So my boss wants me to check in with the hospital to see what the story is." She watched Terry mess around with the tires for a moment then asked Smoke, "Have you got a vehicle? I need a chauffeur until that's fixed."

"I've got a hog."

She looked confused for a second, then understanding blossomed on her face. "You have a motorcycle?"

"No," he said, leading her around the building and over to a big, black machine that looked like it ate the flashy type of motorcycles she saw in the city for fuel. "A hog."

He swung one leg over the seat and kick-started the engine. A dragon's roar came out of it, rumbling through the exhaust pipes until it emerged in a low growl of vibration and smoke.

She stared at him like he'd lost his mind. "I can't ride that. Where am I going to put my collection case?"

"Leave it," he told her, thrusting his chin toward the interior of the garage where Terry was busy jacking up her rental car.

She pressed her lips together but went to the car, mumbling something he couldn't quite catch under her breath. She popped the trunk and stashed the box, then closed the trunk and came toward him with her jaw set and shaking her head.

"Do you have helmets?"

He snorted.

"Right. How silly of me to expect a soldier to wear protective equipment while driving this car-eating machine."

"Stop procrastinating," he said and revved the engine.

She sighed. He couldn't hear it, but his eyesight was perfectly fine and her chest rose and fell the same way as any woman's did when she was frustrated with a man.

She slung her purse over her head so it was across her body then swung her leg over the seat and settled behind him. One glance down showed him neither of her feet were touching the ground, and she was also sitting too far back. That would change as soon as he put his baby into gear.

"Hang on," he said over his shoulder and injected the gas.

She squawked and threw her arms around his waist, and just like that she was plastered to him. Her breasts felt just as good against his back now as they did yesterday morning pillowed on his abdomen. He'd missed seeing her today. She'd managed to get up and off to work before he'd finished his shower.

He chuckled as they left the parking lot and headed at a sedate speed toward the hospital.

"Not funny," she yelled into his shirt.

He patted one of her hands tightly gripping his waist.

She sighed again, but aside from snuggling up a little closer, didn't complain.

They turned onto Main Street and drove past the two grocery stores, the hardware store, and three bars as people called out and waved when he passed. He waved back, but wasn't tempted to stop and talk.

First, he was on the clock now and he didn't have time for chitchat. Second, everyone knew he wasn't much for talking anyway. No one was going to be surprised when he rolled on by.

The hospital came into view ahead, and Kini leaned around him to take a look at it.

Smoke rode into the parking lot and found a good spot for his hog, then cut the engine.

Kini got off so fast she wobbled.

Smoke reached out and snagged her with one hand, jerking her up against him.

She squeaked then froze, her face only a couple inches from his.

She smelled like lavender, clean and crisp, her breath hot as it caressed his lips. His cock was a fucking steel rod. Any more pressure and he was going to break his goddamn zipper wide open.

"Sorry," she whispered, the word sounding more like a prayer than an apology.

"What for?" he asked just as quietly.

She gave him a little smile. "Clumsy."

He let some of the lust racing through him bleed into his answering grin and drawled, "Anytime."

He watched her pupils dilate and had to work hard to resist the urge to kiss the daylights out of her. Work really hard.

It did not help him when she sucked in a shaky breath and licked her lips. Was she trying to kill him?

She put her hands on his shoulders, took a half step back, and steadied herself.

He held on to her for a fraction of a second longer then released her slowly.

She stepped away from him, but still seemed awfully wobbly.

"Okay?" he asked, studying her.

"I've never ridden anything so…"

He raised one eyebrow.

A blush spread across her face, giving her a glow he wanted to stroke and pet.

She cleared her throat. "Loud before." She shifted her

weight from foot to foot and her teeth worried at her lower lip.

"Scary, too?" he asked, keeping his tone soft.

Her head came up at that. "No." It was her turn to study him. "No, a little more thrilling than I'm used to is all."

"I guarantee a safe ride," he told her in that deceptively soft tone. "No matter how fast, hard, and loud it gets."

She blinked and her cheeks turned a luscious pink. "Oh."

Oh yeah, he'd given her plenty to think about.

"Ready?" he asked, glancing at the building.

Her expression lost its soft speculation. "Yes. Let's get this mess figured out."

Smoke flicked out the kickstand and pocketed his keys. He joined Kini on the sidewalk, and they went in the emergency room entrance. For a small town, there were a lot of people waiting to see a doctor. All the chairs in the waiting area were occupied, with a few standing or leaning against a wall.

Kini went straight to the admitting desk and leaned over it to speak to the receptionist quietly.

"No, I'm sorry," the receptionist said, not looking away from her computer screen. She spoke loud enough for the entire room to hear every word. "We only have one doctor on duty right now. You'll have to wait until tomorrow morning to talk to the hospital administrator."

"Isn't he working today?" Kini asked, matching the other woman's volume.

Yup, she wasn't happy with this chick.

"All I know is that he isn't in the building."

"What about your chief of staff?"

"The chief is on duty."

Kini drummed her fingers against the desk. "I have to talk to him about the pneumonia cases."

"Look," the receptionist said, dropping the thin veil of

politeness she'd been hiding behind. "Our exam rooms are full, our waiting room is full, and our ICU is full. He doesn't have time for a chat about our programs or anything that isn't an emergency."

"I'm not here to talk about programs, I'm here to find out the facts surrounding your pneumonia cases."

"Are you a reporter?"

"No, I'm a nurse."

"Who do you work for?"

Smoke glanced around and noted how many people were listening in to this conversation. Things were about to get interesting.

Kini sounded pissed off when she answered, "I'm with the CDC."

Chapter Five

The nurse stared at Kini, horror chasing all the blood out of the woman's face, and she said much too loudly, "The CDC is here?"

Behind her, the sudden and complete lack of noise from the rest of the room told Kini a large portion of the people waiting had heard the receptionist's question.

So much for keeping it on the down-low.

"No." Kini really had to work to keep from clenching her teeth and shredding every word out of her mouth. "I'm here on behalf of the CDC. Where is your chief of staff?"

She pointed over her shoulder. "In the back."

Well, wasn't that helpful. *Not.*

Hanging on to her temper with both hands, Kini stepped around the desk and went through the doorway behind the reception desk. If that idiot's inability to lower her volume started a panic, she was going to say something…unpleasant.

She passed through a hallway that opened out into a circular bullpen with exam rooms radiating off of it like spokes on a wheel. A half dozen people, all in scrubs, were working like the room was on fire.

No one seemed to have noticed Smoke or her.

One of the women seemed calmer that the rest, typing with a speed that should have had the keyboard giving off radiation. Kini strode over to her. "I need to speak with the doctor on duty."

The woman glanced up, a frown on her face. "I'm sorry, you can't be—"

"My name is Kini Kerek," she said, interrupting the other woman. "I'm a nurse with the CDC."

"Oh." The woman's posture relaxed a bit. "Thank God Dr. Flett called you in." She turned before Kini could correct her assumption and called across the room to a tall, lean man with salt-and-pepper hair. "Dr. Flett. The CDC is here."

Did everyone think the CDC showed up in force at every suspicious infectious hot spot? They didn't have that kind of money.

God didn't have that kind of money.

Dr. Flett looked at her then gave Smoke a quick once-over. "The CDC?" He didn't sound impressed or happy to see them.

Kini walked toward him. "Kini Kerek, CDC Public Health department." Smoke stood so close behind her she could feel the heat radiating off his body. "This is Lyle Smoke—"

"CDC Outbreak Task Force," Smoke finished for her.

She had to work to keep her attention on Flett because she really wanted to gape at Smoke and ask, *really*?

He gave her a brief nod and said one word. "River."

River had managed to recruit Smoke already? "That was fast," she said under her breath.

"Who called you?" Dr. Flett demanded. He pointed an accusing gaze at the woman she'd just spoken to. "Did you call them, Janet?"

"No, sir. I thought you called them."

Before he could accuse anyone else, Kini spoke up. "No one called us. We're following up on a tip from a member of the public."

Flett rolled his eyes. "You investigate every crackpot and conspiracy theorist in the state?"

She gave him a tight smile. "When they assault me and accuse me of killing people with an infection I know nothing about, yes."

The doctor shook his head and went back to the chart he'd been looking at. "People are overreacting. It's just the start of flu season."

"So, you admit you have patients with flu-like symptoms? What about breathing difficulties? Pneumonia?"

He stared at her like she was asking for military launch codes.

Idiot.

Kini gathered all the patience she could muster and tried to project it into her voice. "Right now, it's myself and Mr. Smoke investigating. If all you've got is a few people with the flu and nothing more serious, we'll be in, out, and gone before you know it. If what you've got is more than that..." She paused to lean toward him and lowered her voice. "You want us on the ground here early."

"This is my hospital," he said, his tone sharp, contempt curling his lip.

Don't go there. Do *not* go there.

"These are my people." He continued looking down at her as if he were standing on a pulpit and she was a lowly petitioner. "*I'm* in charge."

He went there.

Moron.

Kini managed to hang on to her temper well enough to say, "Not my call to make, but the CDC doesn't take over if it doesn't have to. We'd rather work with you behind the scenes.

Things stay calmer that way."

He stared at her for a couple of seconds then glanced at Smoke before, finally, saying, "We've had three deaths in the last couple of weeks, all from rapid onset pneumonia. Testing hasn't come back yet on whether it's bacterial or viral."

Finally cooperation.

"Any current cases?"

"Four. I just admitted a new one about ten minutes ago." He paused and cleared his throat. "There may be more in the waiting room."

If he suspected more, what the hell were they doing in the waiting room? Gleefully infecting all those other people?

Saying that out loud would not lead to continued cooperation. She sucked in a breath and held it. No telling the idiotic man he was not only narcissistic, but stupid, too. He'd just get all arrogant and whiny.

By the time she was done talking to this jackass she was going to have a hernia.

Behind her, Smoke shifted his weight.

When had he gotten that close?

He tapped her on the shoulder. "A word?" He didn't wait for her response, looking at Dr. Flett and giving the man a nod before guiding her away.

"What is it?" she asked him. "Did you get a text from River?"

"No." He glanced at a couple of nurses who'd paused to read charts a couple of feet away.

They moved off.

"You looked like you were going to go boom."

She winced. "That bad, huh?"

He nodded once and gave her a thorough visual examination that left her with a full-body blush. "Okay?" His gaze was…hot, possessive, and completely inappropriate.

She wanted more.

No. No. *No*. More was bad. More would lead to another morning of waking up naked on his chest. Her libido had barely survived the first time; it couldn't take a second time without tying the man down and having its wicked, wicked way with him.

She cleared her throat instead of fanning herself. "I'll try not to have a stroke." She practically ran back to Dr. Flett. "My apologies. Would it be possible for me to obtain your patients' recent histories and take blood samples?"

He looked at her like she'd just crawled out from under a rock. "Fine, but stay out of the way of my staff."

"Of course." She pinched her lips together to prevent the words, *prick* and *dick,* from coming out of her mouth. Her mother would rise from her grave to stick a bar of soap in it.

Flett called over a nurse and ordered her to assist Kini, then turned on his heel and disappeared into an exam room.

Kini gave the woman a commiserating smile. "Sorry to disrupt things, but all I need is the histories on the patients with pneumonia. I'll also need to come back to take blood samples from them."

"Okay." She led them over to a stack of charts, grabbed four, and handed them to Kini. "Why do you need to come back for the samples?"

"I didn't bring my collection kit with me," Kini said. She would have, but Smoke's monster machine would have needed a sidecar. "Will returning later for them be a problem?"

"We'll mention it at shift change if you're not done before then."

"Thanks." Kini looked at the charts then at her new colleague. How the hell had he gotten hired in just one day?

He met her gaze with a self-contained *I'm innocent* expression that was beginning to drive her crazy.

She took the charts, found an unoccupied bit of space on the counter, and began reading.

Three of the four patients all reported having flu-like symptoms for the last week. Fever, tiredness, achy muscles in the chest and back. What drove them to the ER was a worsening shortness of breath. One patient described it as feeling smothered by heavy blankets.

Blood had been drawn for chemistry and blood cell analysis, but the results weren't in the chart yet.

An alarm went off in the one of the exam rooms. Two nurses and Dr. Flett rushed over and went inside. The alarm was shut off, but the nurse who came out of the room ran to a cart of medical supplies and pushed it at a run back to the room.

Kini glanced at Smoke then headed toward it.

She didn't need to go inside to see Flett inserting a trach tube down the patient's throat and into their lungs, then connect that to a ventilator. The patient had lost the battle to breathe on her own.

She looked at the room number then at the charts in her hands. It was one of the hantavirus possibilities.

Another nurse came over and poked her head into the room. "Lab results are back."

Flett nodded at her but didn't pause as he listened to the patient's chest.

"Is the patient's hematocrit elevated?" Kini asked. When the nurse hesitated, she added, "I'm with the CDC, evaluating this patient."

"Um." The nurse turned away and consulted some paperwork on the desk. "Yes, it's slightly elevated. White cell count is up a little too."

She winced. Well, that wasn't good news. "Thanks."

The nurse returned to her work.

Smoke stepped into her space. "What does an elevated hematocrit mean?"

"Hm, oh, often at this stage, the body overreacts to the presence of the virus by flooding the lungs with fluid. It shows up in the blood as a kind of dehydration, which raises the hematocrit. It's one of the diagnostic criteria for Hantavirus Pulmonary Syndrome. That would be the official diagnosis if the patient has the hantavirus. Most non-health-care people would just call it pneumonia."

"So, it's here."

"Very possible."

He looked at her. "Now what?"

She squared her shoulders. "Dr. Flett isn't going to like the now what. So, I'll have to be sure I follow procedures perfectly. I need to go over these charts and write an analysis/summary of them, take samples, and make my recommendations."

"Doesn't sound quick."

"I can't afford to make mistakes." Mistakes could kill. "How long will it take before the tires are fixed on my rental?"

Smoke's answer was to take out his cell phone and call his uncle.

"Twenty minutes," he reported after a series of one- and two-word sentences.

She looked up at him. "How do you do that?"

"What?"

"Say in a couple of words what most people have to use entire sentences to communicate."

He shrugged, his wide shoulders stretching the fabric of his T-shirt. "Talented?"

He was going to drive her crazy.

She pulled out her tablet from her purse and began making notes. It took her about fifteen minutes to finish, and Smoke stayed with her the entire time. He didn't wander around, pace, or ask questions. He watched the entire room like he expected bad guys to stroll in looking for an argument.

"Stop it," she hissed at him.

"Stop what?" He sounded confused.

She glanced at him. He looked it, too.

"You're like a coiled cobra ready to strike, and it's making me...edgy."

"Coiled cobra?"

She sighed. "You know what I mean." She waved her hand in front of him, indicating all of him. "You're ready to go into battle, only there's no one here for you to beat up."

He grunted, seemed to consider her complaint, then spoke softly. "That's who I am. My grandfather says I live up to my name. A silent watcher who knows to wait until the right moment to make my move."

A shiver went down her back and she stared at him.

"I'm not a nice man." It almost seemed like an afterthought. A confession he hadn't thought to make until now.

"Are you trying to scare me?"

"You...you're the last person I want to scare." He smiled and it was so full of sexual promise it devastated her.

It took two deep breaths for her to recover and say, "You're a menace."

"Yep," he said, drawing the word out.

Kini focused her gaze on her tablet. Work. She had work to do, and salivating all over her partner shouldn't be on her list. As she made note of this last patient's name and address, she realized she'd seen it before. Or something close.

She scrolled through her notes and wondered if she was seeing connections where there weren't any.

"Smoke, would you look at these addresses? Are they close together?"

He went through them. "Yeah, they're all within a five-mile radius."

"Oh." Damn, she'd thought she'd found something useful, but five miles was a lot of space.

"They're all on the edge of the Zion National Park. There isn't anyone else out there, just them."

Understanding animated her voice. "*Oh*."

Chapter Six

Kini had an expressive face. Smoke watched as surprise, understanding, then dismay rolled across it. She glanced at her tablet then stared at nothing, thinking. A little nod and a lift of her chin told him she'd made a decision.

He'd bet fifty bucks she was going to want to check in on the family members of each patient to see if they were showing any symptoms.

"I need my collection kit and my car."

Yep, they were going for a drive. "Okay." Smoke angled his head at Dr. Flett, who'd just come out of the exam room. "What about him?"

"He isn't going to listen to anything I have to say." Her tone was flat. "I'm just a nurse."

"Dumb."

"Yeah," she said, her voice dry. "But no surprise there." She moved off to talk to one of the nurses then returned. "We can go now."

When she would have gone back out through the ER waiting room, he put a hand on her shoulder and nudged her in the opposite direction. "Back door."

Surprise flitted over her, making her seem...brighter. "Excellent idea."

"Do you compliment everyone?" he asked as they walked down the hall.

"Only when people deserve it." She glanced at him. "Thanks."

"For what?"

"Backing me up in there."

He frowned at her. He hadn't done much.

Though he hadn't spoken out loud, she said, "You didn't try to take over, and you didn't say anything; you stood behind me and looked irritated. You were perfect."

They reached the door and he opened it for her, raising one eyebrow as he looked at her. "Perfect, huh?"

"At looking threatening," she qualified quickly, a blush spreading up her neck.

He leaned down to whisper in her ear as she went past him and through the doorway, "I aim to please."

Her back went ramrod straight and she stomped ahead of him, muttering something under her breath that sounded suspiciously like, "*Men.*"

They rounded the building until they arrived at his bike. He got on, kicked the engine into life, and looked at her.

She'd crossed her arms over her chest and was scowling at him. "We need to talk."

He lifted one shoulder to tell her to get to it.

She looked pointedly at the engine, so he killed it.

As soon as the rumble ended she said, "Stop with the innuendoes. It's disrespectful to both of us."

The blush on her face was red hot now. Did she think he was doing it to get a rise out of her? That he was just playing with her? If he told her what he wanted, to go back to the first time they met and do less talking and more kissing, she'd probably run like hell.

But she'd asked for honesty, so she'd get honesty.

"No disrespect intended," he said. "I've been hard since I woke up with you draped over my chest."

She rocked back on her heels like he'd hit her. "Is that a threat?"

See what honesty got him? Into shit, that's where. "No."

She narrowed her eyes. "A promise?"

Those eyes, along with pinched lips, told him she really meant *threat* again. "No."

She stared at him, the frown on her face growing more and more pronounced. "Then what?"

Fuck it. "Yesterday morning, when I woke up with you half naked and plastered to me was the first time in two years I didn't wake up with the urge to kill someone." He watched her face as her blush dissipated.

"Oh." A furrow etched its way between her eyebrows along with something suspiciously close to sympathy.

No thanks.

"I'm not looking for a pity fuck."

That erased the awkwardness in about a second. "I wasn't…" She groaned and rolled her eyes. "You're such a guy." She climbed onto the bike behind him. "Let's go."

He waited until she'd wrapped her arms around his waist before starting the engine and leaving the parking lot at a sedate, legal speed. He gave the gas a kick once they were on the street and she hung on to him harder, pressing her breasts into his back.

He knew she'd liked what he'd done and not done while she was negotiating with Flett. He'd let her do her thing while he did his, convincing the asshole he'd beat the crap out of him if he was disrespectful.

Then he'd become an asshole himself. Why? Because he wanted her attention, her mind picturing them on his bed completely naked? Why not just give her a stupid one liner? *Hey baby, forget my bike, take me for a ride.*

She'd knee him in the nuts, and he'd deserve it. He wasn't that guy, so why was he acting like it? Was she right? Was he acting like an asshole because getting close to her meant facing all the shit he'd dragged home with him and all the shit waiting for him here?

They arrived back at his uncle's shop, her car with its new tires ready and waiting.

Kini hopped off the back of the bike and took a step toward her car. Smoke put a hand on her arm.

He made eye contact and said, "I was an asshole."

Both her eyebrows rose.

"Can't promise I won't be again, but…" He shrugged. He wasn't going to swear to something he couldn't deliver, but he'd try.

"Okay," she said after a couple of seconds. "I'll try not to be so bitchy." She let out a sigh. "It's been a pretty weird day."

He nodded and she gave him that brilliant smile again before she turned and walked toward her car.

They were okay. She'd understood him and that was it. They were okay.

He couldn't keep his eyes off the little wiggle that was part of her stride.

Something in Smoke's stomach tightened into a sizzling ball of heat. Shit, all she had to do was walk ten feet, and he was hard and ready to go.

But a pretty little gal like her wasn't going to be interested in a beat-up soldier with eight years of death, destruction, and desolation in his head.

He should leave her alone. Do his job, keep her safe, then walk away with a *nice working with you* wave.

That possibility had ended the moment he woke up with her sleeping on him. Her scent and the softness of her skin was in his blood and in his head so deep he wasn't sure it would ever leave.

He'd never wanted a woman like he wanted Kini.

He was absolutely bad for her.

She was too good for him.

It would never work.

He was so fucked.

Christ, when had he become a mopey Marty? His teammates would have razzed him to death if they saw him right now.

Smoke got off his bike and joined Kini and Terry.

"—brand new, all four tires," Terry said to her. He gave a nod to Smoke and kept talking. "You're good to go."

"Thank you. How much do I owe you?"

"Nothing. Smoke picked up your tab."

She turned, her mouth open, but he managed to speak before her. "The CDC is picking up the tab."

She closed her mouth, nodded, then stuck out her hand to Terry. "Thank you."

They shook. "No problem, and good luck." He turned away to work on another car.

"I'm going back to the hospital to get those blood samples," she said to Smoke.

"After that?" he asked.

"I'd like to visit the homes of the patients, check on their family members, ask more health history questions."

He thrust his thumb at his hog. "I'll follow."

The ER waiting room had doubled its occupancy since the first time they walked through it. The crowd actually made it harder for people to ID her as the nurse from the CDC, and they made it to the bullpen without incident.

When one of the nurses on duty informed them one of the patients with the suspected Hantavirus Pulmonary Syndrome had died in the time they'd been gone, Kini's face settled into a combat stare.

He knew what went on inside a person's head as they prepared to enter a live firefight—wrap all their emotions and stuff them into a concrete box in their head. All that was left was cold, calm calculation on what the next offensive in the battle was going to be.

That was all kinds of hot.

A body didn't develop that mind-set overnight. It was a coping mechanism some people acquired after they saw too much shit.

What shit had she seen?

Without speaking to him, Kini went about collecting samples from the live patients, then he followed her down to the morgue. He watched her convince the pathologist to give her a swab from deep inside the deceased's lungs and a blood sample.

They returned to the ER and Kini told Dr. Flett she was done and that she was going to check on the families of the patients.

He barely acknowledged her, his attention on the stack of charts in front of him.

When this was all over, Smoke was going to come back and have a conversation with the asshole about basic decency and politeness.

"Tell me this town has a FedEx office," she said as they left again.

Smoke shook his head. "Sorry."

"Any courier service besides the post office?"

"Nope."

"What are the chances the staff at the local USPS will keep their mouths shut?"

"About as good as seeing a dinosaur walk down the street."

"That sucks."

"Could send it with a guy I know," he said. "He could take it to Las Vegas now and put it on a plane to Atlanta."

"Vegas? How far away is that?"

"About two hours door to door."

"You trust this guy?"

"Yeah."

She thought about that for a second. "Okay."

Something was off. Her speech was clipped, and she held herself at rigid attention. He watched her out of the corner of his eye.

"How close is this friend of yours?" she asked. Too calm. Too composed. She'd put on a cloak to show the world that she was everything they expected and wanted. Underneath, her true self was fighting to get out.

"About a ten-minute drive."

She swept her arm toward the road. "Lead on, Macduff."

Invoking Shakespeare's Macbeth was never a good sign. Things hadn't turned out so well for Macduff or Macbeth.

Now wasn't the time to find out what was going on inside her head. But soon.

Smoke got on his bike, and she dutifully followed him in her rental car. They drove through town until they reached the opposite side and what looked like the last row of houses before the desert took over.

He pulled into the driveway of home that looked like it should have been on the set of one of those 50s TV sitcoms where the world's most perfect wife and mother held court in her kitchen wearing high heels and a string of pearls around her neck.

There was a truck in the driveway and a couple of later model jeeps parked out front.

Smoke got off his bike and waited for Kini to join him.

She looked at the Zen rock garden that was the focus of the front yard and the white picket fence surrounding it and the house. Then she looked at the rest of the houses on the street, none of which could hold a candle to this place.

"Your guy lives here?" She sounded incredulous.

"Yeah, he lives with his grandparents."

"He's old enough to drive, right?"

"He's twenty-two, and I taught him to drive myself." Smoke opened the door and went inside. "Hello," he called out.

"Smoke, is that you?" his grandmother asked from deeper in the house.

"Yes, ma'am."

The rapid pace of steps came from the left of the front door, then a gray-haired woman with skin the color of cream dressed in jeans and a western-style shirt came down the hall. "About time you showed up here, young man."

"Sorry," he said, folding her into his arms.

He'd never get tired of her hugs. They were powerful and lasted as long as they needed to.

She didn't seem in a hurry to let go, and he was fine with that.

More footsteps came from the other direction, and his grandfather and cousin joined them by the door.

"Hey," Tommy said, giving Smoke a back-thumping hug as soon as their grandmother let him go. "Been dull around here without you."

"Grandson," his grandfather said giving him a nod. "Good to have you home."

There were more words in his grandfather's eyes. Questions mostly, but also love, acceptance, and welcome.

Smoke soaked it all in. Maybe he should have come here first, but if he had, he wouldn't have met Kini yesterday morning. That experience wasn't something he'd ever give up.

He turned her and said, "Kini Kerek, these are my grandparents, Harold and Maggie Smoke."

Chapter Seven

Smoke had his grandmother's eyes and his grandfather's features, but Kini couldn't picture either one as a courier.

"Kini?" his grandmother asked, laughter in her gaze as she held out her hand. "So nice to meet you."

Kini smiled and shook the woman's hand. "It's good to meet you, too, Mrs. Smoke."

"Please, call me Nana." The elder woman's smile reminded Kini of her own grandmother. "We were just about to have lunch. Join us." It wasn't a suggestion.

Her lungs tightened as if wrapped in layers of barely flexible rubber. Yesterday, she could have taken the time to eat and chat. Today, every tick of the clock meant the possibility of more people getting sick and dying. "Oh, thank you, but—"

"No buts," Nana said, leading the way to the kitchen. "You can't do your job if you don't eat. You might not be a construction worker, but all that running around and talking to people takes energy, too."

"We'll be quick," Smoke said to her, his expression

confident.

All right. She turned her attention back to his grandmother. "You know what I do?"

"Of course. Jim and Susan mentioned it when they offered their home to you."

Lunch was on a large round table in one corner of a massive kitchen. Two loaves of bread, a variety of sliced cheeses, deli meats, and vegetables were laid out on platters. Condiments crowded around the food like paparazzi after a celebrity salami.

"Make your own sandwich day," Smoke said to her.

Kini hung back, but Smoke nudged her forward with a hand on the small of her back. She wanted to lean back and let him carry her weight for just a second. Would that be bad? Probably. She went to the table instead and made a sandwich.

Nana Smoke was waiting for her with a beckoning hand, leading her out of the kitchen and outside onto a covered deck. An outdoor table surrounded by chairs waited for guests.

By the time she was seated and Nana gone inside, Smoke was taking the chair on her left.

"Holy crap," she said when she caught sight of his sandwich. It was at least three inches thick. "Did you put one of everything on that thing?"

"Two," he said. He opened his mouth and took a monstrous bite. "Hmm."

Smoke's cousin Tommy pulled out the chair on her right and sat down. His sandwich was just as large as Smoke's.

Kini shook her head and took a bite of her own lunch.

It was a few moments before anyone said anything.

Finally, Smoke glanced at Tommy and said, "Got a job for you."

"Yeah?" the young man sat up straighter. "What kind of job?"

"Delivery to Las Vegas. Got to get a package to Atlanta ASAP."

"Okay. What is it?"

"Blood samples," Kini answered. Smoke's grandparents joined them. "For the CDC."

"Whoa, the CDC? Really?"

"Smoke works for them now." What she didn't know was if he'd leaned on his buddy River for the job, or if River approached him. Either way, it seemed too damned convenient. She did *not* need a babysitter.

Tommy seemed surprised. "When did that happen?"

"This morning," Smoke said. He looked at his cousin. "Yes, you get paid."

Tommy's grin was wide. "Awesome."

Kini glanced at Smoke and read the questions on his face. *Can we tell my family anything? How much can we tell them?*

How much did they really know? A series of bad luck incidents and a single digit uptick in hospital admissions and deaths did not equal an outbreak. Not for certain, anyway.

"May I make a suggestion?" Kini asked no one in particular.

"Of course," Nana Smoke said.

"You might want to stay close to home for the next day or two." She paused, considering her next words carefully. "And stay away from mice."

The faces of Smoke's family went uniformly blank.

Smoke shifted in his seat. "We just came from the hospital." He took another bite and chewed. "Town is full of conspiracy theorists."

"Well, no wonder you want Tommy to take your package into the city," Nana Smoke said, her tone hot. "Those bitches at the post office would probably look at the package's address and push the big red panic button they seem to think they own and scream, 'Anthrax!' or some other nonsense." She shook her head. "You'd end up with the FBI, State Police, and Homeland Security here before you could blink."

"You'll have to excuse Nana's language," Tommy said into the shocked silence at the end of her tirade. "The post office *lost*"—he put air quotes around the word—"a package Great Aunt Francine sent from Scotland for a whole week last month."

"Tommy, enough," his grandfather said. "Don't apologize for your grandmother. She can do that herself."

"Only when there's a reason to apologize," the woman in question said with great dignity. "And there isn't any reason to." She stood and patted Kini's hand. "Tommy will take your package to where it needs to go while Harold and I watch old movies and neck like a couple of teenagers."

"Ew," Tommy said, covering his ears. "Don't say things like that in front of me." He got up, grabbed his plate, and took a couple of steps away. He stopped and turned. "Actually, don't say them anywhere. Don't think them either." He disappeared into the house.

"He's a lot different than your other cousin," Kini remarked.

"You mean Nathan?" Nana Smoke asked. "Night and day those two. Brothers. Tommy is younger by a couple of years." She winced. "Their parents, our daughter Joyce and her husband, Roger, work for one of the international aid groups that are trying to get supplies into Syria. Nathan has his own place, but Tommy's been staying with us." She waved her hands at Kini and Smoke. "You two go on and get your business done."

"Thank you for lunch."

"Come back next week. You never know what you're going to find on the table on *make your own sandwich day*."

Kini stretched her lips up into a smile. "I'll try." This house was a foreign country to her. A place filled with laughter and love and light. All of it no more real to her than the perfect families portrayed in sitcom television shows. Safe, secure, and sheltered.

She got up, managing to keep the smile pinned to the corner of her lips until she was out of sight. Smoke followed her into the house.

Tommy was waiting for them in the kitchen. "So where's this package?"

"I'll get it." She brought it in from the rental car and explained what she needed him to do. She gave him the address of the shipping company that would transport it to Atlanta, and gave him enough cash to cover gas and coffee. He'd be returning late.

"Do not open the package," she said, caution adding depth to her tone.

"I won't," he promised. He left with an enthusiasm she couldn't remember ever feeling, driving off in one of the jeeps parked in front of the house.

"I don't think I was ever that...young," she whispered.

"I was," Smoke said. "I thought I was going to change the world."

"Did you?" she asked, afraid to look at him.

He sighed. "Not so far."

She glanced at him despite herself. "Do you want to give it another try?" She held up her tablet. "I've got three addresses that need to be checked out."

He studied her for a moment. "I suppose you want to split up."

"We'll cover more ground."

He held up a finger. "Graffiti." He lifted a second. "T-boned." A third. "Dogs." A fourth. "Slashed tires." A thumb. "Idiot."

Sure, bring all that up. "The law of averages says the next one will be fine."

He stared at her. "Bullshit."

She threw her hands in the air. "It's the only way to talk to everyone before it gets too late." She paused, then added, "Please."

"Well," he said slowly. "Since you said please."

She blinked. "Really?"

"No."

"Smoke," she said with a sigh. "We really don't have a choice."

He didn't look happy when he held out his hand. "Phone."

She gave it to him and he gave her his.

"Put your number in," he said as he did the same with her phone. "You get into any kind of trouble, even a hint of trouble, you call me."

She wasn't a moron. "I will. You do the same if you see anything suspicious. Or anyone sick. Or mice."

He nodded.

"We could meet at the third address together."

He must have been thinking the same thing, because she got an actual, real, noncynical smile from him. It hit her right in the gut with enough power to knock the wind out of her.

Jesus, she'd thought he was handsome *before*.

Smoke took the first address and explained how to get to the second one, a little farther away.

She got in her car and followed his bike down the road to the highway. Riding behind him had been fun once she got the hang of it. More than fun. He'd been warm against her body, his muscles firm under her hands.

Stupid. Getting involved with a man she'd just met was *stupid*. She knew nothing about him, and her job kept her on the move. He also carried around more anger and fury than any other ten people combined. The thought of all that rage detonating…no, she couldn't go there again. It would break her. A relationship deeper than the surface was absolutely out of the question.

As she watched him ride his bike in front of her car, the desire to feel him under her hands again grew until she had to force herself to grip the steering wheel.

She imagined him on horseback and realized if she ever saw him on one, she'd probably attack the poor man and rip his clothes off. Nope, not going there either.

He slowed down and drew level with her car.

Kini rolled down the window.

"The second right will take you to your address," he yelled. "I'll try to meet you there or at the connection to the highway."

"Okay," she yelled back.

Smoke decelerated and turned off. The highway looked desolate without him.

The second right was a long, narrow gravel road that led to a valley and a small, square two-story house. A couple of older model half-ton trucks were parked out front and a variety of children's toys were strewn across the brown grass that made up the yard.

Kini parked the car, shut off the engine, and got out.

The silence that greeted her seemed to coat everything in a suffocating blanket.

She checked her notes. This was the home of a twenty-eight-year-old mother of two. She presented with early symptoms of Hantavirus Pulmonary Syndrome that worsened until she'd been placed on a respirator about six hours earlier.

Kini walked to the front door and knocked. She knocked again, then when no one answered, tried the knob. The door opened.

"Hello," she called out. "Anyone home?"

"Mama!" A toddler came around the corner at Mach 3 and barreled into Kini's legs. The child grabbed hold of

Kini's pants with both hands and yanked, crying alternately for Mama and food.

Kini picked up the little girl. "Hi, sweetie, who's looking after you?"

The girl stared at Kini for a long couple of seconds then poked her nose. "Not Mama."

"No, I'm not. I'm Kini."

"Ki," the child said, then pointed imperiously toward the interior of the house.

Kini walked around the corner and discovered why the child was so unhappy. Someone had added Velcro straps to the door and side of the refrigerator so little hands couldn't open it.

"Hello?" Kini called out, raising her voice. "Hello."

No answer.

Where was this child's babysitter? Family members?

Small hands landed on either side of Kini's face and turned it so the little girl could press her nose against hers. "Hungy."

It took effort not to laugh. "I get the picture."

Kini opened the fridge, and the girl dove for the yogurt tubes in the door. She held one out and demanded, "Open!"

"Yes, Your Majesty."

As soon as the child got the open tube, she plopped onto her diapered butt and began to eat.

The kitchen was a mess. Dirty dishes covered the counter, sink, and small dining table.

"Hello," Kini called out again. "Anyone here?" Someone had to be looking after the child, right?

The little girl pointed toward the hallway to the left of the kitchen. "Gampa."

No sound or movement from down that hall.

"Stay here, okay?" Kini said to the girl.

The child nodded, but didn't stop gobbling up the yogurt.

Kini moved down the hallway. "Hello," she said as she walked, going slow so she didn't surprise anyone. "My name is Kini Kerek, I'm a public health nurse."

No response.

The first door she reached led to a bathroom.

The next room felt larger, the door open halfway. She knocked and said, "Hello?"

There was no answer, so she pushed the door open, bracing herself for anything. The room was empty.

She released a pent-up breath. *Stop scaring yourself, stupid.*

There was one more room to check, then she would search the rest of the house. Someone had to be here looking after the child.

She knocked on the last door and called out a hello just in case, but it was empty, too.

"Ki," said a voice behind her. "Hungy. Num num?"

"Well, your mother has good taste in snack food," Kini said to her new best friend. "Why not. More num num."

"Yay!" the child ran into the kitchen and waited by the fridge, jumping up and down and waving her arms like it was game day.

Kini got her another yogurt, opened it, and left her little friend to enjoy her snack. Around the corner opposite the hallway was a living room with the requisite big screen TV, a couple of gaming consoles, and a laptop computer sitting on the coffee table.

The coffee table was also covered in pop cans, dirty plates, and two empty pizza boxes. All the evidence of teenagers without the actual teens.

Where was everyone?

She continued searching, but found no one. Finally, she went back to the kitchen and spied another door hidden behind a coat rack. It was narrower than all the others, probably a closet, but she opened it anyway.

Stairs leading down into darkness. A basement.

She looked around. There had to be a light switch somewhere. She eventually found it, a string hanging above her head. One yank had the light on.

She looked down the stairs. Steep.

She paid attention to where her feet were going rather than examining the rest of the space. That was probably why she didn't see the body until she reached the dirt floor.

Chapter Eight

A man lay, face down, on the floor. His arms were by his sides and his legs were straight, as if he stopped suddenly and pitched forward rather than fell down the stairs. No injury, wound, or blood was evident.

The scent of earth predominated, but Kini could detect a trace of decomposition in the still air. Only a trace. He hadn't been dead long.

Long enough for the toddler upstairs to get hungry. If Kini hadn't come to investigate when she did... *Nope, not going to think about the what-ifs when they haven't happened.*

She pulled out her cell phone and tried to dial Smoke but nothing happened. *Damn it, no signal down here.*

The patter of little feet. "Ki?"

"Stay right there," she told the child. "I'm coming."

At the top of the stairs, the little girl waited with sticky hands and a sad face. "Gampa?"

Kini told the first lie she thought of. "He's sleeping." She picked up the child despite the food on her clothes, carried her into the kitchen, and plopped her on a chair. "I'm going to make you something to eat."

The child clapped her hands and said, "Hungy!"

As she looked in the fridge, Kini tried calling Smoke's phone again.

He picked after one ring. "Smoke."

"Hi, it's me." There wasn't much in the fridge. She closed it and opened the nearest cupboard. "Can you come to my location?"

"Trouble?"

"I found a toddler all by herself, and…" She grabbed an open box of crackers and shook it. Bingo. "There's a dead body in the basement."

After a moment's hesitation he said, "Stay put." The call went dead.

Kini found a can of vegetable soup and held it out to her restaurant-for-one customer, who smiled and clapped her hands.

She put her phone away and began searching for a pot.

• • •

Smoke strode out of the house, got on his bike, and roared down the road back to the highway. He'd managed to say thank you to the wife of the deceased patient for talking to him. He hoped that would be enough of the niceties. Unexpected dead bodies went to the top of his priority list.

Kini hadn't sounded too freaked out. In fact, she'd sounded distracted, but he'd take that over…okay, so Kini wasn't the hysterics kind of woman. Hell, all she'd done the morning after waking up in bed with him was tell him to mind his own business.

That didn't make it any easier to hang on to his patience as he tore up the road toward the house she'd gone to alone.

He knew that place. Same family had owned it for years.

A friend of his father's, with a daughter who'd had kids young. She was in the hospital now, a respirator keeping her alive. Who'd be at the home? Her kids were, fuck, one of them was in his teens by now. The other was a lot younger, a girl.

He reached the highway and was able to put on more speed until he hit the turnoff. He didn't slow down much, even after he hit the gravel.

Dead bodies were never good.

He pulled up out front of the house, and Kini was coming out of the door before he'd gotten off his bike. With a baby on her hip.

He thought of her, large with child, and a wave of need washed over him. *Damn.*

"Smoke." She rushed toward him then came to an awkward halt before she could reach him. She glanced at the baby, as if just realizing she was carrying the little girl.

Kini's hands were busy, but Smoke's weren't. He reached out and touched her shoulder and that of the child's. "You two okay?"

"Who dat?" the little girl asked, pointing a finger at Smoke.

"Smoke," he said, gesturing at himself with his whole hand. "Kini." He did the same to Kini, then he extended his hand toward the little girl.

"Bity," she said with a wide, toothy smile.

He remembered now. "Brittany."

She clapped and laughed.

"Call the police yet?"

"No, I've had my hands full."

"Anyone else around?"

"Not that I can see. I knocked and called out before entering the house. Brittany came straight to me asking for something to eat." The expression on her face was sad and concerned. "She was very hungry."

"Call 911. I'm going to look around, make sure no one else is taking a dirt nap."

"What killed him isn't obvious," she said. "It might not have anything to do with the hantavirus."

"Eyes open," he said with a nod.

It was harder to walk away from her and the baby than it should have been. She could look after herself and a toddler for a few minutes. The body was *dead*.

Aside from an assortment of tools, a couple of bicycles, and junk, the garage was empty. Behind the house were a couple of sheds. No one was in either. His body went on alert as the sound of a vehicle engine, but no sirens, became audible.

Smoke walked back to the house and checked the back door. Locked. Good. One less way for someone to get in. The vehicle engine died as he strode around the house. A visitor or someone he didn't know come home?

"Who the fuck are you?" a young masculine voice yelled.

Smoke's heart rate and breathing skittered, jittered, and jumped like it never had in combat. He broke into a sprint.

"I'm a nurse," Kini's voice was high with concern, or was it fright? He pushed for more speed. "My name is Kini—"

"I don't give a fuck who you are, put my sister *down*."

Smoke rounded the corner. He couldn't see Kini. Two young men stood between him and her and one of them was struggling with something. Someone. *Kini*. One of the boys was trying to take the baby forcibly from her.

"A nurse?" the kid grappling with her said, his voice a snarl. "Are you the one everyone is saying brought that sickness to town? The sickness that's *killing* my mom?"

"No, I'm trying to figure out what's made your mother sick."

The teen pulled the baby away from Kini and stepped back. The little girl began to cry and extended her hands toward Kini. The other kid stepped forward, his body posture aggressive and hostile.

"No," Smoke said in a bark he'd learned during basic training years ago. It was an order *and* a threat, and the two teens turned almost as one to meet it.

"Who the fuck are you?" the mouthy one asked, putting the little girl down and taking a step toward him with his hands clenched into fists.

The baby made a beeline for Kini, who picked her up.

"Smoke." He stopped a few feet away, keeping his shoulders deliberately relaxed while balancing on his feet, ready to repel an attack.

Or initiate one.

Both kids frowned. "You related to Nate?"

"Cousin."

The two boys separated, moving farther apart, their steps slow and measured. "Never seen you around."

They were trying to flank him. He almost smiled. "Army."

They halted as both their jaws dropped. "You're the guy who's some kind of Navy SEAL?"

Smoke shook his head.

"Didn't think so," the mouthy kid on his left said.

"SEALs are in and out," Smoke said. "Special Forces go in and stay there. Scouting, teaching, supporting." He waited a second for that info to soak in then angled his head at Kini. "She's not a threat."

They looked over their shoulders at her.

"Is she with you?"

"Yes." He examined the sniffling little girl. "You made your sister cry."

The boy sneered. "She'll get over it."

They slid toward him like a pair of hunting cats, certain of their prowess and success.

He could take them easily. They thought they knew how

to fight but had no concept of the extent of his training. "Did you do it together?"

"Do what?" mouthy asked.

"Kill the dead man inside the house."

They stopped cold. "What the fuck are you talking about?" Mouthy snarled.

"There's a body in the basement," Kini said. "An older man. He looks like he had a…"

Both boys dove toward the door.

Kini, with the baby in her arms, flattened against the wall, letting them pass. "…heart attack."

As soon as they were out of sight, Smoke signaled her to come to him with the little girl. "Police?"

"On their way."

Male howling erupted from inside the house. A few seconds later, both boys threw themselves out the door, murder in their eyes.

"You killed my grandfather!" Mouthy shouted at Kini.

"No," she said in a tone that allowed for no argument. "I found him at the bottom of the stairs. I didn't touch him."

Sirens wailed in the distance.

The teens heard them, too. They looked at each other then launched themselves at Kini and Smoke.

Smoke swept between them, pushing both off-balance and into each other.

Kini ran for the house.

The boys saw her go and untangled themselves enough to follow. Smoke kicked the feet out from under one and upended the other with a Judo throw.

He heard the door slam and focused on the two little shits. The sirens were close now, and their wail seemed to enrage the boys. They dove at him, one going for his legs, Mouthy for his face.

He blocked the punch while shifting his weight so the

other one didn't knock him off his feet. The kid wrapped his arms around Smoke's knees and held tight. He threw his weight to one side and Smoke allowed himself to go with the pull of gravity, rolling free.

Mouthy was waiting with a malicious smile and a fist.

"No you don't!" Kini's yell was close. Too close.

Before the teen could turn to locate her, a sneakered foot came up from behind between his legs and landed a solid hit to his balls.

He dropped like stone, clutching his groin.

Smoke wrestled the other one into a headlock just as a police car and an ambulance rolled up.

Two cops spilled out of the car, their guns drawn, and pointed right at him.

"Hands up!" one yelled.

"Let him go, sir," the other ordered. "Let him go now."

Smoke released the kid, held his hands up, then backed away a few steps.

"I'm a nurse with the CDC," Kini said. "The gentleman with his hands up is Lyle Smoke, who also works for the CDC."

"They murdered my grandfather," Mouthy said, wheezing.

"No." Kini's voice was a whip. "I came to get medical histories and blood samples from the family members of three patients at the hospital suspected of having Hantavirus Pulmonary Syndrome."

"We heard a rumor that the CDC was doing something in the area." His tone was skeptical, suspicious, and sarcastic.

"Don't tell me," Kini said, her nose wrinkled in disgust. "You stopped at the post office today."

The cop rocked back. "How did you know?"

"They've been telling a lot of people that. One man sicced his dogs on me and another tried to punch me in the face."

She put her hands on her hips. "The CDC is not conducting any experiments or making people sick. We're attempting to research immune statistics in this region for the hantavirus."

Smoke, the cops, and even the teenagers looked completely confused.

"We're exploring the possibility of creating a vaccine."

"So, you have nothing to do with the dead body inside the house?" the lead cop asked.

"Other than discovering his body, no. The only person who was in the house when I got here was my little friend." Kini pointed at the baby. "Which brings me to you two." Kini pointed at the two boys, her voice vibrating with rage. "Where were you? The child was alone with the deceased for a long time. *Hours*."

Chapter Nine

"We were in town," the boy on his feet said. "Aren't you going to arrest her? She kicked Matt in the balls."

Sniveling bullies. She'd like to smash the other one's balls, too. "You both attacked Smoke. Two on one isn't fair."

"Kini," Smoke said, his voice full of censure.

One of the emergency responders approached. "Can we go inside now? If there's a dead body and not a live patient, you don't need us, you need the coroner. We need to know for sure."

"We have to clear the house first," one of the cops said.

"I'll call for backup," the other said and headed to his car.

The first cop looked at Smoke. "On your knees, hands behind your back."

As soon as he complied the officer put his gun away, pulled out a set of handcuffs, and approached Smoke.

What? They couldn't do that. Confusion tossed her into a shallow, cold pool she had to fight herself to get free of. She and Smoke had a job to do.

She glanced at the teens. They were both grinning. "I don't understand. What's happening?"

Smoke glanced at her. "We're getting arrested."

"But—"

"*All* of us."

She looked at the two teenagers.

Their grins were gone. They looked from the policeman in the car to the one putting the handcuffs on Smoke and bolted. The two boys sprinted past the house and out into the scrubby bush and untamed land beyond it.

The officer with Smoke finished putting the handcuffs on him then followed the boys at a jog. *A jog? This has to be a joke.*

But the other officer stood outside their cruiser, his hand on his weapon, watching Smoke like he was an escaped felon.

Smoke kept his head down and didn't move.

The other cop came back a few seconds later.

"They're long gone," he told his partner.

"Shit."

"Guess they're not pressing charges."

Kini crossed her arms over her chest. "We ar—"

Smoke interrupted her. "Aren't."

"Hold your horses, lady," the first cop said. "There's still a dead body to deal with."

"That's got nothing to do with him," she said, gesturing at Smoke.

"Kini," Smoke growled the warning again.

She ignored him. "He never saw the body. He didn't even go into the house."

The two cops looked at each other then at Smoke. The first one shrugged while the second one nodded.

He came over and took the handcuffs off Smoke and said, "For what it's worth, you have my condolences."

"Yeah." Smoke sighed.

The officer approached her. "Turn around ma'am, and put your hands behind your back."

"You're arresting me?"

"Ma'am," he said again, an overabundance of patience in his voice. "Turn around."

"But—"

The baby started to wail and ran over to cling to Kini's legs. She looked down at the little girl as the officer handcuffed her. "So," she asked the three men. "Which one of you is going to look after the baby?"

Smoke strolled over, crouched down, and opened his arms.

The baby looked at him, her bottom lip quivering. "Ki?!"

"I'll take care of Kini, too," he promised her.

She scooted over and he picked her up, cradling her against his wide shoulder.

The officer who cuffed her waited with Smoke, the baby, the EMTs, and her while the other went into the house. He came out after a minute.

"Clear. The body is in the basement."

The two EMTs went in with the cop and came back out a couple minutes later. "Call the coroner," one of them said.

"How long has he been dead?"

"We don't do time of death, that's the coroner's job, but the body is cold to the touch."

"I only got here about twenty minutes ago," Kini said to the cop babysitting her.

"Can you prove it?" he asked.

"Yes. Smoke and I were at the hospital, then his grandparent's home for a quick bite to eat."

The two cops moved aside to talk. They came back after a minute. "Ma'am do you have ID?"

"In my purse, which is inside the house, along with my collection kit."

One of the officers went in, while the other took the handcuffs off her.

She held out her arms to the baby.

She came and gave Kini a kiss on the cheek. "Hungy."

"I think she was left alone for more than just a couple of hours," Kini said to the officer. "She keeps saying she's hungry."

He stared at the child, dismay obvious in his expression. "We'll have to call child services."

"Her mother is in the hospital on life support," Kini continued. "You may have to do some digging to find a relative who can take care of her."

The other officer came out with Kini's purse and kit. "She checks out," he said to his partner. "We can call the CDC to confirm, but her ID looks legit."

"What the hell is really going on?" the other cop asked Smoke and her. "You have any idea why people are suddenly deathly ill or dropping dead?"

"No," she answered. "That's why I'm out here trying to ask questions and collect blood samples. If this is an outbreak of hantavirus, I need to confirm that and figure out where people are coming into contact with the virus."

Another police car pulled up, and two officers got out.

"Okay," the lead cop said. "I'm going to call all this in, then I'll let you know what the sheriff wants to do."

"How long will that take?" Kini asked.

"An hour, maybe two. Depends on what else is happening in the county."

Kini glanced at Smoke. "Might as well finish making that soup for the baby."

He nodded and walked beside her into the house. One of the cops came along, as if it were an afterthought on his part.

She ignored him.

The pot of soup was still sitting on the stove. She'd turned the burner off when she left the house, so she turned it back on and went to the fridge. Milk…the baby was young enough that she must drink milk every day. There was a carton at the back of the fridge, three-quarters empty.

Kini found a glass and gave her young friend a full serving of the white stuff.

Smoke settled on a seat at the table next to the baby and seemed content to simply watch her move around the kitchen. The police officer wandered the house, looking in on them often.

Impatience jerked at her focus repeatedly. The delay in her fact-finding mission could result in a big problem if this was an outbreak. More cases, more deaths that could have been prevented.

She checked her watch. "It's been a couple of hours since we left the hospital. I'm going to call, see if there's been any change in the condition of the other suspected HPS victims."

"New cases, too," Smoke said, getting to his feet and walking toward her. He stopped only one foot away and slowly reached out a hand to take the spoon she was using to stir the soup from her. "Call."

"You don't say much, but you're still a little pushy."

He gave her a half smile and lifted one shoulder.

Not an apology, but recognition of her role. Cocky man.

She gave up the spoon to him and pulled her cell phone out of her purse. First, she called the hospital ER. The receptionist wouldn't tell her anything and put her on hold. The next person to talk to her was one of the nurses she'd met earlier.

The nurse confirmed that both of the other suspected cases were still alive but that their conditions had worsened. Another six suspected cases had been identified, with more possibilities coming in the door all the time. They'd run out of beds and had called in extra staff to deal with the influx of sick. No one was saying Hantavirus Pulmonary Syndrome, but that was the prevailing theory.

The chief of staff was still wavering on calling in the CDC officially, despite knowing a call would bring in more help, more supplies, and more medical staff to deal with whatever this was. He obviously didn't want to lose control of the situation, staff, or hospital, because he refused to allow anyone to use the word "outbreak."

The man was a moron, but there wasn't anything she could do about him. She needed to focus on getting her job done, so the appropriate decisions could be made.

Kini explained that she'd be longer than initially thought and hung up. She turned to give Smoke a synopsis of the conversation and found him feeding the baby with all the patience of a man who had several of his own children and loved being with them.

It made her heart ache to see him, this rough, rugged man, play with the little girl like she was the center of his universe. A memory surfaced of her father before he'd gone overseas, of him playing with her like that. His smile had been so bright…her breath got tangled up at the base of her throat. She cleared it and wiped her eyes before Smoke noticed the tears on her face.

He was making a game out of eating the soup, pretending to put the spoon in his own mouth so the baby would grab his hand and force him to put the spoon in hers. She crowed in delight every time she got the spoon in her mouth, like she'd scored the winning point in a championship title match.

"Good news," Smoke asked her. "Or bad?"

"Bad. No new deaths, but everyone is worse, so it's likely only a matter of time. They've got a bunch of new cases, too."

"They call in the CDC yet?"

"Nope. Not enough evidence for the chief of staff."

Smoke sighed. "Ass…jerk."

"Nice save," she told him. She watched him get another spoonful into the baby's mouth. "Do you have nieces and nephews?"

"No. I used to play this game when I fed my boy," was his

answer after a moment's pause.

Boy? He had a son? She opened her mouth to ask him but paused when she saw his face.

The playful man feeding the baby was gone. In his place was a stranger with a tense mouth and angry eyes.

"Your son?" she asked cautiously.

He flinched. Something had happened to his child? Did she want to know?

"He...died."

Oh no. A double-edged sword, recognition on one side, comprehension on the other stabbed her lungs. What he'd lost equaled the empty places in her own heart.

It took five long seconds to figure out how to breathe around this new piece to Smoke's puzzle.

"I'm sorry," she finally managed to say.

"He died because I wasn't here," Smoke said with a hard edge to his voice.

"I don't believe that," Kini whispered. No matter how it happened or who was to blame, losing a child this young would open a wound that might never heal. "Don't believe that."

Smoke held himself so still with such cold resolve he appeared to be carved out of glacial ice. Frozen between layers of tragedy and horror until all that was left of him was strong enough to wear down stone. But an attempt to heat that ice—he'd melt away into nothing.

"I'll never know." His voice was scored by the rough gravel glaciers ground into dust. "I wasn't here."

Pain was etched in every line of his body, every muscle and nerve and bone. A pain no drug could stop or medicine could heal. She knew it, recognized it, suffered it. Running away from it was futile.

She'd tried that, too, but it hadn't helped, only made things worse.

"It's hard," she said, fighting to breathe through the heavy weight of knowing he'd been hurt right down to his soul like she had been. "Don't give up."

The police officer who'd been shadowing them came into the kitchen, and Kini had to consciously pull her thoughts back to the problem at hand.

The officer looked…irritated and resigned. "Okay, we've confirmed your credentials," he said to her. "You're to finish whatever you were doing and report back to the CDC as soon as possible."

He sounded grumpy. Someone had bitched to someone else's superiors.

"The baby?"

"Someone from child services will be here shortly. We'll keep an eye on her until they arrive."

"Hmm, let me try something." Kini wet a cloth and wiped the baby's face clean then held out her hands to the little girl and asked, "Nap?"

The child reached for Kini.

She picked the little girl up and headed toward the bedrooms. Next to the master bedroom was a smaller one with a crib, diaper changing station, rocking chair, and dresser.

Kini put the child into the crib, covered her with a blanket. The baby wiggled into a comfortable position and blew her a kiss.

"Trouble," Kini said. "That's what you are." She smiled and kissed the little girl on the cheek then left the room.

Smoke met her in the hallway. "I'm not leaving you alone this time."

She studied his face. It was so blank she knew he'd been told something more, something she didn't know. "What? What's happened now?"

When he didn't answer, she said, "Just tell me."

"That asshole ER doc has a fever."

Chapter Ten

"Holy shit," Kini whispered, her jaw hanging open for a moment.

Smoke had to agree. "Time to go."

"Let me grab my stuff." She led the way through the kitchen, picking up her purse and collection kit as she walked toward the front door.

None of the cops said anything to them or even cast a curious glance their way.

Kini put her equipment in her rental car then paused with the driver's door open and one foot on the floorboard. "Meet you at the next address?"

"We're not going back to the hospital?" he asked.

"I need these samples to show or refute a pattern and, hopefully, a timeline of infection. I need to find the source. Dr. Flett's infection is significant, but so is this."

Smoke wasn't sure he agreed. "Okay, you're the boss."

She frowned at him then started the car's engine and departed the yard about thirty miles an hour too fast. He waited a minute for the dust from the gravel road to settle before starting his hog and riding after her.

It was about ten minutes before he pulled up to another ranch-style home. Unfortunately, this place seemed just as quiet and serene as the last one. Except, the last one had a dead body in it and a little girl who was probably going to rule the world when she grew up.

Smoke scanned the house and yard. Kini wasn't visible anywhere. The car was here, but she wasn't.

He walked to the front door and knocked. Feminine laughter echoed through the house. He could hear more than two people in there having a conversation.

Footsteps alerted him a second or two before the door opened. A woman in her forties scanned him then shouted over her shoulder, "Kini, I think your man is here."

"My what?" Kini's voice came from deeper inside the house, out of sight, and sounded scandalized. "I distinctly recall *not* acquiring one of those while visiting your fair state."

Yes, she had.

"What I acquired was a babysitter. A fist for hire, really."

"Ooh! You're paying a mercenary to take care of you?" The woman sounded more and more excited with every word she spoke. "That's hot."

"It's annoying, is what it is. He won't let me go anywhere alone."

"A guy like this could take me anyplace and I'd be *happy*."

He was standing right in front of her. How could she talk about him like he was some kind of…object?

Or was this some sort of cosmic karma wherein he got heckled as a stand-in for all the men in the world?

"Kini?" Smoke called out. "Done?"

"Give me two minutes."

"Two words?" the woman asked. "You only used two words, yet she was able to understand what you meant." The woman looked him up and down again. "I could get used to that."

Holy shit, it sounded like this lady was about to proposition him.

"Kini?" he repeated. He'd faced armed militants, terrorists, and men driven insane by loss and hate without flinching, but this woman scared him.

He took a step back from the door then spied Kini walking toward him.

"It's going to take me another ten minutes to finish here. Feel free to head back to town," she said.

"I'll just wait..." He cleared his throat and managed not to glance at the woman while he pointed at his motorcycle.

"Suit yourself."

Smoke moved away, letting himself lean on his ride and study the landscape. Their enemy was too small to see and too quiet to hear, and no amount of hypervigilance could change that. He was wound right up, and nothing would loosen until this shit was over.

The worst kind of war.

Maybe he shouldn't have taken the job River offered. Nah, he'd be here doing the same thing, job or not. Kini needed someone to support her. Protect her. That's all he was good for now.

Her voice reached across the yard, pulling his attention back to the house.

"Thanks, Mary, for taking the time out of your day to answer my questions and provide a blood sample."

Smoke met Kini as she stepped out of the house.

"No problem." Mary smiled and pointed at Smoke. "The scenery was worth it."

He kept pace with Kini as she strode to her car. Very close pace.

She gave him a frown and sidled away from him, but he

followed.

From the house came the sound of laughter. Wicked, naughty laughter.

"What's the matter with you?" she asked him.

"I don't want Mary to think I'm available for...whatever she's laughing about."

"You can't tell me women haven't hit on you before. I won't believe it."

"Why not?"

"Because you're everything a woman looks for in a man."

Smoke forgot Mary. Forgot the illness they were investigating and forgot the dead body Kini had found not an hour ago.

She kept talking, her hand indicating all of him. "Big, muscular..."

He stepped toward her, one hand coming up to play with a tendril of hair that had escaped her ponytail.

Her words fizzled out as her face grew red. "Never mind."

Oh no. She'd started this explanation, she was going to finish it. "Keep going."

Her breathing sped up, and she licked her lips. "Um, what was I saying? Oh, right, you're big, muscular, and..." This time, she stopped talking to breathe. Hard.

He waited, his hand stroking over her cheek then tucking the tendril behind her ear. "And what?"

"Hot," she said. Her tongue darted out to wet her bottom lip.

He couldn't stop himself from lowering his head so his tongue could follow the path of hers.

Her bottom lip was as plump and sweet as it looked. Better. He tasted her again, just to be sure. Fuck, she was sweet and tart at the same time. A flavor that gave him an adrenaline hit and his body demanded more.

His hand slid behind her head, cradling it at just the right angle for him to kiss her deep and long.

A low moan came out of her throat, then her hands were on his shoulders, hanging on to him like he was the only reason gravity hadn't pulled her flat to the earth.

Raucous laughter from the house had her jerking away from him, but he didn't let her go. Not when her face drained of all color right before his eyes.

She tried to retreat, but at some point during their kiss, he'd put his other hand on the small of her back and pressed her to him. He most definitely didn't want her going anywhere.

"Smoke," she said, breathing heavy, eyes glassy. "Let me go."

Those words dumped ice water over his head, and he released her suddenly. She staggered, and he grabbed her by the shoulders to steady her.

"Sorry," he said, though it came out as more of a mumble.

She nodded, the movement jerky.

Smoke cleared his throat. "Now what?"

"We get these samples packaged up and on their way to Atlanta." She blew out a shaky breath. "I'll meet you at your grandparent's house?"

Smoke nodded and watched her get in the car and drive off.

He wanted her.

He'd wanted her since waking up with her on his chest, but this *want* was different. He wanted more than a hookup or even a short-term fling. He wanted to kiss her with no time limit, no audience, and no distractions. That first taste would never be enough. He was already addicted to her sweet-tart flavor.

Yeah, like he was relationship material. Liam's mother, Lacey, had complained bitterly about how he was never around when she needed him. When his son needed him. No matter how much he wanted to be a part of their lives, he hadn't been able to take that last step to total commitment. It had felt like a noose around his neck, choking the life right out of him.

Kini wasn't anything like Lacey, though. She wasn't looking for *happily ever after*, and maybe *happy right now* might last long enough to work her out of his system.

He got on his hog and roared after her. Her reaction this morning told him he'd have to be cautious and careful as he found a way through her emotional defenses. She'd been hurt, to the bone, by someone she trusted. That trust wasn't something she offered lightly to anyone, if she offered it to anyone at all.

At the house, Tommy was outside talking to Kini, the two of them standing next to the young man's jeep. Kini held a box in her hands. As he joined them, she opened the box and began explaining what made this box different.

"It's not made of regular cardboard. It's composed of plastic-coated cardboard designed to resist punctures and tears. It also has a Styrofoam interior that protects the tubes of blood and includes freezer packs to keep them cold."

"So, if I drop it…?"

"I would try to avoid that if possible, but if you do drop it, the samples will probably be fine."

"No drop kicking it through the goal posts. Got it."

"Give me your phone, and I'll enter the address for the courier."

He did, and she put in the information into his contacts.

"Drive safe," Smoke said. "You get stopped by the cops, you tell them to call me."

Tommy got in his jeep and drove away.

Kini was standing close. Close enough that if Smoke reached out he could put his arm around her shoulders and pull her to him.

Resisting the urge to touch her, he asked, "Next?"

Kini turned to him then had to tilt her head back to meet his gaze, but she didn't back away.

She took in a breath and opened her mouth.

"Smoke, Kini?" his grandmother called to them from the front door of the house. "You'd better come in and see this." She retreated inside.

Smoke followed Kini into the living room where his grandfather was watching the TV.

"...received a video from an unknown source claiming to be from a group called Free America From Oppression. In the video the FAFO threatens to use biological weapons to achieve its goal to force state and federal authorities to scrap the national health care plan. They have this message for state and federal law enforcement: *We will not be cowed into silence or inaction. The government's attempt to manipulate and control the free marketplace and personal liberty is as insidious as a virus. It is criminal and must be stopped. This is the only warning you will get. Continue to interfere and you will learn the true meaning of the word plague.*"

Domestic terrorists.

Holy fuck.

Kini's cell phone began to ring. As she reached for it, Smoke's rang, too.

He pulled it out of a pocket and accepted the call. "Smoke."

"River. We've got a problem."

"Free America From Oppression?"

"You saw the news report?"

"Yeah. Idiots."

"Idiots who are fucked in at least two different ways."

Smoke grunted his agreement. "You think they're here in Small Blind?"

"Don't know, man, but we're not taking any chances. Did Kini get those samples?"

"They're on their way. My cousin Tommy is driving into Las Vegas and dropping them off at the courier."

"Good. The powers that be here are chomping at the bit to get their hands on them."

"We're not seeing an obvious pattern to the infection," Smoke told him.

"So no way to know how the sick came in contact with the virus?"

"No, but before anyone even suspected the hantavirus, there was a rumor going around town that Kini and the CDC had deliberately gotten people sick. Three people have died in the past couple of weeks. Another person died today."

"We need to know if this is hantavirus or some other pathogen."

"I might tangle with local law enforcement."

"I'll see if I can keep you out of jail. It would help if you didn't kill anyone."

"No promises." Smoke hung up.

Kini had hung up a few seconds before him and looked at him. "No promises?"

Smoke shrugged. "Not to kill anyone."

Chapter Eleven

Smoke was serious—Kini could see it in his set jaw and determined eyes. See it in the half step he took toward her, his body angled to cover hers, to protect her.

If he had to, he'd kill.

He'd kill because he'd done it before.

Oh, *hell*, no. No one was committing murder on her account. "That's a promise you need to make to me," she said in a low tone and surprised herself with how angry she sounded.

She had every right to be pissed. The man was making decisions without consulting her.

His shoulders stiff, he glanced away and said something to his grandfather in a language she wasn't familiar with. His grandfather nodded and went outside through the back door.

There was only one reason to use a language one person in a group of people didn't understand in front of them—he didn't want her to know what he said.

A hot wave of anger and embarrassment swept over her. He could have just asked her to step out of the room. She turned to do just that.

Smoke pinned her in place with one look. An expression that contained both fierce suspicion and purpose. "Five minutes."

He could say a novel's worth of words with one or two, but he'd already decided to shut her out of one conversation. She'd run out of patience in an attempt to read between the lines in this one.

Time to write her own story and let him figure it out. She took a step away from him. "Okay."

He examined her face. His frown intensified. "Stay here."

She was just going to leave the room, not the house. "Okay."

He didn't move.

Now he was just being insulting.

"Where am I going to go?" she said. "I've been ordered to stick with you."

"Ordered?" His shoulders stiffened even more.

That bothered him? She crossed her arms over her chest. "Ordered."

He paused another second. His gaze searched her face then, finally, he followed his grandfather outside.

Kini turned to his grandmother. "What did I miss?"

"He might not say much, our Smoke," she replied. "But he takes his responsibilities seriously."

"I'm his responsibility."

It was a statement, not a question, but his grandmother still answered. "Yes."

A responsibility. There was a definition she had never wanted attached to herself. A burden. All part of the job.

Despite the fact that her boss had ordered her to stay with Smoke, ordered her to work with him and rely on his military training to identify threats, she wanted to rebel. The last man with a military background she'd trusted had broken that trust so completely, there had been nothing left of it by the time that man was gone.

Smoke's grandmother studied her. "He will do whatever he has to to protect you." She sounded like she was trying to be reassuring.

She wasn't.

Smoke walked back into the house. He looked at her, his grandmother, then her again.

"Are you ready to go?" Kini asked him.

He waited a second, staring at her, before saying, "Yes."

His habit of attempting to read her soul was pissing her off. She turned on her heel and headed for the front door.

He followed close enough to heat her back.

She opened the front door just as a small truck raced up way over the speed limit. It slid to an abrupt stop right next to her car, spraying dirt and dust into the air.

"What…?" she began.

Smoke slid in front of her, forcing her back a couple of steps.

A man with dark hair and sunglasses in the back of the truck leaned over with a crow bar in his hand and smashed her car's front passenger window.

"Hey!" She took a step forward, intending to confront the assholes in the truck, but Smoke blocked the way with his body.

Something flashed bright.

The interior of her car exploded, making her duck.

The smell of burning plastic and metal soured the air.

She blinked, straightened up, and looked past Smoke. Her car was on fire.

Her car was on *fire.*

Flames shot out of the driver's side and front passenger side windows, building and growing with each passing second.

Smoke's body shielded her from the rising heat. She

needed to get around him, try to salvage her collection kit from the vehicle. His palm connected with her chest and shoved her back.

She stumbled backward through the doorway just as the windshield shattered and one of the tires popped. Smoke turned, picked her up like she was a piece of furniture, and moved her farther into the house so fast she didn't recall how exactly he got her inside.

Off-balanced and with too much momentum, she tripped, rolled, and ended up on her back.

A larger explosion shattered the front window and shook the house. She threw her arms up in front of her face just as a shower of glass shards rained on her. Pain bloomed in multiple places on her arms and neck.

A shadow blocked the flickering light of the fire outside. She pulled her arms away to see who was there. Smoke's blue eyes seemed to glow. "Kini? Kini!"

He didn't even give her a chance to respond before grabbing her by the shoulders and yelling at her again. "Kini!"

She thrust her face toward his and bellowed, "I'm okay."

He bared his teeth and snarled, "You're bleeding."

Blood beaded on his forehead and began to trickle down the side of his face. "So are you."

He growled at her, *growled* and said, "Stay here."

This, *again*?

"Where am I going to go?" she said, *again*.

He snarled at her one last time then charged down a hallway she assumed led to bedrooms. When he came out, he carried a scary-looking rifle, the kind she'd seen on the news in the hands of military soldiers. He had the butt in the hollow of his shoulder and the muzzle raised for a target man-high.

He paused at the doorway, scanned the area outside, then went out in a smooth motion that would allow him to shoot and hit a target even while moving.

Smoke's grandmother came over to her. "Kini, let's get you up and into the kitchen." She extended a hand and Kini took it, allowing the older woman to give her the leverage she needed to stand.

Smoke's grandfather appeared, also carrying a weapon, but this one was a simple hunting rifle. He followed Smoke outside.

"The people who bombed my car are gone," Kini said to Smoke's grandmother as they went into the kitchen. Why did her voice sound so...odd? Confused, unfocused, dazed.

"Where there's one enemy, there are probably more." It sounded like a proverb. Smoke's grandmother pulled a tall stool out. "Sit."

Kini sat and waited while the older woman opened a door that led into a pantry. She came out with a large first-aid kit. Kini glanced down and noticed for the first time all the blood on her arms. *Whoa*. It looked a lot worse than she expected since the pain was...manageable.

"I'll get to those," Smoke's grandmother said. "You have a few cuts on your neck I want to check first."

Kini brushed her neck with the tips of her fingers and they came away wet with blood. "They don't even hurt." She gave Smoke's grandmother a wobbly, wry smile. "Adrenaline is a great thing."

The older woman snorted. "Enjoy it while you can." She examined Kini's neck a little closer. "Be right back."

The sound of sirens got closer and closer. Police, fire, and ambulance if she wasn't mistaken. And she was covered in blood. Lovely. There wasn't time for all the red tape this was going to generate.

Her car had been blown up. She had a few extra supplies for collecting samples in her personal luggage, but not enough for what she needed. *God damn it.*

Smoke came into the room with the ferocity of a storm. When he caught sight of her on the stool he stopped cold and stared.

Fury pulled his lips back from his teeth.

With that deadly looking military rifle in his hands and blood all down one side of his face, he should have been a threat.

He should have scared the shit out of her.

He should have been in control of his emotions. He'd had years of discipline drilled into him from his time in the military, but this was not a man in control.

He'd taken one look at her, cut up and bloody, and lost it.

All that fury was for her.

Her.

The room spun and narrowed to Smoke's flame blue eyes. Darkness encroached, hunting her consciousness, but his gaze, hot and bright, became her beacon, leading her to safety.

To him.

Desire awoke a different kind of fire inside her, one that licked its way over her skin, momentarily erasing pain and leaving her breathless and dizzy.

Anyone else looking at him would see a madman. The police would probably throw him in jail if they saw him, certain he was a man on a killing spree.

They were partners with orders to look after each other. He'd done his job; now it was her turn to look after him.

She sighed and managed a small smile. "So..." she said, letting the word hang for a moment. "What are the chances the rental company will let me have another car?"

She watched him as her words sank in. His face relaxed first, then his stance, and finally he answered, "Zero."

"Yeah, that's what I think, too."

Outside, the sirens were loud and steady. A whole lot of

people in uniforms were about to descend on them.

Male voices, raised and stressed, filtered into the kitchen from outside.

Smoke sighed, went to the refrigerator, opened it, then stuck his weapon inside and closed the door.

Two more steps took him to where she sat on the stool. He examined her face, neck, and arms.

"I haven't seen the damage," she said. "Does it look like I'll need stitches?"

He considered her question for a second or two too long. "No."

Had he just *lied* to her?

Booted feet thundered toward them.

"Here come the clowns," Smoke said in the same inflectionless tone he'd used since coming into the kitchen.

She had to convert her laughter into a snort as two police officers came boiling into the room.

The officers had their gun hands on their weapons. Those weapons were still in their holsters, but they both looked twitchy enough to draw at any provocation.

"Sir, put your hands up," one of the officers said to Smoke.

"What for?" Kini asked, frowning at them. "He was with me when the guys in the truck destroyed my car."

Smoke, however, raised his hands and looked at the officers. The cops spread out, staring at him, examining him.

"How did you get injured?" one of them asked Smoke.

"Shielding me from the explosion," Kini said, disbelief coloring her tone.

"Ma'am, there was a report of a man matching his description with a semi-automatic rifle threatening people."

Kini rolled her eyes. "What about the guys in the truck that threw some kind of explosive into my rental car and blew it up? Are you looking for them, too?"

"Ma'am—" the same man began, his voice now devoid of

patience.

"Check my ID," she interrupted. "It's in my purse, which is in the living room, I think."

They hesitated.

"It might answer a few questions for you."

One of them left and returned with her purse. He rummaged through it, pulled out her wallet, and opened it. His eyebrows rose. "You work for the CDC?"

"We *both* do."

That knowledge did not reassure them.

Pain came roaring back as her stomach clenched. What the fuck was going on?

"As you can see, we're not going anywhere at the moment," she said, frustration making her voice sound harsher than was polite. "Why don't you call this mess in and see what the sheriff wants you to do?" And give all of them a chance to calm down.

They thought about that for a few seconds then nodded and called for the paramedics to come inside the kitchen.

It took the medic checking her over several minutes to clean all the blood off her face, neck, and arms.

"A couple of these lacerations could use a stitch or two," he said, looking at her neck and right arm.

She looked at what she could see without a mirror. "Could you close them with butterfly bandages?"

The medic looked at her. "Nurse?"

"Yep."

"Are your shots up to date?"

"Yep."

"I'd still like you to see the ER doc."

She shook her head. "Not today." She leaned around the medic to check out Smoke. "How are you doing?"

"He's got fewer lacerations," his medic said. "But one of them really does need stitches."

"Smoke?" she asked.

"No."

"How long is it?"

No one answered her. Her medic smirked. So did the one cleaning up Smoke.

"The laceration," she said with a shake of her head. "Not his dick."

Chapter Twelve

The two paramedics chuckled but didn't stop working on cleaning and patching up Kini's and his wounds. The tension in the room did drop several notches, though.

Shouts from outside ricocheted into the kitchen—a male voice, raised with a sharp edge. A voice he knew.

"Shit, it's Deputy Blackwater," one medic said.

"Doesn't sound happy," the other put in.

Smoke checked their faces. No trace of mirth now. Both men appeared completely absorbed in their work as a man in a deputy's uniform walked into the kitchen.

"Someone tell me what the fuck is going on," he demanded, then he caught sight of Smoke and grinned.

Smoke's grandmother opened her mouth, but Blackwater saw her and apologized before she could complain. "Sorry, ma'am."

Kini started talking. "Some assholes took a crowbar to my rental car, busted in a window, threw in a Molotov cocktail, and destroyed the vehicle," she said in a tone that was so even, Smoke knew better than to trust it. "I hope you catch those guys because, otherwise, my insurance premium is going to go through the roof."

Blackwater glared at her. "Lady, I advise you to stay away from him." He angled a thumb at Smoke. "Women who get mixed up with him have a tendency to die."

A threat to her and a taunt to him all rolled up in one and delivered in front of witnesses. What the fuck was Blackwater thinking?

"What are you talking about? This is my coworker Lyle Smoke," she said, glancing at him.

"Coworker?" Blackwater asked with a sarcastic laugh. "They let women into the Special Forces now?"

"Discharged," Grandfather said, coming into the room, rifle in hand. "One week ago."

Blackwater's hand strayed toward his weapon.

Grandfather put his rifle on the counter. "I got the first half of the license plate number off that truck."

Blackwater frowned at the older man before turning to Kini and giving her a malicious smile. "What, *exactly*, are you doing in Small Blind?"

"A public health study. The CDC has any number of them ongoing across the country for a variety of reasons."

"A *study*?" He said the word like he'd never heard it before.

"Yes. That's what I do. Collect medical histories and samples. I also track infection, recovery, and vaccination rates across the country. If needed, I may also be one of several public health nurses who conduct educational seminars for hospitals, health centers, and other care providers."

As she spoke, the deputy's gaze became more and more interested. "What are you studying?" He seemed to catch himself, then asked with a sneer, "Or are you not allowed to say?"

"Of course I can answer your questions. I'm doing a

study on the local population and rates of immunity to the hantavirus."

"How do you do that?" Blackwater asked with a raised eyebrow. "Give people the disease, then see how many die and how many don't?"

Kini's mouth dropped open. "No." Her voice rose with fury. "I take a blood sample and we test it for antibodies." She stopped, gathered herself, and said in a tone that was less heated, "Giving people a disease, *for any reason*, is unconscionable."

"Sounds like something a conspiracy theorist would throw around," Smoke said into the silence following her words. He got to his feet and stepped away from the medic who'd worked on him and was now packing up his gear. Smoke gave Kini a once-over, checking to see if her medic had taken care of all of her lacerations. "Where'd you pick up that rumor?" he asked, not looking at Blackwater.

"Probably the post office," Nana said as she squeezed past the deputy into the kitchen. "Those hens in there cluck worse than a dozen chickens." She put her hands on her hips and asked the room at large, "Who wants coffee?"

"Me," Kini said, putting up her hand.

Smoke nodded at his nana.

"What about you, Deputy Blackwater?" Nana asked.

He ignored her, watching Smoke with an avarice and anticipation that was out of place. "I have a report that says a big man was running around with a military-grade weapon."

"Wait a second?" Kini asked. "What about the bombing of my car?"

"I'm investigating that, but—"

"*But*?" Kini asked, her voice rising. "But what? I'm injured." She hooked her thumb at Smoke. "He's injured, and that rifle over there doesn't look all that complicated to me." She pointed at Grandfather's old Remington.

Blackwater looked as if he'd swallowed a chicken bone and it had gotten stuck halfway down. "My information states that the two are connected."

"Information?" Disgust and disapproval wrinkled her nose. "Be specific, Deputy," she ordered. "What information, and who gave it to you?"

"I'm not at liberty to say," he answered, focusing his attention on Smoke. "My source is a confidential informant, but it's clear that someone bigger than your grandfather, with a weapon commonly used by the military, was running down the road out front." He flashed his teeth. "I'll bet that weapon isn't street legal. I'll bet it's in here somewhere."

Kini turned to Smoke. "Is he seriously going to ignore the car bombing?"

Smoke shrugged and deliberately relaxed his body posture. He wasn't going to give Blackwater any reason to decide his accusations had any merit.

"Two other deputies are investigating the issues with your car."

Kini looked at Blackwater and tilted her head to one side. "Are you feeling okay? You wouldn't be running a fever would you?"

"I'm fine," Blackwater said, his tone sour.

"Because that would be a reason for your irrational, single-minded focus on Smoke," Kini said. "Otherwise it's harassment."

Blackwater walked up to Kini until he was towering over her. "Lady, shut up."

"I feel like I'm in an eighties dirty cop movie," Kini said softly, as if she were talking to herself. "Complete with an officer of the law who's completely clueless about how fast Homeland Security would be here with *one* phone call."

Blackwater stared at her like she'd just accused him of being mentally incompetent. "Homeland Security?" He laughed. "They don't give a shit about small towns like us."

"The CDC falls under their command, and we *both* work for the CDC." She paused and said perfectly polite, "They're going to be very interested."

"As far as that military-grade weapon your informant says they saw…" Grandfather pushed away from the counter he'd been leaning on. "There isn't a house in this town that doesn't have a rifle or five." He squinted at Blackwater. "You'd better have a name on the bottom of that report, or you're going to have a hell of a time explaining to the judge why you aren't investigating the crime that's currently visible to everyone within a mile radius."

The deputy looked at everyone, one at a time, including the medics who'd paused in their cleanup of their gear to listen to the whole conversation. "Someone will be in to take your statements." He left as precipitously as he arrived.

No one said anything for a few moments. The two medics finished gathering their gear and left.

"What's his problem?" Kini asked with a deep furrow between her brows.

"Indigestion," Smoke said.

She tilted her head to one side. "Of something he heard or swallowed?"

"Yes."

"Funny." She laughed softly. "You have a sneaky sense of humor, Smoke."

"You're the only person alive who thinks so."

"See, there you go again." Her smile died. "So, as I see it, we have one important question to answer before anything else."

Smoke gave her his complete attention.

"Where am I going to get another car?"

Okay, that wasn't what he thought she'd say, but he could roll with it. Blackwater was a waste of time and energy. "We'll use mine."

"Your hog is not going to work."

"Jeep."

Her jaw dropped. "Why didn't we use your jeep before?"

"I wanted to ride with the wind in my hair."

Kini glanced at his military short hair then narrowed her eyes. "You're just digging yourself a hole."

"Kini," Smoke said.

"Yeah?"

He looked at her cell phone, the one in her hand. "Call it in."

She pinched her lips together. "I've been successfully avoiding that until now."

"Why?"

"Besides the fact that I'll never be able to rent another car again?" She looked at herself and huffed. "How am I going to explain all this? It's like a shit storm descended on me, and it doesn't make sense."

"It makes sense to someone."

"I hate it when people say that. Sometimes bad luck is just bad luck, but repeated assaults and someone blowing up my car…that's not luck. That's—"

"Sabotage," Smoke finished for her.

"I'm not doing anything worth sabotaging." She sounded aggravated, annoyed, and at the end of her rope. "This is a standard, routine public health survey and research assignment. It's only supposed to take me three weeks. It only took that long in Arizona."

She stared at him as if waiting for an answer, but he had none.

"Could I have insulted someone by accident?" she asked.

"Insulted someone enough to make them bomb your car?"

"That would have to be a big insult, wouldn't it?" She

shook her head. "I don't remember insulting anyone." She tilted her head to one side. "The guy with the dogs this morning—I never had a chance to do more than introduce myself. As soon as I said I was performing a health survey, he blew up at me."

She was right. It didn't make sense. Unless...

Before he could say anything, two sheriff's deputies called out from the front door, asking for permission to come in and take their statements.

Grandfather went to deal with them while Grandmother poured Smoke and Kini a cup of coffee each.

Kini cradled her cup and held it near her face like it was her own personal campfire and she was cold and tired. When the two cops came into the kitchen she didn't lower the cup, not even while answering questions.

Smoke kept one ear on her conversation and one on the cop interviewing him, but it was quick and straightforward.

After about ten minutes, the two police officers left.

He examined Kini's face. Some of her color had returned, and her eyes didn't have that beat-up look to them anymore.

"Time to call this in," he said to her. "You call your boss, and I'll call mine."

"Fine," Kini muttered as she got out her phone and stabbed it repeatedly with her index finger.

"Now you're in trouble," Nana said.

He frowned. "How?"

"When a woman says 'fine' but she's visibly upset." His grandmother winced. "She's not fine."

The woman in question was talking softly with someone on the phone and pointedly not looking at him.

Great.

He got his own phone out and called his boss.

"River."

"It's Smoke. Shit blew up in our faces."

"I was about to call you. Some deputy in Small Blind, Utah, just called."

"Yeah?"

"Complaining about a gun-toting vigilante who was stirring up trouble. The description matches you to a T."

"Did he mention Kini's car getting assaulted by a crowbar and blown up by a Molotov cocktail?"

River paused. "No, that never came up."

"We were about to leave. Got the front door open in time to see the whole thing. Three guys in a beat-up truck pulled up beside the car, bashed the window in, and tossed a lit bottle of something in there. Instant fire and a nice explosion."

"You didn't happen to chase the dudes in the truck did you?"

"I might have. Grandfather also went after it and got a partial plate number."

"Where's your weapon?"

"In the fridge."

River laughed. "Okay. Good. Give me a couple of minutes to call the sheriff's office back and get this straightened out. That asshole deputy is going to be sorry for leaving details out of his complaint."

"Good," Smoke said and ended the call.

Kini had headed to the bathroom a half a minute earlier, so he waited in silence.

Three minutes later, River called back.

"I told him that if he didn't get his shit together and look after you and Kini properly, we'd be arriving in force with Homeland Security in tow. At that point, the only thing he'd be in charge of is looking stupid in front of the media."

Chapter Thirteen

While she was in the bathroom, Kini could hear Smoke talking to someone on the phone. No actual words were clear, just the deep rumble and rasp of his voice. It purred over her skin, soothing something battered and bruised deep in her chest.

Her reflection—sliced, slashed, and smeared with blood—only made her tense up again, so she closed her eyes to the bandages, blood, and bruises that were all she could see and just listened. His voice soothed her anxiety, slowed her breathing and pulse, and allowed her muscles to go lax.

After a couple of minutes, his voice disappeared. *Damn.* He had finished his conversation.

Her conversation with her boss had been better and worse than she had anticipated.

Better because no one was blaming her for all the punishment her cars had taken, and worse because she'd been tasked with a face-to-face visit with a community leader. A woman who'd called the CDC a couple of hours ago and requested assistance on behalf of the local Navajo.

Arriving covered in bandages and looking like she'd lost a fight with a porcupine wasn't going to instill confidence in anyone.

She left the bathroom and found Smoke talking with his grandfather.

Actually, the two men weren't talking so much as standing in close proximity, both apparently deep in thought.

Her coffee was still hot. Good. "How do you guys do it?"

The two men stared at her blankly for a moment before Smoke finally said, "Do what?"

"Communicate telepathically like that?"

They did it again, glanced at each other, then stared blankly at her.

She gestured at them. "You just did it again. Spoke to each other without speaking."

"That's not telepathy. It's body language and knowing how someone else thinks," Smoke told her.

"I don't know, I'm thinking you have some kind of Vulcan mind meld going on."

Smoke's grandfather snorted, but he was smiling.

Smoke shook his head. "Ready?" he asked her.

"For what?"

"Emmaline Haskie."

"Oh yes. Sorry." She gulped at bit more coffee down. "So, where is this jeep of yours?"

"Other side of town."

Did he think she could ride on that monster bike of his and hang on to her tackle box and him at the same time? "Um—"

"I think we can lash your tool box to the back of the bike."

"Oh." It wasn't like there was much choice. "Okay."

Smoke turned to his grandfather, but the older man spoke first. "A couple people are on their way to fix the window good enough to get us through the night. Take care of Kini."

Smoke nodded and led the way out of the kitchen.

Kini didn't immediately follow. She stood up a little straighter and said, "I'm really sorry for bringing all this destruction to your door."

Smoke's grandfather shook his head. "Don't blame yourself for the decisions of others. You have a job that's necessary and important."

He really thought that way. She could see it in the way he met her gaze head-on, in the set of his shoulders.

Intellectually, she knew what she did had value, but it was also a role that ensured she was never in the same place for more than a few weeks at a time. Most people who did her job, only did it for a couple of years before moving into a role that allowed them a permanent address they actually lived in.

She'd kept her head down, worked hard, and worked even harder at not thinking about all the crap in the back of her head. Was she a...coward?

"Thank you. You're very kind."

That earned her a crooked smile and a bellow of her name from Smoke from somewhere outside.

She rushed out and met him coming back in. "I had no idea you could be loud like that."

"I save it for special occasions."

How did he say stuff like that without the least hint of a smile?

She didn't know what drove her to do it, but she said in a tiny voice, "And it's not even my birthday."

He blinked then said, "I've got something much better lined up for your birthday." His voice had a smooth, chocolate quality that made her hungry.

Wait. Was he flirting with her? *Now*? They both looked like they'd just broken out of prison. She wasn't touching that with a twenty-foot pole. "Do you know where we're going?"

"Emmaline has lived in the same house her entire life."

"I'll take that as a yes, then." She hid a smile. "Did you hit your head during the explosion, because even though I just met you, you don't usually willingly give that much information out?"

He gave her a startled glance but only shook his head.

"Nope, not gonna fly," she told him with a grin. "That genie is out of the bottle."

Smoke put a hand behind her back and urged her out of the door.

Firemen surrounded her rental car, still working on extinguishing the blaze. Smoke guided her past them and to his bike. He used a couple of rubber tarp straps to attach her kit to the back of the bike and got on the machine.

Kini got on behind him and scooted up until she was plastered against his back and could wrap her arms around his waist.

God, it felt good to hold him like this. His body heat gave her a level of comfort so strong tears threatened and she managed to get a tiny bit closer, hugging him with her arms and legs.

He put one hand over hers and pressed them to him. That just made her want to cry even more. He had to take his hand off hers to start the engine and get the bike rolling, but as soon as he didn't need two hands on the bars, he was covering hers again.

Giving her the comfort only touch could provide.

Establishing a connection.

No questions asked.

Tears rolled down her face, and she closed her eyes so she didn't have to see the faces of the onlookers who'd gathered across and down the street. Couldn't see their expressions of curiosity, condemnation, and suspicion.

She didn't open her eyes until Smoke took his hand off hers again to stop the bike at a stop sign. No one was around.

All the excitement was behind them.

Her head hurt and the various lacerations on her body were making themselves known with sharp, jarring jabs.

They drove through town to his parent's house, and he parked in front. For several moments, neither of them moved.

He got off his bike, so very careful not to jostle her. His gaze was sharp as he looked into her face. "Okay?"

"Not really," she managed a weak smile anyway. "I'm starting to feel it." She pointed at various lacerations.

He studied her for a couple of seconds then nodded. "After this, we'll come back here for food, painkillers, and rest."

"Sounds like paradise to me."

He gave her a crooked grin. "You need to get out more."

"Ha-ha." She got off the bike and had to steady herself.

The door to his parents' house flew open, and his mother came out at a run. "Oh my God, are you two okay?" she called as she hurried toward them. "I just got off the phone with your grandmother and—" She'd obviously gotten close enough to see both of them clearly, because her jaw dropped.

"It looks worse than it is," Kini said.

Smoke turned and gave her a look that clearly said, *"You're full of shit."* But he didn't say anything out loud.

"What *happened*?" Susan demanded, almost as if it were their fault.

"I thought you spoke with Grandmother?" Smoke asked.

"She didn't say you lost a fight with an entire squad of ninjas throwing pointy knives at you."

"Pointy?" Smoke sounded scandalized by her choice of words.

"None of your sass." She shook a finger at him. "Get in the house, both of you. Some TLC is what you need."

"That would be lovely, but we can't," Kini said with a wince. "We're under orders to interview Emmaline Haskie.

She called the CDC to demand some answers. And the CDC has a few it would like to ask as well."

"Emmaline is a tribal elder," Smoke's mother explained. "She not listed anywhere official, but she's respected."

"We'll be back after we speak with her," Smoke promised.

"Fine, but if I don't see you walking in the front door within an hour, I'm sending out the hounds."

"Yes, ma'am."

Smoke nudged Kini toward the garage and she took the hint. Inside was a tarp-covered vehicle. He pulled the cover off to reveal a jeep, one that looked like it had seen action in WWII, Korea, *and* Vietnam. It was beat up, bent, and had a few bullet holes in the driver's side door.

Smoke grabbed a set of keys off a peg, got in, and started the engine. She'd expected it to sound as rough as it looked, but the engine hummed.

"Wow."

"I put a new engine in it the last time I was here," he said.

She got in the passenger side. "Are you going to work on the body next?"

"Nope." He smiled at her. "I like the contradiction of the body looking a little like a battlefield wreck and it running like it's brand new."

"A *little* like a battlefield wreck?" she asked. "This thing looks like it's going to fall apart as we're driving."

"Don't insult my ride. Looks aren't everything; what's under the hood is far more important."

Kini rolled her eyes at him. Men and their cars were weird.

Smoke backed them out of the garage and headed for the highway. Emmaline's house wasn't far, but it was distant enough that she couldn't hear the sirens anymore.

They pulled up in front of a house that looked like it had been built in the 70s with the cheapest building materials available. No one was visible, so she and Smoke walked up to the front door. A rickety screen door was the only thing keeping the bugs out.

Smoke knocked hard on the frame and called out, "Emmaline?"

"Come in." The voice sounded rough and old. Sickly.

That voice had Kini bracing herself as she opened the door, Smoke right behind her. A few steps in, a ragged cough led her to the right into a tiny kitchen occupied by a gray-haired Native American woman who looked weathered, lined, ancient.

Smoke sucked in a sudden breath.

So, this wasn't normal then. "Emmaline?"

"Thank you for coming," she said to both of them. "Have some tea."

On the table in front of Emmaline was a pot of tea along with cups, cream, and honey. The old woman looked both of them over and began to chuckle. It was a dry sound, like the wind rustling husks of corn plants after the harvest. "And I thought"—she paused to take in a breath—"I was the sick one."

"Ma'am, we need to get you to the hospital." Kini could hear her lungs rattling from five feet away.

The old woman shook her head. "You work for the CDC?" she asked Kini.

"Yes, ma'am. Smoke does, too, but that's not important right now."

"Child," Emmaline said with what sounded like infinite patience. "Nothing at the hospital is going to help me." She turned to Smoke. "I hadn't heard about your new job."

He lifted one large shoulder up and down. "Got hired yesterday. Phone interview." He cleared his throat. "Kini is right. I'll call an—"

"Lyle Smoke, sit your ass down in a chair and listen." She

leveled the same glare at Kini until she sat. "Some strange goings-on in the desert."

"Ma'am?" Kini asked.

"Lights on all day and night, and a bad smell in the air."

"Where?" Smoke asked.

Emmaline smiled. "The old Rogerson place."

"That heap of wood?" Smoke shook his head. "I can't believe it hasn't been blown over by now."

"Nope, still standing." She took a sip of her tea. "Some developer from Arizona bought it from the bank a couple of years ago. They haven't done much more than survey the land and put a big-assed fence around it." She paused to breathe. "People are living in the house. Men who shoot at you if you get within sight of the fence." She took another sip and a smile lifted the corners of her lips. "I could see a couple of fresh graves in the dirt not far from the house."

What? Kini stared, open mouthed at the old woman, her stomach so cold it was another ice age in there.

"Did you tell the sheriff?" Smoke asked.

"I complained when one of the assholes living in the house took a shot at me. The sheriff told me to mind my own business and stay away. He said he'd talked to them, and they had a garden with a potato patch." She shook her head. "That idiot couldn't find his ass without three deputies with maps and the fire department holding the lights on the situation."

"Why did you call the CDC?" Kini asked.

"Because none of those people died of natural causes," she said sharply. "They died because they couldn't breathe." She had to stop and take several breaths herself. "I've seen this before." A few more labored breaths. "Twelve years ago, my youngest boy played in one of the sheds out back and ended up in the hospital with that virus. He died the same way those people did."

"How do you know this?" Kini asked.

"I came back later, climbed the fence, peeked through the windows, and watched."

Kini could not have heard that correctly. "You snuck up to a farmhouse populated by armed men doing suspicious things, and sick with an illness you know kills, and watched them?"

Emmaline looked at Smoke. "Is she hard of hearing?"

"Not that I know of."

"That was dangerous," Kini said.

"Not as dangerous as getting sick." She smiled, but it held no humor. "As you can obviously see."

"How many?" Smoke asked in his traditionally brief way.

"Live, four or five. Dead, two." She frowned. "Though there could be more. The air smelled of rotting meat, so they might not have had time to bury any recently dead bodies."

"When were you there?" Kini asked, horrified at the thought that this frail-looking lady had gone investigating on her own.

"A couple of days ago. I talked to that jackass of a doctor at the hospital. Told him to call in the CDC, but he told me I needed to come in for a checkup. He thought I was seeing things, and that it was a medication problem." She laughed, but it quickly became a body-wracking cough that refused to let go of her.

"May I listen to your chest?" Kini asked.

Emmaline stared at her for several seconds, her breathing so loud it seemed to echo through the kitchen. "I'm not going to that damned hospital."

"I won't make you do anything you don't want to do."

Finally, the older woman nodded.

Kini opened her box and took out her stethoscope. She put the ends in her ears and the diaphragm of the chest piece against Emmaline's chest. She didn't really need the device to hear what was happening inside. Fluid popped as Emmaline breathed and forced air through it, sounding like an old-fashioned coffee percolator. That was in the upper parts of her lungs. In the lower areas, there was no sound at all.

She pulled away, took the stethoscope off, and put it back in the box. "You have pneumonia. I can't hear anything from deep in your lungs. They're too full of fluid." She considered the older woman. "If you don't get treatment, it could kill you."

That made Emmaline laugh, but it was a wet sound and it sounded...wrong. A sound that shouldn't have come out of anyone living. "I've been dying since the day I was born. This ain't nothing new."

"This time it might be permanent," Smoke told her.

Chapter Fourteen

Smoke watched Emmaline struggle to take in enough air to satisfy her body's needs. She was sweating with the effort, and something in her eyes told him she knew, *knew* death was coming. Soon.

He saw acceptance in Emmaline's gaze, but it gave him no comfort. People weren't supposed to welcome death; they were supposed to fight it.

"We need you to be a voice in our community," Smoke said. If he had to remind her of her place as an elder, as a leader, then he wasn't going to pull his punches. "We need your words to convince the sheriff and hospital people that the time to act is now. Not tomorrow or the next day. *Now.*"

"That's," Emmaline said slowly, taking a breath with every syllable, "your job, Lyle Smoke. You're already a warrior; now you need to be a leader, too."

"You're just going to give up?" Her words, all that she said and didn't say, were a spear to his gut. It tore him open, leaving him in a winter of weakness.

Emmaline tried to speak, but she was wracked with

cough after cough.

Kini scooted around the table to lend a hand, but Emmaline waved her off. Kini looked at him and angled her head toward the doorway. Smoke followed her out of the kitchen.

"Agitating her won't help."

"She's committing suicide," he countered, clenching his fists tight and holding them rigid against his sides so he didn't put holes in the walls. "Slowly, but it's the same thing."

"We can't force her to go."

"Can't we?" Emmaline might have decided it was her time to die, but a couple of people might be able to talk her out of it. "She has family, grandchildren."

"Oh, that's…" Kini thought about it and grimaced. "She won't thank you for it."

He'd faced down scarier people than Emmaline. "I can live with it."

He strode back into the kitchen to confront the old woman again. She was face down on the table. *Shit*. "Kini."

She was already darting around him, rushing to Emmaline's side to put fingers against the unconscious woman's neck. "She's got a pulse, but it's fast. Too fast."

Kini dove for her tool box and pulled out her stethoscope and wasted no time to listen to Emmaline's lungs. "It's worse." She met his gaze. "Call 911."

Smoke had his phone out already, so he punched the numbers in and made the request. He was told the ambulance would be there in ten minutes.

He and Kini stood vigil as those minutes ticked down, Kini listening to Emmaline's chest and back the entire time.

It wasn't until the sound of sirens became audible that she spoke. "I can literally hear the difference between now and ten minutes ago." She looked so sad, so fucking helpless that he wanted to yell at the old woman for making a martyr of herself.

"She made this choice," Smoke told Kini, his anger turning his voice into a sharp-edged blade. There wasn't any softness in him to dull the edge. "Suicide doesn't end the pain, it just reassigns it, and that's not fucking fair to everyone she leaves behind."

Kini stared at him, all the color draining out of her face. "How old are her grandchildren?"

"Not old enough," he said with a grunt. "No one is old enough for this."

"I didn't mean—"

Smoke cut her off. "I know." He rubbed a hand over his face. "I know," he said more gently.

The paramedics came in then, the same two who'd bandaged them up an hour before. They gave Smoke and Kini long looks before focusing on Emmaline.

Kini told them the timeline of events since they arrived, and the medics got the old woman on a gurney and into the ambulance in short order. They were gone a few minutes later.

"Now what?" Kini asked.

Smoke looked at her, taking in her slumped shoulders, the lines of pain and stress bracketing her mouth, and the dark circles under her eyes. He probably didn't look much better.

"Now, we talk to the sheriff then get some rest before we both fall over."

"What are we going to tell him? That jackass deputy has probably told him all kinds of shit."

"Trespassing is a crime. Maybe the people she saw in the house didn't look like any kind of developer."

"Oh," Kini said with more enthusiasm. "That might work."

Or the sheriff could ignore what Emmaline said as the

ramblings of a sick old woman. They'd cross that bridge if they came to it.

He phoned the sheriff's office and was told he was at the scene outside his grandparents' home.

He and Kini drove there in the jeep and found the man talking to two of his deputies. Neither man was Blackwater.

"Sheriff Davis," Smoke said.

The man looked up, saw them, and his face hardened. "Lyle Smoke and Kini Kerek?"

"Yes, sir. Emmaline Haskie was just taken to hospital," Smoke said. "Breathing problems."

The sheriff stared at them. "Unfortunate, but I don't see why that warrants you two tracking me down."

"She became suspicious of increased traffic near her at the old Rogerson place. Said there were strangers in the area at odd hours."

"I told her to stay away from there. There are a couple of guys living in the house until the developer begins building some kind of lodge for corporate retreats." The sheriff swore. "Don't tell me. She took a look herself."

"Yep. She thought they looked like squatters, and the place stank." Smoke left out the graves and the smell of decomposing bodies.

The sheriff scowled at them. "Emmaline told you all this?"

"Yeah, she'd asked to see Kini."

Sheriff Davis turned a confused gaze on her. "What for?"

"She'd heard about my health study and wanted to participate."

"Participate?"

"Yes."

The sheriff studied them both for a couple of long seconds with tired, suspicious eyes. "Did she say anything else? Did she see drugs or anything illegal going on?"

Interesting that the sheriff brought up drugs. "No," Smoke said. "She collapsed after that." He watched the sheriff's face as he suggested, as tentatively as he could manage, "The bioterrorism threat from FAFO is all over the news."

The sheriff waved it away. "Utah doesn't have enough people to make us a target. Those assholes will go after something shiny like New York or Washington, DC."

"Lots of sick people right here," Smoke pointed out.

"Fine." The word shot out of the sheriff's mouth. "I'll send a couple deputies to check it out. Jesus, if it isn't Blackwater yammering in my ear about ex-military crazies, it's..." His voice died mid-sentence. He glanced at Smoke, sighed, and rubbed his face with both hands. "I'm too old for this shit."

"Thank you for your time," Smoke said, forcing one corner of his mouth up in a *yes, we're all in this together* smile. He put a hand on Kini's back and guided her back to his jeep.

"Where can I find you two if I need you?" the sheriff asked.

"My parents' house," Smoke told him.

They left him standing on the sidewalk staring after them as they drove away.

"I don't like him," Kini said after they were out of sight. She had her arms crossed over her chest.

"Yeah, he's an ass."

"It's not just that," she said, glancing at him. "He wasn't happy with Emmaline or the fact that she got that close to the house."

"No, he wasn't." Smoke considered the sheriff's reaction—he'd been more concerned about what Emmaline might have told them.

"Maybe we should investigate it, ourselves."

Smoke grunted. "My mother isn't going to allow us out again tonight."

"Part of me wants to argue, another part wants to fall

asleep on the spot."

"No sleep equals bad decisions."

"Okay, fine, I get it."

Her huff made him smile.

They arrived at his parents' house, and both of them were given a bowl of thick stew with bread to eat as well as some over-the-counter painkillers.

Kini nearly fell asleep at the table.

Smoke picked her up and, despite her squawking that she was too heavy, carried her to his room and set her on the bed. He looked into her sleepy gaze and asked, "Do you need help undressing?"

She snorted. "No. Nice try though."

He shrugged. "Nothing ventured." He went to the door.

"Where are you sleeping?" she blurted out the question in a rush.

"On the couch. Goodnight, Kini."

He left the room and crashed on the couch in the living room. It wasn't long enough. He tossed and turned for a long time, hours. At about two in the morning, Kini came into the room, wearing one of his old T-shirts as a sleep shirt, her bare legs taunting him.

She had bruises blooming under the cuts on her face and arms. Her hair was a mess. Damn, if she wasn't the prettiest thing he'd ever seen. He had to restrain himself from wrapping her in his arms. He wanted the scent of her hair in his nose again, her weight against his chest, and the silk of her skin under his hands. Wanted with a strength that tested his control.

"You can't sleep either?" she asked him softly.

"No," he said.

She stared at him for a moment, her hands rubbing up and down her arms like she was cold. She padded over to stand in front of him then grabbed his hand. "Come on."

"To where."

"Your room."

That was a fantastic idea.

What? No, no it wasn't. Not touching her would tie him up in knots so tight he'd be lucky if he didn't strangle himself. "No, you sleep there." He had to clear his throat. "I'm good out here."

She frowned and huffed. "Stop arguing with me. I'm not suggesting either of us sleeps out here."

"Then what—?"

"It's a king, we'll both fit."

Jesus Christ, the word *fit* took him someplace he didn't think was on her radar. "Kini—"

"I promise to keep my hands to myself this time."

"It's not your hands I'm worried about," he muttered, feeling his cheeks heat.

"I trust you." She tugged on his hand again. "You're too much of a gentleman to…you know."

Did she think he was some kind of Prince Charming riding to the rescue? He had a hard-on like a steel bar and was dying to get a taste of her. The images his brain kept coming up with of her wearing nothing but skin were far from gentlemanly.

He yanked on her hand so she fell into his lap, then he slid his arms around her so she was plastered against him hip to hip. His erection was pressed into her belly, but he wanted to be sure she understood the enormity of the situation, so he dragged her upward across his body, letting her feel all of him.

She gasped and planted her hands on his shoulders, giving herself some leverage to hold herself away from him. Not enough to get away though. Not nearly enough.

"Does it feel like I'm a gentleman?" he asked her in a low, dangerous tone.

She breathed hard and a small, frightened sound came from her throat.

"I can't sleep," she whispered. "I keep feeling the force from the explosion again and again. Getting knocked over, the glass stinging, and the heat of the fire as we watched my car burn." She sucked in a breath and kept going. "The only time I've been able to relax at all was when we rode your motorcycle and I had my nose buried in your shirt." She shuddered. "I feel like I'm going to fly apart. Please help me."

Ah, fuck. He couldn't say no.

Smoke eased his hold on her until she was on her own feet next to the couch, then he got up, towering over her. "I still think this is a stupid idea."

She flashed him a smile, took his hand again, and dragged him toward his room.

"My mother is going to give me shit," he said. "Again."

"Stop worrying. I'll explain everything to her."

"You might think that's going to happen, but I doubt it's going to work. It never does for me."

They reached his room. She dragged him inside and closed the door.

He lay down on the right side of the bed first, near the edge to give her plenty of space, and closed his eyes. His body remembered how soft her skin was under his hands, the scent of her hair, and just like that, he was hard and shaking with the effort to stay where he was.

The mattress dipped as she took the other side.

Waterboarding had nothing on this as a form of torture, but he was damn well going to do what he promised and leave her alone.

It took a few minutes, but eventually her breathing evened out.

Maybe it was the deep trust it took for her to sleep next to him that helped him relax.

He was just about asleep when she rolled over, ending up with her nose against his arm. Another shift and she was hugging his arm to her torso.

So much for getting any sleep.

Fuck.

Chapter Fifteen

Kini woke, warm, rested, and safe. Still tired, but considering the shit she went through yesterday, not bad. She snuggled into the blanket a little more, loving the spicy masculine scent.

The blanket moved beneath her.

Moved?

Kini opened her eyes and took stock. She wasn't sleeping on a blanket, she was on top of Smoke, cradling one of his legs between hers, her head against his chest.

For the second time in three days.

It was too comfortable for such a short amount of time. Something inside her had relaxed for the first time since her father destroyed their family, and it felt so good. She'd been marking time for years, never settling, never looking for more than short term. Smoke wasn't a short-term anything. He was an all-in bet.

He'd been hesitant about sleeping here with her. *Oh no.* Had he slept in this bed with the mother of his son? Were they married? It was entirely possible that he was the one feeling stressed and unhappy.

She'd only had a couple of boyfriends, both of which had been shy, geeky types who couldn't have threatened a fly. She hadn't been able to sleep comfortably with either of them. She'd wanted to, but something in her subconscious refused to trust a man sleeping next to her.

Until Smoke.

He was dangerous in every way imaginable. He made her want something she'd never entertained before—a real relationship. He challenged her view of the world, made her see there could be something new, something better.

He was so very dangerous, yet her hindbrain didn't seem to agree. How else could she explain her current, cozy position?

Her hands flexed on his chest, and she had to restrain the urge to pet him. Her whole body quivered with the need to rock against his.

Smoke shifted beneath her again and she glanced up, opening her mouth to apologize, but his eyes were closed.

He looked peaceful.

She put her head back down on his chest. She'd let him sleep a little longer. They'd had a rough day yesterday, and today didn't look to be any better. Their list of things to do was a long one.

Investigate and determine the cause of so many sick people.

Finish her health survey, or cancel it, depending on what her boss decided.

Squash the rumors going around that she was to blame for the sickness spreading through the community.

Investigate the farmhouse Emmaline said had bodies buried next to it.

She shifted her leg and realized the hardness under her knee wasn't Smoke's hip, but an erection. From what she could tell, he was blessed in that respect. So *very* blessed.

Her body tightened, wishing she could explore him further, but after his declaration last night, she wasn't sure she was ready to deal with the probable results of that exploration. He wouldn't be the kind of man she could have a short-term affair with, then walk away from without regret. He had *complicated* written all over him, with a protective streak that was three miles wide. She liked it.

She wanted him. More than that, he made her feel safe. He shouldn't be able to do that. Not a military veteran, a man who'd been trained to use violence as a solution for… anything. Still, she felt no apprehension, anxiety, or tension with him. None. Lying here with him only made her feel… safe. Content. Free.

It was confusing.

He'd already made it clear he wanted her. Tried to scare her away with it even.

Casual sex wasn't her thing. Her relationships might have all been short, but she didn't enjoy it if there wasn't an emotional connection with the man she was with. She'd only met Smoke the day before yesterday, but that connection was there.

Day three.

It seemed impossible, felt more like they'd known each other long enough for her to know that though he presented a gruff exterior to the world, he cared. She could see him in uniform. Tall, strong, and dangerous. Smoke would be the one man she'd run to if she needed help.

Her job kept her on the road most of the time. Who knew where River would send him? A relationship between them would never work.

Kini had to hold in a snort. Listen to her, jumping the gun. Just because he had an erection didn't mean he was interested in more than an hour's pleasure.

Smoke shifted underneath her, and she lifted her head to

wish him a good morning and an apology for not staying on her side of the bed. She touched his shoulder with her free hand and found herself on her back, her wrists in his grip, and shoved over her head. He settled between her legs, his weight pinning her to the mattress.

His erection was a long, hot brand against her, and she found it impossible to calm her breathing. He stared down at her, frowning, his blue eyes focused on her, her face, her lips.

"Smoke, I'm sorry—"

He kissed her. His mouth taking advantage of the fact that hers was open by flicking his tongue against hers, tasting her, teasing her.

His kiss sent an arrow of fire through her veins, tightening her body, increasing the want to a level that made it impossible to keep still. She moved under him, rocking against that wonderfully hard cock. Why had she been hesitant to touch him, be touched by him?

He groaned and kissed her harder, angling his head so he could taste all of her, and pressed his hips harder against hers.

She wasn't sure how long they kissed, long enough that she had her legs wrapped around his waist while she rocked with him. The sharp crash of a dish shattering in the kitchen brought all of it to a halt.

Smoke wrenched himself away, and he stared down at her like he didn't know where he was or who he was with.

"Fuck." The word came out of him like an explosion.

"Yes, please," she replied without thinking.

He blinked slowly, his blue eyes dilated. His breath came in a fast and hard pant, like he'd run a mile in record time.

He looked at her like she'd lost her mind, then lowered his head so he could whisper in her ear, "My mother might hear us."

"Not if we're quiet," she whispered back.

Wait. What had she just said?

He thrust himself against her and shuddered, his face tightening with desire. "Be sure, because once I have you naked, I'm not sure I can stop."

The words just fell out of her mouth. "Doesn't look to me like you're going anywhere."

He frowned then glanced over his shoulder at her legs, holding him down. The groan that came out of him started deep in his chest and rumbled out as he put his forehead against hers. "Holy Mother of God, I'm going to go to hell."

"Only if I can come with you," she whispered.

"This is a bad idea, Kini."

"The worst," she agreed. Her body was alive with tension and need. She couldn't help a little wiggle, and it pulled a moan out of both of them.

Smoke shuddered and tightened his hold on her wrists, his gaze hot on hers. "Last chance."

"Shut up," she said, staring at his mouth. "And come here."

"I'm on top," he growled against her lips. "I give the orders." He took her mouth before she could argue, his lips and tongue pulling her under in a sensual undertow she had no wish to fight.

His hand released her wrists, and she wound her arms around his neck. Something tugged near her waist then a hot hand skimmed up her side to stroke the sensitive swell of her breast. She moaned softly as his fingers explored her, rubbing, then pinching her nipple. She bucked, the pleasure swamping her, making her needy and greedy for more.

She wanted his mouth on her. Needed him to suck and tease her with his teeth. She pressed his hand against her with her palm. "Your mouth," she whispered, her voice raw. "I need your mouth on me."

His response was a groan so deep she felt it more than

heard it.

He reared up, pulling the T-shirt up and over her head, leaving her naked except for the panties she wore. He stared at her breasts, his hands cupping and shaping them, then he dipped his head and tasted her.

The pleasure swept over her, and she willingly drowned in it. He sucked hard and she arched under him, her hand behind his head. She wanted to moan, order him to suck harder, but if she let any sound out, it would all come out and the whole house would know what they were doing.

The need for silence intensified the pleasure somehow. Ratcheting up her response to his slightest touch.

He switched breasts, and she found herself stuffing the heel of her hand in her mouth to keep from crying out. He was destroying her, utterly wrecking her, and she didn't want to be the only one.

She ran her hands across his shoulders and down his back as far as she could reach, but it wasn't enough. She wanted to explore the rise and fall of his muscles, discover the places on his body that gave him pleasure.

"I want," she whispered, barely able to catch her breath, "to touch you, too." She tried to wiggle down and sent her hands over his shoulders.

He paused, tilting his head so he could meet her gaze. His eyes burned with an inner heat that matched her own. "I won't last if you touch me," he said, in a subvocal voice that seemed loud, even though it wasn't.

How was that fair?

She darted her hand toward his nipples.

He grabbed her wrist and planted it to one side and above her head. "Keep it here."

"But—"

"I give the orders, remember?"

She narrowed her eyes. "I get to be on top next time."

A slow, hot grin spread across his face, right before he took her nipple in another hard suck.

She was going to die of pleasure.

He teased, rolled, and pinched her neglected nipple until she was thrashing her head back and forth against the pillow. His lips caressed the skin beneath her breast, then lower and lower still.

His palms followed the path of his mouth until he reached the edge of her panties, then he began to tug them down, slowly exposing her to his white-hot gaze.

Despite her best efforts to remain silent, she made a noise.

He looked at her face. "Do you want to stop?"

She shook her head in a frantic motion that had nothing to do with fear and everything to do with how close to the edge she was.

He kept eye contact with her as he tugged the fabric down her legs and off. Only then did he look down at the curls at the juncture of her thighs. His big hands took hold and spread her apart, holding her open for his perusal. He stared for what seemed like hours, but was probably only a couple of seconds before he petted her gently, his fingers seeking out her warm, wet center.

He circled her opening with a finger, over and over, and it pushed her to the very precipice of orgasm.

"Smoke," she whispered. "I need...stop teasing...fuck." She shifted her hips, trying to encourage him to thrust that finger inside her, but he pulled his hand away.

"No," she panted. "Please don't stop."

He kissed her, open mouthed with teeth and tongue driving every thought from her head.

One of his hands still held her open for him, while the other seemed to be doing something, but she wasn't sure what.

His briefs had kept him from connecting with her below the waist. Suddenly, they were gone and a hot bar rubbed over her pussy.

He shifted, getting both knees between her thighs then guided his cock to her, rubbing the broad head in her wetness and rimming her vagina again.

She grabbed at him, rocking her hips against him, hoping he would just take her.

"Kini?" He was giving her one more opportunity to stop.

"Take me before I die of frustration."

He put himself against her, pushed the first inch in, then swore, backed up, and got off the bed.

Oh no. He wasn't going to leave her hanging like this. She made a grab for him, but he was moving too fast, grabbing something out of his duffel bag.

A condom.

She'd been so far gone, it hadn't even crossed her mind.

He tore open the packet, rolled the condom over himself, then returned to his former position. He took his cock in his hand to rub it over her, making her absolutely crazy. He watched what he was doing to both of them, the exquisite torture, until his breathing was as far from normal as a man could get without blowing up his lungs.

He stilled, snared her gaze with his, then buried himself inside her in one long thrust.

So full, almost too full. She sucked in air like a bellows for several seconds. When she didn't see spots in front of her vision, she wiggled beneath him to indicate she was ready. More than ready. For the love of God, if he didn't move, didn't do *something* she was going to scream.

He pulled out, starting a hard, fast pace that sent her into orgasm within a minute, but he didn't stop there. He fucked her through her first orgasm, his rhythm strong, smooth, and steady. As she came down from the high, he began to speed up, then pulled out suddenly, surprising her.

He flipped her over onto her belly, pulled her up by the hips until she was balanced precariously on her knees, then thrust himself inside her again.

She buried her face in the pillow and screamed.

He came over her, trapping her beneath his body, his pace fast and hard. She could feel it building, a second orgasm, deeper than the first, building to a crescendo she wasn't sure she'd survive. His hands were planted on the bed on either side of her head. Wrapping a hand around each of his wrists, she held on as the orgasm detonated inside her.

He thrust once, twice, three times, then stiffened and shuddered.

The pillow beneath her face was damp when she lifted her head, her eyes wet. Her breathing took a long time to calm, but since Smoke seemed in no hurry to leave her, she didn't worry about it too much.

He finally pulled out, and she rolled over onto her back while he left the bed and discarded the condom.

She got her first real look at him. Lord, he had more muscles than any man had a right to. A streak of white near his shoulder caught her attention. And scars, too.

He turned and stopped cold, frowning. "You're bleeding."

"What? Where?"

He knelt on the bed so he could trace one of the lacerations she'd received on her neck yesterday. He didn't put any pressure on it, but it was tender, nevertheless. His finger came away with blood on the tip.

Kini touched the spot, wiping to see how much blood was there. Not a lot.

"I shouldn't have touched you." He sighed and pulled away.

She should have agreed with him. If she wanted to stay untangled, it was the smart thing to do. The reasonable thing to do, but she wasn't feeling either. "As I recall, I touched you first."

He stood next to the bed and stared down at her for a long moment. "Go ahead and shower. I'll get breakfast on the go and check in." He pulled on a pair of jeans, the same ones he'd worn yesterday, and left the room.

She was treated to the sight of his muscled back and shoulders and wanted to go back to where they started. Not going to happen.

She rolled off the bed and got to her feet. Dizziness forced her to sit down on the bed and put her head between her knees. After a few seconds, the vertigo passed. She got up, put on the borrowed shirt, and walked to the bathroom.

Food would help.

After a shower that revealed more bruises than she thought she had, she was careful to make sure all the lacerations she had were held together with butterfly bandages and Band-Aids. She probably could have used a stitch or two on a couple, but that was going to take time and attention away from the larger problem.

What the fuck was making people sick here?

She got dressed in Smoke's room and called her boss before going out to face whoever was home besides her new coworker. Holy crap, she'd just had amazing, mind-blowing sex with a *coworker*.

Dummy.

"Rodrigues," her boss said.

She had to clear her throat. "Good morning, this is Kini."

"How are you? Do I need to pull you out, or are you well enough to continue?"

"I'm okay. I'm going to look colorful for a week or two, and I've got bandages all over my face, neck, and arms, but it's nothing that will get in my way."

There was a long pause before Rodrigues said, "All

right. Smoke talked to River this morning and mentioned a farmhouse he wants to investigate. I looked into it, and it's on private property. We would need more than a rumor or the suspicions of a single resident to justify a visit. Not when two more people died overnight at the local hospital with another ten showing symptoms. Meaning, it's not seeming like there's a single source of the virus. We could be looking at a new strain or a new vector/rodent carrier. Your samples arrived late last night, and we're waiting for definitive results before declaring the pathogen a hantavirus. We need to know the species of rodent that's carrying this particular virus. I'm bringing in a second epidemiology team to help investigate. Hopefully, we can find answers quickly."

"Yes, ma'am."

"Assist with patient care and check in with me every two hours. Good luck." Rodrigues ended the call.

Kini put her phone in the pocket of her jeans, pulled on another public health nurse T-shirt, and left the bedroom.

Smoke was in the kitchen cooking eggs and bacon.

"Wow, you're brave," she said to him. "Cooking bacon shirtless."

"No," he said with a shrug that drew her gaze to his muscled chest. "Lazy."

His mother came in with some tomatoes. "Stupid might be closer to the truth." She put the vegetables on the counter then came over to give Kini a long once-over. "Are you sure you should be working?"

"I look that bad, huh?"

"Yes."

"I hope I don't scare anyone."

"They're more likely to call an ambulance than the police."

"Mom," Smoke said. "Stop picking on her."

Susan turned on her son. "She's covered in bruises and

cuts, has two black eyes, while the rest of her looks like she was dipped in white paint."

"Thanks," Kini muttered. "I feel so much better now."

"Mom." Smoke's voice was a warning.

But Susan appeared to warm to her topic. "She looks like she's been beaten to a pulp and you expect her to work?"

"I'm fine. Really."

"Do you think I'd let her work if I didn't think she was okay?" Smoke asked, sounding angry now.

Was no one listening to her?

"It's your job to protect her. Isn't that what you said?" Smoke's mother barked. "So *protect* her."

Smoke opened his mouth, looking like he was about to explode. At his *mom*.

"Hey!"

They turned to look at her.

"I've survived much worse than this," Kini said, pointing at herself. "I'll be fine."

Mother and son stared at her, their eyes wide.

Her own words hit her broadside with the punch of an armored car.

Shit.

Fuck.

She didn't just open her mouth and tell them both she'd been...beaten...before.

"Worse?" Susan gasped.

Smoke closed his mouth. "Who hurt you?" The words came out of his mouth like they'd been crushed in glass.

Yep. She opened her mouth, all right. Wasn't that wonderful? *Idiot.*

"No one alive," she said, hoping that would end the entire conversation.

Smoke's jaw clenched and unclenched.

His mother stared at her like she was a pity case.

If she didn't have a job to do, if she didn't need Smoke backing her up, she'd grab her stuff and walk all the way back to Atlanta.

Blue smoke rose from the frying pan behind Smoke.

"Your bacon is burning," she said.

Smoke and his mom turned to look at the stove.

Kini used their break in attention to duck back into his room and gather up her stuff. She could at least prepare for a quick getaway, even if she couldn't actually go anywhere.

She picked up her dirty shirt, shaking her head at the blood stains all over it. No amount of washing was going to save it.

A draft washed over her as someone opened the bedroom door behind her then closed it. She glanced over her shoulder.

Smoke stood behind her. "I'm sorry."

"For what? Burning the bacon or talking about me in front of my face like I wasn't there."

He cleared his throat. "No. More like wishing I could strangle the person who hurt you worse than this."

"You're apologizing for thinking about committing a homicide?" she asked. "You're a soldier. Kind of late for that, isn't it?" She went back to packing.

"Going somewhere?" he asked, sounding only mildly curious.

She'd heard that tone from him before. It was a lie. He used it to calm an opponent so when he attacked, they were surprised into making a mistake.

She straightened up and turned to face him. "Tell me you don't have a go bag ready at all times."

He froze. It was only an instant before he relaxed again, but she saw it and knew she'd turned the tables on him.

"You think we're going to need them?" he asked.

"I think there's too much we don't know about the situation to be unprepared."

He nodded slowly. "Agreed."

She gave him her back again and continued to pack her clothing into her bag.

"I'm sorry," he said again, but this time he sounded like he really meant it, really was apologizing for something he'd done.

"Is this a different apology or the same one?"

"I didn't mean to bring back bad memories."

She faced him again and shrugged. "We all have them— bad memories. The trick is to not let them take up any more real estate inside your head than they're entitled to."

Chapter Sixteen

"Easier said than done," Smoke said with a grunt as he watched Kini pack her bag with an efficiency that could only come from a lot of practice. "Some nightmares become a part of you."

She'd been moving smoothly, but at his words, she hesitated and caught herself reflexively before continuing on. "Yes," she said without looking at him.

She zipped up her bag and set it on the floor next to the bed. Her gaze met his. "I need to eat."

The anger he saw in her punched him in the throat. He stepped back and opened the door, letting her go through it ahead of him. Her body was stiff, her shoulders back.

Note to self: *don't talk about Kini in front of Kini unless you want a fight.*

His mom already had two plates on the table filled with scrambled eggs, bacon—unburnt—and toast. Kini sat in front of one plate; he sat in front of the other.

She shoveled the food in so fast there was no way she had time to taste any of it.

He ate steadily, finishing just after she did then followed her into his bedroom. "I want to check some of those lacerations before we head out."

She turned, her gaze as hot and angry as before, but she nodded and sat down on the edge of the mattress.

He bent over, taking a good look at her neck, palpating the skin around the bandages. "Any pain here?"

"No."

He poked at all the wounds he could put his hands on without getting slapped, but her response was the same.

Almost all her visible skin was either cut or bruised to one extent or another. He looked over the worst areas carefully. "I'd be happier if you had some x-rays done on your arm and ribs."

"I've had broken bones before," she said in a tone so controlled he knew she was still spitting mad. "Nothing feels like that."

That didn't mean the pain she was feeling wouldn't get in the way of doing her job. "If your pain gets worse, becomes hard to manage, tell me."

"So you can have me shipped off for my *safety*?" she asked like "safety" was a dirty word.

What the fuck? "Yes. Your safety as well as the public's. We can't afford to make mistakes or delay in doing our job because of injury. You will tell me if you're not well enough to perform at an acceptable standard."

She stared at him, her lips pressed so tightly together they were white.

"And I will do the same," he added.

That surprised her jaw into dropping open for a count of two seconds before she said, "As long as it goes both ways, agreed." She got to her feet.

He followed her out into the kitchen then watched her down half a cup of hot coffee in one go. "Where first?"

"Several people died in the hospital last night."

"Start there?" Smoke asked.

She nodded. "That farm Emmaline talked about is bugging me. She seemed so certain…"

She'd also been so sick. "Let the sheriff clear it first."

She stared at him like he'd lost his mind. "He and his officers don't know what to look for. Besides, Deputy Blackwater is an asshole, and he's probably spun our encounter with him to make *us* look like the assholes."

"Stupid, too," Smoke agreed.

"Yes, and I hate dealing with stupid people. I dealt with several of those yesterday, and look at me." She held her arms out, covered in bandages, and gave him a wry smile. "I think I'm allergic to them."

It wasn't funny. She'd been cut, beaten, and bruised. She should be off work and restricted to bed rest at home. Instead, she was investigating the source of a disease that had killed several people and sickened many more.

Someone had started a rumor she was responsible for the illness and destroyed her car.

"The CDC is a threat to someone," Smoke said slowly, considering her value, skills, and knowledge as a single unit. "*You* are a threat to someone."

"That's crazy," she said flatly. "I'm just a nurse."

"You're not *just* anything. You work for the CDC. You represent the Centers for Disease Control."

Her eyes widened. "But the only people who would fear the CDC are people doing something—"

Smoke finished the sentence for her. "Exceptionally stupid."

She sighed theatrically. "I hope that doesn't mean my *rash* will get worse."

If it got any worse, he might have to kill someone after all. "Help is coming."

"When help gets here we'll be sent home. We're both injured." She shook her head. "At least *I* will be sent home. You're already home...and none of this is relevant to our immediate problems. I want to swab everyone possible. Try to figure out where the majority of cases are coming from. I have more swabs and sample containers. Hopefully enough."

He was armed in case it wasn't. "Hospital?"

She nodded, dragged her bag onto the bed, and pulled out a handful of specimen collection swabs. "Have you got something I could put this in? Something portable."

Smoke opened the bedroom closet. He'd gotten rid of a lot of crap after Lacey cheated on him, but he'd kept a few useful pieces of gear at his parents' house. He pulled out an old backpack, one he hadn't used in years and had seen better days. It wasn't large, which made it a good size for Kini.

He put it on the bed next to her bag.

She picked it up, stuffed a few things in it, then paused to give it a cautious examination. "You went to Princeton University?"

He shrugged.

"What did you take?"

"Engineering."

"Right," she said, muttering to herself. "And I'm *just* a nurse."

He hid a smile as he went back to the closet and pulled out a few items he could see possible uses for. First was a folding knife in a rugged pouch that clipped to a belt.

"Here," he said to Kini. "Put this on."

She took it like it was a live snake and dropped it into the backpack. "I'm not wearing a knife."

"It's not just a knife. It's got a fire starter, flashlight, and even a whistle."

"I'll keep it in the backpack, but I'm not wearing it."

Stubborn woman.

He bent down, lifted his jeans pant leg, and slid another knife and sheath on so it hugged the outside of his lower right leg. A longer knife.

"Why would you need a knife that big for anything legal?"

"It's for illegal problems, not legal ones."

He removed the last item he wanted from the closet, its paracord-wrapped handle reassuring in a way that should have been uncomfortable, but wasn't.

"What is that?"

"A tactical tomahawk." He set it on the bed.

She watched him shrug on the leather shoulder holster for his Beretta, check his weapon, then holster it.

"You need a knife, a gun, and an axe?" Her voice sounded incredulous. "Just how many illegal situations do you think we're going to run across today?"

He met her gaze and held it. She couldn't be that naive after all of the injuries she suffered yesterday. Which reminded him... He went back into the closet and came out with a first aid kit, stuffing that into her backpack, too.

She sighed. "It's going to be one of those days again, isn't it?"

"Hope not," he said with shrug. "Not getting caught unawares, if it is."

She closed the backpack and slung it over one shoulder. "Thank you for making me paranoid on top of everything else." She led the way out of his room, waved at his mom, and opened the front door.

Deputy Blackwater stood in the doorway, his hand raised to knock. "Looks like I got here in the nick of time," he said, his voice vibrating with rage.

She glanced over her shoulder and said to Smoke, "Can I go back to bed and start this day over?"

"Not sure it would help," Smoke said, examining the

deputy's expression and body language. The man had his teeth clenched so tight, there were white lines of tension painted on his skin along his jaw. His entire body was rigid, nearly vibrating with some strong emotion, and his right arm was bent at the elbow, ready to draw his weapon.

"We're going to the hospital," Kini said to the other man.

"Neither one of you are going anywhere until I get some answers," Blackwater said, glaring at both of them and taking a step forward. "Six more bodies are in the morgue this morning." He took in a breath and snarled, "Two of them are fellow deputies."

The muscles of Smoke's back twisted and tightened. That explained the fury, but not the accusation on his face.

"I'm sorry for your loss," Kini said, her combat-ready stance and voice softening. "How can we help?"

Smoke restrained his need to move in front of Kini, shove her back and out of the way of a man on the edge of violence. His instincts beat and screamed at him, demanding he protect her, but she'd made it clear she wouldn't tolerate him treating her like she was a potential victim.

Blackwater leaned down, invading her space, and said in a menacing tone, "You can tell me where his AR15 is."

She leaned back, almost unbalancing herself. "His what?"

"The civilian version of an M16. He has one registered to him, along with several other weapons."

Smoke opened his mouth to correct the idiot, but Kini beat him to it. "Wait. Are you accusing Smoke of sneaking out in the middle of the night to shoot two of your coworkers?" She shook her head. "Are you serious? After all the injuries we both suffered?" She pointed at Smoke. "Does he look like he's up to that kind of cloak and dagger bullshit?"

"He's a soldier," Blackwater barked. "I think he's capable of anything."

"I haven't shot anyone," Smoke said before Kini got the idea to punch the deputy in the face. "Recently."

Blackwater glared at him, while Kini glanced at him over her shoulder and mouthed, *What the fuck?*

"Where were you last night between 2:00 a.m. and 4:00 a.m.?" Blackwater demanded.

"Here. Sleeping."

A smile came and went on Blackwater's face. "Can anyone testify with one hundred percent certainty that you were home during those hours?"

Shit, here it comes.

"I can," Kini said, turning so she could put her hand on his chest. "I was touching him all night. He didn't go anywhere."

Damn, he liked her claiming him.

Blackwater's face got so red it looked like he was about to explode. There could be only one reason why he was so focused on Smoke as the culprit.

"Who told you I was the one who shot your boys?"

Chapter Seventeen

"A friend of the sheriff's from Washington gave him a call," Blackwater said to Smoke. "Told him a few things about you."

Kini couldn't believe how calm Smoke was in the face of the idiot. He didn't move, didn't even blink.

"A friend in law enforcement?" Smoke sounded only mildly curious.

"Used to be." Blackwater smirked. "He's a consultant now, but he's still got his contacts."

"What did this friend say?"

Blackwater crossed his arms over his chest and puffed himself up. "You weren't anything special, like you tell everyone. You were just an army grunt."

"Nope. Engineering Sergeant," Smoke corrected. "Special Forces."

"Special Forces?" Blackwater snorted a laugh. "Your record says you're not a team player. You and a few of your buddies went AWOL a couple of years ago, assaulted several other soldiers, and stole a helicopter. Your record says you got an honorable discharge, but the truth is, trouble follows you around like a bad penny. Mental health issues finally resulted in your departure from the military."

"Colorful," Smoke said, his expression not changing at all. "Untrue, but colorful."

"Hmm, who should I believe?" Blackwater asked in a mocking voice. "A meathead who enjoys blowing shit up, or a friend of my boss's who's one of the smartest men I've ever met?"

Smoke shook his head. "He's given you some bad intel."

Blackwater's smile got wider. "How so?"

"The only things not classified on my record in the last six years are my medals and my honorable discharge. Everything else—deployments, training, missions—won't appear on anything official for at least a couple of decades, if ever."

"Where," Blackwater growled, "is your AR15?"

Smoke didn't reply.

Kini didn't blame him. The deputy had already made up his mind, and if Kini had to bet, nothing but a court order was going to change it.

"What is going on out here?" Susan yelled from inside the house.

"A murder investigation," Blackwater yelled back. He reached behind himself and pulled out a set of handcuffs.

He was arresting Smoke?

"How did those deputies die?" Kini asked, injecting confusion and concern into her voice. "Were they *both* shot? Who found them, and where were they found?"

Smoke shifted on his feet while Blackwater paused with the handcuffs in his hands.

"They were shot outside of their vehicle on the I-15 thirty miles northeast of here just after 4:00 a.m. It looked like a traffic stop gone bad."

"Were they the men assigned to check out the farm?"

"Yes." Blackwater's lips were curled up with disgust.

"And your *coworker* is my number one suspect."

"Call the United States Army Special Operations Command in Fort Bragg," Smoke said, all evidence of sarcasm gone from his tone. "Neither of us has time for bullshit."

"What's that supposed to mean?"

"I'm not your shooter, but someone wants you to think I am, which means there's more to this than we're seeing."

"Like some kind of conspiracy theory? Why the fuck would anyone go to that much trouble?"

"That's the real question, isn't it?"

Blackwater seemed to consider Smoke's words, then his face hardened and Kini knew he'd disregarded it all.

"You're under arrest on suspicion of murder. Turn around and put your hands on the wall."

Smoke sighed, turned, and did as he was instructed.

The man cuffed Smoke's hands behind his back.

"Blackwater," Smoke's father said from inside the house. "You're making a huge mistake."

"Stay out of my way," the man snarled. "Or I'll arrest the rest of you for obstruction." He began reciting the Miranda rights.

Smoke looked at his father, at Kini, and shook his head. *Back off*, that head shake told her. That was a suggestion she was most certainly going to ignore.

Blackwater hauled Smoke to his cruiser, shoved him into the back seat, then drove away.

Anger was a hot spike in her gut. Kini watched them leave.

Susan touched her arm and urged her into the house. "They won't be able to hold him long," she said in a tone that was probably meant to be reassuring. It wasn't.

The hot spike twisted painfully, robbing her of breath. What the *fuck* was going on?

Susan put a hand behind Kini's back and guided her to

a chair at the kitchen table. "I think another cup of coffee is in order."

Kini pulled out her cell phone and called, not her boss, but River. She'd only met him once, but he'd seemed smart and his reputation, while new, stated that he backed his people up 100 percent.

As soon as he answered, she identified herself then said, "Smoke has just been arrested for murder."

There was a two-second pause. "Did he do it?"

Kini was abruptly tired of everyone assuming the worst of a man who, if he'd had his way, would have taken every cut and bruise she'd suffered. "No, he didn't do it," she snapped. "He was asleep thirty miles away when it happened, but the stupid sheriff's deputy arrested him anyway, because of secondhand information from some old buddy of the sheriff's. Said Smoke's service record wasn't good, or something like that."

Another second of silence. "Who died?"

"Two of the sheriff's deputies."

"*Fuck*."

An accurate description of what had occurred. "Can you talk to Sheriff Davis? Get this cleared up?"

"I talked to him last night. He's backing one of his deputies, Blackwater. I think he needs to hear from someone with more clout than I've got."

"Get whoever is necessary to make these idiots listen." She paused as an idea occurred to her. "Blackwater said a friend of the sheriff looked at Smoke's military record, mentioned him going AWOL and stealing a helicopter. Did that actually happen?"

The pause was even longer this time. "Yeah, but it's classified info. The list of people with access to it is relatively small, and all of them know better than to share it with a county sheriff."

"That's what I thought."

"I'll look into it and find someone suitable to give your sheriff and his deputies an attitude adjustment."

"Thank you."

"How are you doing? Smoke said you were injured last night."

"I hurt, but it's nothing I can't handle. I'm not sure what the situation at the hospital is. We were just about to go there when Blackwater showed up."

"Can you assess the hospital's status on your own?"

Bumps, bruises, and a few cuts didn't render her an invalid. It would be a miracle if she didn't end up strangling someone today. "Yes, I'm fine to do that."

"I'll call when I have some news," River said, then hung up.

Kini put her phone away and stared at the top of the table. She still had a job to do, but no partner. She glanced at Smoke's father. "Jim, do you have a set of keys for the jeep?"

She arrived at the hospital's parking lot without incident. A fucking miracle, given the shitty shit that had already gone on this morning.

Walking into the ER was another thing entirely.

The place was packed, literally wall to wall to wall, with people coughing, yelling, and crying. Unfortunately, they were doing it all at once.

How could anyone even think in this cacophony?

She bypassed the line of patients waiting to see reception and headed for the examination rooms and diagnostic area of the ER.

Someone grabbed her arm and yanked her to a stop. "The back of the line is way over there."

Kini looked at the woman dressed in scrubs and said, "I'm not a patient."

The woman shook her head. "Either get back in line, or

I'll call security."

"I'm with the CDC," Kini told her, hauling out her identification and showing it to the woman. "I'm expected." She hoped.

The woman stared at Kini's CDC ID then jerked her hand back. "You look—"

"I know. I look like I barely survived an argument with a pissed off porcupine, but it's nothing to do with why I'm here," Kini interrupted. "Okay?"

The woman nodded, and Kini hurried toward the knot of medical personnel she could see through the doorway.

She glanced around but didn't see anyone she recognized from the day before. That wasn't a good sign. She approached a group of three women and one very elderly man, all dressed in identical mint green scrubs, and introduced herself, showing them her CDC ID as well.

"The CDC is here?" one of the women asked. "Oh thank God."

All four of them stared at her with varying degrees of relief. So much relief she feared one of them might faint.

"How many people came with you?" the man asked.

"*I'm* here," Kini said. "To assess the situation. I spoke with Dr. Flett yesterday. The last I heard, he had a fever. Where is he?"

"Dead," the man said. "I'm Dr. Gordon, retired. The staff couldn't reach anyone else, so they called me in." He looked around and shook his head. "We're overrun."

"By what, exactly?" When Dr. Gordon looked at her like she'd said something incredibly stupid, she continued with, "I need to be certain and specific when I call this in."

"Some kind of viral pneumonia. It's very fast." His voice caught in his throat, almost a sob. "Even the people we manage to get on a ventilator are dying before we can do anything to stabilize them."

"Sir," Kini said with respect. "The CDC can help, but it has to be invited in."

"Please," he said to her. "Help us."

Kini nodded and offered a smile. "Is there a staff member who can work with me to coordinate their arrival?"

"I'm not sure…" His voice trailed off as he looked at the women huddled next to him. "Who?"

"Sonja," one of them said. "She's the charge nurse right now." The woman turned and dashed off toward one of the exam rooms.

"What kind of help will the CDC send?" Dr. Gordon asked.

"All kinds. Medical, diagnostic, logistical. They'll bring people, equipment, and supplies. I think we can safely declare an outbreak for whatever this is, which allows for emergency funds and manpower."

"How soon will they be here?"

"Quicker than you might think." She kept her tone professional and confident. "I tried to get Dr. Flett to request assistance yesterday, but he refused. Even so, they've been preparing for this call since my report yesterday afternoon."

"We've called in everyone," one of the nurses said. "Every single staff member is here, either working, sick, or dead."

Dr. Flett was an asshole, and it was a good thing he was one of those dead. She would have torn him a new one otherwise.

"Are you using your emergency protocols?"

"No," Dr. Gordon said. "But we should be." He turned to one of the two remaining women. "Get on the public announcement system and tell everyone that with the number of people looking for care, we're initiating our emergency response protocol. All sick people who have yet to see a doctor or nurse will receive a number and be triaged as soon as we can."

"Yes, sir." She ran off to do that.

Another woman hurried over to them. "You sent for me?"

"Sonja," Dr. Gordon said, "This is…"

"Kini Kerek, CDC public health nurse," Kini supplied.

Sonja found a quieter corner for Kini to make the phone call and stayed to supply answers to several questions Dr. Rodrigues at the CDC had. Afterward, Kini spent the next ten minutes watching for Smoke and explaining the timeline and the CDC's response.

Where was that damn man? Every time she looked around and didn't see him, her stomach wound tighter and tighter.

It took a ruthless kind of attention to keep her focus on Sonja and explain than an advance team of frontline care providers, nurses, doctors, and support staff would be departing Atlanta within the next hour. They would be traveling in two mobile clinics along with several other vehicles containing supplies as well as people.

"That's the good news," Kini told her. "The bad news is…it's going to take them twenty-seven hours to get here. An advance team will arrive in about eight hours, depending on available flights, but that's only a half dozen people."

"How are we going to keep up with all the new cases?" Sonja asked in a tone on the verge of panic. "There's a never-ending supply of them."

"You do the best you can with what you can." She gave the nurse a half smile. "It's all any of us can do." She caught sight of Dr. Gordon talking to a couple of other nurses. "Call whoever you need to."

"I think I've contacted everyone on my list, but I'll check it again," Sonja said as she hurried away.

Kini headed for the doctor and filled him in.

"Dr. Gordon, would it be possible for you to talk to

the mayor and sheriff? Have them inform the public in the area of what to do? Avoid gathering in groups to prevent the spread of the disease, wash their hands often, and wear a dust mask when cleaning."

He nodded slowly then asked, "Quarantine?"

"I'm not authorized to issue a quarantine order, and enforcing a mandatory one in an area like this would be next to impossible without a lot more manpower." She glanced down at herself, at the bruises and cuts visible on her arms and hands. "I'm not sure a quarantine would work, even with enough bodies to enforce it. Some of the people I've met here have had...an adverse reaction to me." Look at that, she could be diplomatic once in a while. She tried to smile. "Is it possible for an entire town to be allergic to someone?"

Dr. Gordon's gaze took in her bruises and sighed, no smile in sight. "No, but we're not used to having strangers arrive asking personal, and often painful, questions. Add a sudden outbreak of a deadly disease, and the result is suspicion and distrust." He shook his head. "I'll do what I can, but I don't know how successful I'll be at calming people down or getting them to cooperate."

The next hour went by in a blur of noise and activity. Kini answered a stream of questions, first from hospital staff, then from the town mayor and other community leaders. No one liked the quarantine option, but she was careful to stress that it was *voluntary*, to stay home if they didn't need to go out for the next few days. Thanks to Dr. Gordon's support, most of them promised to spread the word.

From the expressions of disgust and contempt on their faces, though, a couple still believed this outbreak was her fault.

Finally, she ran out of people trying to question her, giving her an opportunity to check her phone for texts or voice messages. The texts were all short notifications from her boss, but nothing from Smoke. The cold fingers of dread walked their way up her spine. He'd been arrested by a man who hated him. Images of Smoke, beaten to within an inch of his life, filled her head, and her breathing turned ragged. No, there wasn't time to panic.

Wait. Someone had called her from a local number and left a voice message.

"The sheriff is charging me with murder," Smoke said, his tone so calm and even only a fool would believe it. "Know a good lawyer?" The message ended there.

A cold sweat coated her skin. This was bad, very bad, and she was done waiting. *Done.*

About to call River and demand to know why he hadn't found a general or admiral, or whoever to shout some common sense into the sheriff's head, she noticed the time stamp on the call. Almost an hour old. Maybe the sheriff had been forced to see the light?

If so, where was Smoke?

She tried calling him; it went straight to voicemail. Damn it. She, the sheriff, and Deputy Blackwater were about to have an unpleasant conversation.

The reception desk in the building housing the jail was manned by a young-looking man with a large mustache wearing a police uniform and a name tag that read: Domingo.

"Hello," she said with a polite smile. "My name is Kini Kerek and I'm wondering if I can talk to the sheriff?"

Officer Domingo returned her smile. "Pleased to meet you, ma'am. I'm afraid the sheriff is busy with a prisoner right now. How can I help you?"

That didn't sound good.

She upped the amperage on her smile. "Would that prisoner be Lyle Smoke?"

Chapter Eighteen

"I don't care if the fucking Pope calls me," Deputy Blackwater bit out, spitting on Smoke's face. "You killed two of our officers, and you're going to pay for it in every way I can come up with."

And Blackwater was determined to make sure everyone believed it. Normally, Smoke would just wait the bastard out. He was good at waiting. Patience was a prized trait in a soldier, and he had it in spades.

But Blackwater was too angry, and if it weren't for the sheriff and three or four deputies hanging out in the small dark room he was being questioned in, Blackwater would likely act on that anger. Not that the other men would stop him, but they were witnesses.

Kini had better be taking care of herself, or he was going to tan her bottom when he caught up to her. That woman wouldn't hesitate to work herself to the bone, make herself sick. Sooner or later, someone was going to go over Blackwater's head, give the sheriff a clue, and he'd have to release Smoke. He hoped it would be sooner.

Someone knocked on the door.

Blackwater ignored it to get into Smoke's face again. "I want to know why you did it."

Another knock, along with a man calling the sheriff's name.

"Fuck off, Domingo," Blackwater shouted. "We're still questioning this piece of shit."

The sheriff left his position, leaning against a wall, and went to the door. "What?"

The door opened wide enough for the guy to say, "Sir, Dr. Gordon is on the phone for you. He says the CDC is on its way and that he needs you to convince people to stay home."

"Dr. Gordon?"

"He was the only doctor in town for years," Blackwater said. "He's retired."

The cop in the doorway said, "The doc on duty died during the night, so they called Gordon in," the fresh-faced officer standing in the doorway said. "There's also a Kini Kerek here to see the prisoner."

"That bitch is working with this asshole," Blackwater snarled.

"Language," the sheriff said, a warning note in his voice.

The deputy cleared his throat, "Sir, one more thing. An agent Dozer from Homeland Security called. He spoke to me and said that if you don't call him back in the next ten minutes, he'll be on the first plane out here with a dozen of their agents and twice that from the FBI."

"Is that so?" The sheriff looked thoughtful as he glanced at Blackwater. "Anything else?"

"And," Officer Domingo continued in a small voice, "he also said he'll set up his command post in your office."

Shit, Dozer was pissed off.

Smoke had to work not to laugh.

"Everyone is sure in a goddamned hurry to start a ruckus

today." The sheriff strode out the door.

Blackwater's face looked hot enough to start a fire. "Fuck." He paced away then came back to the table to hiss at Smoke, "Fucking Homeland Security. This is my town and no snotty asshole is going to take over just because they work for Homeland Security." Blackwater leaned closer and said very softly, "You're going to pay for what you did to my sister."

"Didn't do anything."

His words made Blackwater madder. "That's right, *nothing*. You didn't do a fucking thing for her. Always gone and never here when she needed you. Then you re-upped. Instead of coming home to take care of your family, you chose to stay in the army. It was your fault Lacey started drinking. Your fault she and Liam died."

Smoke didn't react. Anything he said or did would be viewed as an attack. He couldn't tell Blackwater that Lacey had had a problem with alcohol from the beginning. Couldn't tell him she refused marriage. She hadn't wanted to be tied down to one man. Every time he'd been home, she had a new boyfriend and *he* wasn't welcome.

Blackwater stormed out of the room, shoving another deputy out of the doorway and slamming the door against the wall. The silence resulting from his departure was a relief. Smoke closed his eyes and catnapped.

Until he heard Kini shouting, "You can't arrest me for doing my job!"

Smoke's eyes popped open, and he realized the door to the room was ajar.

"You're the cause of the fucking outbreak," Blackwater yelled back. "You and the CDC created this mess, and now you expect us to cooperate?"

"We didn't create anything. My being here and the outbreak is a coincidence, nothing more."

"Bullshit."

Smoke could hear Kini's frustrated sigh from where he sat. "Why won't you believe me? You've been accusing me of being the cause of the outbreak since the moment I met you. Why?"

"I've got friends. Friends in interesting places. One of them told me the CDC was conducting experiments out here designed to make people sick."

"That's unconscionable, illegal, not to mention ridiculous." Her voice rose as she asked, "Why would we do that?"

"Money, why else." His voice was filled with a sneer. "Your employer wants a bigger piece of the budget pie."

"I don't know anything about the funding we get from the government, but making people sick on *purpose*?" She paused, and Smoke could hear her breathing as she tried to control her emotions. "I took an oath to do no harm, and I take that oath very seriously. Everyone I work with has dedicated themselves to the pursuit of fighting disease in an ethical manner. Your friend is *mistaken*."

Blackwater was silent for several seconds.

Kini had been smart to avoid accusing this source/friend of lying outright.

"He said there was proof." Blackwater didn't sound any closer to believing her than when they'd started arguing.

"What proof? No...wait." She paused. "Unless your friend is a health professional with experience in infectious diseases, any documentation he might have would be difficult to interpret correctly on his own."

"He's not a dummy."

"Neither am I, but though I drive a car, I wouldn't know the first thing about rebuilding its engine. Show me this proof."

"I don't have it," Blackwater said through his teeth.

"There is no proof that Smoke is your killer, either." She

sounded ready to rip his face off.

"Deputy Blackwater," interrupted the sheriff. "Take a coffee break. Now."

Blackwater swore as he walked away, the sound of his footsteps retreating. Smoke relaxed for the first time since he'd arrived in Small Blind's police station.

Kini's head popped around the doorjamb. Relief surged through his system, leaving him high on just the sight of her.

"There you are," she said, her voice heavy with relief. "You okay?"

"Yeah," Smoke said dryly. "They haven't had time to get the tar and feathers out yet." He crossed his arms over his chest. "Baiting Blackwater in front of the sheriff isn't going to win you any points."

Her bruises had gotten more colorful, making her look sick. He wanted to make her sit, preferably on his lap so he could hold her, but her jaw was set and he knew she'd shoot any such suggestion down.

She got stubborn when she was angry.

"I wasn't baiting him. I meant everything I said." She harrumphed. "It's officially an outbreak. The CDC is on its way, and you and I are supposed to be assisting local health care until they arrive."

Shit, that alone was going to keep them busy.

Kini glanced at the door, so Smoke did, too, but no one was there.

"What do you think that agent is telling the sheriff?" she asked in a whisper.

"To rein in his boy and pull his head out of his ass," Smoke said, not bothering to lower his voice. He didn't care if the sheriff and every cop in the building heard him. They'd screwed things up so bad, they'd put themselves into shit creek without a fucking boat. "Arguing with him doesn't help," Smoke said with a pointed look.

"Excuse me?" she said, frowning. "I was defending you."

"I know that, but I can defend myself just fine. Having them pissed at both of us is just stupid."

"Stupid?" she asked in a soft voice that told him he was in big trouble. "Really? Well, fuck you very much."

"Kini, wait—I didn't mean that you're stupid, just the situation—"

"Don't apologize when you're not sorry."

Smoke rubbed his hands over his face. Anything he said now was only going to make it worse. "What's the ETA of our backup?"

She stared at him before looking at her watch. "It'll be another seven hours before the advance team gets here."

"That's a long time."

"Too long."

Yeah, she was still mad.

"Kini—" Smoke began, but the sheriff stormed into the room.

He glanced at Smoke then at Kini. "Out. Both of you." He looked Smoke square in the eyes. "Stay out of trouble, or I'll let Blackwater have another crack at you."

Smoke got to his feet and urged Kini out the door with a hand to the small of her back. This close to her, he could feel her body heat, and he tried not to let it show how much he liked it.

Officer Domingo handed him his ID, his weapons, and cell phone, but didn't say a word.

Smoke nodded at the kid and said quietly, "Watch your six. I didn't kill your guys, but someone did."

Domingo glanced over his shoulder, but neither the sheriff or Blackwater was in sight. "It was up close and personal," he said, swallowing hard. "There was gunshot residue on their foreheads."

"What does that mean?" Kini asked.

"Whoever shot them stood within five feet." Smoke shook his head. "And was familiar with police procedure if they got that close."

"That's the part that has me worried," Domingo said.

"Good," Smoke told him. "Use it to stay focused and aware."

"Is the CDC really coming?"

"Absolutely," Kini said. "The advance team will be here this afternoon. The rest will arrive tomorrow."

The kid looked relieved.

"If anyone asks, tell people not to panic. Stay home if they can and stay away from any environment that might contain mice or mouse droppings."

"That's like, everywhere."

He heard the fear in the young officer's voice and agreed with him. Nowhere was safe.

They left the building.

His jeep was parked near the door. "Have you been to the hospital?" He unlocked the doors and got in.

She nodded, a jerky motion as she got into the passenger seat, but didn't say anything. The cold expression on her face, along with her arms crossed over her chest, could have set a block of ice on fire.

"What?" he asked, key in hand, but not in the ignition.

She turned her glare on him. "Those idiots are going to get people killed."

Smoke raised a brow and waited for her to explain.

She stared at him, then rolled her eyes and sighed. "Blackwater, the sheriff, they aren't listening, they aren't thinking, they're reacting, and those reactions are... dangerous."

He found nothing to disagree with in her assessment. "Yeah." He started the jeep and pulled out of the lot.

"What are we going to do about it?"

He shrugged. "Nothing."

"Excuse me?"

"The sheriff doesn't believe us. Won't believe us, so we leave him to those he will believe." He considered that, then revised his statement a little. "We leave him to those whose orders he has to follow."

When she didn't respond, he added, "You and I don't have time to hand-hold the sheriff or Blackwater. We have other responsibilities."

It took a few seconds, but she finally relaxed a fraction. "Stupid assholes suck."

Smoke allowed one corner of his mouth to rise. "Yup."

A couple of minutes later, he pulled into the hospital parking lot, but there wasn't a single spot left open. He was forced to park on the street a block away.

As they went inside via the emergency entrance, they grabbed surgical masks from a large box sitting next to the door and put them on.

The waiting room was standing room only. Some people slept in the chairs that were scattered around the space while others yelled at the staff, demanding help, drugs, a doctor, or in the case of one elderly lady, anyone with enough brains to switch on a light.

Smoke had to use his size to create a way through the crowd. Kini grabbed hold of the back of his shirt and hung on. It made him want to smile, which in the middle of this disaster was a fucking miracle.

They eventually broke through the throng and walked into the exam area, but the scene here wasn't much better. Only the staff were doing most of the yelling.

Kini came out from behind him to approach an old man dressed in scrubs and a lab coat. He wore a surgical mask, so Smoke couldn't see most of his face, but he looked familiar.

"Dr. Gordon?" Kini asked. "Has anyone been assigned

to lead the CDC team in when they get here?"

Shit, Dr. Gordon was something close to ninety years old. He'd retired years ago. What the hell was he doing here?

He looked at her blankly for a moment before blinking and saying, "No, I don't think so." He glanced around. "We have so few people working, I haven't been able to spare anyone…"

"Smoke and I will take care of it."

His hand landed on the small of Kini's back. "A moment?"

She led the way to an unoccupied bathroom, went inside, and held the door open for him. "I figure this is as much privacy as we're going to get."

He followed her in, and she closed the door. He captured one of one her hands. "You tell me when you need a break or something to eat or drink. Keeping yourself healthy is important."

She blinked up at him. Surprise and something else, sadness maybe, crossed her face. "Okay. Thank you."

Why would a reminder to take care of herself make her sad?

They left the bathroom and dove into the fray, both of them assisting in organizing the incoming patients.

The next few hours were a blur of names and faces filled with fear. Twice, Smoke made Kini take a few minutes' break to eat something. The first time, about two hours in, her face went bleach white and she swayed on her feet. He took her by the arm, walked her out of the ER altogether, and made her sit on the front step of the building in the sunshine.

He handed her a bottle of water and a granola bar he'd gotten from the vending machines and ordered, "Eat, drink, rest."

She frowned at him. "You're not the boss of me."

The image of her face from this morning as she climaxed hit him square in the chest and he smiled. "Sometimes I'm the boss of you."

Her pale cheeks infused with pink, and she swiped the water and food out of his hands. Her gaze seemed caught on the ground, as if something there was speaking to her, then she chuckled. "You make me laugh."

"Do I?"

She glanced at him. "Yeah. It's a surprise every time, too."

"Why?"

It took her a minute to respond, and when she did, it was barely above a whisper. "My father was a soldier. He came home a different person. A broken person. He tried to put himself back together, but some of his pieces weren't just broken, they were missing." She inhaled deeply, like something sat on her chest, making it impossible to take in another breath. Finally she said, "I don't know what the last straw was, I only know he shot my mom, then himself in front of me."

"*Fuck*." The word came out of Smoke's mouth like a bullet out of a gun. "I must be your worst nightmare."

"No." The answer came out of her with surprising certainty.

He searched her face for evidence of polite lies.

"My father had no control over himself, no connection with us, and no conscience to guide him." She pulled her knees up, wrapped her arms around them, then laid her head on them. "It was as if something had been ripped out of him or died, leaving the rest of him without an anchor. So when he crashed and burned, he took us with him." Tears leaked out of her eyes.

Smoke watched her. "How old were you?"

"Ten."

"A child."

"Yes."

"I don't know which of us is in a worse place," he said at last. "You, a victim of violence, or me, a man who uses violence as a tool and a weapon. Only, I'm scared that if I pick up that weapon, I'll forget how to put it down."

"Forget how to…what does that mean?"

"I know a few guys who, after leaving the military, discovered the military wouldn't leave them. They began taking small protection jobs and security details. But without the structure, support, and a supervisor they have to answer to, eventually, most of those guys ended up dead, here." He tapped his temple. "After that, it wasn't long, and they'd be all the way dead. You get me?"

"Yeah, I get it. All those men who'd gone to war hoping to change the world, and ended up broken by it." Her expression closed down, leaving her shuttered.

He didn't like that, not a bit, but if he wanted more than a casual fling with her, he was going to have to open up to her, too.

What did he really want?

He wanted her, lock, stock, and barrel, but he had so much fucking baggage to deal with he needed a transport truck just to move it. It wasn't fair to ask her to deal with his shit. That didn't mean he couldn't get to know her better in the hours they had left. Maybe in a few months…

He studied her, shouldering the horrors of her childhood like any soldier and carrying on.

"I lost…" Goddamn, the words didn't want to come out of his mouth. "My son a couple of years ago."

Kini put a hand on his thigh and rested it there, lending him something he hadn't been offered by anyone outside his battle brethren. Strong, silent, steady support.

He took in a breath and let the words flow out of him. "Lacey and Liam were on their way home from a friend's house when they drove head-on into an eighteen-wheeler on the highway. She was driving and drunk."

Kini's hand on him tightened. "I'm so sorry," she whispered.

"It's my fault, and it's why Blackwater hates me. Lacey was his sister."

She recoiled. "What do you mean, it was your fault? Were you here?"

"No. I was deployed."

"Then you couldn't have—"

"I wasn't here," he said, his voice breaking. "I wasn't here." His voice dropped to a whisper. "I was never here."

"You aren't responsible for the actions of anyone other than you," she told him. "Trust me, I know."

Silence sat between them, an unwelcome ghost filled with grief and guilt.

"I don't want to be one of those guys looking for a way to die," he whispered after a few minutes. "But I don't know how to live this life"—he pointed at the ground—"anymore. After my son died…I couldn't…I can't let my emotions go. I'll fly apart."

She took one of his hands in hers and stroked her thumbs over that taut skin until he relaxed and tangled his hand with hers.

"The worst part of surviving when someone you love dies is the guilt," she said softly. "It invades every organ like a cancer and tears you up inside until you're as dead as the one you mourn."

Her words battered the ice wall around his heart and lungs.

"Take me for example," she said, with a smile that wavered. "I work a job that keeps me constantly on the move. It's the only way I feel safe, but it's not what I want. I want children, a home, and a man who loves me despite my weirdness."

That sounded pretty good, but to a soldier like him, a

man who could never unsee or undo the things he'd seen and done, it was just a dream. A good and noble and honest dream, but one that would be always out of reach.

"I think that's what any of us want." He put an arm around her. He didn't have all the right words to make any of this easier, but he did have a couple of shoulders she could cry on.

Tears streamed down her face as her body shook with silent sobs. Her arms went around his neck, and he pulled her close. Close enough for her scent to invade every cell in his body. Close enough for every hiccup and shake of her body to feel like they were coming from inside of him.

Eventually, she quieted, wiped her face, and nodded to tell him she was ready to go back to work.

The second time Smoke had to make her take a break, she didn't resist at all. She drank the water and ate another granola bar with robotic motions, then got back to work.

He watched her close. She was running out of energy and it showed.

About seven o'clock in the evening, her cell phone began to buzz.

"Hello." She nodded. "Yes, ma'am. We'll meet you at the main entrance." She ended the call. "That was Dr. Rodrigues. They're ten minutes away."

"Good." It was about time they got here. There wasn't much between Small Blind and Las Vegas but flat highway and the odd tumbleweed.

Kini looked at herself and groaned. "She's going to take one look at me and order me off this outbreak."

"That's bad?" Hell, he *wanted* her ordered off this outbreak.

"I've been chased by dogs, had my tires slashed, then someone blew up my car, leaving me looking like I've been attacked by a serial killer. I'm invested, Smoke. I want to know what the hell is going on."

Chapter Nineteen

Kini had to pause and rein in her temper. If it turned out that this whole mess was caused by people in some way, as opposed to mice, she was going to hurt someone.

Smoke didn't say anything, just paced along beside her as they walked to the main entrance of the hospital. There were lots of people around, many of them coughing, all of them going toward the emergency room.

Outside, the sun hadn't set yet and beat down with an unrelenting heat, which could be its own kind of killer.

She wanted to do something, *anything*, so badly her hands shook. The problem wasn't finding something to do, there was too much. A dozen different things crowded into the number one priority spot in her head, until she wasn't sure which to do first.

It left her in a state of impotence she didn't like at all.

Down the road, two vans approached, the sun reflecting off their windshields. Both vehicles came to a stop in two of the parking spaces allocated to the police next to the entrance and disgorged six people each.

Kini knew them all. River, Dr. Rodrigues, and four members of the doctor's advance team members, whose job it was to create order out of chaos.

Rodrigues and River strode up the short set of stairs and came to an abrupt halt in front of Smoke and her.

"Good God," Rodrigues said, staring at her face. She glanced at Smoke, and her lips tightened into a thin white line. "This is what you call minor injuries?"

"I know it looks bad, but—" Kini began.

"*Looks* bad?" Rodrigues shook her head. "You're both off this case. Go back to Atlanta, get checked out by medical, and don't return to work until I say so."

"But—"

Rodrigues ignored her to train her focus on Smoke. "River tells me you're very good at your job, Mr. Smoke."

"Smoke," he corrected. "No mister."

Rodrigues flashed an irritated look at River. "What is it with you guys and your irrational attachment to one-word nomenclature?"

"Irrational?" River asked.

"Nomenclature?" Smoke asked.

Her stare turned razor sharp. "Your job is to make sure you and Kini follow my orders. Understand?"

He nodded, his face taking on all the flexibility of a block of granite. "Yes, ma'am."

Rodrigues flashed her palm at them all and said to Kini and Smoke, "Go." Then, she turned and strode through the front doors.

River shrugged and mouthed, "Sorry, man," before following her inside with the other team members.

That was it? She was just supposed to forget about everything, toss it out of her head, and go home? Emmaline, baby Brittany, even that idiot Dr. Flett, she was just supposed to forget all of them? How was a person supposed to do that?

Smoke stood as still as a statue for about ten seconds then said in a flat tone, "Time to go."

His words started a slow drip of anger deep inside her gut. "I don't like leaving a job half done."

"Same."

"They need all the help they can get."

"Help is here and more is coming."

Kini glanced down, realized her fists were clenched into tight balls, and decided to show him a truth about herself. "I hate this."

It wasn't until he turned to look at her with a deep frown that she realized she might have given him more truth than she intended.

She sighed. In for a penny, in for a pound. "I care too much."

He was silent, waiting for more, but there wasn't much more.

"Too much?" he finally asked.

"It's why I'm assigned to public health surveys and fact-finding work, and not outbreaks. I get attached to people and I prefer them to stay...alive and healthy."

He stared at her, his gaze so intense she was sure he could see all the way to the bottom of her soul.

"When I first got out of nursing school, I wanted to work in an ER. Helping people in distress, victims of accidents, heart attacks, and strokes. What I got were small children with fevers, battered housewives, and drug overdoses." She stopped to take a breath and found she didn't have the energy to continue.

Smoke, silent as ever, seemed to watch her and the world at the same time. "Ugly," he said.

She laughed, at first, but it morphed to tears which, when they dripped onto her hand, were pink with blood from the wounds on her face. "You know how first responders are supposed to be able to put all that ugly stuff into boxes in the back of our heads?" She could hear the hysteria in her voice but didn't feel connected to it. It was as if she were two different people. One in pain, the other so far past pain she was numb. "Well, it turns out I don't have any boxes."

He gave her a narrow-eyed look of disbelief. "Or maybe," he said. "Your boxes are all full."

He couldn't have hit her harder than if his fist had connected with her stomach. She struggled to breathe and found she couldn't. The earth tilted oddly to one side and Smoke grabbed her by the shoulders, forced her to sit on the cement steps, and put her head between her knees.

The world narrowed into a thin line with high black walls and a ceiling that seemed to lower with every passing moment.

Now was not a good time for a new fucking box to show up.

A voice whispered in her ears, urging her to breathe.

What a fabulous idea. Her diaphragm seemed to work when she concentrated on it. In and out, in and out. The walls retreated, the ceiling rose, and a little more of the world became real.

Hard, warm hands rubbed her shoulders, while two massive knees hemmed hers in. A deep voice kept speaking to her, rumbling low with words she didn't understand. No, that wasn't right. Some of them were familiar.

Rest. She knew that word.

Heal. She knew that one, too.

Safe. That word was...dangerous. So attractive, so wonderful she wanted to believe in it, but the thought of knowing it, experiencing it, threatened to reopen wounds so deep and wide inside her they would kill her.

No, safe was not something she could ever believe in.

Still, that voice called to her, soothed her in a way that

was unfamiliar. Soft, smooth, and with a strength that made her curious. What kind of creature could heal and entice with his voice alone?

"My people have been healing with song since the beginning of the world," the beautiful voice said.

Had she asked her question out loud?

"It isn't the same as the songs of my Scottish grandmother, whose people use it as a battle cry. Song is how we speak with spirit. Our medicine men can sometimes sing a person's wounded spirit to a place where it can heal itself."

"Are you a medicine man?" she heard a voice, hers, ask.

"No, I'm a warrior, but even warriors need to know when to rest. When to live in the quiet so they can heal."

Rest was something she didn't understand. She kept busy in an effort to stop dwelling on things she dare not discuss, even with herself. How had he gotten so wise?

"You meant it, didn't you?"

He tilted his head to one side.

"When you said you'd kill whoever hurt me."

He nodded slowly.

"It's too late." She tried not to cry, she really did. "The pain lives inside me now."

One of the hands on her shoulders cupped her face. "No," Smoke disagreed. "If it did, you wouldn't try so hard to fix everyone else."

Was he right?

Hope, something she also tried to avoid, flirted with the edges of her understanding.

"Come, little bird. Let's go to a place where we can rest, and where the shadows of the dead can't hunt us." His hands urged her to stand, but the dizziness came back in a rush.

"How about I sit here and wait until you get the jeep?"

When he didn't answer immediately, she tilted her head up enough to make eye contact with him and tried to smile.

"I'm just a little dizzy."

He stared at her for a moment, searching, judging. "Don't move."

She snorted. "Not even if I wanted to."

He cupped her face briefly then stood and jogged toward the car.

Kini rested her forehead on her knees wondering if she'd ever get a lid back on the crypt containing her emotions. Maybe he was right. Maybe that box, and every other one in the catacomb at the back of her head, was full.

A shadow fell on her, blocking out the eye-blinding sun.

She glanced up, expecting to see Smoke, but it wasn't him. Two young-ish men stood over her. The kid she'd kicked in the nuts after discovering her flat tires, Freddy Alvarez, and someone she didn't know. But the expression on their faces…she'd seen anger like that before.

She opened her mouth, but something flashed past her and a ball of cloth was shoved between her teeth. They grabbed her arms and restrained her before she could pull the gag out of her mouth and scream for help.

The men wrenched her to her feet and carried her into the hospital.

Smoke, where was Smoke?

She struggled, but someone growled in her ear, "Keep struggling and we'll knock you out."

In a crowded hospital? She struggled harder and managed to yank one arm free. She sent her fist toward the throat of the unknown man and was gratified when he made a pained noise and let go of her.

"Stupid bitch," a male voice said then her neck was grabbed from behind and squeezed.

Pain overwhelmed her then dizziness sucked her into a black hole.

Chapter Twenty

Smoke got in the jeep and started the engine. He turned the vehicle around and drove toward the hospital. A crowd of people going up the steps to the main entrance blocked his view of Kini.

When they passed, no one was left sitting on the steps.

He'd told her to stay there, damn it. It was hot, so maybe she'd gone inside where the air conditioning could take the edge off.

The parking lot was even fuller than before, with a couple of trucks now parked on the groomed, gravel landscaped areas adjacent to the sidewalk on either side of the steps.

He parked next to one of the trucks, got out, and ran up the stairs.

The air was far cooler inside, but no Kini was in sight. Scanning the lobby and a couple of the hallways leading deeper into the building, he couldn't see her.

Something caught his attention and he did a double take. One of Kini's shoes lay on the floor of one of the hallways.

He strode toward it and picked it up.

The blood splatter across it was all too familiar. These were her shoes. *Kini*.

He looked around and saw a caretaker washing the floor farther down. "Excuse me," Smoke said. "Did you see the lady who lost this shoe?"

"Yeah. Her friends didn't bother to go back for it when it fell off. Not even when I yelled at them to stop and come back to get it."

"Friends?"

"Two of them were carrying her."

"Those weren't friends," Smoke growled.

"I thought she was having a seizure," the caretaker said, horror turning his expression slack. "One of them shoved something into her mouth, I thought it was to keep her from biting her tongue, you know? She flailed around, hit one of them, then seemed to fall unconscious."

"They took her."

The hallway wasn't a direct route to an exit, but it wouldn't be hard to get to one.

Smoke turned and sprinted for the front door, dodging a line of people coming in. Seconds later, he was in the jeep, gunning the engine and peeling out of the parking lot.

The hospital had many doors, but only two ways a vehicle could get to it. He drifted the jeep as he forced it to speed into the staff parking area and commercial drop-off zone, hoping to confront whoever had taken Kini. He braked, angling the jeep so it blocked the exit.

No one was in sight, inside or outside a vehicle.

No one.

Smoke waited. He was supposed to be good at that, but the weird groan from the steering wheel told him he'd better stop taking his frustration out on his ride.

Why would anyone take her? She was a nurse, not someone with authority, privileged information, or launch codes.

Who benefited from her kidnapping? What could they hope to gain from Kini? Was it an angry local who'd lost a family member?

Smoke pulled into a parking spot and called River's cell.

"Kini's been kidnapped," he said as soon as the other man answered the call. "Two men took her about five minutes ago, made it look like she was having a seizure or something."

"You're shitting me."

"I shit you not."

"What the fuck for?"

"That's what I'm trying to figure out. She's not in charge of anything." They hadn't really talked in depth about work, too distracted by all the crap going on around them. Had she kept the true scope of her job from him? "Is she?"

"No. She's mostly independent. Travels a lot, does her job, goes on to the next one. Rodrigues likes her because she doesn't need anyone to hand-hold her, but she doesn't go off half-cocked either. This is the first time she's ever been involved in an active outbreak."

"Doesn't make sense," Smoke murmured, considering the entire situation. His heart rate had slowed, the adrenaline in his bloodstream reduced enough to let him think.

"It doesn't track for me either. I mean, she was firebombed last night. What the fuck was that about?"

"We don't know what the fuck, because the sheriff is listening to one of his deputies, who just happens to be Lacey's brother. He's looking for a way to bury me. Kini was attacked before the light show last night. Graffiti, getting T-boned, dogs, slashed tires, and a dumb fuck all tried to mess with her in the last two days."

"Is there a pattern?"

That was the question he needed to ask.

"Yup," Smoke said as his brain finally, *finally*, saw them.

"After she'd been in town for a week, a rumor started going around about the CDC experimenting on people, making them sick on purpose. At about the same time, people started getting sick and dying from the hantavirus."

"Either someone wants to make her the fall guy, or they're using her as a distraction."

"That's how I'm reading it."

"So they take her and the distraction continues."

"Got any intel on this Free America From Oppression group?"

"Surprisingly little. The name has popped up in a few places on social media, but aside from the threat they sent to the news, nothing organized."

"Nothing about this feels organized either," Smoke said. "Whoever grabbed her, took a big risk in doing it in a public place."

"Who started the rumors?"

"I don't know, but I do know where to find out."

"Where?"

"The post office."

"Uh..."

Smoke started driving. "The women who work there are a bunch of gossips. Better than taking an ad out in the paper. I'll call you as soon as I learn anything." He ended the call and focused on driving.

The post office was in an adobe-style building that had been there for about one hundred years. It had operated as a jail at one time and still had bars on the windows.

He pounded on the door.

A middle-aged woman with her gray hair cut in some kind of bob came into view. "We're closed," she hollered.

Smoke ignored her large hint to leave and waved her over. "I need to know who you talked to about the CDC nurse."

She looked at him like he'd asked for the moon to be

delivered on a silver platter. She came over and opened the door. "Smoke? When did you get home?"

"Doesn't matter," he said with a shake of his head. "The CDC nurse?"

"There's been talk all over town about that nurse and the disease she brought with her."

Smoke leaned closer. "She didn't bring anything other than a rental car with her, and she sure as shit didn't get anyone sick."

The woman reared back. "But—"

"No," Smoke ordered. "Whatever you think happened, you're wrong. Thanks to the gossip, she's been attacked by dogs, idiots, and had her car firebombed." He smiled his shark's smile. "I would take it as a personal favor, Sylvia, if you'd put a stop to those rumors."

She crossed her arms over her chest. "How do you know that nurse didn't bring something with her? No one got sick until she showed up."

"She doesn't work in a lab or anything close," Smoke told her. "She collects information and a small blood sample. That's it."

Her frown returned. "Oh."

He widened his smile. "So, who's unhappy?"

She shrugged. "Who's not unhappy would be a shorter list."

"Anyone stand out as particularly pissed off? Someone with a sick friend or relative?"

Sylvia threw her hands up. "That's everybody."

"I'm looking for two fuck-ups."

Her brows rose.

Shit, he was talking to a civilian postal worker. "Idiots who act before they think."

"That narrows it down a bit." She bit her lip and said hesitantly, "One of them is your cousin, Nate."

Nate? What the fuck? "Anyone else? I need all the names."

"What for?"

Smoke just looked at her.

Sylvia rolled her eyes. "You always were good at keeping your mouth closed." She said it like it was an insult. From her, it was a compliment.

"Freddy Alvarez." She thought for another moment. "A few others, but Freddy and Nate were the worst of the idiots."

Smoke nodded his thanks, turned to leave, then glanced over his shoulder. "Stay healthy."

She didn't respond.

Freddy wasn't a surprise, but Nate hadn't been that big a moron when Smoke had been home last.

For his son's funeral.

His gut tightened as his memory flashed pictures of his little boy. His smiling face as he ran toward him in what he called a *sneak attack* hug. His son's tears as Smoke left on his last deployment. His face, still and pale in the coffin. Smoke forced those images away.

So maybe he'd been a little distracted; he'd have still noticed his cousin turning stupid.

Would Nate be stupid enough kidnap a nurse? No. So, Smoke would put him on the back burner and focus on the guy who might be dumb enough to kidnap Kini.

Freddy.

He still lived with his parents, as far as Smoke knew, despite the kid being...he had to think about it, add up the years. Twenty-three.

Christ, he was getting old.

Smoke drove to the Alvarez place, a medium-sized house one street off of Main Street. The dirt and gravel front yard featured a couple of clusters of junk. A rusted and pitted washing machine sat in one corner near the outside of the house surrounded by a broken shovel, a bicycle missing both tires and the seat, and three horse shoes.

A wagon wheel, which was probably supposed to look decorative, sat at the intersection of the driveway, and the street was almost completely shrouded by tumbleweeds. An old TV sat behind the wheel with a cactus growing through the middle of it.

The house looked quiet, shades drawn against the sun, and driveway empty of vehicles.

Smoke parked the jeep, walked to the front door, and knocked. Twice. When no one answered, he went around to the rear and found the back door open with only the screen keeping the bugs out.

"Hello," he called out loudly enough to wake someone who might be sleeping. He knocked good and loud, too, and called out again. No answer.

Fuck it.

He opened the door and went inside.

No movement or sound. He walked farther inside until he reached a crossroads of hallway, kitchen, and living area.

Air movement inside the house was almost at a standstill, but he caught the slightest scent of decay down the hallway. He walked cautiously forward, hands loose and ready to move if a quick reaction was needed.

The smell became thicker with every step, coating his tongue in putrefaction and rot. Death was the only resident here; the only questions left for him to answer were how many and who they were.

The first bedroom he came to was empty, the bed rumpled and clothes strewn across the floor.

The second bedroom revealed a person-shaped mound under the covers, a patch of black hair visible near the pillow.

Odd. He expected the smell to be stronger this close to a body.

The body moved, coughed weakly.

Smoke strode to the bed and flipped the blankets back, revealing a girl who looked to be ten or eleven years old. Her eyes were closed, her clothing and hair wet with sweat. He put a hand on her forehead. Fuck, she was burning up.

"Hey," Smoke said, putting a hand on her shoulder and giving her a gentle shake. "Wake up, princess."

She didn't respond. At least she was alive. That meant he hadn't found the source of the decomposition.

He pulled out his cell phone and called River as he left the room, heading for the last door at the end of the hallway. It was closed. As he neared it, the scent of death grew stronger.

As soon as River answered, Smoke said, "I've found a sick kid in a house with no visible adults present. I couldn't wake her, and she's got a hell of a fever. Can you spare an ambulance?"

He opened the door and took a step into the room. It was all he needed to find out everything he didn't want to know.

A woman lay on her side on the bed in the fetal position, facing toward the door. She wore underwear and a T-shirt, both soaked with sweat and possibly other fluids resulting from decomposition. The room was hot, so maybe that had sped things up, because the skin at the ends of her fingers was black, her fingernails oddly long, her lips pulled back from her teeth.

She looked like she'd been dead for days, but given the temperature, it could have only been hours since she passed.

With a child in the next room.

"There's no family present?" River asked.

"No one alive," Smoke replied. "One corpse. Adult, female."

"Shit. Just give me a second." River didn't put him on hold, and he could hear the man talking to someone else, relaying information.

"No ambulances are available," he said, coming back. "But one of the sheriff's deputies is going to pick up the kid and bring her here. Give me the address."

Smoke provided it then said, "Explain to the officer why I can't stick around. Kini is out there in the hands of someone desperate. This was just my first stop in trying to find her."

"I will. Call back if you run into anyone else who needs assistance."

"Will do." Smoke ended the call and left the house.

He checked Freddy's aunt's house, but no one, dead or alive was there. After that, he stopped at a couple other homes belonging to other members of the Alvarez family, but no one had seen him, and there was no evidence to indicate he'd been by lately.

Smoke worked to keep himself calm so he could think rationally, but it was hard. It didn't fucking make sense.

Where the fuck had Kini been taken?

Chapter Twenty-One

Kini was going to strangle someone. Two someones, to be specific.

The idiots who'd grabbed her had dropped her into the back seat of a grimy Cadillac that couldn't be younger than the Nixon era. The floor of the car was covered in a disgusting, threadbare carpet smelling of things best left unsaid, and the engine sounded like it was a few drops of oil away from seizing solid.

Her arms were awkwardly tied behind her back. *God*, the sock in her mouth better be clean or she was going to rip someone a new one. Hah. She was going to rip someone a new one anyway.

Freddy and his friend were smoking joints with both windows down.

Dust entered the car and funneled back and down to where she lay. It clung to her clothing and hair and clogged up her nose. Her tongue felt like it was coated in chalk, and she wished for a tub full of water to rinse out her mouth. Grit got into her cuts, letting in sweat, making her feel like she was an unwelcome guest inside a hornet's nest.

Someone's phone rang. Freddy answer it with a *yeah*, which was then followed by several more *yeahs* and a *see you there* before he hung up.

He turned left onto another road and kept driving.

A headache was developing behind her eyes and in her temples, thanks to the bumpy road and lack of water. She hadn't heard another vehicle for a long time.

Where the hell were they?

They slowed down then came to a stop. Freddy and friend got out, the sound of their footsteps getting softer and softer. She tried to sit upright using the edge of the seat behind her, but the sound of voices and laughter got louder along with returning footsteps.

Were they coming back for her or were they going to drive somewhere else? She let herself fall back onto the floor and braced herself for whatever was coming.

A gunshot, too close, made her whole body flinch. She'd have screamed if she didn't have the damn sock in her mouth. She dragged air in through her nose as a second shot ripped through the dusty air.

Footsteps approached. Kini squeezed her eyes shut and braced herself for pain.

"Hey, lady? Are you okay?"

She opened her eyes and turned her head as far as she could to see who was talking to her. Mostly, all she saw was the back of someone's head and shadows.

"Hey, man," someone said. "Those assholes have a woman tied up in the back seat."

More than one man, and it sounded like they were coming to her rescue, but someone had pulled a trigger twice. Maybe they did it to scare the boys off?

The door opened and sunlight hit her in the eyes, making it difficult to see. Hands reached in and pulled her into a sitting position, then all the way out of the car.

Two men, a lot older than the boys who'd taken her, dusted her off, as one of them worked on getting her hands free. The other took the sock out of her mouth.

She gagged and coughed. "Thank you," she managed to croak out as the guy behind her cut whatever was around her wrists. The man in front of her stepped to one side and she saw them.

Two bodies on the ground, blood, brain matter, and bone spattered on hair, skin, and clothing.

She sucked in a breath, her heart faltering for a beat before trying to sprint out of her chest. She stumbled backward and hands grabbed her by the shoulders.

"Easy, now," the man in front of her said, glancing at the bodies. "They pulled guns on us." He smiled at her, but it creeped her out even more. He patted her on the shoulder. "Self-defense. The little fuckers kidnapped you, right?"

She managed a shaky nod of her head.

"On a crime spree it seems." He smiled again. "Why don't we get you out of here, huh? Get you some water?"

She was nudged past the bodies and toward a larger truck. The man speaking to her had blond hair under a faded ball cap, a farmer's tan, and straight white teeth. "I'm Bruce and the gentleman behind you is Gary." He shook her hand.

The other man held his hand out for an almost too-firm handshake. He gave her a smile that had an edge to it. She blinked. *Edge*? But the sharpness was gone, leaving only polite curiosity behind.

"What happened?" He opened the passenger door and helped her onto the front bench seat.

"It's a long story." Hell, she didn't even know where to start. Didn't want to think about it, or anything, at all.

"You live out here?" Bruce asked as he started the engine and began driving away.

Why were they leaving? Wasn't this leaving the scene of a crime? Neither had a phone visible. Weren't they going to report what happened?

Shivering, she said, "No, I'm ju...just visiting." Jesus, she sounded scared to death.

"Visiting, huh? No houses around here."

"Those two took me from the hospital in town."

"A lot of sick people there, a lot of them dying. The cops are saying everyone should stay home and not go *visiting*." Bruce's voice was dipped in an oily coating of sarcasm. A slick, scary warning that sent a cascading crash of panic through her body, only she was boxed in by men and machine.

There was nowhere to go.

"What kind of person goes visiting while everyone is sick?" Gary asked, his tone a mockery of concern.

"Sounds nefarious, eh?" Bruce said with a chuckle.

"Real cloak and dagger," he agreed.

"Just how involved are you with that disease in town?" Bruce asked, all humor disappearing from his face.

She stared at him, then darted a look at his friend and found the same expression there, too.

Understanding was a cold stone at the pit of her stomach. Those shots hadn't been self-defense, and these two men weren't rescuing her.

"I think she's very involved with that disease," Gary said, his gaze so cold she shivered. "I also think she's been sticking her nose into things that are none of her business."

"Who are you?" she asked before she could censor herself. Her voice wavered with the fear that she'd just gone from the fire into the frying pan.

Bruce shrugged. "We're no one important."

Something brushed her arm, and Kini shrank away from Gary's hand. "Don't," she said sharply.

A slow, serrated smile crept across his face.

"Why did you decide to come to this area now?" Bruce asked at the same time as Gary wrapped his hand around her forearm.

"Let go of me," she ordered from between clenched teeth. *Don't scream. Don't scream.* Something told her these two would like it too much.

"What brought you here?" Bruce asked again.

She tried to twist her arm out of Gary's grasp, but his grip tightened, and he pinned her shoulder to the back of the seat.

"Answer the question."

"My job," she said.

"You're that nurse." Gary inched closer and leaned toward her, putting his face only a couple of inches from hers. "It's all over town that you work for the CDC. Why would the CDC send you to this little pissant place?"

Stomach roiling and holding on to her cookies and her sanity with everything she had, she said, "I get sent all over the country to do population studies, see what pathogens are endemic in a region, and look for patterns of disease transmission. This was a routine assignment no different than the dozen or more others I've done."

The two men exchanged glances.

"You weren't sent here because of the hantavirus?" Gary asked.

"Yes and no." The information wasn't a secret. In order to perform the study, the CDC was required to fully explain the purpose of it to anyone who might be a potential subject in the study. Anyone could ask for this information. "This study was to get a sense of how many of the people who live in this part of the state have developed antibodies to the virus without developing the illness. The CDC is considering the possibility of developing a vaccine."

"Why?"

She resisted rolling her eyes. "I don't know. I'm just a

field nurse. They give me the general parameters of what they want and set me loose to get it done."

Gary's lips tightened along with his grip.

Pain shot down her arm and she gasped.

"Why are they looking *here*?"

"I don't—"

"Speculate," he snarled, squeezing her arm again.

"Just tell him," Bruce advised. "He likes hurting people a little too much, and women most of all."

She stared into Gary's eyes and saw the truth there, cold, sharp, and coiling like a snake made of razors. No matter where it hit, it was going to make her bleed.

"There have been," she began, "several small clusters or pockets of infection in the population outside of the normal areas where hantavirus is endemic. My boss looked at all the cases and couldn't find a common denominator, other than the possibility of the rodents carrying the virus, moving into new territory."

"So what?" Gary hissed.

"So, if the virus is moving into more populated areas, the time, cost, and effort of creating a vaccine might be warranted."

"There's no other reason?"

"None that was shared with me."

Gary smiled and it sent a shiver of fear through her. "I don't believe you."

Chapter Twenty-Two

Smoke hurried into his parents' home and found his mother watching the news on her tablet.

"What are you doing here?" she asked him as she got to her feet. "I thought you'd be at the hospital—"

"Do you know where Nate is?" Smoke interrupted.

"Why?"

"I need to find him."

"I haven't seen him since yesterday."

"What about a cell phone? Do you have his number?"

"Yes, I've got it. Just give me a second to grab my phone." She picked it up from the table. "What's going on?"

"Kini has been taken."

"What?" His mother stared at him like he'd dropped a hand grenade on the table and asked her to defuse it before it blew up.

He rubbed a hand over his face. "I know. It sounds crazy, but that's what I think happened."

"What's this got to do with your cousin?"

"She and I had an altercation with Freddy Alvarez. He's

my number one suspect, and Nate probably knows where to find him or has his phone number. They were tight."

"Yes, a couple of years ago, but not so much anymore."

"It's the only lead I've got, Mom."

She read him Nate's number and Smoke added it to his contacts, then he called his cousin. After two rings, it went to voicemail. He texted a simple message: *Call me, Smoke* and hit send.

Now what? Standing around waiting for a phone call wasn't going to help Kini, but running around like a chicken with its head cut off wasn't any better.

His phone chose that moment to ring. River's ringtone.

"Smoke," he said.

"There's a Deputy Blackwater here. He says two young men were found in the desert about six miles from town. Dead, shot execution style. One of them, a Freddy Alvarez, filed a harassment complaint against you yesterday."

Shit. Freddy was dead? *What the fuck is going on?*

Smoke balanced precariously on the edge between action and complete shutdown. If Freddy was dead, where was Kini? Cold fingers wrapped around his neck, strangling his ability to breathe.

Get a grip, asshole. Losing his shit wasn't going to help. *Focus.* "So?"

"So, the police are asking nicely if you'd answer some questions."

"I never touched him."

"Harassment, not assault." River paused, then said, "We need this cleared up, so it doesn't distract us from the important shit."

"Blackwater wants to bury me."

"The fucker has a serious hard-on for you. We've got someone here who has volunteered to act as your...advocate."

"Not a lawyer?"

"Nope, doctor."

"She's out there—" Smoke's throat closed, making speaking, breathing impossible. If this shit with Blackwater ended up harming Kini in anyway, the asshole was going to disappear. Permanently.

"We'll find her," River said. It was a promise from a battle brother.

"On my way," Smoke said, heading for the door as he ended the call.

"Smoke?" his mother asked.

"Backup is here." He didn't wait for any more questions.

He parked his hog outside the hospital entirely illegally on a strip of landscaped rocks rimmed with drought-hardy plants. He'd driven there, somehow, but didn't remember a second of the trip. All he could think about was Kini covered in bandages and bruises, lying in a dry ditch somewhere.

The sun was going down, and soon it would be too dark to see much.

Smoke strode through the building, heading for the ER, where he figured someone in charge would be, but there were so many people in the waiting room, he literally couldn't get through the crowd.

"Hey, Army," someone called out from behind him.

He turned to find River waving at him. Smoke followed the other man until they were away from the worst of the crowd.

"We're in the human resources office. It's the only place in the whole building that's not in use in dealing with the outbreak."

"Officially?" Smoke asked.

"Yep. Rodrigues announced it ten minutes ago." He looked at Smoke sidelong. "Ready?"

He shrugged. What was there to get ready for? He hadn't done anything to anyone.

Yet.

"Rodrigues reached her bullshit limit two seconds into her conversation with Blackwater and the sheriff," River said in a satisfied tone. "Told them that if this was a fishing expedition, she was going to use their balls for bait."

Huh, that was going to piss Blackwater off. Big time. The sheriff…Smoke didn't know the man well enough to say.

River stopped in front of a door, opened it, and went in. Smoke followed, noting the sheriff and Blackwater standing at the rear of the room next to a desk.

Another man, wearing scrubs, a hospital gown over top, booties on his shoes, and a plastic hat over his hair stood with his arms crossed in the middle of the room.

"Dr. Gunner Anderson, this is Lyle Smoke." The doctor nodded at him, but offered no handshake.

"Oh, isn't this nice. We all know each other now," Blackwater drawled. "Do you want to exchange cell phone numbers, too?"

"Dale," the sheriff said softly. It was a warning.

River's cell phone pinged. He checked it and swore. "I've got to go." He was gone a second later.

"Well?" Dr. Anderson said, looking at his watch. "Get on with it?"

"In a hurry, Doc?" Blackwater asked.

"Yes, you effing moron," the doctor said, giving Blackwater a hard stare.

The deputy stared back, or tried to, but the doctor never flinched. Finally, Blackwater looked at Smoke. "Where were you an hour and a half ago?"

"At the post office."

Blackwater frowned. He hadn't expected that answer. "And after that?"

"I went to Freddy Alvarez's house, found two of his relatives, one alive, the other dead. Called that in, then went to his aunt's home. Didn't find him there either."

"So you could have—" Blackwater said, his tone triumphant.

"Why were you looking for him?" the sheriff interrupted.

Blackwater scowled at his boss, but didn't say anything.

"My partner, Kini Kerek, has been kidnapped. She'd kicked him in the balls yesterday, so I thought he might be stupid enough to take her."

"You saw no sign of him?"

"No."

"She was taken about thirty minutes before we think he was killed," the sheriff said. "It fits."

"Sir," Blackwater began. "This man—"

"If he'd killed Alvarez, he'd have that nurse back safe and sound," the sheriff said, his voice certain.

"He could have killed her, too," Blackwater shouted.

"I don't think so," the sheriff said. "He looks like a man ready to rip your fool head off for wasting his time. He looks like a man who cares for this woman." He turned to Smoke. "Sorry, son, but we don't have the manpower to deal with this outbreak, investigate several murders, and look for the nurse. River said we'd have more hands by tomorrow, but the clock's ticking now."

"I know. I'll find her."

"Any ideas on where to look next?"

Smoke shook his head. "Nothing solid. My cousin Nate and Freddy used to be good friends. I'm trying to find him."

"All right," the sheriff said. "Keep my office informed. As soon as I can spare a few men to help you look for her, I'll let you know."

"But, Sheriff," Blackwater said, his voice only a decibel or two below a shout.

"No, Dale, we're done here." The sheriff looked his man in the eyes. "Done." He nodded at the doctor then Smoke as he left the room.

Blackwater stared at Smoke, his mouth twisted with hate. He didn't say anything, but his gaze promised death.

Smoke allowed the trained killer inside him out so the other man could see the bastard on his face. *You're not so tough, asshole.*

Blackwater left.

"Thanks," Smoke said to the doctor.

"That guy hates your guts."

Smoke snorted and turned to leave. He should get a fucking award for acting the part of a rational human being in front of Blackwater. Wouldn't be able to hang on to the calm for long. If he didn't find Kini soon, he was going to lose control and start hurting people.

"Watch your back. He's a coward," the doctor said. "They never come at you straight on."

Smoke saw the jagged edge of horror on his face. Not a combat stare—that said you were willing and able to fight, to kill. What was on Dr. Anderson's face was the look of someone who's seen and endured terror, torture, slaughter, and was powerless to stop it. "Where did you serve?"

It was the doctor's turn to snort. "I wasn't military. Doctors Without Borders, three years working in Syria."

"Shit. That was some rough time."

"I wasn't in prison," the doctor snapped. "I chose to be there."

"Whether we choose it or not, Dr. Anderson, when you've lived through nightmares, you take the prison with you."

"Gunner or Dr. Gunner, your choice." He studied Smoke for a moment. "Do these cops have any idea what you are?"

"What am I?" Smoke heard the threat in his own voice and flinched.

Gunner smiled, baring his teeth. "I've had many conversations with your friend River. He's intelligent, skilled, utterly unafraid, and can think his way out of shit most people would drown in. I thought he was the deadliest man I'd ever met, until you."

What the fuck was he supposed to say? *No, I'm a cream puff.* "Sorry, man, I'm just not that into you."

Gunner laughed. "Okay. Just remember, even idiots get lucky sometimes."

Good advice.

Smoke left to track down River. He tried to call his cousin again. Still no answer. That left him with only one option.

He found River talking to Dr. Rodrigues.

"Do not get into a pissing match with the police," Rodrigues ordered without preamble.

"No, ma'am," Smoke agreed.

"Having said that, find Kini. She's running out of time."

"I will."

She turned on her heel and disappeared into the crowd of people.

"When does our backup get here?" Smoke asked.

"About sixteen hours."

"I've got my cell phone, but there may not be service where I'm going," Smoke said.

"Do you know where you're going?"

"Only one place that's come up that doesn't belong. One of our tribal elders ran across an abandoned farm with squatters living in it and some dead bodies buried nearby. No one has had a chance to check it out yet."

"Is there anyone in town I can ask for help to look for you, if you don't show up in twenty-four hours?"

"My dad or grandfather. Either of them knows where I'd go to ground."

"Need anything else?"

Smoke thought about it. He had his weapon, ammunition, water, and food all at his grandparents' house. The rest of his stuff, what he needed for this operation, was at his folks' place. Kini had been right. He always had a go-bag ready. "I'm good."

River nudged him with one hand. "Stay that way."

Smoke gave him a nod and left.

He went home first, grabbed his backpack, then took a couple of minutes to explain to his parents what was going on.

His father grabbed his rifle.

"No," Smoke said. "I work for the CDC. If you or anyone else gets involved, there could be trouble." He paused. "If I do need help, I'll get in touch, but this is my hunt. My fight."

"You call if things get too hot." His father smiled, but it was cold. "There's more than one way to fight this kind of stupid."

Once, when he was about thirteen, a man had shot up the grocery store in town then taken off into the desert to hide. This man had lived in the area for a few years and thought he knew the desert, thought no one could find him.

Smoke had gone out with his father, grandfather, and a few other Navajo. They found him within the first day but hadn't done anything but watch the hidey hole the man was in. When he tried to leave to get food or water, they fired at him, not to kill or even wound, just to force him to stay in his hole. They kept him there for three days. On the fourth day, the man had begged to be arrested. Had whined that he was going to die of thirst if they didn't let him out.

So they called the police and he was arrested, charged, convicted, and served time.

He never came back to Small Blind, Utah.

There were lots of ways to hunt and trap whoever had taken Kini. The army had sharpened some of those skills into fine, almost invisible, points.

He went to his grandparents' place. For all he knew his

AR15 was still in the refrigerator stashed behind the jug of milk.

It took him about five minutes to gather everything he wanted and fit it into his pack. Unfortunately, he also managed to acquire his very own babysitter sitting in a dinged-up truck parked a couple of doors down the street. Not far at all from his jeep.

He recognized the guy as a relative of his ex, Lacey. Blackwater wasn't giving up.

The jeep wouldn't do him much good after a certain point. But a dirt bike, now that would be a lot handier. Tommy had one he usually kept in the shed behind the house.

"Who's that?" his grandfather asked as the two of them looked out the partially repaired front window. Only half of it had glass, the other half was still covered with plywood.

"Blackwater," Smoke said flatly, turning away from the window and going into the kitchen. "Is Tommy's dirt bike running?"

"Yes. You'll need gas, but there's a can out there." His grandfather smiled grimly. "Let me check to see if anyone is watching the back of the house. There's nothing between us and the desert other than a runoff ditch."

Grandpa went out, fooled around with the barbeque, and unhooked the propane tank. He took it to the shed and came back with another one he connected to the barbeque.

"I didn't see anyone," he said when he came back into the house.

"I take it we're having burgers tonight?" Grandma asked.

She got a smile for an answer.

Smoke shouldered his pack and weapon and went out to the shed, filled the bike's tank, then walked it into and out of the ditch. He watched for anyone following him but saw no one as he pushed the bike deeper into the desert.

The Rogerson place was about ten miles from town at the

end of a dirt road. He'd start there. Beyond the buildings was a dry canyon that ran hard with runoff when it did rain. Past the ravine was about a hundred miles of unoccupied desert bordered by the Grand Canyon on the south. It looked like the whole area was uninhabited, but it wasn't. There was lots of wildlife that made their home in the desert. Deer, coyotes, rabbits, vultures, and men. The native people had been in the area for thousands of years.

If Kini was out there, he would find her.

Chapter Twenty-Three

Kini saw pain in Gary's gaze. Not his pain. Her pain. This man was going to hurt her, not because he wanted information, but because he liked it.

"Why do you care what the CDC does? Everyone is dealing with the outbreak. No one has the time or manpower to do anything else."

"How long is that going to last?" Bruce asked.

Gary's leer hadn't changed. Nothing she said was going to stop him from doing what he wanted to do. She winced at the sudden added pressure as Gary squeezed his hand around her arm. "A couple of days. More help is coming."

"What kind of help?" Gary asked.

"Medical assistance and…some law enforcement."

"*Fuck*," Bruce said.

Gary grabbed her by the neck with his free hand in a chokehold. "How do we get rid of them, bitch?"

She couldn't breathe, couldn't answer, couldn't save herself. A charged, cold chill whispered over her skin. Her hands scrabbled at his, trying to loosen his hold, but he just smiled and squeezed.

"If you strangle her now, she can't tell us anything." Bruce paused as if thinking about it. "Or be a useful hostage."

Gary let her neck go. "Answer the question, bitch. How do we get rid of them?"

"I don't think you can," she said, her voice raspy. "Not since those two deputies were shot."

"That has nothing to do with the outbreak," Bruce said.

"They won't assume that," Kini said. "They'll turn over every stone in this desert until they find out why all of it happened."

"*Fuck*," Bruce said again. He glanced at Kini. "Cover her eyes."

Gary reached around behind the seat and grabbed something. A paper shopping bag. He put it over her head.

Dammit. Now she wouldn't know where she was or how to get back to the highway, let alone town. That was *if* she managed to escape these two lunatics.

Gary kept a tight grip on her arm, but not as tight as when he'd been asking her questions. Her fingers were swarmed by pins and needles, but she didn't complain. The pain told her he hadn't done any lasting damage. She was just glad he hadn't put his hand anywhere else.

They bounced down the road, the potholes seeming to increase exponentially by the minute. To give herself something to do, and stay calm, she counted the seconds. When they stopped, eight hundred and forty-four seconds had gone by. Fourteen minutes. Given the distance a truck could cross in that time, the search area was going to be huge.

No one knew where she was or who she was with.

No one was going to find her in time.

They yanked her out of the truck, dumping her onto her hands and knees. The ground beneath her was packed hard with uneven gravel on top.

Gary swore and used his grip on her upper arm to haul her to her feet. He pulled so hard her arm nearly came out of its socket, and she cried out.

He jerked her forward and she staggered again.

"Get up, you stupid bitch," he growled at her.

"I can't see where I'm going," she said. "How do you expect me to stay on my feet?"

The paper bag was ripped off her head.

The first thing she saw were three body-sized mounds only a few feet in front of her.

What the…?

She stared at the edge of one mound. The dirt had been disturbed by something small, leaving a human finger visible. A finger with bite marks all over it and some flesh torn out.

Gary leaned down, his breath coating her ear in an invisible slime she wasn't sure she'd ever clean off. "If you don't want to end up in the next hole, you'll do exactly as you're told." He gave her a shove. "Get up."

Kini got to her feet and didn't resist when he pushed her toward a rundown house. Paint had begun peeling years before, leaving only the faintest hint of white on its weathered boards. There was a porch with a section of the roof covering it, but the corner supports were leaning to one side, giving the impression that the whole thing would collapse in the next stiff wind.

There wasn't a window in the place that didn't have at least one hole in the dirty glass.

Gary pushed her up the two steps to the porch, then through a screen door barely hanging onto the doorframe by one hinge.

The smell hit her first. A bitter, acrid scent combined with something she identified as cat urine burned the inside of her nose. The mess was the next assailant on her senses. There were empty beer bottles, matchboxes, and lighters all over the floor. Along the wall on the left was what looked like an old picnic table covered in hot plates, glass jugs, and a variety of chemicals and kitchen utensils.

Okay, so, crystal meth lab. Should she be horrified or relieved?

A glance in the opposite direction had her stopping cold. A map of Utah had been adhered to the wall with a large number of the state's towns and cities marked with tacks. Above the map was a single sentence written in black marker: *HV first stage infection targets.*

Targets?

Infection?

An icy wave of fear broke over her, coating her body with frost and freezing her lungs solid. *The outbreak was no accident.* If she read the map correctly, things were going to get worse. A lot worse.

Gary put his hand between her shoulder blades and shoved.

So angry her hands shook, she glared at him. "You're insane."

He pushed her again. "You're here for only one thing." He gestured with the gun. "In the bedroom."

Her jaw fell open for the second time in ten seconds, but he shoved her toward a doorway to the right before she could respond.

There were a couple of cots in the room; one was occupied, the other wasn't.

"He's sick," Gary said, waving a hand at the occupied cot. "Take care of him."

Kini raised her empty hands. "With what?"

"You'll get some stuff," he told her giving her another push toward the cot. "But if he dies, you'll be next." Gary gave her a serial killer's smile and left the room.

Kini reluctantly approached the cot. The smell of

unwashed male almost overpowered the cat urine smell from the other room. All that was visible was brown greasy hair, so she pulled the sleeping bag back.

A man, late twenties to mid-thirties, unconscious and with labored breathing. His face shone with sweat and when she peeled more of the sleeping bag away she saw that the fabric was damp. An indicator of a prolonged fever.

Footsteps approached.

Kini glanced up as Gary came back into the room with several large cases covered in EMS symbols. The words just fell out of her mouth. "What did you do, rob an ambulance?"

Way to go, idiot. Goad the asshole into hurting you.

Gary flashed his teeth in an unveiled threat but didn't do more than ask, "Can you help him?"

"I don't know yet." She'd been in the room less than a minute, and he thought that was long enough to diagnose an unconscious person? "When did he start getting sick?"

"Yesterday. Started complaining about a headache and coughing a lot. A couple of hours ago, I tried to wake him, but he wasn't all there, you know?"

This was someone Gary cared about. A friend or brother? She raised an eyebrow.

He scowled at her with a suddenness that told her he wasn't happy with revealing how important this man was to him.

She didn't say anything, just opened the case of supplies closest to her.

It contained a blood pressure cuff, stethoscope, and other assessment tools. In another, IV tubing, needles, suture kits, and other tools for treating wounds. The third case contained antibiotics, painkillers, and other medications.

Gary watched her investigate the contents for a minute then turned to leave.

"Wait," Kini said. "What's his name?"

"Don," the man said before he disappeared.

She returned to her patient, listening to his heart and lungs, and talking to him as she worked. "Hi, Don, my name is Kini, and I'm a nurse." She took his pulse, found a digital thermometer in one of the cases, and stuck the business end in one of his ears.

So far, the signs weren't good. His pulse was fast at 110, his lungs were full of fluid, especially his right lung, and his temperature was 105 degrees. She found a blood oxygen monitor in the first case.

Kini clamped the small device over one of his fingers. It read 82 percent, low, but not deadly. Combined with his fast pulse rate though...he needed advanced medical care no amount of goodies stolen out of an ambulance could provide.

She got up and went to deliver the bad news. Hopefully, they wouldn't kill the messenger.

Gary and Bruce were talking in the living room, but they went silent as soon as they saw her.

There wasn't any point in trying to sugarcoat any of it. "He's got a fever and pneumonia. He needs to be on a ventilator and treated with medications used in an ICU, not an ambulance."

"He has that hantavirus?" Bruce asked.

"I don't know for sure, but with all the cases in this area"—she shrugged—"it's the most likely cause."

Gary stalked toward her. "You're not even going to try to help him?" He walked around behind her, grabbed her by the hair, and hauled her back against him. He whispered into her ear, "Do you have a death wish, bitch?"

He thought he was scary. He had no idea the kind of scary she'd already faced down and watched die. "Would you prefer I lie to you? You're wasting *his* time. He needs advanced life support. If you take him to a hospital now, he's got a chance."

"And if I don't?"

"He's got no chance."

"Take him," Bruce said. "I'll stay here. Maybe she can help the others."

"Others?" she asked. There were more sick people here? "You should take them all to a hospital."

"Shut your face," Gary said as he shoved her so hard she landed on her back. He raised his fist and she flinched, bracing herself for the hit.

"Go," Bruce told him.

Gary hesitated, sneered at her, then walked toward the bedroom.

Kini met Bruce's gaze. "You're making a mistake."

He tilted his head, studying her as if she were an interesting insect he'd never seen before. "Gary's right. You do have a death wish." He angled his head toward what she'd assumed was the kitchen. "Get up. You have other patients."

Kini clambered to her feet and preceded Bruce into the kitchen.

No one was there.

"Keep going," he ordered, pointing at the back door.

Outside was a large tent. Someone inside sounded like they were hacking up a lung.

"How many people need medical attention?" she asked. That tent was big enough to hold half a dozen people.

"Three."

She turned. "I'll need the medical supplies—"

"I'll bring them." He pointed at the tent.

Damn it. So much for a dash to freedom while everyone's back was turned. She entered the tent to find four cots, three occupied by people coughing.

Even the inside of the tent stunk of unwashed bodies and urine. Did the smell of the chemicals they worked with seep into their pores, so they sweated it out later?

"Who's this?" one man asked, sitting up to look at her. Skinny as a rail with pale skin and bloodshot eyes, he looked more than half dead.

"A nurse. She's going to take care of you guys, hopefully make you better."

Skinny let out a cackle that scraped across her nerves endings like a cheese grater. "Make me better? The Pope doesn't have a chance in hell of doing that." He flopped back onto the cot. "You're wasting this sweet young thing's time." He laughed again.

Kini winced and tried to swallow, but her mouth had gone as dry as the desert around them. Her usefulness as a nurse was the only thing keeping her alive. "Do you mind if I attempt to give you a second opinion?"

"Whatever, lady." His laughter descended into a wheeze.

Well, she had at least one semicoherent patient. After a glance at the other two occupied cots, she approached them cautiously.

Standing a couple of feet away, she said tentatively, "Hello?"

She got a snore for a response. At least he was alive.

When she queried the last cot, a rough and irritated voice barked, "Will everyone please *shut the fuck up*."

Two complainers and a snorer. Better than three dead.

Movement had her spinning around, preparing for a fight. It was Bruce with the medical supplies. He handed her the stethoscope with a frown that told her he'd noticed her reaction.

"I'm not going to kill you," he said in not much more than a whisper. "Not now, anyway."

"Gee, that's so reassuring."

Wait, had those words come out of her mouth?

Kini closed her eyes and waited for the inevitable reaction and resulting pain.

A couple of seconds later she opened her eyes to find Bruce staring at her like she'd put her crazy pants on backward.

"When I'm tired and sore I get snarky."

He just stared at her coldly then walked away.

It took her twenty minutes to take the vitals of all three men and document them in a notebook she'd found in one of the cases. Of the three, Skinny was the healthiest, but none of them were well.

She spent a long time listening to their lungs. They didn't have pneumonia, but the sound coming from them wasn't right, either.

Bruce came back at that point, and she saw no reason to lie to him.

"All of them need proper medical care." She pointed at the stolen medical supplies. "This isn't enough."

"Get them up and able to work," he ordered. "I don't care how."

She opened her mouth to protest, but the cold expression on his face, so completely devoid of emotion, scared her. It took her a couple of seconds to get her vocal chords working again. "I need to know what got them sick in the first place, before I can give them any kind of treatment. What were their symptoms?"

He shrugged. "They started coughing and constantly complained of having a headache."

She sucked in a breath. "The chemicals used to make the meth. Did any of you wear any kind of mask or breathing apparatus?"

He raised one eyebrow. "You're kidding, right?"

"Those chemicals are dangerous. They may have damaged lung tissue."

"So they don't have that damned disease?"

"Their lungs don't sound right, but they don't sound like

pneumonia, either." She looked at the three men. "I could be wrong though."

"Can they work?"

"I don't know." She studied Bruce. "Can they?"

He glanced at the house then at his watch. "We have a quota to meet."

"If the damage is the result of the chemicals, making them work will only hurt them further. It could kill them."

He barked out a laugh. "This isn't a union. They don't get sick time or anything else for that matter. They produce or they die."

And she'd thought he was the nice one. "What are you going to do with me?"

Chapter Twenty-Four

Smoke walked the dirt bike a quarter mile out from the Rogerson place. Ever since they'd talked to Emmaline, he'd had a bad feeling about this place. The murders of the two deputies and Freddy getting himself and his buddy shot cemented his opinion that nothing good was going on.

He'd stayed away from the road, coming toward the property at an oblique angle. When he got to the fence, he used his knife to unhook the bottom of one link from its neighbor. Once started, the process to completely unravel the steel link only took a minute and he was through. As soon as the buildings came into view, he hid the machine under some scrub brush then found a good place to watch the house and the ragged tent behind it.

The sun was going down. Soon darkness would turn this dangerous game of hide and seek deadly.

A tall, skinny guy came out of the back door of the house and headed for the tent, coughing hard enough to wake the dead.

"Hey, lady," the guy called at the tent. He cleared his

throat, or tried to. "Uh, Nurse?"

"My name is Kini."

Smoke jerked his small binoculars up and watched her come out of the tent, a stethoscope around her neck. "What do you want?" Covered in bandages, and bruises, and with bags under her eyes, she'd never looked better.

She was alive.

She was okay.

A burned, twisted wire deep inside his spine unwound and cooled off a little. She was *okay*.

"Bruce wants you." Skinny dude angled his thumb at the house.

She backed up a step. "Why doesn't he come get me himself?" She sounded defensive, cautious. She didn't want to go into the house.

"He's on the phone." The guy gestured toward the back door again. "Hurry up."

With a huff, Kini walked around the guy and went into the house.

The sick grin on the skinny dude's face didn't give Smoke the warm and fuzzies. Getting her out of there was his only priority, but how many men were in the house and how many in the tent?

Had they taken her to treat their sick? He couldn't see anyone on a watch detail, and he would have seen someone if there was anyone to see.

As soon as the skinny dude disappeared into the tent, Smoke moved, silent and sure, until he stepped on something oddly squishy.

Looking down, he realized it was a hand, partially eaten and withered by daytime heat, but a human hand. On the middle finger was a ring, its shape familiar. The last time he'd seen it was two days ago on Nate's hand.

For a long moment, Smoke's brain refused to make the

connection. Then, with rage raining white noise inside his skull, he flung the dirt off the face of the body and had to snuff out a snarl.

Nathan. A bullet hole between shadowed eyes.

These fucking assholes had killed his cousin. The same assholes had Kini inside this hovel of horror.

She wasn't going to end up in one of these shitty, shallow graves. He would do anything, *kill* anyone to prevent it.

The lock on the lessons he learned in foreign deserts and lost jungles, lessons that kept him alive, but could only bury him at home, disintegrated.

A vicious, violent joy filled him.

The fuckers were dead. Every last one of them. *Dead.*

His soul all but sang, *justified, justified, justified kills.*

Smoke took the endorphin rush and used it to focus on what he had to do next, and next, and next. Kini wasn't safe yet.

He left the body of his cousin and moved into a position where he could look into one of the windows to the front room of the house. Someone was turning on a couple of lights.

A whole lot of glass jars, plastic tubing, and other shit made seeing anything clearly impossible, but with the window busted, he could hear everything just fine.

"You want me to what?" Kini asked someone in a tone filled with a caustic combination of hostility, fatigue, and pain.

"Work," a male voice, sounding pissed the fuck off, said. "My people are too sick." A Texan accent.

"Your people are dying and doing *this* is what's killing them." Her voice scraped across Smoke's nerves, with jagged, sharp edges. He'd heard that kind of strain before in the life he'd left behind weeks ago. It took days of witnessing violence and death with little sleep to achieve. Years of training couldn't guarantee a soldier could handle it. How close to her breaking point was she?

"Get. To. *Work*," the Texan ordered.

"No."

Fuck. This conversation was going downhill fast. A distraction needed to happen yesterday. He tensed, preparing to be that distraction.

A cell phone rang.

That was a little too convenient.

There was a two-second silence then the asshole said, "What?"

Smoke waited. Should he take the Texan out now while he was distracted by his phone call? Or instigate a larger disruption with a greater likelihood of separating Kini physically from the men he'd seen?

"I've got it under control," the Texan said, his voice vibrating with anger. "Just keep the Feds too busy to come out here."

Another pause.

"I don't give a shit if it's the fucking Marines. Keep them away from here, because if I go down, so do you."

Smoke had to get her out of that house and away from the Texan and Skinny, and he had to do it now.

He went back to where he'd left his dirt bike and walked it to the road leading to the buildings, maybe 150 feet away. The moon was nearly full and the sky was clear. Good conditions for what he wanted.

Once he was around a corner and behind a collection of stones, trees, and the remains of some kind of rusty farm equipment, he kick-started the bike. After revving the engine several times, he dropped it and disappeared into the landscape. The back country only looked barren. To someone who'd spent most of their life here, it was traversable. To an outsider, it could be a death sentence.

Smoke moved fast and made it back to a spot where he

could watch the house in time to see the Texan hauling ass down the road toward the bike.

Kini wasn't visible anywhere.

"Get your hands off me!" The sharp words and the unmistakable crash of broken glass had him heading for the house at a sliding run he'd perfected as a kid while hunting with his father and grandfather.

Fast and silent, he went in through the front door, his rifle in his hands.

Kini was struggling with the skinny dude, but he had her pinned up against the wall and was using his body to hold her in place.

The asshole laughed. "Fight me, baby. I *like* it," he said as he mauled one breast through her blood-stained shirt.

Adrenaline hit Smoke's system and he detonated. He slung his rifle behind his back, freeing his hands as he ran. A bullet was too good for the asshole. One arm went around Skinny's throat while he pummeled the other man's kidney with his free hand. Smoke ignored the choking sounds coming from the asshole's throat and kept hammering away. By the time he was done with Skinny, he'd be lucky if he could piss blood. "How do you like it now, *baby*?"

Kini staggered a couple of steps, knocking over a couple of metal buckets with a splash and clatter.

Smoke dragged Skinny farther away from her and began hitting his face.

"Smoke, I think you've convinced him to stop."

Really? The image of Skinny, his body pinning Kini's, passed through his head. *Nah.* He kept beating the shit. He got to kill whoever he wanted.

Kini frowned. "Smoke, he can't breathe."

Gee, that's too bad.

"Smoke," Kini said in a severe tone. "You're killing him."

And that was a problem, how?

Small, warm, bloody hands wrapped around his wrist. "Please, Smoke."

Behind her, the floor around the buckets she'd upended began to smoke.

He looked into Kini's warm chocolate eyes, a gaze so full of hurt it made the killing rage that had hijacked him retreat enough for him to think.

Those delicate hands pulled at the arm clamped around Skinny's neck. He released the asshole and stepped back, pulling Kini with him.

Skinny flopped onto the pitted wood floor like a sack of potatoes.

Kini reached out with one hand toward the asshole's neck. Smoke took another step back, taking her with him. She glanced at him. "I need to see if he's still alive."

"Doesn't matter."

She stared at him, turning even paler than she already was. "Because you're going to kill him anyway?"

He didn't respond. He didn't have to.

"No," she said, determination putting some color back in her face. She laid one hand along his jaw. "I don't want his death on your conscience."

"Won't bother me." It wouldn't, but something was wrong with that truth, even though he couldn't think of what it could be.

"No," she said again, a tear clearing a track through the blood splatter on her skin. "Please don't become one of the monsters."

But that's what he was.

She put a hand on his chest. "I'm tired and sore and I want to get away from this..."—she glanced around—"horror movie."

Reality smacked him upside the head. The Texan would be back soon, and ready for a fight. This time, when she reached for Skinny's neck, he let her go.

The smoke coming from the spill site intensified.

"Still alive, but…"—she looked around the room—"if he stays here, he isn't going to stay that way."

Smoke went to the front door.

Movement on the road.

He strode over to Kini and snagged her hand. "The Texan."

The smoldering floor burst into active flames.

He hustled her through the house.

She sucked in a breath. "What about—"

"No time." He kept her moving.

At the back door, Smoke paused to observe the tent, but if anyone was watching them from inside it, he couldn't detect them.

He headed into the desert at a trot, needing to get her away from the burning cesspool as quickly as possible.

He pulled out his cell phone and swore.

"What's wrong?" Kini asked.

He held out the phone. At some point during his scuffle with Skinny, his phone had taken a hit. The screen had been shattered and the battery case caved in.

He dropped it in the dust.

With the dirt bike no longer an option, they either had to flag down a ride back to town, steal a vehicle, or walk. Hitching a ride was out, there was no other car or truck in sight, and Kini was already at her physical limit.

He needed to find a place where they could hole up for a couple of hours or more. Somewhere the ass-wipe they'd left behind, who was inside the house yelling like a two-year old, and firing his gun like he had shares in Remington, wouldn't find them.

Unfortunately, the area they were in wasn't noted for its abundance of hideouts.

Except for one.

He guided her down into the canyon that formed the northern border of the Rogerson property. Though the creek bed was dry right now, it saw enough water to support more robust brush and trees.

Better cover.

Behind him, Smoke could hear Kini's breathing, fast and deep. He was pushing her, all but dragging her down the steep slope, but they had to get some distance between the Texan and them.

He stepped over a rock sticking out of the dirt.

She tripped over it then tried to hide a pain-filled noise as she attempted and failed to stay on her feet.

Smoke planted his boots in the sandy earth and caught her on his back.

An uncomfortable "oof" came out of her, but she didn't move for a couple of seconds.

"Hurt?" he asked her quietly.

"No, just…give me a second to catch my breath."

They didn't have a second, but if she passed out and he had to carry her, his hands would be too busy to use his rifle. So, he waited.

More rifle shots, then a flash of light so bright he could see it halfway down the canyon, and a boom.

"Was that…" Kini began.

"The house," Smoke finished for her. "Yeah."

"There were two men in the tent out back," Kini said, her voice strained.

"Doubt we have to worry about them anymore."

She made a sound, something sad, angry, and afraid all at once.

Smoke was about to move when running footsteps became audible from the lip of the canyon above them.

"*Fuck*." The Texan hadn't spoken all that loud, but it was

still clearly audible.

Damn it, he'd hoped the Texan had been a victim of the explosion. If he was going to try to catch them, they weren't moving fast enough.

Kini sucked in a breath then managed to lever herself off his back and stand on her feet. She touched his shoulder, patting him a couple of times. A signal she was ready.

He began walking again, watching for, and avoiding, footing problems. The farther they went down, the denser the foliage got until they were at the bottom. The vegetation was thick enough here to easily hide them from anyone searching for them from above, but they were a long way from safe.

"Okay?" he asked as he picked a way through the prickly trees and undergrowth.

It took so long for her to answer, he stopped to take a good long look at her. Blood was splattered across her shirt and some of her cuts had lost their bandages. The bags under her eyes were so deep and dark that, in the moon shadows, they made her eye sockets appear empty.

Her hands shook and she was limping.

She wasn't going to stay on her feet for very long. He needed to find a place for them to hole up until she'd gotten some rest, water, and food.

A gunshot echoed through the canyon. Another and another, along with the *thunk, thunk, thunk* of bullets hitting trees and dirt.

Damn fool might end up shooting them despite not knowing exactly where they were.

"Come out, come out, where ever you are," the Texan called. He was on the canyon floor now, too. "I don't know who you are, dirt bike guy, but you've got yourself mixed up in some very bad business. I've got more guns coming and *when* we catch you, we're going to make you pay for making such a mess in my house."

Smoke kept moving, trying to recall the topography of the canyon floor. It had been at least four years since he'd last been down here.

Texan sent a few more random shots in their direction, one of them ending up in a tree trunk a couple of feet from Smoke's head.

Yeah, he was going to have to do something about that moron.

A rocky outcrop became visible and, if he remembered right, it was concave on the other side, a place where water pooled when it ran. A protected place to hide.

He led Kini into the shaded hollow. "Stay here. Got to lose the paparazzi." He pulled out his backup weapon, a Berretta, and handed it to her. "Do you know how to use this?"

She checked the safety and held it in a two-handed grip. "It's been a couple of years, but yes."

Watching her hold the gun, handling it with confidence despite the pain and exhaustion he knew had her at her breaking point, made him hard. That was all kinds of messed up. "Don't shoot unless you have to."

"Right back at you, big guy," she said with one eyebrow raised and expectant.

If ever there was time for a justified kill, this was it.

She snagged his hand before he could move, and, still panting, whispered, "Be careful."

He nodded once and tugged his hand free. Not what he wanted to do. He wanted to wrap his arms around her and hold her while they both slept.

More random gunshots.

First, he had an asshole drug dealer to deal with.

Locating the Texan wasn't hard. The moron made more noise than an entire class of kindergarteners with all his shouting, shooting, and swearing. None of it made sense beyond the promises to kill Kini after he hurt her and hurt her and hurt her.

The bastard needed to die. Needed to pay for Nate's murder and terrorizing Kini. Needed to pay for bringing poison into Small Blind.

So many sins, too little time.

He managed to circle around and get behind the Texan, who was stumbling around like a drunkard. Was the dude high on his own shit? His clothing was sweat stained, dirty, and...*fuck*, he smelled like he'd gone swimming in a shit lake.

Getting rid of him wasn't going to hurt the world one bit. The memory of Kini's face, bruised, battered, and cut reminded him of his first priority: keep her *safe*.

Smoke aimed his rifle and fired.

Chapter Twenty-Five

Kini had to admit, the spot Smoke had found for her to rest and wait for him was a good one. Sheltered and relatively safe, she was able to roll back the hypervigilant state she'd been in since those boys had put a paper bag over her head.

Why was the world so full of stupid people?

Bruce was still making all kinds of noise in the trees, shooting off his mouth and his gun. *In the trees.* He'd made it down into the canyon.

A single shot rang out, different than all the ones that had echoed through the canyon before. This one had a deeper pitch. A different weapon.

Smoke.

Had he killed Bruce? He hadn't made her any promises, and maybe he didn't have a choice, but the thought made her want to scream at the injustice. The first man she'd met who made her inner demons go quiet was now the man with the gun.

Nausea rolled over her, making her muscles ache and shake, and a light sweat to break out over her skin. *No, Smoke.*

He didn't need the cost of another soul on his conscience.

A high-pitched scream echoed around her then was cut off abruptly. Who was that?

Seconds turned into minutes before a figure, tall and broad shouldered, came around the outcrop. Full dark had descended, and it made him look more like shadow than a man.

"*Smoke*?" she asked, barely above a whisper, terrified she was wrong. Again.

"Who were you expecting, Mary Poppins?"

What?

Her jaw had dropped. She closed it, trying to grasp why he looked so angry. At her.

She hadn't done anything but sit where he put her and wait for him.

"It was an honest mistake," she said with a fake smile. "I mistook your rifle for an umbrella."

He'd been moving toward her at an even pace, but at her words, he stopped and stared at her from underneath his eyebrows. And said nothing.

She sealed her lips shut, determined to make him say the next word.

He'd had a lot more practice than she did at this particular contest, though. His face never moved.

Finally, she couldn't stand it. She leaned forward and hissed through clenched teeth, "I thought *you* might have gotten shot."

Now he frowned. "Oh." He glanced away then cleared this throat. "I didn't kill him. Just shot him through the leg a little."

I didn't kill him, four little words, one big result. Smoke hadn't killed. His moral compass hadn't been destroyed. Dented, dinged, and dirty it might be, but he still had it.

Warmth spread out from her chest through her entire

body, wiping away the pain of her lacerations and bruises and the fuzzy edges of exhaustion. *He hadn't killed.*

Then the full meaning of his words registered. "You shot him through the leg a *little*?" she asked, incredulous. "How does one do that? I mean…a little, what…" She sputtered and waved her hands around. "What does that even mean?"

"It means he's alive, and he'll stay that way." Smoke tilted his head to one side and considered the ground thoughtfully. "Probably."

"*Bleed to death* kind of probably?"

"No, I bandaged the bullet wound, but…" He glanced away with a distinct guilty expression. "The bullet fractured his leg."

"So, by probably you mean he needs someone to find him and take him to a hospital."

"Yep." Smoke gave her an almost smile. "But not for a couple hours. Maybe even three or four. The asshole deserves that much."

Well, this was better than just murdering the man.

"Fine." She huffed out a breath as the endorphin rush began to ebb. "Can we go now? I'm so tired I don't even know what day this is."

Smoke opened his mouth, looked at her, then closed it again without saying anything.

Smart man.

She extended her hand, offering him the gun he'd given her. He took it and holstered it—tucked inside the rear waistband of his jeans.

She grabbed his outstretched hand, and he pulled her to her feet. Dizziness made gravity optional, and she found herself plastered up against Smoke's body, his arms around her as he held her up.

"Sorry," she said, breathing deep, trying to stave off unconsciousness. "My knees have apparently gone on strike and the negotiations for a new contract aren't going well." Damn it, she couldn't fall apart now; they were in no way safe.

"Would an incentive package help?" he asked.

She raised her head to meet his gaze. "Wha—"

He kissed her. A long, lingering slide of his lips against hers. He sucked on her bottom lip, coaxing her mouth open, then licked at her tongue. Slowly, like they had all the time in the world.

She hung on to him, her hands gripping the back of his shirt to keep herself upright, to keep him close.

One of his hands cupped her butt, pulling her into full contact with the erection inside his jeans.

She wiggled and was rewarded with a groan emanating from deep in his chest.

His breathing grew as fast and choppy as hers. He ended the kiss and rested his forehead against her. "Good to go?"

She chuckled, still trying to catch her breath. "My knees have voted to accept your incentive package on the condition that it's delivered on demand."

He laughed out loud. Then he took her hand and they continued down the canyon.

After a few minutes, the adrenaline wore off to such an extent her muscles shook with the effort to keep her upright. A couple of times she caught herself falling asleep while walking, waking only when she began to list too far to one side.

"Smoke?" Her foot caught on a root and she would have fallen if it weren't for his grip on her hand. "I don't think I'm going to last much longer." Disappointment in herself turned to despair. She was going to get him killed. "I'm slowing you down. It will get us both caught. You should lea—"

He spun, got within a couple of inches from her face, and said in a low growl, "No."

"But—"

"No." There was no give to him. No compromise. A muscle in his jaw jumped, telling her he was good and angry. At her.

She swallowed and blinked away the burning sensation in her eyes. "What do we do?"

He stared at her a moment longer, as if daring her to suggest he leave her behind again. When she just waited, he relaxed a little.

"There are a couple of spots along the canyon where we could rest for a bit." He took a step closer. "No complaining if I decide to carry you."

She rolled her eyes and started walking again. Smoke caught up and passed her, but kept within a few paces, checking on her often as he scanned the way ahead and monitored for activity behind them.

After about fifteen minutes of walking, Smoke went down into a crouch and pulled his rifle up so he could look up through the scope at the north edge of the canyon. Though it was dark, it was a clear night and the moon was bright enough to allow him to see.

Kini joined him, crouched a foot or two away, listening hard. At first, she couldn't hear anything that might have set off his alarm bells, but within a few seconds, distant but distinct voices sounded. Male voices.

"...repeated gunshots," one voice said.

"It's probably a local out hunting," another said.

"Hunting what?" the first man asked. "There's nothing out here but that broken-down farm on the other side of the canyon."

Kini glanced at Smoke. She'd bet a year's salary he'd find something to hunt, other than people, out here.

So, what were these two city guys doing out in the desert?

"It's probably that asshole at the farm, then. He likes to think he's middle management rather than a number on the factory floor."

The voices sounded close. Through the foliage, two men stood at the top of the cliff face, looking out over the canyon and beyond.

"I don't hear anything now, but something is burning," the first man said. "Is that smoke?"

"I'll give the asshole a call, make sure he isn't fucking around," the second said. "And I'll tell him to stop shooting at shit for fun. We have enough to do." The two men turned and disappeared.

Smoke didn't move from his crouch, didn't so much as breathe for a couple of minutes. His hands remained steady, his rifle pointed at the space where the edge of the canyon met the sky.

The muscles in Kini's thighs and butt burned from holding one position for so long. A trickle of sweat ran down her back. The temperature had gone down with the sun, but she was still thirsty. At least now she didn't feel like every molecule of water was being yanked out of her throat every time she opened her mouth.

Eventually, Smoke relaxed and stood. He held out his hand and helped her get to her feet all while scanning all around them and above them, for…what? Enemies? Bad guys?

A phone rang. She'd heard that song coming out of Bruce's phone. Though they'd been walking a while the sound carried a long way.

She stared at Smoke, the bottom of her stomach gone and gravity pulling the rest of her into a black hole.

He met her gaze, nodded once, and set off at a ground-eating pace she doubted she could keep up with. Her whole body hurt and every laceration stung, thanks to the sweat coating her skin. Her feet seemed to weigh twenty pounds each, and every step pushed her closer to unconsciousness.

She stumbled, but caught herself and kept going. The second time she stumbled, Smoke caught her.

She put her hands on his biceps and stared at her shaking hands like she'd never seen them before. "I think I'm tapped out."

Smoke didn't say anything, didn't make a sound, just picked her up and cradled her close to his chest.

"I know you're in shape, but...how long do you think you can carry me?"

"Long enough," he said, his breathing perfectly normal.

Show off.

He walked along the creek bed at the base of the canyon and somehow managed to not lose his footing once. She dozed off, put to sleep by the steady rocking motion of his stride and the safety in his arms.

Never had a man felt as safe as Smoke did. Safe, dependable, and strong—qualities she'd never expected to find in a man, not after the betrayal of her childhood. Maybe she was so desperate for hope, for a *good* man, she was seeing things in Smoke that weren't really there.

Trying to understand herself and someone else would have to wait until she'd had more sleep.

Time took on a hazy quality, and the next thing she knew Smoke was kneeling on the ground, still holding her.

"Kini?" he asked in a soft voice that nonetheless got her attention.

She tried to sit up and he let go of her legs. A glance around told her she had no idea where they were.

"How long did I sleep?"

"About fifteen minutes."

It felt longer than that. "I think I can walk on my own now."

"Good, because company's coming."

"What?"

"The Texan was found faster than I'd hoped," Smoke whispered. "We're being tracked."

She looked at her feet and his. "I'll probably make a trail a mile wide for anyone to follow." *And get you killed.*

"That's what I'm counting on."

"Huh?"

"A false trail for the city boys to follow while we go another way."

The plan was probably supposed to reassure her, but she couldn't seem to wrap her brain around it. She was so *fucking* tired.

Her despair must have registered on her face because Smoke cupped her jaw with one large hand and leaned close to say, "You'll be able to rest soon."

As in *dead*?

He saw the unspoken question as soon as the thought surfaced in her head and scowled at her.

Geez, she might as well be wearing a neon sign tacked to her nose.

"*Safe*," he growled.

She sighed and waved her hands at him. "Let's go before I think something unforgivable."

His only answer was to grunt and take her hand, pulling her along next to him until her body accepted the forward momentum and kept moving of its own accord.

"In my defense, I think I'm tired enough to plead mental incapacitation."

He didn't say anything for so long she was sure he wasn't going to, until he slanted her a scorching hot look. "Too bad. I was going to eat you out later."

Her jaw dropped as a wave of heat and longing rolled over her and dumped energy into her overtired muscles. She pictured his head between her thighs all too easily. His blue eyes watching her watch him as she writhed beneath him.

She tried to take in a breath, but her diaphragm didn't seem to be working. After a brief struggle to convince her body to function somewhat normally again, she managed to ask, "Could I take a rain check?"

The shit-eating grin on his face erased all the hurt from her body, leaving nothing but anticipation behind. For about two minutes. Then the dull ache settled over her like an unwanted blanket on a hot day.

She stumbled, weaved, and wobbled all over the place. Smoke nodded in approval at one point when she tripped and fell to her hands and knees. At least one of them was happy with the drunken trail she was leaving.

He angled his head to the south side of the canyon. "See that washout? It goes all the way to the top of the canyon. That's the false trail."

"Where are we going really?"

"A spot farther to the west."

"And why aren't we using the washout to get out of here and go for help?"

"It's the obvious choice. The easy choice. The only choice in sight to someone who didn't grow up here."

"You're assuming that the bad guys don't have someone who grew up here on their payroll."

"Yeah, but they know you didn't."

"True."

She stared with bleary eyes at the steep washout. "I have to climb that and make it look like I did it myself?"

"Yup."

Her thighs ached already. "You suck."

Chapter Twenty-Six

Smoke allowed himself to smile at Kini's aggravated tone, more to keep her calm than to communicate how he really felt. There was a spot between his shoulder blades that twinged in warning. Someone was on their trail.

He was a hair's breath away from following the urge to circle around behind their pursuer, or pursuers, and commit however many murders it would take to wipe them out. The only thing that kept him from doing it was Kini.

She was in no shape to be left alone, not even for a few minutes. Too tired to take more than two steps in a straight line and muscles shaking with both exhaustion and pain, she needed him. More than he needed to kill.

He got her to the base of the washout, but she ran out of gas. No surprise there. She'd gotten farther than he'd expected. He helped her get another twenty feet when they finally got lucky. Evidence of other people, footsteps and a granola bar wrapper on the ground.

He looked at Kini, about to tell her the good news, and discovered her on the verge of passing out completely.

He scooped her up and whispered in her ear, "Sleep, you're safe."

Her answer was to cuddle up to him and drop off into unconsciousness like a stone thrown into a pool of deep water.

His fellow soldiers, the men he worked and fought with for years, trusted him enough to sleep while he was on watch. Same as he trusted them. All of them heavily armed and ready to fight if attacked.

Kini had no weapons, no idea where she was, and no energy left. A body couldn't be more vulnerable, yet she trusted him enough to take care of her, to carry her to a place of safety.

His eyes burned because of that trust. He didn't think he'd earned it, and he sure as hell didn't deserve it, but he was damn well going to do everything he could to live up to it.

The spot he had in mind for them to lay low in was a little more than a quarter-mile away, down canyon.

There was a national park a little farther on where some of the ancient native peoples who'd come before his ancestors had built homes in the canyon walls and pit houses. They'd dry farmed or channeled water to corn crops, but a long drought had forced change and they'd never returned.

There were still one or two pit houses as yet undiscovered by the archeologists. His grandfather had shown him where they were when he was a boy and told him to stay away from them, as the spirits of those people might still reside there. It was disrespectful to go in and poke around for what might be left behind.

So he'd built his own. Sort of.

Smoke moved carefully but quickly, noting that others had walked down the canyon floor since the last rain or windstorm. He hadn't seen any signs of people before the washout, so maybe folks were using it to gain entry to the canyon. Hiking to the park?

He'd just about reached the spot where he was going to have to climb up a narrow side gully and the chimney at the end of it, when the echo of gunshots reached him.

He stopped under an aspen tree, crouched, and balanced Kini's weight on his knees and chest while he used the scope on his weapon to see what was going on behind him.

Four men climbed out of the wash and stood at the edge of the canyon, looking in the direction of town. None of them looked like they had a broken leg.

What happened to the Texan, or was he the reason for the shots? Would they give up the search for Kini or assume she found a ride?

A moment later, the answer became obvious in a rhythmic thrumming against his skin. The sound followed a couple of seconds later as a helicopter flew over the canyon by the wash, heading for town.

Son of a bitch. Whoever was looking for Kini had enough money and brains to use a helicopter?

He got moving, leaving little trail as he eased his way down the narrow gully. At the back wall, he squeezed past a rock that looked like it was solidly anchored into the cliff. It was, but the rear side of it had ridges that acted like ginormous stairs going up to a ledge.

Even from close up, the ledge looked shallow. He'd taken great pains to ensure it appeared to be a solid wall of rock and dirt to hide the entrance of a modified pit house formed from a screen of stones and soil.

He was going to have to wake Kini in order to get her up there.

"Hey," he said, giving her a bounce in his arms. "Wake up."

She moaned. "Why?"

"To get into our hideout."

"Bad guys again?" She sounded barely awake.

"Yeah."

Her eyes blinked open, and she looked even more tired. He put her on her feet. With a hand under her ass, he shoved her up the stair rock then followed her up to the next step and the next and the next. With careful hands, he guided her to the ledge then pointed at the shadow, all while watching to be sure no one was observing them. The ledge was well hidden, like the internal space of a snail, the landscape around it curled in on itself. Kini crawled into the shadow he'd pointed out, and disappeared from view.

A second later, her head came back out, a huge grin on her face. "Cool."

He handed her his backpack. "There's water and food in there. Eat something and drink. I want to backtrack us a bit to be sure we won't lead anyone here. Okay?"

She nodded. "Do you have some kind of light? I can't see past my nose in there."

"There are glow sticks in one of the pockets." He waved at her to go back inside.

He climbed down and listened hard before he moved, retracing his route to the entrance of the gully and into the canyon.

The *thwap, thwap, thwap* of the helicopter beat against his skin, sending him to ground in a thick clutch of trees and bush. The bird overflew the wash then circled the canyon several times in an obvious search pattern. They had a search light, but that wasn't going to help them; there was too much brush.

Idiots. The backwash from the rotors stirred up all kinds of dirt and dust, erasing recent footprints like they'd never been there. Made his job easy.

The helicopter flew around for another twenty minutes while the men who'd gone up the wash came back to the edge of the canyon and searched it with binoculars. Finally, they moved off toward the Rogerson farm.

Smoke stayed low and got back to the gully and up the stair rock before any more searchers arrived in the area.

It was a tight fit to get inside the camouflaged entrance of his hideout. As soon as he was in, he scattered dirt and rocks across the ground so no drag marks were visible.

A soft snore had him looking at Kini curled up on the dirt floor of the structure with a pale-yellow glow stick in one hand. Though it didn't give off a lot of light, it was enough to reveal the dimensions of the room.

Roughly circular in shape, it measured about fifteen or sixteen feet across. The floor was mostly loose dirt and appeared empty. It didn't look like anyone had been in here in years. Good.

Next to Kini sat an empty water bottle and a granola bar wrapper. She'd followed his orders almost to the letter. Too tired to argue.

He checked his watch. Nine o'clock at night. They could rest and stay out of sight in here until the search cooled down, then they'd make their run for town and help.

Smoke studied the sleeping woman. So much energy in such a small body, yet that body, with all its curves housed an indomitable will and restless intelligence he found just as attractive as the rest of her.

Fatigue was making itself known through muscle aches and the deep desire to lie down next to his sleeping beauty.

No reason to resist. He pulled out another water bottle from his pack and drank it down then ate a granola bar. It was enough for now. He curled around Kini's sleeping form and dozed off.

The deep rumble of an overflying helicopter shook the room, waking them both.

She jerked and sucked a breath.

"You're okay." Smoke tightened his arms around her. "Safe."

Her rigid body relaxed, despite the sound of the helicopter repeatedly flying over the canyon in multiple directions and in no discernable pattern.

"Huh," Smoke grunted. "Sounds like someone is having a temper tantrum."

"In a helicopter?" she asked, her voice hoarse.

"Wouldn't be my first choice, either," he admitted. "It's going to attract attention."

They lay still, Kini wrapped in his embrace until she asked, "How long did I sleep?"

He checked his watch. "A couple of hours."

"Okay, that goes along with the way I feel."

He waited for her to finish. When she didn't, he asked, "How do you feel?"

"Like shit."

Two hours of sleep wasn't enough, but he needed to check her over, get more food and water into her before letting her grab another nap. They'd wait until whoever was out there trying to flush them out, had settled down a bit.

A soft snore came out of her.

"Hey," he said, rubbing her arm with one hand. "Don't sleep."

"So tired," she mumbled.

"Food, water, and a first-aid assessment first." He grabbed his backpack and began pulling everything he'd need to do a thorough inspection of every cut, scratch, and bruise on her body.

"In that order or can we do all of it at once?"

The pen light he shone at her face showed puffy eyes surrounded by bruised skin. A number of the lacerations she'd gotten yesterday were oozing watery blood, thanks to a near constant exposure to dust and dirt. Infection was a real concern.

He handed her a bottle of water and a protein bar then pulled out a package of baby wipes and began washing away the gritty, gummed up scabs on the largest of her cuts. The one on her neck. The one that had come way too close to her jugular. He'd closed it with butterfly bandages and they'd held, more or less.

The skin around the laceration was an angry red, and he could tell by her flinches his attempt to clean it hurt.

He hesitated, his hands, his gut, his heart refusing to add to her pain. "Some of this dirt is in there good."

"It's okay," she said, her voice barely audible. "You're remarkably gentle."

Logic tried to argue with the lodestone in his gut and convince the rest of him that cleaning her wound was absolutely necessary. His gut wasn't buying it. "That's not what most people say."

"What do they say?" she asked, sounding genuinely curious.

"I hit like a freight train."

Both of her hands closed around one of his. She studied his fingers, rubbed the callouses, then placed a kiss on the center of his palm. "They're a bunch of idiots, whoever they are."

One little kiss. One tiny press of her lips to his skin was all it took to rev his heart rate up until he was vibrating with the need to kiss her. Not a nice safe peck on the cheek, either. A no-holds-barred, all-or-nothing claim was what he wanted. What he needed.

She was in no shape for that. Injured, exhausted, and on the verge of collapse. Only an asshole would attempt a seduction now.

Her lashes lifted and her gaze met his as her lips hovered over his palm. Those lips were curved up into the sexiest smile he'd ever seen. *Ah fuck, sweetheart.*

A puff of warm air hit the sensitive center of his hand. Her tongue peeked out from between her lips, as if about to lick.

"Don't do it." It came out as a harsh rumble he would have flinched from, but Kini...she just cocked her head, the question clear.

"I'm on the edge of losing my shit," he told her, unable to keep the bone-deep need for her out of his voice. "And you don't need me tearing your clothes off and fucking you sixteen ways to Sunday."

Desire flared in her gaze and she sucked in a breath, lowered her head, and licked his palm.

The touch of her tongue and lips, the look on her face, sensuous, sexy, and naughty, ripped the thin veneer of civilization he'd managed to maintain clean off of him.

Growling, he slid his right hand behind her head, holding her in place so he could take her mouth. She opened for him, her tongue tangling with his, her hands fisting his shirt tight as if she were afraid he might try to run away.

No fucking chance of that.

He wrapped his other arm around her waist and hauled her up against him, grinding his erection against her soft stomach.

She made a gasping, inarticulate sound, and flinched.

He felt it jerk her body, realized the noise she'd made had an edge of pain, and tore his lips from hers. *Son of a bitch*, he'd hurt her. He had no business touching her with his blood-stained hands. Because the blood wasn't just on his hands. It had been ground into his body, his heart, and soul until no part of him would ever be clean.

He pulled away and would have put more space between them, so he could see what he'd done to hurt her, but the grip she had on his shirt only got tighter.

"No, no, *no*," she chanted. "Don't stop, please. I need—"

Yep, he was *that* fucking asshole.

"I did something that hurt you," he said, realizing only after the words were out of his mouth that he sounded fucking pissed off. "Where?"

She let go of him so fast he nearly fell on his ass. "I'm fine." She wrapped her arms around herself. "I'm sorry for... throwing myself at you." Her eyes were locked on the dirt beneath their knees.

"Do *not* apologize for—" He cut himself off.

Think asshole, think.

She was injured, tired, and had been through enough hell to drive most people off the deep end. "I practically jumped you, and I hurt you doing it." He went nose to nose with her. "Now, show me where it hurts."

Her glare could have melted all the snow at the summit of Mount Everest.

She turned on her knees, so he could see her back, and lifted her shirt to reveal a large bruise about the size of a man's fist.

Rage roared through him. "I will kill that son of a bitch."

"I think he's already dead."

"Then I'll revive him so I can kill him again." Smoke reached out and cupped the black-and-blue mottled skin, lending his warmth to her.

"You'd start the zombie apocalypse just for the chance to kill a guy who's already dead?" A smile lurked at the corners of her lips, but he was beyond finding any of this funny.

"I'd go to war with the whole world for the chance to kill him again."

Chapter Twenty-Seven

"Why?" Kini couldn't have stopped the question coming out of her mouth if she tried. Smoke knelt in front of her, only inches away, a dark brooding form she wanted to stroke and kiss. But he didn't want her, not really. Not for keeps.

He cupped her face again with his big, sexy hands and leaned down until his mouth was only an inch from hers. "He hurt you."

She swallowed the lump in her throat. Her whole body ached from the struggle with Freddy and his friend and the rough handling Bruce had given her, no sleep, and their dash to escape. If they hadn't found this hideaway, they'd probably be captured by whoever was looking for them or dead. She wanted to feel alive, to taste him again, to have him on her lips, to feel him stroking her inside and out. Just touching him was a pleasure, but she wanted it all.

She couldn't have him. Not for long. Every single relationship she'd ever had died an inescapable death thanks to the disaster that was her childhood.

Trust. Her father had destroyed her ability to trust a man, *any* man, with her whole self. And yet, this man had saved her life more than once.

Her heart wanted her to stay with him, care for him, while her soul feared what might happen if she did. If she gave herself to him, trusted him, and he later threw her away or broke that trust, something inside her would break, too. Into so many pieces no one would be able to put her back together again. He had so much pain inside him, so much anger. Violence hovered like a vulture over his every move. Could she live with the threat of that vicious carrion bird watching her through his eyes?

But walking away, now, when he needed her and she needed him, seemed cowardly and wrong.

"I hurt," she admitted. "And I probably look like I just walked out of that zombie apocalypse you want to start."

When all he did was frown at her, she carried on. "It's no wonder you don't want..." Her face was so hot he could probably feel how embarrassed she was, throwing herself at a man who was too good to take advantage. The strain of meeting his pitiless gaze finally became too much and she looked away.

"Don't want?" The words were spoken in a dangerous purr. "You think I don't *want* you?"

She glanced at him and flashed a smile, though all she felt was disappointed. "Who would?" she extended her arms and examined them. With so many bandages, she looked like a casting call reject for the latest *Mummy* movie reboot.

"Stupid woman."

The words, growled in a tone that sounded like he had a mouthful of crushed glass, had her gaze snapping back to him.

"What?"

He leaned over her. "You think I'm losing my mind, fighting my need to *fuck* you, because I'm some kind of polite, whitewashed *hero*?"

"Obviously not polite," she shot back. "But, yeah. Guys like you—"

"What the fuck do you know about guys like me?"

"Good guys," she snapped, sticking a finger under his nose. "Honorable guys. Guys who, when meeting a woman for the first time, offer to hunt down graffiti and car-crashing assholes." She poked his chest with her finger. "*You.*"

He grabbed that finger and tugged her forward in a quick motion that unbalanced her. She sagged against him, and he crashed his mouth down onto hers.

Oh no, not this.

She'd made him angry, given him something to prove.

She wiggled and pushed and ignored his mouth's demand she let him in, but it wasn't until she let out an aggrieved squeak that he lifted his head.

"I don't want a pity fuck," she snarled at him.

"I do," he snarled back, shocking her. "You have me tied up in so many knots, so desperate to be inside you, I'm losing my fucking mind."

She studied his face, his body, and hands. He shook all over, and the erection tenting the front of his jeans looked like a steel bar.

"Have pity, sweetheart," he whispered, his voice raw. "Don't push me." He swallowed hard. "I'm scared I'm going to hurt you, and that would fucking gut me."

He meant it. She could see it on his face and body, feel it in the firm, but gentle hold he had on her arms.

"I need you so bad, it hurts more than all the rest put together," she confessed. "Please, Smoke. I want to feel alive."

He blew out a breath, shaking even harder than before. "You'll stop me if I—"

This time she interrupted by kissing him with an open mouth, sucking his bottom lip, then nipping it before soothing the small pain with lavish licks.

With a groan, he took over the kiss, making love to her mouth the way she prayed he'd do to her body.

His hands were so gentle she didn't realize he was pulling her torn and battered shirt up over her head. She was all for that. When he pulled back to get the fabric out of his way, she helped by lifting her arms and wiggling.

"I'm dying," he muttered as he tossed her shirt aside and stared at her bra and the breasts they hid. "Fucking dying."

"Then you'd better hurry up and fuck me," she ordered as she all but tore off her bra.

The second it was out of the way he had his hands around her rib cage, lifting her chest up so he could suck a nipple into his mouth.

He sucked hard and she gasped as the pleasure came out of nowhere to fry every brain cell she had left. "Oh *God*," she groaned, holding his head to her.

He released her nipple so he could attack the other one, and she had to lock her vocal chords to prevent crying out. The man's tongue was lethal. His mouth gradually licked, sucked, and kissed its way up her torso and neck until he reached her mouth.

After God only knew how long, he lifted his head. "Naked," he growled. "I want you naked."

"Sure," she said, her gaze taking in his broad shoulders and muscled arms. "You, too."

He stood and began taking his clothes off. She managed to get her pants and panties down her legs then went to lie down, but he shook his head hard and took her hands.

Frowning, she waited while he lay on the floor and pulled her to straddle him.

"I want you in control this time," he told her, his gaze taking in all of her.

She froze, surprised. Smoke was a man who liked being in

control. A man with a protective streak so wide she couldn't see the edges of it. For him to cede that control to someone else, *anyone* else, was a demonstration of trust she'd never expected.

How long would it last?

Unwilling to miss a second of this gift he'd given her, she eased down until she sat on his lower belly. With her hands planted on the dirt on either side of his head, she leaned down until her breasts hovered over his mouth. "What will I do with you?" she asked.

"Anything you want." His voice was low and rough, and as soon as he finished talking he lifted his head and put his mouth on her, sucking hard.

The pleasure was so intense she had to lock her jaw closed, hissing out instead of screaming.

One of his large hands slid around her waist, holding her to him with the other brushing over her clit as it tested her readiness.

"Wet." The word was a rumble against her skin.

"I need you," she whispered, unable to hide her desperation any longer. If he didn't fuck her soon she was going to cry.

He switched breasts to torment the other while his fingers circled her clit. Around and around, but never quite touching.

"Smoke, *please*." She'd beg if she had to.

"Shift back," he ordered.

Allowing her to slide backward, he held his cock in place while she wiggled and rotated her hips against the head of his penis.

Her breathing deepened and increased in speed until she felt dizzy, but teasing herself and him felt *so* good.

"Are you trying to drive me insane?" he asked through clenched teeth, as she kept up the tantalizing torment of her hips and his cock.

"Both of us." A breath shuddered out of her. "Almost... there."

"Watching your face as you drive us both crazy is the sexiest thing I've ever seen," he told her. "I'm hanging on to my restraint by a thread, sweetheart."

She went nose to nose with him. "Fuck restraint."

His body jerked under hers, his eyes wide, his teeth bared. Just one more little push and he'd lose it.

She stared at him and saw his face twist with pleasure. "Do it," she ordered. "Do it."

He set his jaw and slammed up into her.

She threw her head back, stifling the scream.

Smoke growled as he held her hips and fucked her hard and fast. One hand released her hip so he could press his thumb against her clit and the orgasm rolled over her with the strength of a tsunami, holding her rigid before releasing her to collapse on his chest.

He took her mouth in a carnal kiss as he sped up his thrusts, then groaned as his hips jerked against hers, his own orgasm seeming to last a long time.

His heart beat so fast she couldn't keep up with it, so she didn't, closing her eyes and allowing herself to truly relax and rest for the first time since she'd gotten up this morning.

• • •

The floor moved and she jerked awake.

"Shh," Smoke said, cradling her as he sat up. "You can sleep, but we should get dressed first."

She nodded and yawned and tried to get up, but her legs didn't want to work.

He watched her struggle for a second then gave her a crooked smile and lifted her off of him.

They hadn't used a condom.

She stared at his softened cock, covered in her wetness. "Oh."

"Are you on the pill?" he asked.

"Yes, and I'm clean. Until you, I hadn't been with anyone in a couple of years."

Giving her a smugly satisfied look he said, "Same here."

That surprised her. "You haven't? Wow, you must have women hanging off you."

He raised an eyebrow.

"I mean, you're incredibly good looking and..."—she stroked one hand across his shoulder and down his arm—"muscles," she said with a sigh.

He flashed her the biggest grin she'd ever seen on his face. "Muscles, huh?"

"Yeah."

He reached out and cupped one of her breasts. "You'd better put clothes on before I fuck you again."

Her breath caught as he played with her nipple, and she leaned toward him.

He growled at her. "Clothes, Kini."

She sighed again but got dressed. That took all the energy she had left. "Do you have more food and water?"

He nodded and, after pulling up his jeans, he opened his backpack and pulled out two bottles of water and protein bars.

She helped herself to her share of the food and water then sat back to watch him finish dressing. The man was *fine* with a capital F.

"Do we have a plan?" she asked once he'd started eating.

"We wait until the people searching for us settle down, then make a run for town."

"Won't they expect that?"

"They expect we'll probably head for the highway, but we're not going that way. We'll go across country."

"They have a helicopter."

He shrugged. "So we'll hear them coming."

"Who are *they*?" she asked. "I figured out that Bruce and his crew work for *them*, but who are they? Where do they come from? What are they doing out here?"

"When you were in the Rogerson house, what did you see?"

"They had a drug lab, probably meth, but they could have been making other stuff besides that. There was a map on one wall. It had tacks in it, marking towns and cities throughout the state. Infection targets. This outbreak wasn't an accident, but I didn't see anything about why." She rubbed her face with one hand. "Bruce seemed to be the leader, and he had three men working there, but they were all sick. There was another man, Gary, who struck me as psychotic in a serial killer sort of way, but he took a man who was really sick into town to the hospital." She paused to take another couple of swallows of water.

"At first, all Bruce wanted was for me to take care of his people. They all showed signs of lung damage. Not pneumonia, more like emphysema. I think the chemicals they used to make the drugs destroyed their lungs. Bruce wanted me to do the same work."

"That much I heard," Smoke said, his face settling into angry lines.

So that's what had made him attack with such ferocity.

"Anything about Free America From Oppression?" he asked.

"No, but I only got a quick look."

"Doesn't matter. If they think you saw anything…" His voice trailed off.

Bruce and whoever else was involved wouldn't want her to report what she'd seen and heard—it would bring not only the local police, but state and federal law enforcement as well. "They're not going to stop looking for me. For us."

"They have limited time." He smiled grimly. "Homeland Security and the FBI will be here in force, in about ten hours.

Any stunts with a helicopter are going to be noticed and investigated."

"Will River come looking for us?"

He nodded. "He knows no news is bad news."

"So, how long are we staying in here?"

"Maybe a couple of hours. I'll do an advance recon to make sure it's safe."

"Okay." Still time to rest, to recover from the worst day ever. The beat of the helicopter's rotors seemed to be gone, even after she listened hard. "What is this place? Did people actually live in here?"

Smoke shook his head. "No. I built it when I was just a kid. I based it off a kiva, the ancient Native American version of a church and man cave all rolled into one."

"So, this is your idea of a tree fort?"

"Yeah." Smoke lay back on the dirt with his hands behind his head. "My grandfather thought I was a bit crazy for building it."

"Why here?"

"There weren't any ancient kivas in this part of the canyon. There are a couple remains of pit houses farther down, but they were destroyed when the first white men came to this part of Utah. It was a popular Sunday afternoon activity to go for a picnic and blow up a pit house or cliff dwelling with dynamite."

"Seriously?"

Smoke smiled. "Yep."

"People can be so stupid."

"Truth." Smoke grunted.

"Speaking of stupid people, who are these guys? The ones with the helicopter and guns? Some kind of domestic terrorist group? Other than that one mention of FAFO on the news, I've never heard of them."

"I don't know, but you can be damned sure I'm going to find out."

Chapter Twenty-Eight

Despite the feeble light from the glow sticks, Smoke could see quite clearly what Kini thought of his intent to bring the assholes down. Concern was written across her face in the sea of wrinkles on her forehead. Concern and more than a little fear.

"After we reach help," she said, the words an order. "And, with the assistance of River, Homeland Security, and the FBI."

He didn't answer, didn't want to confess that waiting for River, Homeland Security, and the FBI might give the assholes time to escape. He wasn't going to let that happen. They were going to pay for whatever bullshit they were involved in that made them think murder was just part of business.

"Right?" she asked, expecting an answer.

"If Homeland and the alphabet soup are fast enough to keep up with me," he finally said.

She crossed her arms over her chest and lifted her chin. "No. You're going to wait for them. They're law enforcement."

He sat up, put one hand on the dirt, and thrust himself into her personal space bubble. "If I have to wait for two or three different federal agencies to decide who has jurisdiction, those fuckers are guaranteed to get away."

"One man isn't capable of taking on a group with enough people to launch a foot and aerial search." She leaned toward him until she was all but kissing him and poked his chest with an index finger. "It's *suicide*."

Probably, but he wasn't going to tell her that. "Thanks for the vote of confidence."

She grabbed his shirt with both hands. "Stop being an ass."

He could argue or he could do what his hands wanted to do—touch her. As if that was a difficult decision.

He kissed her, taking her mouth hard while he wrapped his arms around her and held her tight.

Smoke pulled back to be sure she was with him all the way—he wasn't taking more than she wanted to give him—only to be hauled back into another battle of a kiss.

She nipped his bottom lip hard enough for a bite of pain to jolt him.

He grinned at her. "I like it when you're mean."

"You're lucky I don't kick your ass," she muttered, going for an earlobe, which she proceeded to suck and nibble on.

Fuck. They'd just had sex, and he was ready to go again. He eased her away from him. "Slow down. We have to escape and make it back to town without getting caught or killed first."

"Does River know where you went?"

"I told him, but I don't know if he's aware the Rogerson place burned down."

"Wouldn't the fire be reported?"

"Depends. The bad guys aren't going to report it." He sighed. "Rest."

He lay down and opened his arms.

She scowled at him then inched over and lay down so he could spoon her from behind.

She was asleep in a couple of minutes, her breathing deep and even.

He wasn't going to let whoever was hunting them, hurt her.

Who were they? Only a sophisticated and organized group could have a helicopter at their disposal. Were they involved with the drug lab? It didn't make sense.

Was the drug lab connected to the hantavirus outbreak? What were the odds of all this happening at the same time in the same area without any connections to each other? His gut was telling him everything was interconnected, but he couldn't see what linked them, the common denominator.

He could see Blackwater getting involved, however— the man enjoyed what power he had a little too much. But, until Homeland and the FBI showed up sometime tomorrow, Smoke was pretty much on his own. He needed more intelligence and information, and there was only one way to get it.

Kini was going to go after his balls if he snuck out on her, but before they left the safety of his hideout, he needed to know what their enemy was doing. Decision made, Smoke closed his eyes and napped for twenty minutes before easing away from her warm and curvy body. It fed something violent and wild inside him to hold her, to keep her safe, and what he was about to do was all about her safety.

Smoke left her a small note propped up against his backpack telling her to stay inside, and that he'd be back soon from a short scouting mission. He even promised not to kill anyone. Then, he cautiously crawled out of the structure.

He left the gully, but instead of checking out the wash in the direction of town, he went down the canyon and climbed up the opposite side. Those men and the helicopter came from somewhere. He wanted to know where.

At the top of the cliff, he crouched amongst some sage brush. The cool air did a good job of carrying sound, and indistinct male voices came from the other side of the canyon. Couldn't tell how many men were talking, though.

In the opposite direction, there was a fairly large light source in the distance. More light than one or two houses could produce. Some kind of warehouse or manufacturing plant?

Interesting. No one had mentioned anything like that going up in the area. He brought out his small binoculars from a case clipped to his belt and scanned the area toward the light source, but it was hidden behind terrain. An examination of the land on other side of the canyon yielded at least four men on foot with flashlights in motion, and two on ATVs.

These guys seemed to have a lot of money to invest in equipment.

The sound of an ATV motor grew louder and louder. A single man with a rifle slung over his shoulder was heading straight for his position.

Incapacitate the rider and grab the vehicle, or let the shmuck drive by?

No one else was in the area. Could he hide the body and the vehicle from anyone else who might come along while he got Kini, or was this asking to get caught?

Tempting. But Kini wasn't up to a hard scramble up the cliff, and they'd be on the wrong side of the canyon. The nearest bridge was on the interstate, a site almost certainly under observation.

There were even more men on the other side of the canyon.

He let the ATV and its driver go on by while he observed the other side of the canyon more closely.

There were men on dirt bikes now, at least three in addition to the ones he'd already seen. They appeared to be ramping up their search despite the darkness. He and Kini might have to hide for longer than he'd expected.

The sound of more ATV engines grew closer and closer, coming from the direction of the light source. He hunkered down in the scrub, allowing his body to follow the ebb and flow of the vegetation around him. Two sets of headlights came to a stop about twenty feet away, close to the canyon's edge. The riders shut their engines off and dismounted.

"Why the fuck are we looking on this side of the canyon?" a man asked. "According to that idiot, Bruce, the woman's injured. She's not going to come this way. She's going to try to get to town."

"He also said some huge Indian came out of nowhere, shot him, and blew up the meth lab."

"*If* there was a guy." The second man grunted. "Bruce would blame his mother if he got caught crossing the street. He knows he fucked up."

"Or he could be that ex-soldier Blackwater told us about."

"Blackwater is full of shit on a good day, and this place is crawling with Indians. Blackwater *is* an Indian."

There was a pause. "Good riddance to the meth lab, I say. It was a hell of a risk setting that place up."

Whoever these men were, they'd never been in the military, never been deployed to a combat active area, or they wouldn't be standing around, shooting the shit.

"It takes money to build the shit these guys have put up. Plus, we're expensive as hell."

"Robbing a bank would have been a lot easier, and less complicated."

"Probably too high profile."

"I don't know, man, this shit is getting weirder every day."

"We're being paid a *fuckton* of money, so I don't care

how weird shit gets. Another year working for these guys, and I can retire on a beach somewhere."

There was another long pause.

"Where the fuck *is* the bitch?"

"Gone to ground somewhere in the canyon is my bet. We'll find her. Foreman said that if we don't find her by daylight, he'll bring in some dogs."

"If she gets away, gets to help, we're going to be up shit creek."

"I guess we'd better find her then."

Footsteps, then two ATV engines roaring to life within a couple of seconds of each other. They drove off, following the edge of the canyon in opposite directions.

What the hell was going on? Some kind of high-cost business using drugs as their funding source? If that wasn't the craziest shit he'd ever heard, he didn't know what was.

Helicopters, armed men, and soon, dogs. He didn't have much time to decide on a course of action that would get Kini somewhere safe. Or he could call for help and create a distraction that would keep these assholes busy until help arrived.

The kiva would keep her out of sight—even if dogs tracked her into the gully, the entrance wasn't noticeable unless you were right in front of it.

What he really needed was a cell phone and an armored vehicle. He'd settle for a phone, but to get it, he'd have to go fishing.

Smoke left the safety of the brush, pulled out his pocket flashlight, and began walking toward the large light source to the north, swinging his flashlight back and forth like in a deliberate search pattern. *Just one of the boys.*

He crested a rise and finally got a good look at the place a small army of security people were trying to hide.

Chain-link fencing topped with razor wire surrounded a

large compound composed of one large building and several smaller ones. A number of jeeps and ATVs were parked on the side closest to him. Massive portable light poles stood at regular intervals providing enough light to eliminate anywhere for a person to hide, day or night. There were at least a dozen people visible inside the fence, all of them armed with rifles.

Light flashed at the edge of Smoke's vision, and he turned to see an ATV coming toward him.

Good timing.

He put his binoculars to his face for a better look at the compound as the ATV driver pulled up about ten feet behind him.

"Put your hands on your head."

Sounded like a cop, but there was no way the guy behind him was one.

"I thought I saw someone skulking around, heading for the fence," Smoke said in an excited tone. "Come take a look." He held out the binoculars blindly without turning his head or looking at the guy.

Here, fishy, fishy, fishy.

There was a pause then the man came abreast of him and put his hand on the binoculars.

Smoke let go of them then drove his other hand into the man's stomach, knocking the breath out of him. With him doubled over, it was easy to knee him in the face.

The guy went down hard.

Smoke searched the guy's pockets and found a cell phone and a couple of zip ties, which he used to hogtie the guy. He tore off the sleeve of his captive's shirt and stuffed it into his mouth.

Smoke mounted the ATV and drove toward the compound. Once he was within about twenty feet, he turned and drove parallel to the fence, going all the way around the entire fenced compound.

The main building had a logo and title painted on the east facing side of its wall: *Dry Duck Jojoba and Medical Cannabidiol Farms.* Beneath that was a sentence painted in red: *No active THC marijuana on site. A pilot project of the State of Utah.*

The front gate faced east, toward the interstate, and had a big sign on it:

No trespassing

It was also locked and had a manned guard shack inside the fence next to the gate.

No THC, huh?

Smoke drove around until he was on the south side of the compound then headed toward the canyon as if he were one of the searchers. He stopped at the edge, shut off the ATV, and called River.

"Yeah?" River's voice sounded cautious, wary.

"It's Smoke."

"Where the fuck are you? Did you find Kini?" Relief filled River's answer.

"I found her at the Rogerson place along with a drug lab. See any smoke in the distance?"

"Like I've been outside."

"It's burning."

"Shit. What about Kini?"

"I got her out, but we had to run, and my phone got smashed. There's a canyon on the north side of the farm. We hid down there, but there's at least a dozen guys, some on ATVs, and a helicopter looking for us. We need an extraction."

"The only support I've got is what I brought with me," River said, sounding pissed off. "Fucking sheriff wouldn't recognize a good idea if it arrived at the head of parade."

"I overheard some flunkies talking. Blackwater is in on

it."

"In on it? The drug lab?"

"Yeah, and whatever else is going on at a jojoba and government-sponsored Mary Jane farm north of the canyon. They've got the whole thing fenced off and surrounded by armed guards."

"So, you're telling me we've got a burned-out drug lab, a dirty deputy, a militarized farm, and a viral outbreak?"

Since the question was rhetorical Smoke didn't bother to answer it.

"Got any good news for me?" River asked after a few seconds.

"I haven't killed anyone yet."

"Nice. Asshole. Anyone in town you trust to back me up?"

"My family."

"Stay in touch." River hung up.

Smoke looked at the phone then silenced the ringer and shoved it into a pocket. He got onto the ATV, started the engine, and drove east, away from the part of the canyon close to the gully hiding the kiva. He'd leave the ATV in a dip in the land or by a grouping of rocks then head for the kiva on foot.

He was halfway up a rocky incline when something struck his leg like a hot poker fresh out of a fire. A second later, one of his back tires exploded and the ATV pitched to the right, bucked him off, and rolled on top of him.

Chapter Twenty-Nine

Kini woke with a start, sitting up before freezing in place. A gunshot echoed outside the dimly lit room. The two glow sticks still shone, but their light was starting to fade.

Another gunshot followed the first, then the distant sound of an engine...no, multiple engines...fading as they moved away. The searchers were out there and were shooting at something, or someone.

The spot where Smoke had slept still held the impression of his body in the dirt, but when she put her hand on the soil, no heat remained. So, he'd left more than a few minutes ago. His backpack sat where he'd left it, but the piece of paper propped up against it was new.

Stay inside until I get back.

Gone to scout the way out.

Won't kill anyone.

Smoke.

She snorted. Most people would be slightly horrified to see the promise not to commit murder, but they didn't know Smoke. Didn't know what a huge concession that was. She'd learned nothing would stop him from doing whatever he thought had to be done.

The gunshots that woke her nagged at her.

How long had he been gone? He was an experienced tracker and soldier, probably knew more about sneaking around than any other twenty people. But what if he'd been caught, or shot?

How long should she wait?

Her watch said it was after one o'clock in the morning; she'd slept longer than she thought.

The sound of more engines, not trucks or cars, more like motorcycles or dirt bikes. Multiple vehicles going in different directions.

Something had stirred things up.

She could imagine Smoke and all of his six-foot-three hotness stirring a lot of things up. But her going out there, when he'd asked her to wait, was stupid. So, she'd wait.

She rested in Smoke's spot and let sleep take her under.

It felt like only five minutes had passed when she woke again. The two glow sticks had dimmed significantly but still emitted enough light to read her watch. Four thirty.

Still no Smoke.

Stomach sinking into the dirt beneath her, she stared at his backpack. He wouldn't have left her to go get help, back to town, by himself. No, he wouldn't have taken that chance. So, he was injured and couldn't make it back to his hideout, or he'd been captured by whoever was searching for them. The thought settled over her like a wet blanket, uncomfortable and cold. She wasn't leaving him for the buzzards to finish off.

The backpack had two more bottles of water and several protein bars. She ate one and drank half a bottle of water then examined the rest of the contents. First aid kit, paracord, the knife he'd tried to give her earlier, matches in a waterproof container, a fishhook attached to a length of rolled-up fishing line, and an emergency blanket.

Fishing gear…in the desert?

Was there a super-secret fishing hole not on any map? Well, she'd ask him when she caught up to him. No other outcome was acceptable.

Kini put everything away in the pack and had to hop to grab the edge of the structure and pull herself up, but managed, then wiggled her way out.

Dawn wasn't yet on the horizon, but she had no trouble making out the terrain. Nothing moved. Just because she couldn't see any danger didn't mean there wasn't any. The air outside was cool, almost cold, and the only sounds she heard were the songs of insects. No barking dogs, no dirt bike or ATV engines, or human voices.

After climbing down the dirt face of Smoke's hideout, she moved on cautious feet to the exit of the gully. Still no hint of pursuit or search, yet the cold lump in the pit of her gut only got larger and heavier.

Where were the men searching for her? And where was Smoke?

She entered the canyon and headed in the direction of the washout—she'd decide her next move once she got that far. She tried to emulate the way Smoke walked, but found his silent, easy pace wasn't easy to adopt.

Probably making enough noise to alert the media.

As she passed a large rock, a low, rough voice whispered her name.

"Who's there?"

Smoke's grandfather stepped away from the rock and toward her.

"How do you do that?" she asked, mystified by what could only be family trait to hide in plain sight.

"That?" he asked in a careful voice.

"Are you chameleons or something?"

His white teeth flashed a smile in the darkness, there and gone again. "Where's Smoke?"

"I don't know." That lump in her stomach expanded until she could barely breathe. "You haven't seen him?"

A shake of his head. "He called River a few hours ago, told him you were hiding in his little house, and asked for an extraction. No contact since."

A few hours ago, she'd heard shots. The ball of ice in her gut was so cold it burned.

"No Smoke?" asked another voice from behind her.

Whirling to confront this new evidence that she needed her hearing checked, she discovered Smoke's father, Jim, standing not five feet away, a rifle in his hands.

"How do you...all of you...sneak up on people like this?" she demanded in a croak.

Why bother breathing at all? Every time she got over one shock, another showed up in time to knock the breath out of her again.

"No," Smoke's grandfather said.

She could see his father's face harden with worry as he digested this news.

"A few hours ago, several shots woke me," she told them. "I could hear engines—ATV engines—and men shouting, but I'd made Smoke a promise not to leave his kiva until he got back."

"You think he was caught?" Jim sounded offended.

"I think a bullet can change the dynamics of any situation. He's not bulletproof."

"Who took him?" asked Smoke's grandfather.

"Where did they take him?" asked Jim.

"Smoke said there was some kind of large light source north of the canyon. He went to scout it out, find a way for us to reach help without getting caught by whoever is chasing me."

"That's the jojoba and marijuana farm," Jim said. "Nathan's been working there for the last six months."

When she stared at him in shock, he added, "The government set it up to produce oil without the THC in it."

"Why would anyone from a government-backed farm be involved with an illegal drug lab?" She couldn't imagine a reason to explain the odd connections things seemed to have around here.

"You heard shots?" Grandfather Smoke asked.

"Yes, um, maybe four or five."

"There isn't anything out here besides the farm," Jim said.

Grandfather Smoke nodded once. "We check there first."

"How will we do that?" Kini asked, looking from one man to the other. "Without getting caught by the men searching for me?"

"I'll go to the front door and ask for Nathan," the older Smoke said. "You cut the fence and sneak in."

Jim shook his head. "No, we don't have time for bullshit. I say we all go through the front door."

"But—" Kini began.

"You're right," Grandpa Smoke said. "None of them city boys is going to expect any of us to be much of a threat."

Kini blinked. *He* was including *her* in that statement?

"I'm a threat?" she asked, unable to keep the incredulous tone out of her voice.

Both men snorted.

"I've seen you in action," Jim said. "When you get mad, no man's balls are safe."

"Oh." She hadn't thought about her preference for going for the groin first as something other people might notice. Should she feel bad about that? "I'm still not sure we should just walk up to the front door."

"It will be the last thing they expect," Jim said.

"They'll believe none of us knows they're searching for you," Grandpa Smoke added.

"Besides, you look like hell. We go in asking for medical help, and they're not going to suspect we know they're up to no good."

Was she supposed to feel insulted or complimented? Perhaps she'd stick with middle of the road. "Thanks."

"Dawn isn't far off. We'd best get going."

The two men led Kini to the dry stream bed at the bottom of the canyon and the two horses picketed there. They mounted and Kini got on behind Grandpa Smoke.

Dawn's pale light added hints of coral and pink to the horizon when they trotted up to the main gate for the farm. A man in a uniform with the company name on his chest and the title of security met them as the two Smokes dismounted.

"We found this gal out in the desert," Jim said as Grandpa Smoke helped her get down off the horse.

Holy shit, she'd only been riding for less than an hour and already her thighs hurt.

"She's dehydrated and injured," Jim continued. "And keeps telling us she was kidnapped by some kind of drug dealer. Please call for the police and an ambulance."

The security guard stared at her with his mouth hanging open, so Kini did her best to look like an exhausted, confused, pain-addled woman.

She must have appeared convincing, because the guard attempted to hide his triumphant smile behind a concerned expression and said, "Hold on for just a minute while I call this in." He took a couple of steps toward his shack before he turned and said while walking backward, "I'm sure the shift supervisor will give the okay to assist."

She almost laughed. *Yep, that was probably a given.*

The guard spoke in some kind of handheld radio, then he

buzzed the gate open.

Jim helped Kini walk into the compound while Grandpa Smoke led the horses.

The guard put his hands up, palm out. "I'm sorry, sir, you can't bring your horses onto the property. Safety regulations."

One of the horses chose that moment to lift its tail and defecate on the middle of the road.

The guard's jaw dropped for the second time in as many minutes.

Grandpa Smoke glanced at the pile of poop, nodded sagely, then walked the horses to one side of the gate and tied their reins to the fence. He joined Jim and her.

They kept walking past the chain-link gate as the guard went into his shack and activated the gate. He came running out, yelling, "If you could wait there, a car is coming for you."

"Why would we need a car?" Jim asked. "The building is right there." He waved a hand at the main entrance. They kept going.

A jeep came around the building at a reckless speed. It sped toward them so fast Kini wasn't sure it was going to be able to stop before running them down. It did stop, with a slight squeal of tires on the pavement, and two men scrambled out, their hands on Tasers holstered to their belts.

Jim, who'd done all the talking so far, frowned at them. "Give us a hand. She's severely dehydrated and someone beat the crap out of her."

The two men glanced at each other then approached cautiously.

"When and where did you find her?" one of them asked, extending a hand toward the entrance.

"Down in the canyon about an hour ago," Jim replied.

Grandpa Smoke must be biding his time before saying anything.

"Awfully early to be out for a ride," the other man

commented after a glance at the horses.

Jim shrugged. "We left yesterday. Decided to camp out."

They were almost at the door now.

"Where's your gear?" the same man asked, suspicion turning his tone sharp.

Jim laughed. "You city boys might need a truck load of crap, but it's no hardship for us to light a fire and watch the stars dance while we think."

Grandpa Smoke managed to look like a man who knew all the secrets of the universe.

The two men relaxed enough for one of them to dash ahead and open the door. The second man followed them in.

There was no one behind the large reception desk. Too early. The man in front led the way down a hallway to the left of the desk. Not far down was a door with a red cross on it.

Inside was a typical first-aid room with a cot along one wall, an examination table on the other, and a desk and chair in between.

Jim sat her on the cot and looked at the men crowding the doorway. "Water?"

Grandpa Smoke had to back out the door to let one of the men exit.

"Did you already call for an ambulance?" Jim asked the remaining man.

"Yes, sir. Did that before we met you outside."

"Good. She's been through something awful."

"How do you know that?"

"She keeps talking about an explosion. If she's got a concussion, it might explain why she's so confused." Jim glanced at the man. "You boys seen or heard any kind of explosion or fire?"

"No, sir." The reply was quick, too quick.

The radio on the man's belt went off. Someone said, "ETA ten minutes. Keep the subject contained."

He turned the volume on the radio way down.

Jim stared at the guy.

"Sorry about that, the ambulance is on its way."

"Keep the subject contained?" Jim asked, sounding only mildly curious.

"It's how the security chief talks," the guy said with a shrug.

"Why would your security chief be involved with a medical situation?"

"Security and medical are all one department."

The guy could think on his feet okay, but his body language needed work. His face all but shouted *bullshit*.

The other man arrived with a bottle of water, which he offered to Jim, who opened it and gave it to her. She sipped it, making her hand shake in a way that would have spilled it all over herself if she tried to gulp it.

Jim got to his feet, nodded like he was satisfied with something, and turned to offer his hand to the nearest man. "Thanks for your hospitality. I'll leave her in your capable hands."

The guard made no move to take it.

Chapter Thirty

There was enough light coming under the door to the janitor's room Smoke had been tied up and left in to see all the stuff on the shelves above him.

Stupid, leaving him inside a room with all the ingredients for a homemade bomb and a belly full of anger. He was going to rain stupid all over their lives. Just as soon as he got himself untangled.

That was proving harder than he anticipated. Whoever had hog-tied him had done a good job. Didn't start questioning him until after he was belly down on the floor of the closet, his arms and legs tied together behind his back.

The guard asked why he'd tied up one of their security guards and taken his ATV. Smoke didn't answer. Hadn't said a thing. The asshole patted him on the face. "If this is some kind of prank, you'd be better off talking to us." Then the guy had sneered. "Because if our boss has to question you personally, you're going to wish you stayed at home."

They thought he was a local, and that was fine. The time it would take to call in their boss was time he could use to escape. Everything about this place felt wrong. It was too big, with too many security guards using equipment that cost too much for a legal operation.

A shadow passed the doorway, no sound, just movement. Interesting. So far, none of the people here had demonstrated they knew how to walk softly, so who was this? The shadow came back and the door opened. Smoke only had a moment to see who had cast the shadow before they were inside and it was dark again.

The light switched on.

Nope, his eyes hadn't tried to play tricks on him. It really was his grandfather.

A whisper of sound, then a knife cut through the rope. Smoke rolled over and sat up. "Kini?"

"With your dad." The elder Smoke pointed the knife at his grandson's right calf. "Bleeding."

"Bastards got lucky," Smoke told him, then winced. "I think the bullet is still in there."

His grandfather cut the crude bandage off and examined the leg. "Only an entry wound. Must have been a ricochet or it would have broken bone."

It bled sluggishly. Smoke frowned at his grandfather. "I'm going to leave a trail."

"Is that a bad thing?" The old man smiled and held out a hand. "I know where to get clean, proper bandages."

Smoke took it and stood tentatively, keeping his weight on his good leg.

"Besides," his grandfather said. "I found you by following the blood trail you left when they brought you here." He opened the door, looked both ways, then guided Smoke out of the room.

Smoke slung one arm over his grandfather's shoulders and allowed him to take some of his weight as they moved down the hallway.

A blood drop on the floor caught his attention. A few feet away there was another. Huh, he had left a trail. The one he was leaving now was more than a few drops though.

They turned a couple of corners then walked to a door with a red cross on it.

Smoke flattened himself against the wall to stay out of sight while Grandfather opened the door.

The old man paused, frowned, then waved at Smoke to go in.

The room was empty.

Neither man said anything as they both went in and allowed the door to close. Grandfather engaged the lock.

"They were here?" Smoke asked.

"Yeah, Kini, your dad, and two guards."

Shit. "They've moved them somewhere."

His grandfather quickly bandaged up the wound then looked his grandson in the eyes.

"This is no government farm, is it?"

"Maybe that's not all it is, but yeah, something hinky is going on."

"When will the feds show up?"

"What time is it?"

"About 6:00 a.m."

"Not for a few more hours."

"When your dad and I left town to find you, the hospital was finally getting organized, but there was still a steady stream of new cases of pneumonia coming in. So far, all they're telling us is hantavirus."

Nothing about this situation made sense. A hantavirus outbreak brings the CDC to the area, and who gets nervous? A drug lord and a medical marijuana farm. Why the fuck would a legal, government-sanctioned operation get its hands dirty with a meth lab?

"How are all these people getting exposed to the virus?"

Smoke asked.

"Why does this place care about a CDC nurse enough to hunt her down?" his grandfather asked.

"I don't think we're going to like any of the answers," Smoke muttered. "We have to find Dad and Kini."

"Got a plan?"

"It's an awful big building," Smoke said. "Lots of places to hide a person." Someone was going to discover he was gone from the janitorial closet soon. An alarm would go out and...a grin spread across his face. Simple was always best, as far as plans went. "What's the fastest way to clear a building?"

His grandfather grinned. "Pull the fire alarm."

Smoke extended a hand toward the door. "After you."

"Can you walk on that leg?"

Smoke tested his weight then took a few trial steps. "Yes. I can walk and fight."

His grandfather nodded. "I saw an alarm on the wall at the beginning of this hallway. I'll pull it then come back here. We can see who comes out of the woodwork."

"Or doesn't."

"That, too."

Grandfather stepped out. A few seconds later the fire alarm began its relentless clang.

It was a few seconds before they heard anyone out in the hallway.

Grandfather opened the door a crack then pulled it open farther. He gestured and said, "Excuse me, can you give me a hand? I found this guy wandering the halls." A young man in a security uniform entered, his hand on the Taser in his holster.

"What are you—"

Grandfather held a knife to the guy's neck while he allowed the door to close. He took the Taser and handed it to Smoke.

Smoke gave the guard a thorough once-over then stepped closer. "About the same height," he said.

"You've got a solid forty pounds on him," Grandfather said.

"I'll suck in my gut."

Grandfather shrugged.

Smoke smiled at the guard, looking him in the eyes. "Take your uniform off."

The man swallowed hard, glanced at the Taser in Smoke's hand, then began removing his clothing with shaking fingers.

"How long have you worked here?" Smoke asked in a casual tone, as if just occupying time.

"A year."

"Tell me about the layout of the building," he asked, trying to keep his expression friendly.

"This section has the administration offices. We have a large climate-controlled greenhouse and a bunch of research labs on the west side of the building."

Interesting. "Researching what?"

The guard handed Smoke his shirt and shrugged. "I don't know. I just do my patrol and keep my mouth shut."

There was something in the guy's voice that pulled at Smoke's internal alarm bells. "What happens if you don't keep your mouth shut?"

"You disappear. Permanently." He started to push his pants down.

"That doesn't bother you?" Smoke asked.

"Not really," the guard said, then snapped his arm up with a small gun in his hand.

Grandfather grabbed the man by the hair and jabbed the point of his knife enough to prick his skin at the base of his head.

The guard froze.

"Gun down or you're dead."

Smoke took the weapon from him and set that on the cot, too. Then he got in the guy's face and said pleasantly, "You thought he was just an old man." He dropped the happy act totally, letting all the death, all the pain he'd seen and suffered, show on his face.

The guard paled and his breathing shallowed out like a dying fish.

"He's not, you know," Smoke continued. "He's been killing assholes like you for a long time. I don't recommend giving him any more reasons to shove that knife right through your brain. Got it?"

The guy seemed to have trouble breathing, but managed to croak, "Got it."

Smoke yanked the guy's pants off then took off his own and put on the guard's instead. They were a tight fit, but once he let the belt out a couple of holes they'd do. He inspected the guard's belt equipment. Taser holster, handcuffs, knife, flashlight, and a baton. The gun had come out of an ankle holster. Smoke took that, too, and put it on.

"There was a woman and a middle-aged man in this room not long ago. Where were they taken?" he asked the now partially clothed man.

"I don't know what you're talking about." That answer was too pat, too easy.

Smoke sighed. "Your funeral." He turned and took a step toward the door.

"Wait!" the guard struggled, but Grandfather had a good grip on the asshole's hair.

Smoke didn't say anything, didn't turn around, just waited with a patience he didn't feel. Kini and his dad were somewhere in this building, and he'd burn the whole place to the ground to find them.

"The shift supervisor said something about one of the labs in the restricted area."

"Where is it, and how to you get in?"

"Straight down this corridor to the end, turn right until you reach the doors marked RESTRICTED. My ID badge will get you in."

It was still attached to the guy's shirt. "Anything else I should know?"

The silence behind him was ominous.

Smoke turned his head to stare at the guard. "Is there anything else I should know?" he repeated softly.

The guy shook his head, his eyes bulging out of the sockets. "Don't kill me...please?"

Behind him, Grandfather rolled his eyes.

Smoke grinned. "We're not going to kill you." He paused. "Much."

Sweat beaded on the guy's forehead.

"Go," Grandfather said, twisting his knife. "I'll stay here with my new friend."

His new friend had his eyes screwed shut and was shaking in terror.

Smoke left, following the directions to the restricted area. He found the doors right where the guard had said they'd be, and his ID badge did indeed get him inside. Right about the time the fire alarm stopped blaring.

People were in the building. Security and possibly EMS. Given the situation in town, any EMS had to be from somewhere else. Private fire suppression team? That cost a lot of money.

Smoke walked with as little of a limp as possible. No use letting anyone know he was injured unless he had to.

He walked up to the windows as if on patrol and had to make himself keep walking.

On the other side of the glass was a lab, all right, but there weren't any fucking plants that he could see. There was a man dressed in a hazmat suit looking at something under a microscope. And wasn't the large upright appliance behind the man full of petri dishes? *An incubator.*

The guy in the hazmat suit glanced up.

Smoke nodded at him and flashed the okay sign. *Yup, all part of the same happy family.*

The guy nodded and gave him a thumbs-up.

Smoke nodded again and kept walking.

Holy fuck. Hazmat suits were only needed for some fucking scary biological or chemical shit. The next window held another lab, but the lights were off and no one appeared to be working.

He came to a corner and turned right. Along this corridor were doors, but no windows. He used the ID badge to open the first door. Dark and quiet. He moved on to the next one.

Light spilled out into the hallway, along with an angry demand, "Get out and close the fucking door before I fire your ass."

Smoke hesitated, like any good security guard. "I was told to check every occupied room," he said, then angled his thumb over his shoulder. "The alarm." He opened the door wider and took one step inside. "How many people are here and are they all right?"

The man facing him was dressed in a security uniform, but his was high quality and quazi-military looking. Definitely not off the rack. On his belt was all the same equipment on Smoke's borrowed belt, plus he wore a Glock in a thigh holster on his right leg.

"I said, get out..." His words trailed off as he stared at Smoke and frowned. "Who—"

Smoke smiled and stepped forward, extending his hand. "Oh, I'm—" He punched the asshole square in the jaw.

The guy flopped onto the floor like he was made of rubber.

"What took you so long?"

Smoke turned to inspect his father. A black eye, bruised face, and split lip, and those were just the injuries he could see. His father was seated on a metal chair, his arms handcuffed to the legs. Anger, hot and bright, tried to flare in his gut, but the icy fear kept the fire banked, because his father was alone.

"Kini?"

"Gone. They dragged her, kicking and screaming, out of here after they beat me up, trying to find out what she knew."

"Where?"

"I don't know, but that asshole might." He thrust his chin at the man on the floor, groaning and slowly coming around.

Smoke removed the gun, Taser, and knife from the security guard's belt then found his handcuff keys. He freed his father, then the two of them dragged the half-conscious asshole over to the chair and put the handcuffs on him. He partially slid off the chair, only his handcuffs keeping him from ending up on the floor.

Smoke slapped his face a few times and finally, the guy woke up completely. After replanting him on the chair, Smoke got into his face and growled. "Where is she?"

The idiot blinked a few times before panic had him jerking at the handcuffs around his wrists. "Wha...*fuck*."

Smoke slapped him again. "Where. Is. She?"

The guard began laughing and kept laughing until Smoke punched him a second time, and kept punching.

Chapter Thirty-One

Kini studied the handcuffs keeping her attached to the metal chair she sat on. They looked…substantial, not something you could easily pick. There wasn't anything in the room to use as a tool, anyway.

She slumped and tried to calm frayed nerves, but her heart rate didn't slow; in fact, it sped up. Tears flowed down her face and a sob snuck past the tight ring of fear around her throat.

Poor Jim. When the second security guard returned with water for her, the guards realized Grandfather Smoke had disappeared. They'd forced Jim and her from the first-aid room and farther into the building. She'd lost her sense of direction after the second or third turn and had no idea where they were in relation to any of the exits.

Jim and she had been shoved into a room that had a conference-style table, a dozen metal chairs, and little else. They'd both been handcuffed to chairs.

The security guards left, then came back with Deputy Blackwater. He smiled with practiced ease, a smile that didn't reach past his nose, and said he wasn't tolerant of trespassers.

She'd tried to tell him they didn't know anything, but the creep just smiled and gestured at Jim.

The security guards had beaten him in front of her, all while Blackwater demanded to know what she knew about the farm, the drug lab across the canyon, and the hantavirus outbreak. What had she told the CDC about all three things?

She told him all she knew, denying any previous knowledge of the farm and revealing the limited knowledge she had of the drug lab. The CDC, being a public company, had a duty to inform the public about outbreaks, so telling them what she'd told the CDC, and what the CDC would do about it, wasn't breaking any oaths.

He didn't believe her.

She wasn't sure what was going to happen next, but the fire alarm started going off. Blackwater talked to the two guards for a moment, then he smiled at her, but it was the most evil expression she'd ever seen on a man's face.

He stroked her cheek with one finger, letting it trail down her neck and collar bone to her cleavage. "I suggest you consider becoming more honest and forthright in your answers to my questions," he'd said in a soft voice that was so cold, she shivered. "Otherwise, I might have to resort to a more direct form of punishment."

The guards took her out of the room. She'd fought, yelling at them, screaming for help, but none came.

They hustled her down the hallway and into another room. An office. Unoccupied.

They'd handcuffed her to the desk then left her alone in the stark room with nothing but the harsh ring of the alarm.

For a few moments, all she could do was cry. The exhaustion, pain, and violence were too much. Eventually, her brain began to work again and sort through the questions he'd asked, and the ones he hadn't asked.

Who was he? Who were these people? It was obvious this farm was the window dressing for something else. Something that required a lot of money, if they were using Bruce's drug lab to finance it.

More drugs? *Designer* drugs?

Were they being impacted by the hantavirus outbreak? Was that why they were so worried about the CDC? They didn't want law enforcement to discover what they were doing?

The alarm shut off, and she stared at the door. Blackwater would come looking for her soon, and she still had no idea what she was going to tell him. She'd only gotten here because of bad luck and the actions of idiots. Something he wasn't going to believe.

The door flew open and Blackwater came in, breathing hard. Had he been running?

"You wouldn't know what happened to one of my guards, would you?"

Was he kidding?

She jiggled the handcuffs, making the chains clank. "When have I had time to do anything to your people? If I'd miraculously gotten loose, believe me, I'd run, not hang around looking for an opportunity to do damage to them. So, no."

"Someone is playing a very nasty game with us," he said, one corner of his lips curling up in a snarl. "We shot and captured a man riding one of my ATVs near the canyon earlier, and now he's missing."

She couldn't hide her joy at that news fast enough. Blackwater saw it.

He strode over to put a hand around her neck and squeezed. "Who is he? Is he Smoke?"

She tried to take in a breath to give some kind of answer to his question but discovered she couldn't; he held on to her too tightly. She kept trying to talk—it might be the only reason he'd stop choking her to death.

Finally, he reduced the pressure, allowing her to suck in some air and speak.

"I don't know who you're talking about."

"Is he a cop?"

"I don't know who you're talking about."

He used his grip on her neck to slam her against the back of her chair. "He was hog-tied and left on his belly. A man with a bullet still in his leg." Spittle flew from his mouth to land on her face. "It was Smoke, wasn't it?"

The door behind Blackwater popped open and one of the other guards said, "Sir, the man who came in with her"—he jerked his head at Kini—"the one we questioned, he's... gone."

If she'd thought Blackwater was angry before, it was nothing to the rage he displayed now. "Gone?" he screamed at the guard. "What do you mean gone?"

"I mean, he's gone, but one of our guards, Ferguson, was handcuffed in his place." A wince. "He's been roughed up, too."

Blackwater kept opening and closing his fists. "So, now we have two unknowns running loose around the place?"

"Three, actually, sir. There's an old man we can't find, either."

Sounded like the Smoke family was living up to their name.

Blackwater's lips pulled back from his teeth. "Find them and get this place locked down, or heads will roll."

The guard's face lost all color. "Yes, sir." He left as quickly as he'd come in.

Blackwater paced for a several seconds then turned a narrow-eyed gaze on her. She watched him watch her and saw the moment he made a decision come and go across his face.

A decision she was sure she wasn't going to like.

He stepped behind her, released her from one handcuff, then unclipped the second one from the chair and put it around her other wrist.

"Get up," he snarled into her ear as he wrapped his hand around her bicep and hauled her to her feet. "Make a noise, a sound, and I promise I'll cut you up into little pieces while you're still alive."

His words hit her like a punch to the gut. "What kind of monster are you?" she asked, staring at him.

He smiled that evil smile at her. "A well-fed one."

He was just trying to terrorize her by inferring that he ate…things people shouldn't eat. Wasn't he?

Nausea roiled her stomach, and she had to breathe through her mouth to prevent vomiting all over herself. On second thought, maybe that would quell his appetite.

Blackwater dragged her from the room and down the hall until they reached a dead end. On the right was a door marked MECHANICAL. On the left was another marked STORAGE. He opened the storage door using his ID then shoved her in.

Inside was a ten by ten room lined with shelves full of boxes, plant pots, bags of potting soil, gardening hand tools, and other stuff she didn't have time to identify. Blackwater pushed her farther into the room and kept pushing until they were in front of the rear set of shelves.

He turned a knob. The shelving unit shivered then swung forward a couple of inches, more, until there was a wide enough opening for them to squeeze past.

This was something out of a Scooby Doo movie.

"You have a secret lair?" she asked, then wished she hadn't.

His head jerked around and he stared at her coldly for a terrifying moment, then he started to laugh. "Of course. All the best villains do."

Smiling, he pushed her past the hidden door then closed it behind them.

The room beyond was divided into sections by chest-high counters. Along the far wall was a series of upright appliances that could be refrigerators or incubators or both. On the counters was a variety of lab equipment: analyzers, a couple of microscopes, test tubes, other supplies.

Two chairs lay on their sides, while a third had been left in a corner. Used gloves, plastic containers, pipettes, and glass slides littered the counters and floor.

No self-respecting lab tech would leave a lab in this state. What the hell had happened in here?

"This is where I create the weapons that will destroy the world," he said, his voice becoming more theatrical with every word.

She stared at him, dumfounded. "Really?"

His grin was back, slick, and in no way friendly. "A slight exaggeration. What I produce here will kill hundreds, maybe thousands of people, but not everyone."

"Produce?" What was he talking about? Some kind of chemical or bio weapon? Was this man using the farm as a cover for some kind of black market biological and chemical weapons production?

He grabbed a couple of latex gloves from a box on one counter and put them on. Then he opened the door of one of the appliances taking up the back wall and removed a container usually used for viral samples. He showed it to her, tilting it up and down so the fluid inside sloshed back and forth.

"Is that," she asked carefully, cautiously. "Hantavirus?"

He checked the label on the container. "Yes." He put it back, closed the door on the incubator, and opened the next one. This time, he pulled out a petri dish. "This is one of those flesh-eating bacteria." He put it back with a chuckle.

"Those things will eat anything."

This guy acted...unhinged. The knot of fear around her neck tightened, but she managed to ask, "Why are you telling me all this?"

"Because the two people I had working here died, and I need new staff. Lucky for you, there's a position open."

"Lucky for me?" she asked. It would have been luckier to have been run over by an eighteen-wheeler.

He cocked his head. "Unless you'd rather I shoot you, because those are your choices. Work or die."

Bruce had said almost those exact words.

From the look on Blackwater's face, her choices were: die slow or die fast.

Stall. She had to stall him, figure out what was going on, create a way to escape. "Um, okay. What kind of work, exactly?"

"I run an online shop," he said with a grin that had an edge of maliciousness. "Selling my products to anyone with enough cash to pay the fee. Sometimes they order just enough for a one-time use, but other clients want enough of one product to use in bulk." He laughed at that.

"So, let me see if I understand all this correctly, because I'm not sure my brain is keeping up." She paused, then asked, "You're producing and selling pathogenic bacteria and viruses online?"

He nodded.

"Where did you get them in the first place?"

"This is what's going to happen," he said, ignoring her question. "You're going to do what I tell you to do. If you don't follow instructions, I will hold a bang party for a few of my guards with you as the main attraction. Then, I'll put a bullet in your head and bury you in the desert. Understand?"

"I understand." She was also going to be sick. She swayed on her feet. "Can I...?"

"Can you what?"

"Sleep for a little while?" She winced. "I haven't slept much in the last day or so, and I don't want to make a mistake with those organisms and accidently kill myself."

Blackwater studied her for a moment. "A few hours. That's it." He grabbed her by the arm again and pulled her over to the door. On the wall next to the door was what looked like a long metal countertop. But the hinges were on the bottom.

"What happened to Bruce?" she asked.

Blackwater gave her a razor-sharp smile. "He's dead."

He pulled the metal surface down, revealing a camping mattress. A permanent cot. He released one wrist from the handcuffs then clipped the open handcuff to a small hole in the frame of the cot.

"Sleep well," he said with a smile then left the room.

She stood, chained to a prison-style bed, in a room full of deadly pathogens.

"Well" wasn't a word she'd pick to describe how she was going to sleep.

Chapter Thirty-Two

Smoke raised his fist to bash the asshole in the face again, but someone grabbed his wrist. He whirled, baring his teeth...at his father.

It was enough to douse the red haze he was in with ice water.

"Enough," his dad said in a calm tone he remembered from childhood. A tone that conveyed concern and disappointment in equal measure. "You can't get answers if you break his face."

Answers? *Kini.*

He looked down and realized he'd already broken the guy's nose, at least one of his front teeth, and both eyes were swollen and on their way to black.

He hauled the guy up by his shirt and growled, "Where is she?"

"Probably the back forty," the guard managed to say despite the damage to his mouth.

"She's dead?" Smoke balled his fist. Nothing would stop him from killing this fucker this time.

"It's some super-secret research lab," the guy said quickly. "Cole, the project manager, was the only one who knew how to get in and out. I've only been there twice, and he made me wear a blindfold both times."

Frustration made him want to keep hitting the guy, but that wouldn't be helpful. He glanced at his dad. "Any idea what he's talking about?"

A decisive shake of his head.

"He had people working in there?"

"Yeah, but…" He started laughing again. "They died."

The guy was fucking nuts. He glanced at his father again, the question of what he wanted to do with this weasel on his face.

"No, you can't kill him."

Smoke let him go, and he dropped to the floor like he was weighed down with stones.

"He's not going anywhere." His father studied Smoke with eyes that saw way too much. "Can you keep your shit together?" he asked in Navajo.

"Yes," Smoke replied in the same language.

They left the room, locking it so it would hopefully take longer for anyone to find the guard.

"I supposed we could ask for directions," Smoke said with a sigh.

"Not in a blood-covered shirt you're not."

He glanced down. *Shit.* There went that idea.

"The back forty," his dad muttered. "You know, people aren't all that creative really. I'd check the back of the building to see if there are any restricted rooms."

"The whole area is restricted, but yeah, let's look."

They headed down the hallway, opening doors and checking rooms, but aside from the guy in the lab with the window, they didn't find anyone else. Frustration built a fire in his gut. A fire that got hotter and hotter with every empty room.

His father watched him, his expression more and more troubled as the minutes went by. Finally, he stopped Smoke with a hand on his arm. "Hold up a minute."

Smoke looked at him. "I don't know if she has that minute. Some of her cuts looked like they were getting infected, she hasn't slept more than an hour or two at a time, and she's so fucking fragile"—he cut himself off and tried to control his breathing...and failed—"I've got to find her."

His father asked, "When the hell did you have time to fall in love with her? You only met her three days ago."

"About thirty seconds after I met her." As he stood there, trying to explain things to his dad, and unravel the mystery of where she could have gone, the sound of police sirens gradually penetrated his concentration.

"Shit. That sounds like local law enforcement," his dad said. He looked at Smoke. "If any of them sees you in that outfit, your ass is going to be in jail, and we'll never find her."

They resumed their search, trying every door they came to, but they were all locked. The ID card didn't do them a bit of good.

The sound of sirens got louder and was accompanied by the noise of several people talking and walking. He recognized Sheriff Davis's voice and Blackwater's.

They were out of hallway and options, with only two rooms left to check. Behind his dad was a room marked mechanical. His stolen ID card opened the door, and they both went inside.

A few seconds later, a group of men stopped at the hallway intersection about ten feet from the room they were hiding in.

"Don't smell any smoke or see any evidence of a fire." The sheriff's voice. "Who triggered the alarm?"

"The only people in the building at the time were

janitorial staff, security, and Ben, one of our researchers, who keeps odd hours." Didn't know that voice.

"We still have to clear the building, including the restricted area." Another new voice. Belligerent and suspicious.

"Mike Shingle," his dad whispered in his ear. "Fire chief."

"No one is stopping you, Shingle," the sheriff said, calm and cooperative. "Clear away."

Shingle wasn't done talking. "With that outbreak going on, I don't know why you're here. It's a fire alarm, not a break-in."

Little did he know.

"The city boys those doctors called in are handling all the shit in town. Blackwater was there, too. We're looking after outlying areas." Jesus, Blackwater wasn't just calm, he was making sense. "Don't you have a job to do?" he asked in a condescending tone.

Ah, there was the asshole he knew all too well.

No one answered him, but someone did stomp away with heavy boots.

"Blackwater, finish in here," the sheriff said. "I'm going to have a look around outside. The last thing we need is for this place to go up in smoke."

No noise for several seconds, then there was a thump against the wall much closer to the mechanical room than Smoke was expecting.

"What the *fuck* is going on?" Blackwater asked. "First that stupid nurse gets kidnapped, the next thing I know Bruce has her at the house. Then, she escapes with help and no one can find her, but you do find and shoot a big Indian riding one of your ATVs. Where's the Indian?"

"I don't know. He got loose somehow. There were two others. Some old guy and a dude named Jim."

"Jim? Jim *Smoke*?"

"He didn't give us his last name."

"Where is he?" Blackwater growled so low and angry.

"He got himself out of some handcuffs and disappeared."

A cold angry bark echoed down the hall along with the vibration of another punch against the wall. "Get this situation under control. Find those men or, by God, you'll be the next body at the morgue."

"You need me, *Deputy*," the other guy said, making the title sound like an insult. "I'm the one with the contacts and the buyers. The guy who makes you the real money. It's time you do your job."

There was a scuffle, thumps, then silence.

"You listen to me you little puke," Blackwater snarled. "Your *contacts*, your *buyers*, they don't care who they buy from as long as there's something to buy. They won't care if you disappear into a hole in the desert and never come back."

"You can't touch me," the man said. "I've got an insurance policy. I disappear, and evidence from this place lands in the inbox of every major news outlet in the state."

More thumps and someone made a pain-filled sound.

"You're not the only one with an insurance policy, boy." Blackwater's voice sounded like crushed glass. "I've got enough evidence on you to put you in jail for the rest of your miserable life. I've got friends and those friends have friends in law enforcement, government, and the military. Your policy doesn't mean shit to me. Do what you're paid to do, or I'll put a bullet in your head right now."

"Okay, okay," the man said in a placating tone. "I'll go—"

There was a metallic click, a scuffle, and an incoherent shout echoed down the hallway. More thumps, the smack of shoes trying to find purchase on the floor, the slap of flesh pounding against flesh. A man chanting as bone crunched and the slap's pitch rose with the echo of something...wet. "You. Little. Fucker. *You little fucker.*"

Blackwater was beating his own man to death.

Smoke stared at the doorknob he could barely see in the dark, rage a cold fire in his belly. He had to stop this, had to bring the man down, but the hand on his shoulder, his father's hand, froze him in place.

Smoke gritted his teeth and resisted the incompressible need to throw that hand off of his body, charge into the hallway, and give Blackwater a taste of his own medicine.

"If you go out there now," his father said in an almost silent whisper, "he'll kill you, me, and *Kini*."

He'd known Blackwater was going to be trouble. There was an indelible stamp of cruelty and arrogance on his face. It was the only emotion besides frustration Smoke had seen in the other man.

Blackwater liked killing.

It was in his voice as he caved in the head and body of the drug-dealing lowlife who worked for him. Smoke could almost feel the impact of the other man's fists go through his body like they were his own. The shock of each hit reverberated through his hands and arms.

Power, pleasure, and pain.

Smoke's stomach twisted and heaved. Dizziness forced his hands out to find purchase, to push against the wall to hold himself upright. Was that what he'd become? A sadistic nightmare of a man who got off on other people's pain?

Is that why he fought the desperate urge to kill people all the time?

He wasn't sure how long he'd stood there, breathing through his mouth, his head hanging down like a horse that had run too far, too fast, but as he slowly got his body under control, he realized the noise in the hallway had stopped.

No, not stopped, changed to a *step, step, drag. Step, step, drag*. Then it paused. Right outside the door to the mechanical room.

Had he made some sound that gave them away?

Smoke shifted his weight, sliding to the left, while his father slid to the right. They waited for the door to open, for that moment of surprise that might allow two men armed with knives to win against a man armed with a gun.

The door didn't open.

The one across the hallway, the storage room door, did.

There was a grunt, then Blackwater dragged the body inside. The door closed on its own, leaving nothing for Smoke and his father to listen to but silence.

Neither of them said anything, just waited. And waited. Finally, after several minutes Smoke opened the mechanical room door a crack. No one out there, but on the floor, bloody drag marks and boot prints going into the storage room. There were none coming out.

Smoke's father nudged him out of the way. Stepping carefully to avoid the blood, he opened the door to the storage room.

Inside, the drag marks and footprints led straight to the back wall but was empty of people or bodies.

Smoke glanced at his father and found the same confused expression probably on his face.

"Where—?" Jim began.

Smoke took a closer look at the drag marks. They didn't just lead up to the back wall completely covered in a shelving unit, they appeared to go *under* it.

"*Sonofabitch*," he muttered, approaching the shelves then testing them to see how they were attached to the wall and if they could be moved. The first few were solid, but one seemed shallower than the others. It jiggled. Behind it, at the correct height and location, he found a doorknob.

Elation coursed through his body, feeding him energy and hope. Until he discovered his stolen ID card wouldn't unlock it, then the adrenaline drained away leaving him at the mercy of frustration, exhaustion, and pain.

He was right back where he started—desperate for the kill.

"She's in there, Dad." Smoke didn't even recognize his own voice. It sounded like it belonged to someone broken and insane. "I've got to get her out before that asshole kills her."

"We've got to find the keys or something to pick the locks with," his dad muttered. "Or…hey, there's firemen still in the building, right?"

"Probably. What…?" Smoke stared at his dad's face.

"I'll bet they have an axe capable of getting through that door."

Smoke looked at his father's clothing and his own, both splattered with blood. "They're not going to be interested in giving either of us an axe."

"We don't have time to ask." His dad turned and walked out of the storage room.

Smoke followed, his limp slowing him down enough that his father rounded the first corner a few seconds before him.

"Stop! Police. Hands in the air." The shout didn't sound very far away. "Don't move and keep your hands up."

Smoke froze a couple of feet from the corner, listening hard.

"I said, don't move," said the same voice. Was there only one?

He heard the jingle of handcuffs moving closer to the corner. "How did you get the blood on your clothing, sir?"

He heard the unmistakable metallic zip of a handcuff tightening.

Smoke went around the corner as fast as his injured leg would allow, grabbed the uniformed police officer, one hand on the back of his neck, the other twisting his free hand behind him.

The officer shouted something Smoke couldn't make out

and tried to mule kick his right knee.

Dad turned, grabbing the cop's gun and turning it on its owner. "We don't want to hurt you," he said with calm conviction. "We just witnessed Deputy Blackwater beating a man to death, and we believe he's got a hostage."

"Blackwater?" the cop's voice was high with stress and disbelief. "You've got to be shitting me. You're covered in blood."

"Most of it my own," his dad told the cop.

Blah, blah, blah. This wasn't getting them any closer to getting through the door Kini was probably behind. Trapped and at the mercy of a fucking animal.

"No time," Smoke said to his father.

His dad made eye contact then fished around for the keys to the handcuffs. He unlocked the cuff already on his wrist and put it on the cop, securing both hands behind the man's back.

"Any other police or law enforcement here?" Smoke asked.

The cop stared at him like he was a boogey man.

So, no then.

They started walking toward the front entrance, the *public* entrance, of the building.

"We're going to use your radio in your car to call for help."

"Bullshit," the cop said with a humorless laugh.

"No time for bullshit. Blackwater has an injured woman behind a locked door and very few reasons to keep her alive."

"What the fuck are you talking about?"

"There's more going on here than what the sign says," Dad said. "Something illegal, and Blackwater is involved up to his neck."

"What the fuck have you guys been smoking?" the cop asked as they saw a group of men, firemen, and security guards clustered up ahead.

Someone spotted them and swore, alerting all of them that something not right was going on. As Smoke and his dad approached, the group backed up, then scattered or backed off.

"What do you want?" one of the security guards asked.

"The authorities."

"Dude," one of the firefighters said. "You've got a cop in your hands."

"Not one of these dirty local pigs," Dad said. "The FBI or Homeland Security."

They kept moving at a steady pace toward the front doors.

"You *want* the FBI here?" someone asked incredulously as they went out.

"Yeah. We're reasonably sure they're not dirty," Smoke told the group, then they left the building.

The officer's car was parked on the sidewalk about twenty feet from the door. There were two firetrucks not far away. They shoved the cop in the back seat of his own car and engaged the locks.

Dad got into the front seat. "I'm going to lock myself in here and try to reach an outside law enforcement agency. I'd tell you to stay here and wait for backup, but I know you won't do that, so…" He handed Smoke the gun. "Grab an axe and go get her."

Smoke took the weapon but didn't have to raise it to clear the way between him and the nearest firetruck. He took an axe off the side of the vehicle and headed back into the building.

Chapter Thirty-Three

It was the smell that woke her. Damp, iron rich, and with a hint of decay. Blood and a lot of it, mingled with death.

Kini had learned death's scent as a child, entangled with her memories of her parents and the home that should have been a safe place, but never was.

Now, it woke her fast and froze her in place, curled in a fetal position on the narrow cot. Only her eyes moved, searching for the source of the smell, but there was nothing in front of her that hadn't been there when she'd dozed off.

The overhead fluorescent lights threw enough shadows for her to detect someone moving around behind the half wall at her back. The shadows moved again, and she heard a grunt as something was dragged across the floor in her direction.

Blackwater came into her field of view. He was dragging someone behind him, leaving a wide trail of blood and other...stuff.

This wasn't real, couldn't be real, but the smell only got stronger. Only served to raise her awareness higher. No dream was this tangible.

She studied the person on the floor. Even though they were face up, there was no face left to see. It had been beaten into a pulpy mass of blood, skin, hair, and bone.

Kini sucked in a breath as dread's icy fingers penetrated every muscle and bone in her body.

Blackwater's head whipped around to pin her in place. He dropped the body, roared incoherently, and lunged at her.

She screamed, threw herself backward, covered her head and neck with her arms, and braced for the collision.

The impact of his body hitting hers never came.

Instead, he loomed over, his breath hot and fetid wafting over her neck, her hair. Something tugged at the handcuff attached to her wrist.

Blackwater began to laugh—a mean, mockery of humor. "Not so tough now, are you?"

Even his voice sounded crazy.

She didn't say anything, didn't move, had no desire at all in lowering her arms and facing this...*creature.*

"Now, now, Dale. There's no need to scare the nice nurse."

Kini peeked out from behind her arms and hands. Sheriff Davis stood on the other side of the room, the door behind him clicking closed.

No, no, *no*. The sheriff *and* Blackwater were involved in whatever lunacy this was?

The two men smiled at her as if sharing a joke only they found funny.

"Go on, Dale. Cut up the garbage. You and I can have a conversation with Miss Kerek when you're done."

Blackwater strode back to the body, picked up a leg, and dragged it a couple of feet before the words slipped out of her mouth, "Cut up?"

He gave her a delighted grin. "We've got one of those industrial wood chippers. Comes in really handy for all kinds of"—he glanced at the body then at her—"garbage."

Oh my God.

Blackwater winked, then dragged the body across the room and through the unmarked doorway the sheriff had entered by. The sheriff followed him through the door. It closed behind him.

Despite the steel door between the rooms, she had no trouble hearing the rumble of the wood chipper's motor or the higher pitch whine as...things were fed into it.

Her breathing sped up. They were going to put her into the wood chipper. The sheriff had done everything but say the words. She was going to be ground into bits. Spots swam in her vision as sweat broke out over her body. Her stomach twisted. The roar of her blood rushing through her body blocked out even the sound of the chipper. And other louder sounds.

Blackness reached out and grabbed her.

Kini came to, crumpled on the edge of cot, her handcuffed arm the only thing holding her on it.

She tried to sit up, or shift back, get out of the uncomfortable position, but her brain and her body didn't seem to be speaking to each other.

The wood chipper wasn't running. Her eyes popped open as soon as the lack of sound registered, and she looked around.

The blood trail was still there in all its glory. The lab was still a mess, but there were only two sets of bloody footprints going to the room with the chipper, but none coming out.

Where were Blackwater and Sheriff Davis?

Probably disposing of the body or, rather, ensuring that the method of disposal was completed. What would they do with the remains after they put them through the wood chipper? Was it fertilizer for the jojoba and marijuana plants?

Yuck.

The door opened, and the sheriff strode into the room. But no Blackwater.

The sheriff's face was oddly calm.

"Where's Blackwater?"

"No need to worry about him. He's taking a permanent dirt nap." The sheriff walked to the incubators and began pulling out sample containers and petri dishes, collecting them in an untidy group on the nearest counter.

He'd killed his own deputy.

Pins and needles pricked at the ends of her fingers, numbing first her hands then her arms.

He'd *killed* his own deputy.

Her breathing sped up, attempting to outrun the evidence in front of her eyes. Evidence that the sheriff wasn't just involved in producing pathogens for sale; he was responsible for the outbreak.

He'd killed his own deputy.

There was nothing to stop him from killing her.

A small duffle bag was retrieved from a cupboard, and he stuffed everything into it willy-nilly, without any concern for what might happen if one of the petri dishes lost its lid.

Blackwater had told her what was in some of those containers. Aggressive pathogens, every single one.

"Sheriff, please be careful with those," she said, attempting to sound helpful rather than helpless. "It would be easy to accidently expose yourself to one of those organisms."

One corner of his lip lifted in a sneer, and he pulled out his gun and aimed it at her head. "Shut up."

She closed her mouth and ducked her head.

The sheriff took his bag and opened another cupboard, removing more items she couldn't see and adding them to the bag. Once he was finished, he dropped the bag on the floor next to the door to the wood chipper.

While she watched with increasing dread, he gathered

a couple of lab coats that had been hung on the backs of chairs, dropping them on the floor about ten feet from her. He opened a cabinet with safety warning stickers on it and pulled out a couple of bottles then dumped the contents on the pile of fabric. The smell of strong chemicals, alcohol, and other flammables made her gag.

He was going to burn the building down.

With her in it.

He studied the mess he'd made, nodded once, then looked at her and walked over. He crouched a couple of feet away from the cot. "I'm leaving shortly, but I promise to tell your boyfriend goodbye for you." He said the words like they were part of a normal, average conversation you'd have with a neighbor or acquaintance.

All she could do was stare at him, this monster who'd managed to convince most of the world he was devoted to serving and protecting the public.

He pulled out his gun and shot the light fixture above the pyre he'd created. Sparks flew in several directions and smoke curled and rose from the pile of chemical-soaked lab coats.

The sheriff stood, strode over to pick up his duffel bag, then left through the wood chipper room door.

Flames licked higher and higher from the bonfire, dancing and weaving with the accompanying heavy black smoke.

Kini opened her mouth and screamed as loud as she could. Finally giving voice to her fear, and panic gave her permission to yank at the handcuffs keeping her attached to the cot. She yanked and pulled until the cuff cut into her skin. Her blood, hot and slick, was almost enough to allow her hand to pass through the cuff. Almost, but not quite.

The fire alarm went off again, adding to her panic.

The flames grew and the smoke expanded to fill the room.

Coughing, she slid off the cot and onto the floor where the smoke was at its lowest concentration.

A blow, loud enough to be heard over the alarm, hit the side of the room with the hidden entrance.

Another blow and another and another.

The steel door screeched and buckled near the doorknob. The next blow created a jagged rift in the steel. The next sheared away the deadbolt, and the door was kicked open.

Smoke charged into the room with a fireman's axe in his hands and eyes filled with the promise of retribution and death.

An ice-cold rock that had been weighing her down suddenly melted. *Fear.* She'd been so afraid he'd been hurt or worse, but seeing him on his feet, his strength and ferocity fully intact, pulled her out of the black hole hope had gone into.

"*Smoke!*" She waved her free hand and struggled to get to her feet, but every breath she took ripped at the tissues of her throat and lungs like the air was saturated with razor blades.

He arrived at her side a moment later, body vibrating with violence and searching for a target.

"He's gone," she shouted at him. "The sheriff is *gone.*"

Smoke focused on her, his gaze so hot and heavy she shivered.

She jerked at the handcuffs. "Key?"

He raised his axe. "Right here."

She stretched the handcuff out so part of the chain laid flat against the edge of the cot.

Smoke drove the blade down on the metal and cut the links in half. As soon as she was free, he grabbed her hand, hauled her up, and headed for the door he'd destroyed.

The fire was in the way.

"No," Kini managed to choke out. "Another way out."

She pointed at the door the sheriff had gone through.

Smoke hustled her toward that door, all but dragging her, and he only let go when he reached the door and had to open it.

The second he put his hand on the knob, he snatched it back again, shaking it like he was trying to throw off water. Or a burn.

Kini looked around, but there were only two doors and neither of them were accessible.

Smoke grabbed her hand and pulled her as far away from the fire and smoke as possible. He studied the walls and hefted the axe like he was looking for a good place to start chopping.

Who did he think he was, Paul Bunyan?

He raised the axe, but before he could take the first swing, a blast of heat, light, and metal had her ducking and covering, and Smoke throwing his body over hers.

When nothing else went flying, Smoke let her lift her head to see what happened.

The door to the wood chipper room was embedded in the far wall. There was a giant hole where the door used to be and no obvious flames, just a solid wall of smoke.

Smoke tugged her close and, holding his arm up to his face so he could breathe through his sleeve, got nearer to the hole. He darted a look at her, nodded, and pulled as he edged his way through the dense black cloud.

Kini followed him, glad he wasn't trying to hurry, because there was no way he could see where his feet were going until he was damn near on top of the next bit of floor. Or stairs, as they came up to them, leading down, and if the change in direction of the smoke was any indication, possibly a way out.

Smoke picked up their pace, and in a few more steps they emerged into bright sunlight.

Kini fell to her knees, coughing as soon as they were

clear, but Smoke didn't let her stay there.

"More distance," he told her, his voice scratchy. He looked around. "Out of sight."

That got her on her feet again.

He led her toward several smaller structures—greenhouses and possibly equipment sheds—closer to the field of plants. They got into the nearest shed filled with tools and fire suppression equipment only seconds before a firetruck came around to the back of the building.

Firefighters disgorged from the vehicle and prepared to begin spraying water when the lunatic she didn't want to see, the sheriff, showed up in a police car, jumped out, and started yelling at the firefighters to get back.

A huge boom, followed by towering flames and smoke, erupted from the building.

Another blast, then a third.

Something long and reflective punched a hole through the metal roof of the building and flew across the parking lot toward them. It tore through the wall and ceiling of the shed, raining tools, metal, and building materials over them as it plowed into the interior.

"What—" Kini began.

Smoke grabbed her with his free hand and half carried, half dragged her outside.

"Pressurized tank," he shouted as he pushed them both into a limping run toward a large metal container sitting on the ground about fifty feet away. "There are more of them."

All well and good to get away from things that might explode in your face and kill you, but now they were out in the open where anyone could see them.

Someone like the sheriff, who launched himself into a sprint toward them. He pointed his handgun at them, his expression a death threat.

Kini had thought she'd reached her physical and

emotional limits, her emotions shut down, and not an iota of adrenaline left in her system.

Tapped out.

Done.

But the sheriff was going to shoot them, and Smoke was too focused on finding shelter to see the danger charging at them from behind.

It was *do* or *die*.

Kini ripped into the well of fear and rage she'd kept tightly locked down since the day her father had destroyed his family. Ripped into it and rode it.

She wouldn't let the monsters take another person she loved away from her. She wouldn't let *this* monster steal Smoke's life.

Screaming, she wrenched herself away from Smoke, causing them both to stumble, ass over tea kettle. She sprang up, grabbed the axe, and hurled it with everything she was at the sheriff.

Chapter Thirty-Four

One second Smoke was running with a grip so tight on Kini's shirt he couldn't feel his fingers, the next she was screaming and they were tumbling across the pavement with bruising force.

She shoved him out of the way, rocketed to her feet, grabbed the axe he'd dropped, and, shrieking like a banshee, threw it at something behind them.

The sheriff, who had a gun and was about to shoot them. *Fuck*.

Kini launched herself toward the sheriff.

Oh fuck, no. Smoke tried to grab her, but missed.

"Kini!" he yelled.

Her throw, wild and without any thought of aim, still made the sheriff flinch and sidestep.

Smoke found himself on his feet and running. He had to get to Kini before the sheriff recovered and shot her. Nothing was more important than protecting her. Not even his own life.

One step, two, three, he'd reach her in another step.

His injured leg buckled as he reached out to snag her shirt.

His fingers brushed the fabric as he fell and missed.

The boom of the gun, once, twice, sounded louder than any sound had a right to. Two shots were all the sheriff managed to make before Kini plowed into him, shoulder first, with enough force to knock the man off his feet.

He landed hard.

Kini had fallen on her butt after her shoulder check, but tried to push herself to her feet, her gaze locked on the handgun the sheriff had dropped before he hit the ground. It had skidded several feet away.

Smoke didn't remember getting up, didn't remember the run, but found himself reaching the gun before Kini or the sheriff.

He turned the weapon on its owner.

Kini blocked his shot.

"Down!" he shouted at her.

An arm slid around her throat from behind. In the sheriff's other hand was the axe.

"Drop it," he snarled at Smoke, holding the axe blade up to Kini's throat.

Smoke froze. Behind the sheriff most of the firefighters were focused on the blaze, but a couple, one of them the fire chief, were watching them.

The son of a bitch would kill Kini. Smoke could read it in his eyes. He considered putting the gun down, but he was also sure the sheriff wouldn't just get into his car and leave. He'd take Kini with him.

Not going to happen.

Another police car came screaming around the side of the building, followed by a couple of sedans. They came to a stop a good distance away, and someone in a state trooper uniform opened the driver's side door, pulled his service weapon, and aimed it at Smoke.

"Drop your weapons!" the trooper shouted.

A grin spread across the sheriff's face.

Fuck. If he didn't put the gun down the trooper would probably open fire on him, which wouldn't do Kini any good.

But he'd escape a life he didn't know how to live anymore.

For one awful moment, he gave serious consideration to shooting the sheriff, knowing he was killing himself at the same time.

Kini made a sound, a tired, pained protest as tears cleared tracks through the blood on her cheeks. "Smoke," she whispered. So much grief, so much fear, so much worry packed into his name.

He couldn't do it. Couldn't hurt her. He loved her too much to add his death to her nightmares.

He loved her.

Smoke set the gun on the ground carefully then put his hands up in the air.

The sheriff glanced behind him and saw the trooper moving forward. The grin on his face got wider. "You two are a regular Bonnie and Clyde," he said, raising his voice so he'd be heard by the trooper and the men who'd gotten out of the sedan and were approaching with weapons drawn. "But your murderous adventure is *over.*"

"Let her go, Sheriff," Smoke said. "You don't need that axe anymore."

"Until you're in handcuffs, boy," the sheriff snarled, "she isn't going anywhere."

The trooper stopped advancing as soon as he was in a position slightly behind the sheriff and to his left. A clear shot to either Smoke or Kini if she managed to get away.

One of the men came forward with a set of handcuffs. He wore nothing but black jeans and a black T-shirt, no identifier printed on his clothing to indicate what law enforcement agency he belonged to. He did have a shoulder holster with the butt of a handgun pointed out on his left side.

"On your knees," he ordered Smoke.

Smoke looked into the eyes of a man who looked vaguely familiar and utterly ruthless, and complied with the order.

He met Kini's gaze and sucked in a painful breath. She was covered in a lot more blood than the last time he'd looked at her. Her face had gone ashen and her eyes glassy. Below her left hand he could see a steady fast drip of blood onto the ground.

She blinked and her gaze sharpened, focused on his face. One corner of her mouth kicked up. "You've got that ferocious look again," she teased, her voice barely above a whisper.

The guy in black behind him grabbed one of his wrists and pulled it behind his back.

Jesus Christ, she was in the hands of an out-of-control asshole who held an axe an eighth of an inch from her neck, and she was *bleeding*. "Don't joke."

The guy grabbed his other wrist and twisted it around and pulled it behind his back. Smoke waited for the cool metal kiss of the handcuffs, knowing he was giving up his last opportunity to kill the bastard. No contest. Any chance of getting Kini to safety was worth taking.

"Promise me you'll laugh once in a while," she said, her voice breaking on the last word.

"Shut up," he growled at her. The pool of blood beneath her was getting larger fast. Her only hope was an ambulance, but the fucking sheriff had to let go of her first.

Smoke would do anything to speed this up. Where the fuck were the handcuffs?

"She's been shot," Smoke shouted to the whole world. "She needs immediate medical attention."

The guy behind him pressed metal against his hand and

wrist, but it wasn't a handcuff. It was a gun.

What the flying fuck was this?

The guy behind him said gruffly, "On your feet," then helped him stand, like Smoke was actually wearing handcuffs.

The trooper lowered his weapon a couple of feet but maintained his two-handed grip. One of the other guys from the sedan approached the sheriff and said, "Thank you, Sheriff Davis. I'll take her." He gave Davis a concerned expression. "You look like you need to see the paramedics, too."

The sheriff frowned at the newcomer. "Who are you?"

"Came in with the state troopers," the guy said with a friendly smile, reaching for Kini.

The sheriff backed up half a step, dragging Kini with him. "I'm not giving up custody of my prisoner until I know who I'm dealing with." He glanced around quickly, his gaze going over then coming back to the trooper who'd lifted his weapon a bit higher and was pointing it more at the sheriff than Smoke.

"I'm FBI," the guy said. "Just arrived on scene and responded to a call for backup at this location." The guy glanced at the burning building without taking his focus off the sheriff. "Some serious shit going on here, Sheriff. We're here to support your office in any way you need."

The sheriff studied the FBI agent then the guy behind Smoke, suspicion a permanent resident on his face. "Who called for backup?"

"One of your deputies."

Kini made a pain-filled sound and sagged in the sheriff's hold.

Smoke and the man behind him made an aborted move toward them, but the sheriff caught it anyway.

"What the fuck is going on here?" he yelled at everyone as he hitched Kini higher, covering more of his body with hers. "You're all looking at me like I'm the criminal and not this stupid bitch and her army reject boyfriend."

"We're concerned for the woman's wounds," the agent said. "She looks like she's losing a lot of blood fast."

"So what?"

Everyone was watching him like he was a cockroach they wanted to step on, and no amount of smooth talk from the FBI was going to convince the asshole to let his guard down.

"She can't face justice if she's dead."

"Fine," the sheriff said, taking a couple of full steps backward. "I'll stick her in my squad car and take her to the hospital myself."

Kini's eyelids fluttered and she went limp; the only thing keeping her upright was the sheriff's arm around her throat.

He managed to keep the axe pressed to the back of her ear and neck as he dragged her a few more steps toward his car.

"Sheriff, she's unconscious," the FBI agent said, frustration coloring his tone. "She needs medical attention now."

"I'm not letting you take over this investigation. She stays in my custody." He was halfway to his car now.

The agent pulled out his weapon. "You're not acting rational, Sheriff. Let the woman go."

The sheriff bared his teeth. "I knew it." He tightened his hold on Kini's neck and turned to face the FBI agent. "Someone fed you a load of bullshit and you believed it, didn't you?"

Smoke couldn't let him get any farther away. He'd made Kini a promise not to kill anyone, but if she didn't get her wounds taken care of, she was going to die of blood loss. If he did what he had to do to save her, he'd lose her just the same.

Better that than dead.

He had a shot. Better than the agent or the trooper who

also had his gun trained on the sheriff.

I'm sorry, sweetheart.

Smoke yanked his arm out of the loose grip of the guy behind him, pulled the gun up, aimed, and fired.

The sheriff's head recoiled and he went down, taking Kini with him.

Before his brain could register what happened, Smoke was running toward them. Kini lay across the sheriff's body, fresh blood leaking out of a cut on her neck.

Not a lot of blood, the cut no deeper than any of the others she already had on the other side of her neck.

He gently, carefully scooped her up and lifted her off the sheriff's body. He lay her down on the ground a few feet away from the dead man. Covered in blood from her neck to her knees, there was no way to tell where the bullet wounds were. He grabbed the edges of her shirt and tore it down the middle.

No, oh God, no.

There were two bullet holes in her torso, both of them bleeding.

"Medic!" he bellowed, putting a hand over each wound and applying pressure. "Someone get me a fucking *medic*."

"So loud," a wavering voice said.

His lungs stopped working for the whole second it took to look at her face. "Kini?"

Her eyes were open a crack but widened with surprise as she looked at him. "What did I do this time?"

She was awake, talking to him. Then her question registered. "You got shot," he growled at her. "You ran straight toward that asshole and he shot you." He leaned down until he was just a couple of inches from her face. "*Twice*."

"Of course I did." She smiled at him, so beautiful and sweet. "He would have shot you otherwise." One bloody hand reached up to touch his face. "Love you." Her hand dropped and her eyes closed.

"Kini!" he shouted at her. "Don't you fucking die on me, don't you fucking dare."

Someone put a hand on his shoulder. He jerked away.

"Smoke, the paramedics are here."

All he could see was the ghost of a smile on her face and the blood on her body. If he lost her, he'd go insane.

"Smoke, come on, man, get your shit together, the paramedics are here!" He glanced over his shoulder at the man who'd handed him the gun instead of handcuffing him. Then at the ambulance and the paramedics running toward them.

The next few minutes were a blur as the paramedics fought to stop Kini from bleeding any more than she already had. They put IVs in both her arms, loaded her onto a stretcher, and were gone.

Smoke hadn't moved from where he'd been standing. All he could do was stare at the pavement where Kini had lain. There was so much blood on the ground. So much.

Finally, he turned his head and regarded the man who'd stayed with him the whole time. Henry Lee, an ex-Special Forces soldier, currently employed at the CDC as a lab tech. "What are you doing here?"

"Came with the rest of our people. No one needed me to figure out the pathogen, so River gave me a gun and told me to stay out of trouble."

"Dumb." One did not hand a man like Henry Lee, who'd lost a leg but none of his training, a gun for any other reason than to *make* trouble.

"Yep."

"So you promptly disobeyed his orders just like he expected you to?"

"He's not my boss, but..." Lee shrugged. "Yeah."

Another fire truck arrived, followed by more state

trooper cars and another generic sedan. None of the people who got out of the vehicles paid them any attention. "Why aren't I under arrest?"

"Your grandfather got word to us about the same time the sheriff called in to say the fire alarm was false."

That couldn't be all of it. "What was the word?"

Lee gave Smoke a startled glance then started laughing. "You live up to your reputation."

"Which is?"

"You get straight to the point and only say what you have to." Lee shook his head. "Your grandfather said to look into the owners of this place and a property on the other side of the canyon that turns out to be a drug lab. Both places are owned by a development company, that's owned by a shell company, that eventually leads back to Sheriff Davis."

"That asshole sheriff wasn't just producing meth. This place is a cover for bioweapons."

Lee stopped laughing. "No. Really?"

"Kini told me the sheriff removed some of the pathogens from the building. You might want to check the trunk of his police car."

"Shit." Lee took a couple of steps toward the knot of people talking with the fire chief, then stopped and said, "Don't go anywhere."

At Smoke's nod, he jogged away, only the slightest limp giving away the fact that he had a prosthetic leg.

It didn't take long for Lee's news to rile everyone up. Shit, he could hear the questions from where he stood.

Smoke walked over to Lee and the rest, the pain in his calf reminding him that he had to see a doctor about getting that bullet out.

"You might as well let the fire burn," Smoke said to the group. "Let the heat destroy whatever shit he had in there."

"What the hell is wrong with your leg?" Lee asked,

staring at his torn jeans like he'd hadn't noticed them until now.

Something told him some of these people were going to squawk. Fuck, he was tired of the noise. Still, maybe he could convince everyone it was no big deal.

He shrugged. "I sort of got shot."

Chapter Thirty-Five

Kini floated on an ocean of cold pain. Her whole body hurt. Stupid sheriff had done something; she couldn't quite remember what. Oh yeah, he'd shot her. Twice.

It was Smoke the sheriff wanted to shoot. There would have been no talking him down from the moral ledge he'd teetered on; he'd been determined to jump.

She'd felt the impact of the bullets, but didn't recall any pain until after she'd rammed him, knocking him down.

No wonder she hurt.

That was okay, because Smoke was okay.

He was okay, wasn't he?

She lifted eyelids weighing fifty pounds each, looking for him, wanting to know where she was and what happened. The sound of an active heart monitor and motorized IV pump beeped and hummed next to her left ear. Hospital bed. Hospital room.

Which hospital?

Kini turned her head to see if anyone was around to answer her questions and found Smoke sitting in an uncomfortable-looking chair, asleep.

The last time she'd seen him, he'd been wearing someone else's clothes spattered with blood and burn holes. Now, he was wearing scrubs and hospital booties on his feet. The edge of a bandage peaked out from under one of his pant legs.

"Smoke?"

She couldn't seem to make her voice box work.

Putting as much strength as she could into it, she said, "Smoke."

His eyes opened and he stared at her, his expression blank for a long, horrible second. Then awareness and relief flooded his face and he sat up abruptly in the chair. "Kini?"

"Hi," she said, trying to smile, but her face hurt a lot, too, so she gave up on it.

"How are you feeling?" Smoke asked. Then closed his eyes and grimaced. "Dumb question." He opened his eyes again. "Any difficulty breathing? Headache?"

What? Why would he ask all that? She had a heart monitor attached to her chest and a blood oxygen saturation monitor clamped to her right index finger. Not to mention more cuts and bruises than she could count along with the two bullet wounds.

She made an *isn't the answer obvious* noise. "Everything hurts," she managed to whisper. "How are you?"

"Fine." There was a thread of pain, of something unhappy in his voice.

She didn't like that, not at all. "I hope you punched the sheriff repeatedly in the face," she said, trying to smile. For the two of them to be in a hospital and not under arrest, the sheriff's illegal activities had to have been uncovered.

Smoke pressed his lips together so tight they were no more than a thin white line. He stared at her for so long she became concerned.

"He was caught, right?"

One of the muscles over Smoke's jaw flexed. "He didn't get away, and he's in no position to hurt anyone anymore." He rubbed his face with both hands. "Davis was selling biological weapons on the darknet, black market internet. The FBI is trying to piece together who his buyers were from what's left of the computers at the marijuana farm, but they're not having much luck."

"Damn," she whispered.

"Given what he was doing, the CDC thinks the farm was the source of the hantavirus outbreak. Not sure how yet, but—"

"I think I know," she interrupted. "Blackwater put a body through a wood chipper. What happened to Blackwater? I think he may have done the same with some of the people producing his biological weapons. If he mixed the results with compost or soil then used it as fertilizer or even disposed of it at the nearest landfill, the result could be an increase in rodent carriers all over this area." Out of breath, she found she couldn't keep her head up any longer. "Ask him what he did with...the bodies."

He got to his feet, limped over to the bed, and kissed her on the forehead. "I wish I could," he whispered. "I'm sorry."

"Nothing to be sorry about." She smiled despite the pain, so damned happy they'd both survived far too many people trying to kill them. "You kept your word, kept me safe."

He recoiled as if she'd shot him point-blank in the chest.

What? "Smoke?" Kini reached out with one hand, but he slid away, out of reach.

He swallowed hard, agony and loathing reflected on his face. "I killed the sheriff." His voice sounded like it had been sliced over and over by the words he forced himself to say. "Shot him in the head. I had no choice, he was going to use that axe to...I had no choice."

Oh, Smoke, no. He'd had to kill for her. He'd had to

relive all the horror he desperately needed to put behind him in order to have a life. A good, happy life.

"It's okay," she croaked. Her voice was giving out along with her strength.

He turned away, running one hand through is hair like he was going to pull it out. "It's *not* okay. I promised not to kill anyone, and I broke my word." He turned back to her. "It looks like I'm really good at two things. Killing people and letting the ones I love down."

"You didn't—" she whispered, no longer strong enough to do more than that.

"I did," he said with complete conviction. "I wasn't here for Liam, and I shot that fucking asshole Davis only a few inches from *your* head."

A horrified squeak came out of her. She didn't remember any of that.

He recoiled again, then his entire body changed, and he stood at attention. "I'm a warrior, always have been, always will be. If I have to kill to protect myself and those I've sworn to protect"—he gave her the saddest smile she'd ever seen— "I'll kill."

What was he trying to say to her? It didn't sound like an apology. He didn't have anything to apologize for. "I don't understand."

"I gave you my word I'd keep you safe." His gaze swept over her body. "I did a shitty job."

"Anyone else would have had a corpse on their hands. You did an amazing job."

"You nearly died," he snarled. "Blackwater was right. Bloodshed follows me around. If I stay near you, it's going to happen again." He met her gaze, his own filled with anger, regret, and determination. "I won't put you through that."

"Smoke, no—" she tried to say.

"I'm a ticking bomb. I don't know when I'm going to

go off. I don't know what I'll do when it happens, but it *will* happen." His gaze drilled into hers, holding her still and silent. "I'm not safe, and you…you need someone who is safe."

He left the room before she could say anything.

"Smoke?" she tried to call, but her lungs didn't seem capable of pushing out the necessary air. "Smoke!"

He had to come back, had to listen to her. She didn't blame him, didn't fear him. She grabbed at the wires and tubing within reach. There was a call button somewhere, right? She could get the staff to stop him, bring him back.

The button was clipped to her pillow. She pressed it, pressed and pressed and pressed.

A disembodied voice said, "Your nurse is on her way."

"Get security to stop Smoke from leaving," she said as loud as she could.

"There's smoke in your room?" Alarm now in that professional voice.

"No. Lyle Smoke."

"Someone will be right with you."

Damn it. He was going to be gone before anyone understood what she needed. She needed Smoke.

He used to be good at reading her mind.

At least he looked healthy, well, aside from the limp. But she wanted to know what happened. Had he really shot the sheriff? Did they find all the bacterial and viral samples he'd removed from his secret lab? Were Smoke's dad and grandfather okay? Was the outbreak still going strong?

She had so many questions, but Smoke was gone.

A nurse came in, but she was in that hazy place between awake and sleep. The nurse changed the dressings on her wounds, giving her the outstanding news that both bullets had done very little damage. She'd lost some blood and had been given a couple of units while in surgery, but she'd make a full recovery in a few weeks.

"Smoke," she said to the nurse. "I need Lyle Smoke."

"He's left the hospital," the nurse said. "Is there anyone else I can call for you? Family?"

"No." She didn't have anyone else.

• • •

The next morning, after having her first cup of coffee since waking up, Henry Lee came into Kini's room. She'd met the lab tech a few times and liked his no-nonsense attitude, but he didn't look like a tech right now. Dressed in black jeans and T-shirt, and wearing a gun in a shoulder holster, he looked like a modern-day gunslinger.

"How are you doing, Kini?"

"Okay, I guess." She'd be better if Smoke came back, but she wasn't going to whine at Henry. She'd give Smoke a piece of her mind when she caught up to him. When, not if. She didn't care how long it took to track him down, she was going to have her say, and then have her way with him.

"Smoke shot the sheriff," she said. "Do you know how it happened?"

He studied her for a moment then nodded. "The sheriff had a chokehold on you and wouldn't release you. I slipped Smoke my backup gun. He shot Davis before he could get you to his car."

If that had happened, she would have bled to death. So, why did Henry look so worried?

"Will Smoke be charged with his murder?" She tried to sit up and had to remind herself she had to go slow.

"No, there were plenty of witnesses. It was a justified kill."

Is that how men viewed it? Justified or not justified? If that was the case, why didn't Henry look any less worried?

He met her gaze and what she saw on his face made her

stomach clench. "Then what's wrong?"

"Something has got Smoke spooked."

"Spooked?"

"Agitated, anxious, unsettled, twitchy, worked up. Completely *not* Smoke."

She glanced at the doorway, hoping the subject of their conversation would appear. But there was no one there. "Talk to him. Ask him what's wrong."

"Nobody can ask him jack shit."

"Why?"

Henry didn't answer.

Closed-mouth men were going to drive her crazy. "Henry, just tell me."

"He left."

"Left?"

"Disappeared." Henry surged up to his feet and began to pace. "He sent me a six-word text. *Gone fishing. Back in two weeks.* " Henry kept pacing. "No one has a problem with him taking time off to get his shit together. Hell, he's smarter than I was when I got out, but I'd like to make sure he's not doing something stupid. No one knows where he is. Not his parents or his grandparents. No one."

Hah. His family had lied, because they knew as well as she did where he'd gone. They were assuming he'd come back when he was good and ready. "I know where he is."

Henry stopped pacing. "Where?"

She gave him a tight smile. "Not telling."

He stared at her. "Why the fuck not?"

"He's doing exactly what you think he's doing. Working through the shit in his head."

Henry frowned and plunked himself in the chair again. "River said the same thing."

"Why are you so worried?"

"I went through a rough patch when I first got home

after..." He tapped his prosthetic leg. "If it weren't for a couple of my Battle, I might have done something stupid."

"Battle?"

"Battle brothers. Men you serve with, fight with, survive with."

"I might not have fought with him, but I think I understand why he's doing it alone. He has to get to a certain point before he can talk about it with anyone."

"Smoke, the man who doesn't talk?"

"He talks, he just says more with less."

Henry rolled his eyes. "Thanks for clearing that up not at all."

"If you stop squawking, I'll show you where he is. After I'm cleared for light exercise, that is."

Henry opened his mouth to argue, but she wasn't finished.

"Stop. This is important. There was another bad guy at the drug house before it burned down. His name is Gary and he left to drive a very sick man to the hospital." She could still remember how awful the man's lungs sounded. "Gary is... dangerous. He hurt me for fun."

Henry's face took on a flat expression. "Skinny dude. Looked like he hadn't showered in a while?"

"Yeah," Kini said slowly, a sinking feeling in her gut. "That sounds like him."

"He's dead."

"Did you...?"

"No, I didn't kill him. The asshole walked into the ER waving a gun demanding a doctor, and telling everyone to get out of his way. An older lady who'd been calmly waiting in line shot him in the back with a big-assed revolver she pulled out of her purse." Henry grinned, but it wasn't nice at all. "I guarantee no one will jump any lines in this town for a while."

• • •

One week later, she directed Henry to the edge of the canyon, as close as you could get to the kiva Smoke had built as a teenager.

Kini pointed out the stair rock from above. "That's how you get in."

Henry looked at her like she'd lost her mind then shrugged. "I hope I don't break my good leg trying to get into that nice hidey hole."

"Henry," Kini said, exasperated with the grumpy lab tech. "There's nothing wrong with either of your legs, so stop grousing."

He blinked at her, the question clear. *Are you fucking serious?*

She crossed her arms over her chest. *As a heart attack.*

He shook his head then began looking for an easy route down the canyon. He never made it to the bottom.

Smoke rose out of the canyon faster than any man had a right to manage. He frowned at Henry and scowled at Kini. "What?"

Kini couldn't believe that's all he would say. She opened her mouth to say so, but Henry spoke first.

"You doing okay?"

Smoke seemed to consider the question seriously. "Yeah, okay."

"Coming back to work next week?"

Smoke nodded.

"Good enough." Henry gave him a brief nod and started walking back to the SUV parked not far away.

Smoke looked at her then shouted at Henry, "Forget something?"

"Nope," Henry said, sounding positively cheerful. "She's your problem now."

Smoke turned to her, his scowl turning into a glare.

She glared back. "How's the *fishing* going?"

"Caught something I didn't expect," he muttered.

"Well, you should have." Anger flared hot and bright, giving her more energy than she'd had for days. "You walked out of my room without so much as a goodbye." She walked up to him and poked his chest with an index finger. "That was rude as well as cowardly."

He flinched. "I was trying to avoid this conversation."

"You avoid all conversation," she said, putting her hands on her hips "Yet, I never had any problem understanding you until now and vice versa. What changed?"

He turned his body so he could only see her in the corner of his eye and said with a quiet voice that vibrated with despair. "I broke my word."

"What are you talking about?" Then she remembered the first conversation they'd ever had, in his room, on his bed, with her naked on his chest. "You kept your word. You kept me safe."

He spun and grabbed her shoulders, holding her in place while he bent down until they were nose to nose. "If I'm with you, I can't keep you safe from me."

"What do you mean, from you?" She angled her head to one side. "Smoke?"

"I promised I wouldn't use violence. I broke my word. It's going to happen again, it's just a matter of time."

It was her turn to scowl at him. "This fishing trip of yours didn't do its job."

He stared at her like she'd lost her mind. "Didn't you hear what I said?"

"I heard, now it's your turn to listen to me." She thrust a finger under his nose and shook it. "The sheriff gave you no choice. You had to kill him. If you hadn't, he would have killed me, and many more people. You did the only reasonable thing possible."

He shook his head, so she put her hands on either side

of his face and held him still. "You were forced to make a decision between two horrible outcomes. The sheriff's death or my death. You made a choice to save me, not because it was easy, but because it was hard, and that choice hurt you."

His gaze never left hers, and it was so full of pain and self-disgust she wanted to shake him and kiss away all the hurt at the same time. "You are *not* a monster. You're a man who sacrificed his peace of mind to save others." She took in a deep breath. "You've also taught me that I can't hold what my father did against the rest of the human race. I can't let what he did dictate my life."

He closed his eyes and rested his forehead against hers, breathing deep for several long seconds. "Thank you." He pulled back with a solemn expression on his face. "Maybe... you're right."

"So, what are you going to do about it?"

He didn't answer, just closed his eyes and rested against her as if she were the sun and he'd been freezing his whole life.

She wanted to hold him, kiss him, love him, but she was running out of energy fast. Her limbs seemed to weigh more than they should, and her body ached.

"So, are you done with your fishing trip?" she asked, glancing at the jeep she'd driven. *His* jeep. It had been hidden by Henry's rented vehicle.

When she met his gaze again, it was to find him frowning at her. "You look pale."

"This is my first full day out of the hospital." She put a hand up to stop him from saying whatever put the scowl on his face. "I'm fine, just a little sore, but finding you, *talking* to you, was important to me."

"I'll drive you back to town." He studied her for a moment. "When do you go back to work?"

"I don't know, maybe a week or two from now."

"Wait for me in the jeep," he said.

Would he *ever* stop frowning at her?

"I'll get my gear." He took off down the canyon while she walked slowly to the vehicle and got in the passenger seat.

Chapter Thirty-Six

Smoke hurried to get the rough camp he'd set up inside his hideout cleaned up and all his gear gathered. Kini had looked more than just pale—she looked like she was in pain and about to fall over.

By the time he got his shit together and arrived at the jeep, she was asleep in the passenger seat. He put a hand on her face and found himself shaking. Her skin was as soft and supple as the petals of a rose. His thumb brushed over her plush lips. He wanted to put his mouth on her and devour her for hours, drown himself in her taste and scent until neither of them had the strength to move.

Not going to happen anytime soon, asshole. Recovering from two bullet wounds was no joke, and after…she might be able to forgive his shooting the sheriff, but that didn't change the core problem.

Him. He was damaged. Rage and war were part of who he was, and she'd already experienced enough killing to last her whole lifetime. He could take care of her now, satisfy the primitive thug inside him with that much, and hope that would be enough.

He needed to get his head on straight.

He put in a call to the CDC doctor, Gunner, who'd looked after both of them. The guy was a bit of an asshole, but that just made him easier to work with.

Gunner answered the phone with a barked, "What?"

"This is Smoke. Kini is with me."

"I heard you were hiding out in the desert," the doctor said. "What the fuck is she doing out there with you? She's in no shape to be hiking or anything more strenuous than a walk to the nearest bathroom."

"Not my idea." Smoke sighed, but it was his fault. "She came looking for me. She's asleep now. Should I bring her back to the hospital?"

"Fuck no."

"Hotel?"

"That'll do. Light exercises only. And by 'light' I mean walking at a pace she sets for herself. No lifting, no working, and no wild monkey sex. Got it?"

"No monkeys. Got it."

"She'll have to have her dressings changed in a couple of days."

"I can do that. I wasn't a medic in the army, but I qualify as an EMT."

"Good. Saves me having to track you down."

Smoke cleared his throat. "I need to talk to you."

"We are talking," Gunner said after a moment.

"About…the shit…inside my head." That was harder to say than he'd expected.

"I may not be the best person for that," Gunner said slowly. "I've got a fair amount of shit of my own to deal with."

"That makes us equals," Smoke said.

"Huh." The grunt came out sounding surprised and thoughtful. "That it does. You want this on the books or off?"

"On. I'm pretty sure the CDC would insist."

"I'll make it a mutual thing," the grumpy doctor said. "They've been yammering at me to talk to someone, too."

"Like a support group?" At Gunner's silence, Smoke added, "I'm not holding your hand."

Gunner laughed. "Good, I hate awkward dates." Still laughing, he hung up.

Smoke phoned River next, caught him up to speed, then headed into town. He left the jeep running with Kini in it while he had a fast shower and packed for hoteling it rather than camping out.

His mother told him he was going to get into trouble for not asking Kini what she wanted to do, but he just shrugged. He wanted her someplace comfortable, with all the amenities, not a cheap motel off the highway.

The drive to Las Vegas was uneventful, and Kini didn't wake up until they were almost at the hotel. She blinked several times, looking out the window with a frown. "We're in Vegas? How did we get here?"

Since the answer was obvious, he didn't say anything.

She glanced at him, her gaze lingered on his clothing and clean-shaven face. "How long did I sleep?"

"Three hours."

She stared out the window. "Why did we come here?"

"Better hotels, food, and no outbreak." He kept his tone neutral and unconcerned.

She turned to look at him, her gaze going over him carefully. "What's going on?"

"Huh?" Everything was exactly as it appeared. He was taking her to a nice place to recover from her gunshot wounds.

His hands gripped the steering wheel and twisted.

And twisted.

She squinted at him. "What's wrong with you?"

"Aside from nearly getting you killed?"

She leaned toward him and hissed. "I distinctly recall you *saving* my life."

He'd said that out loud? *Fuck.*

"Is that what's been going through your head for the last week?" she asked, her voice rising. "Are you seriously blaming yourself for anything those greedy, narcissistic, morons did?"

The words blasted out of him with a despair he thought he had locked down. "I sure as hell didn't help." *Way to go, asshole. Bellowing at her is a great way to keep things on the down-low.*

"Blackwater and Davis knew the second they laid eyes on you that they couldn't intimidate, bully, or otherwise control you."

When he didn't respond, she threw her hands up in the air. "For fuck's sake, they set me up to take the blame for an outbreak they and their treasonous friends started."

Smoke already had his mouth open to argue with her when her words registered.

Wait, back up. "Treasonous friends?"

"See? This is what happens when you disappear for a week. You miss out on important information. Sheriff Davis wasn't alone in his production of dangerous bacteria and viruses. The FBI says that there's a whole convoluted trail of shell companies, offshore accounts, and invisible buyers involved. All of which seemed to have found ways to disappear into financial and legal black holes about the time the first cases were reported three weeks ago."

"Is that why Davis went off the rails? He finally figured out he'd been left holding the bag?"

She shrugged. "The FBI and Homeland security have only begun to untangle things, but Henry and River seem to think so."

They pulled into the Bellagio's valet parking line.

Smoke turned off the engine then gave her his full attention. "We'll talk more about this when we're alone. For now, we're staying here for a few days. Doctor's orders."

She snorted then winced. "Okay, fine. Force me to stay at a nice hotel and eat good food. Hurt me again."

He was very afraid he would do exactly that. Still, he didn't want the conversation heading back into emotional territory, didn't want her thinking too hard and understanding just how bad he was for her, so he asked, "Grumpy much?"

She pinned him in place with a laser stare. "Don't start."

"Yes, ma'am."

Smoke got out of the jeep, tossed the keys to one of the valets, then helped Kini out. He'd have carried her, but she gave him such a dirty look he didn't dare suggest it. He grabbed their bags, and they went inside.

Ten minutes later, they were entering the suite he'd reserved. A bedroom and sitting room with a small kitchen. He put her bag in the bedroom, but left his in the sitting area. The sofa bed would be more than adequate for him.

She sat on the sofa and scowled at him.

He handed her the room service menu. "Pick out something and I'll order us up an early dinner."

They ate in silence. Kini seemed just as angry two hours after arriving at the hotel as she'd been in the vehicle.

He didn't know what to say that wouldn't make things worse, so he kept his mouth shut. He wanted to tell her how scared he'd been when the sheriff shot her. How stupid happy he'd been when she woke up, and when he'd seen her standing at the side of the canyon earlier.

If River, Henry, or any of his Battle could see him now, struggling desperately for the right things to say, they'd laugh their asses off.

At eight o'clock, she wished him a cool good night and went into the bedroom. The only thing that gave him any solace at all was that she left the door open a few inches.

• • •

Kini couldn't breathe. There was too much smoke in the room and the hand around her throat was so tight. She clawed at that hand and the arm it was attached to, trying to make the grinning monster let her go, but he just laughed and squeezed harder.

"Kini, wake up. Wake the fuck up!"

Her eyes opened to find Smoke's face only a few inches from hers, and the only hand around her throat was her own.

She coughed. "Smoke? What?"

He buried his head against her shoulder. "*Fuck*." The word shuddered out of him, and his whole body shook. "You were having a nightmare I think, but you were choking and couldn't seem to breathe."

She sucked in a couple of hard breaths. "I'm okay."

He didn't respond, didn't move.

She put her hand on his head and let her fingers pet and stroke him. It seemed to help decrease his shaking so she kept doing it. "Before you chopped your way to me with that axe, which was incredible by the way, I was certain I was going to die in the fire."

He lifted his head to stare at her with sad, sad eyes. "This isn't the first time you've had this dream?"

"No. I scared the absolute shit out of Dr. Gunner a couple of times." She tried to smile. "You know how he likes to work the night shift."

"Did he give you any medication to help you sleep?" Smoke asked.

"No, but he did say there was something better than medication."

Smoke frowned. "What?"

"Sleeping with a friend."

Smoke reared back as if to get off the bed. "He offered to sleep with you?"

"What? No. *No.* He advised me to do it with someone trustworthy. Someone my body and subconscious would recognize as safe."

Smoke stared at her like she'd just told him she had an incurable disease.

"I can think of only one person who meets all of the doctor's criteria," she continued.

His eyes grew wide and he shook his head.

"Yes. You." She snagged one of his hands before he could bolt and tugged on him, whispering, "Please don't leave me."

He stood, staring at her and breathing fast, for several seconds. When he spoke, his voice came out a low rumble, "This is a very bad idea." He disengaged himself from her and stood next to the bed. Was he going to leave?

His hands went to the waistband of his jeans and he shoved them down. His skin-tight boxer briefs were molded to his muscled thighs and ass.

Lord have mercy, he was a beautiful man.

He crawled under the covers with her and coaxed her to roll over so he could spoon her from behind and put an arm over her waist.

The heat, scent, and feel of him did something to her insides, relaxed muscles she hadn't realized were tense. "Thank you."

"Bad idea," he murmured in her ear.

"Bah humbug to you, too," she said, her eyes so heavy she couldn't keep them open.

She woke up on Smoke's chest again.

This is a neat trick. Here she was in Las Vegas, in bed with the best-looking man she'd ever met, and neither one of them was wearing a whole lot of clothes.

As super powers went, it wasn't bad.

Should she be a good girl and remove herself from her somewhat compromising position?

Sheesh, where would the fun be in that?

Kini wiggled until she was a little higher on his chest before tracing the outline of his cock through his underwear. He was already hard. And thick. It would feel so good when he took her. So very good.

His hand clamped down on hers. "Kini."

"I need you," she whispered.

His face twisted like he was being tortured. "You're injured. Two bullet holes. *Two*."

She went nose to nose with him. "I only need one thing to make me feel better and it isn't any damned pill."

"I don't want to hurt you."

"Then don't." She kissed him. "You can be on top. Do all the work." She kissed him again and again, teasing him with her lips and tongue show him how much she needed him.

He released her hand and carefully rolled her over. "You will tell me if I hurt you."

She nodded. "Yes."

"Even if it's a little bit."

"Yes, I promise."

He helped her take her T-shirt off, one of his, before he kissed her. His mouth took hers as if he were desperate to taste her, know her, yet his hands were gentle, his arms a cradle for her wounded body.

His mouth tasted her everywhere, her neck, between her breasts and even around her bandaged wounds. He spent a lot of time teasing her nipples by not quite touching them, then a little flick of his tongue to get them wet, before starting all over again.

She finally resorted to begging. "Please, Smoke, I need you to suck on them. Bite them. *Something*."

He hovered over her chest. "Do you?" His voice was low and rough. "Poor baby."

She made an inarticulate noise and began to struggle. She needed him to touch her.

He put his mouth on one nipple, sucking it deep and hard, while he pinched the other, and she nearly came then and there. The pleasure rolled over her in waves and she lingered on the precipice of orgasm.

"Smoke, please," she whimpered. "I need you inside me."

His answer was to slide one hand under her panties and part her private flesh. "So wet," he growled, angling away so he could pull her panties off. When he moved over her, settling himself between her legs, he was naked, too.

His cock nudged the entrance to her body, then he pushed inside, rocking back and forth until he was all in. "*Fuck*," he hissed as he pulled out then pushed back in.

Kini tried not to move. Her promise held her down, and it seemed to amplify her pleasure.

"Harder," she ordered. "I'm so close."

"I don't want to hurt you," he said, gritting his teeth.

"You won't," she gasped.

Picking up the pace a little, he gave her what she asked for, and she went over the edge. Pleasure detonated deep inside her, erasing all the pain and exhaustion from her body, leaving only sleepy contentment behind.

As the last ripples went through her, Smoke groaned then gave her several hard thrusts before pressing deep and shuddering over her.

He opened his bright blue eyes. "You okay?"

She couldn't help but smile at his worry. "I'm *awesome*."

He shifted, checked her dressings, then cuddled her close and said, "Sleep."

The next time Kini woke, she was alone again, but the sound of the shower running told her where Smoke was.

A shower sounded really good and the doctor had told her she could have one as long as it was short and fresh dressings were applied afterward.

Smoke came out of the bathroom then, a towel wrapped around his waist.

She had to bite her lip to stop herself from moaning at the sight of him. Then her gaze reached his face and all the naughty thoughts died premature deaths.

"What's wrong?" When he didn't answer right away, just stood near the end of the bed looking at her with a lost puppy expression, she tried to sit up and found she couldn't.

Smoke was at the bedside a second later, putting a hand on her uninjured shoulder to keep her on the bed. "Stop."

She grabbed that hand. "What's *wrong*?"

He shook his head.

"Oh no you don't," she said, tightening her grip on his hand. "You looked absolutely *broken* a moment ago. Why?"

"I shouldn't have brought you here." The words landed between them, dead.

"I don't understand."

"I thought if I had one more taste I could let you go, live your life, be happy, but the thought of doing it..." He lifted one hand and they both stared at it as it shook. "I'm a selfish bastard for what I'm thinking."

Things were getting interesting. "Tell me."

When his gaze met hers, the blaze she saw damn near scorched her. "I want to keep you, look after you, and fuck you until you never want to leave."

What the hell was going on in his head? "Sounds good to me," she said. "When do we start?"

He frowned. "It's not possible. You know it's not."

"No I don't. Unless..." No, she couldn't believe it of him. "Is there another woman?"

He shook his head. "No. I'm..." He sighed and started

again. "There's a part of me that's all aggression and anger, and it has a hair trigger. I think I need..." He took in a deep breath and said, "Help."

"Recognizing that you can't do it alone is the first step toward healing." She poked his chest. "*You are* a good man, Lyle Smoke. I know we haven't even gone on a single real date, but there's nowhere else I'd rather be than with you." She cocked her head. "Unless this is your version of a gentle brush off?"

His next word burst out of him, "*No.*"

She raised his hand to her lips, turned it, and kissed his palm. "We have all week to decide *how* we want to be together, as long as we're both clear on the fact that we *are* together."

He studied her for several seconds, then his eyes grew wide with surprise and joy. "Crystal."

"Good," she said, pulling on his hand. "Come back to bed. I don't sleep well unless I'm sleeping on you."

He slid back under the covers and under her, the beginning of a real smile on his face. "Yes, ma'am."

Epilogue

Smoke buried his nose in Kini's hair and inhaled. He would never get enough of her scent, the softness of her skin, and the caress of her voice as she whispered how much she loved it when his hands touched her.

He needed to let her go, open his arms to allow her to leave. Instead, he tightened his hold.

"I know," she said softly. "I don't want to go without you either, but someone has to drive your jeep and all your stuff to Atlanta."

"Ride with me." He kept his voice low, but couldn't keep the growl out of it. He hated the idea that she was taking this flight to Atlanta alone.

"I wish I could." She pulled away from him, patting his chest as she left the circle of his arms. "Rodrigues needs one of us to work with Homeland Security now. She's afraid, they're afraid, there could be multiple incidents of bioterrorism here inside the United States, thanks to Davis and his online shop of evil." She lifted her chin so she could meet his gaze.

He could look into her eyes for hours, days, years and be

happy. Because she saw all of him, and she didn't shy away from the darker parts of his soul.

"I don't have to like it," he said.

She grinned at that and poked his shoulder. "I would have never guessed, oh grumpy one." She leaned forward and whispered, "The security people here would probably relax a little if you smiled."

He obligingly flashed his teeth.

She sighed and shook her head. "That's not a smile, that's a declaration of war." She hugged him again, squeezing tight. "I'll see you in three days. Don't be late."

"I won't," he said, attempting to imprint the feel of her body against his. "Stay safe. Don't overdo it."

"Yes, sir," she said, pulled out of his arms, turned, and entered the line to go through security.

Smoke didn't stay to watch her wind her way through the circuitous line. It wouldn't help, and it might make him feel even crabbier than he already did.

His jeep waited for him. It was time to go.

He drove back to Small Blind, parking in front of his parents' home. He walked in to find his grandparents and his cousin Tommy as well as his folks. He told them all he was heading to Atlanta to officially start his new job with the CDC's Outbreak Task Force. They didn't pepper him with questions, but it was close. Mostly, they wanted to know how Kini was, and if the two of them were together or not.

His mother, in particular, had a gleam in her eyes that made him wary.

"Don't go planning the wedding," he told her. "Kini might decide I'm not worth the work."

"Lyle Smoke," his mother said with her hands on her hips. "That's no way to talk about yourself."

"Mom, I've seen and done some bad shit."

"So what?"

"So, I'm still carrying that shit around." He tapped his temple. "Don't know if I can shovel it elsewhere or if it'll be there for the duration. No point in pretending otherwise."

"Does she know about the shit?"

He nodded. She knew, and that scared the fuck out of him.

His mother snorted. "That girl loves you. Give her and yourself time to heal."

He offered her a small smile but couldn't help wondering how Kini would feel after a few days apart from him.

· · ·

The drive took two and a half days. He could have arrived faster if he'd driven without stopping, but he had orders from Kini to sleep, so he stopped and slept. Twice.

Just before he entered Atlanta, Smoke called River and gave him his ETA. When he pulled into the CDC's headquarters and parked, River was waiting for him. His official parking pass, ID, and shit in River's hands.

He got out of his vehicle, shook River's hand, and asked, "Kini?"

River grinned, handed him his stuff, and angled his head at the building. "She's been talking to Homeland Security since she got here. It's been fun to watch."

What the fuck did that mean? "Oh?"

"She's gone up and down them so many ways, they're damn near covered in tire tracks. A sheriff operating a bioweapon factory inside a government-funded greenhouse." River laughed. "I've never heard the word 'incompetent' used so many times in my life."

"She's...okay?" His stomach was oddly unsettled, like he couldn't decide if he was relieved to hear this news or worried.

"Yeah, she's fine." River patted Smoke's back. "Tired,

cranky, but fine." He started walking. "Come on, Rodrigues wants to see you."

He sighed. His boss probably wanted to sit and talk. Fun—*not*.

Rodrigues was a tiny thing, maybe five feet; her hair was pulled back into some kind of knot that looked like something a sailor would tie. Her hair was gray, but her face didn't quite match. Not enough lines or wrinkles.

"Ma'am," Smoke said with a respectful nod.

She glanced up from her computer. "Come in, Lyle. River, please check on Kini. See if she and the Homeland agents with her will be finished in about…" She consulted her watch. "Thirty minutes."

"Will do, ma'am." He turned and left.

That left him with Rodrigues staring a hole through his head.

"My name is Smoke," Smoke said after a couple of seconds.

"Yes, sorry, I forgot." She sighed and muttered something about men and nicknames. "In your professional opinion, is Kini ready to go back to work?"

Professional? "I'm not a doctor."

"No, but you've had extensive first-aid training and your experiences in the army give you a uniquely qualified perspective useful in gauging what people are capable of."

Sounded like a load of bullshit to him, but if she was giving him a voice on the subject of Kini's health and safety, he wasn't going to throw it away. "No. She needs at least a couple more weeks before even considering putting her on desk duty." There had been so much blood on her, on the ground, too much.

"Are *you* ready?" The question sounded far away, not in Kini's voice.

He wrenched himself out of the past, forcing his vision to

show him the here and now, rather than one of the nightmares plaguing his sleep.

Rodrigues was watching him, her gaze sharp and focused on his face.

He didn't know this woman, but River trusted her. Henry trusted her.

He sucked in a breath then stuck out his neck, saying, "No. I need to talk to..." Who *could* he talk to? It had to be someone who'd gone through similar shit.

Rodrigues smiled, a Cheshire cat smile. "I have just the man. It took some doing, but I finally bribed him away from the El Paso Transit Authority."

Transit? Then it came back to him. "The drill sergeant who helped River during the terrorist attacks in El Paso?"

"Yes, him."

"You hired him for his services as a therapist?" Smoke couldn't keep the surprise out of his voice. That cantankerous old man had a gold star potty mouth and only one volume setting on his voice: shout.

She laughed. "Not exactly." Rodrigues studied him for another moment then said, "The Outbreak Task Force is made up of a number of people with different backgrounds. We operate both inside the USA and internationally. We often have to work within cultures that are very different than our own. Many of those cultures offer greater levels of respect and attention to what an older male says versus what a younger female might say. The drill sergeant, or DS as he likes to be called, is excellent at organizing people and situations. He's also turning out to be a valuable sounding board for many of our more...technically inclined people."

That was a nice way to say *lab rat*.

"As well as our military veterans. He's been with us for a month," she continued as she picked up her phone and texted something. "But he's still settling into his office."

"He didn't strike me as an office kind of guy," Smoke said. He'd only met the man once, but that was plenty long enough to get his measure.

"He isn't," she said absently. "Thank God he doesn't mind using his cell phone or I'd never know where he was." She put her phone down. "He's on his way." Rodrigues gave him another long look. "Do you want to be partnered with Kini?" She put up a hand. "Don't give me the answer you think I want; give me the answer that's best for you *and* her."

She didn't pull her punches. His preferred kind of commander. "Understood, ma'am, and yes."

"Why?"

So many reasons, but most of them were none of his boss's business. "Trust. Respect. Intelligence. Competence."

She studied him for another moment and said, "Your first task, then, will be to convince her to take the minimum of two weeks to rest and heal. You will be doing the same with her."

"Yes, ma'am," he said again. That was it?

Someone knocked on the door.

"Come," Rodrigues said loud enough for the person one the other side of the door to hear.

The door opened and a deep, rough voice asked, "Is this my new recruit?"

Smoke turned. The retired drill sergeant stood in the doorway, an evil grin on his face.

• • •

Kini's entire body ached like she'd been sat on by a sumo wrestler. The exhaustion weighing her down didn't help. She hadn't slept well since she'd left Las Vegas and Smoke. It took hours for her to go to sleep, then, when she finally dozed off, nightmares terrorized her until panic woke her. That would be it for sleep.

Thank God Homeland Security was done grilling her about what she saw at the drug house that burned down and at the jojoba plant before it burned down. They called it an interview, but it was nothing short of an interrogation. Three agents had questioned her since the hour she'd arrived at the CDC's headquarters. Almost three eight-hour days ago. Only one of them, Agent Dozer, had made any effort to make her more comfortable while they asked her question after question after question.

Now her only goal was finding Smoke. It shouldn't be hard. He was in the city. The man had dutifully sent her a text every time he stopped along the route to Atlanta. Texted her with his current GPS coordinates, not the name of the town or even of the highway he was on, just the numbers.

Some men might bring their girlfriend flowers; Smoke told her *exactly* where he was.

She checked her cell phone for his latest set of coordinates then entered the numbers in the app on her phone. According to the app, she and Smoke were at the same location.

He was *in* the building.

She sent him a text: *Where are you inside CDC HQ ?*

He replied: *Cafeteria. Coffee. Drill Sergeant.*

She'd met the DS before Homeland began its marathon of questions. She liked him. He had a gruff exterior, a good heart, and he'd told her she could chat with him about anything at any time.

She texted back: *Incoming.* Then made her way to the cafeteria.

It was after one in the afternoon, so the space was relatively empty. Smoke and the DS were seated at a smallish table in the back corner of the room, cups of coffee sitting in front of them.

Both men saw her coming and watched her approach,

angling their bodies in a way that signaled welcome. She didn't walk fast—that was still beyond her ability—so there was plenty of time for Smoke to grab a chair for her before she arrived at the table.

She had to work not to stare at him too long, memorize his features and body all over again. She wanted his big hands on her, caressing her, cradling her. She wanted to touch him everywhere, ensure herself that he was okay.

Jumping the man in the cafeteria probably wouldn't go over well.

"How are you doing, Miss Kini?" the DS asked, a smile on his face and in his voice.

"Tired and a little sore," she said, surprised at how out of breath she sounded as she sat down.

Smoke lifted her and her chair, tucking her comfortably close to the table. He returned to his own seat, moving close enough to hers for his knee to come into contact with her thigh.

She met his gaze. "How was the drive?" There, that was a nice normal question.

He stared at her, his gaze hot, his body curved toward hers. One of his large hands covered one of her smaller ones, and the heat of that connection raised the temperature in the room by several degrees. "Took too long." His voice stroked over her skin, deep and rich and full of sexual promise.

"Much too long," she whispered.

"Ack," the DS said with a shake of his head. "Love birds." He held up a stern finger and pointed it at Smoke. "I'll see you tomorrow morning for that run you promised me."

"He can't run," Kini protested. "He has a bullet wound in his calf that's only a week old."

"He says he can do a light run, so that's what we're going to do," the DS said. "As for you, missy, I want you to start doing some stretches a couple of times a day. As soon as you're cleared for exercise, you're going to join us on our runs."

"Oh." That was a surprise. "Um, why?"

"Physical exercise is an excellent way to work out the shit in your head. But that's just the start. You people working for the CDC, you see and do some seriously dangerous work. Part of what keeps soldiers from losing their shit constantly is the sense of safety and security a team gives you." He pointed a finger at her then at Smoke. "This lone wolf shit isn't going to happen anymore. You're to be part of the team, and you're going to know your teammates as well, or better than yourself." He looked at her as if waiting for a response.

"So when we get shit on, we know where to turn for support?" Kini offered.

The DS smiled at her, the smile of a proud father. He looked at Smoke. "You've got a smart woman here." He leaned closer to Smoke and said in a stage whisper, "Don't fuck things up."

Smoke turned his head to meet her gaze, held it, and said, "She's the only woman I want." His voice rolled over her like hot chocolate. Easing muscles she hadn't realized were knotted tight at the base of her head and deep in her chest.

The DS left the table, but Kini hardly noticed.

She couldn't look away from Smoke. His gaze held her captive, giving her something she hadn't had since before her father had destroyed their family. A place to belong, a person to love, and be loved by in return.

He cupped her face with one large hand. "I missed you."

She was absolutely certain she had a ridiculously goofy smile on her face, and didn't care one bit. "I missed you, too."

The heat coming off his body made her want to fan herself. Or maybe that was just her own reaction to being this close to him. Only a few inches of air between them. She wanted that space to be zero, she wanted them both naked, and she wanted them in a bed so she could touch him skin to skin.

"When are you finished for the day?" he asked, his voice making her breathing catch.

"Now. You?"

"Finished," he agreed. "Do you want to go..." He frowned. "I don't have a hotel room yet, but—"

"I've been staying at a hotel not far from here," she said quickly. "I was offered an apartment in the same building where some of the other people on the task force live, but I wanted to talk to you about it first." She waited for him to speak, to show some enthusiasm for the possibility of living together, but he seemed frozen in place. "Unless, you want to get your own place?"

"No," he replied abruptly. "No, I'd rather live with you." He swallowed. "If that's what you're suggesting, I mean." He sounded tentative, nervous even.

It hit her between the eyes. Good grief, they were both scared the other one had changed their mind about being together.

She leaned forward and kissed him, light and sweet, then retreated for only part of a second before returning to suck on his lower lip.

One of his big hands cradled her head as he took over the kiss, showing her in no uncertain terms that he was *all in*.

They broke apart, both breathing hard.

She said, "I love you."

"I love you, too." He smiled, a sinful expression promising all kind of naughty things. "Wanna shack up with me?"

She sighed, happiness fizzing through her bloodstream. "I can't wait."

He took her hand and they walked slowly out of the building. He cleared his throat. "So, our boss wants you to take a couple more weeks to recover."

"And she asked you to make it happen?" Kini asked, laughing.

At his nod, she said, "She told me to do the same for you."

"Huh. Sneaky."

"Two whole weeks together, with no one bugging us and nowhere to go. Whatever will we do?"

He wrapped an arm around her and drew her close for a kiss. "I think we can come up with something."

Acknowledgments

Special thanks to the tireless staff at the Centers for Disease Control and Prevention for their ongoing work to identify, surveil, treat, educate, and prevent disease inside the United States and around the world.

About the Author

Julie Rowe's first career as a medical lab technologist in Canada took her to the Northwest Territories and northern Alberta, where she still resides. She loves to include medical details in her romance novels, but admits she'll never be able to write about all her medical experiences because "Fiction has to be believable."

Julie writes romantic suspense and romantic military thrillers. Her most recent titles include *Viable Threat*, the first book in the Outbreak Task Force series, and *Viral Justice*, book three of the Biological Response Team series. You can find her at www.julieroweauthor.com, on Twitter @ julieroweauthor, or on her Facebook page: www.facebook.com/JulieRoweAuthor.

Discover more Amara titles...

THE MAN I WANT TO BE
an *Under Covers* novel by Christina Elle

DEA agent Bryan Tyke hates weddings. He hates them even more when he's forced to travel to a hot as hell resort to watch his best friends say I do, while acting happy about it. Forever isn't in the cards for Tyke. It hasn't been since he joined the army years ago and lost everything. That is, until the woman he's never forgotten shows up as a bridesmaid and puts herself into immediate danger.

HARD PURSUIT
a *Delta Force Brotherhood* novel by Sheryl Nantus

Trey Pierce has spent years helping the Brotherhood, using his computer skills to dig out secrets and help deliver justice. But there's one mission he's yet to finish—finding out who killed his best friend. A chance meeting with Ally Sheldon gives him a new lead, one that comes with some baggage. Never in his life has Trey been more attracted to a woman, but she's hiding something. And that something may just destroy them.

Girl in the Mist
a novel by S T Young

Infamous for infiltration and *becoming* her undercover identities, Nina Hernandez disappeared without a trace. Three years later, Naval Intelligence agent Rory O'Donnell finds her in a tortuous mental hospital. He's unsure if it's really Nina, or if she's undercover and faking it. Either way, he's pretty sure something sinister is going on... Between car chases, flying bullets...and Nina's mercurial changes, sexy come-ons, and exasperating independence, this might just be Rory's toughest assignment ever.

Witness in the Dark
a novel by Allison B. Hanson

Deputy Marshal Garrett McKendrick does *not* get involved with witnesses he's tasked to protect. Can you say *off limits*? But as they run for their lives and he battles to keep Samantha Hutchinson safe from the powerful and influential people out to silence her—permanently—he finds she's strong, feisty, and willing to risk everything to tell the truth. And totally irresistible.

Made in the USA
Columbia, SC
20 March 2018